Dump

14. Billy Thunder
15. Tommy Gifford
16. Florence Walker
17. Dump Sign
18. Dump
19. Mama Sal Gifford
20. Blanche's Cafe
21. Rita & Henry Plunkett
22. Harry Plunkett
23. Booster & Dorie M.
24. Jurassic Park
25. Buck Fennelson
26. End of Tarred Road

Praise for *The One-Way Bridge*

"Here's great news for readers: Cathie Pelletier has driven the pickup back to Mattagash, the New England outpost of her wild and fertile imagination, and she's invited us to ride shotgun. How does Pelletier do it? How does she manage to satirize the feisty folk of this rural Maine village and, simultaneously, to make us care so deeply about them? Cathie Pelletier is one of my favorite novelists, and she's at the top of her game with *The One-Way Bridge*."

—*Wally Lamb, author of* She's Come Undone *and* Wishin' and Hopin'

"In her new book, Cathie Pelletier's brilliantly drawn, true-to-life characters break your heart and make you laugh at the same time, a rare talent indeed."

—*Fannie Flagg, author of* Fried Green Tomatoes at the Whistle Stop Café

"*The One-Way Bridge* is the novel Cathie Pelletier fans have long awaited. Her Mattagash, Maine, is one of the most fully realized fictional locales I've ever visited, its geography as vivid and precise as any actual place, its citizens as real and compelling as our own friends and neighbors."

—*Richard Russo, author of* Empire Falls

"If you liked *Olive Kitteridge*, you'll love *The One-Way Bridge*. Maine writer Cathie Pelletier is a national treasure, her lovely prose filled with grace and humor. She understands the complicated issues of loneliness, family, and community—and the kinds of accommodations we all make in the name of love—better than anybody else."

—*Lee Smith, author of* The Last Girls

"*The One-Way Bridge* is a striking novel, both humorous and elegant. Although set in a small town, its concerns reach across the vastness of North America and into the jungles of Vietnam. It is about change and pain and the legacy of history, an elegant testimony to its place and time. The writing is lyrical and intense. The characters and landscape are presented with the sure hand of an established author. It's a splendid novel."

—*Alistair MacLeod, author of* No Great Mischief *and* Island

"Cathie Pelletier can conjure up an entire town full of people who are hilarious, wise, and wonderful. This is an exciting novel, and I wish I'd written it."

—*Chuck Barris, author of*
Confessions of a Dangerous Mind *and* Della

"Cathie Pelletier's *The One-Way Bridge* is elegantly wrought, and the characters are finely drawn, and yet all of them and everything in this story surges with life in its full wildness and messiness. The way these people are inextricable from each other, and from their landscape and collective history, makes this novel both profoundly universal and meticulously specific. Oh, and it's also very funny, sometimes quite darkly so, sort of like the Coen brothers if they'd grown up in northern Maine. You will remember this book for a long time, and you will be very glad to have read it."

—*Matthew Sharp, author of* Jamestown

"Cathie does a wonderful job of capturing [her characters'] moods and loves and losses and yearnings… Her writing is lovely and so descriptive."

—*Annie Philbrick, Bank Square Books, Mystic CT*

"I have just finished reading *The One-Way Bridge* by Cathie Pelletier. I loved it. Her characters, with all of their flaws and synchronicities, are all believable and lovable. I've looked forward to a new book by Cathie for some time, and she hasn't disappointed with this one. Can't wait to pass it around to others in the book shop for their reactions. I am looking forward to selling this original, touching book!"

—Susan Porter, Maine Coast Book Shop, Damariscotta, ME

Praise for Cathie Pelletier

"Nobody walks the knife-edge of hilarity and heartbreak more confidently than Cathie Pelletier."

—Richard Russo

"Cathie Pelletier generates the sort of excitement that only writers working at the very top of their form can provide."

—Stephen King

"Imagine a modern-day Jane Austen with a wildly ribald sense of humor."

—Howard Frank Mosher

"One of the funniest authors in the country today..."

—Florence King

"Cathie Pelletier is a writer of great craft, with a unique ability to be simultaneously sympathetic and wickedly funny."

—Newsday

"Pelletier is excellent at illuminating ordinary lives within nature's context, bringing out the beauty and complexities they contain."

—Rebecca S. Kelm, Northern Kentucky University Library

"Cathie Pelletier accomplishes what every great novelist should. She creates a place, invites you in, walks you around, talks to you, lets you see and feel and hear it, allows you to get to know the people."

—*Fannie Flagg*, New York Times

The One-Way Bridge

a novel

Cathie Pelletier

Cover design by Kathleen Lynch and Lynn Buckley
Cover illustration by Tom Hallman
Endsheet design by Carl Hileman
Author photo by Leslie Bowman

Published by Sourcebooks Landmark, an imprint of Sourcebooks, Inc.
P.O. Box 4410, Naperville, Illinois 60567-4410
(630) 961-3900
Fax: (630) 961-2168
www.sourcebooks.com

Library of Congress Cataloguing-in-Publication data is on file with the publisher.

Printed and bound in the United States of America.
BG 10 9 8 7 6 5 4 3 2

For **CARL HILEMAN** of Tamms, Illinois.
The word *friend* falls short.
The better word is *brother*.

In memory of **PATSI BALE COX**
of Nashville (formerly Kansas)
and
DEAN FAULKNER WELLS
of Oxford, Mississippi.
Heaven will never be the same.

My sister, **JOAN ST. AMANT**,
who has been reading since I was nine years old.

BRIDGE:

n. a structure spanning a river, road, or chasm

v. to reduce the distance between

MATTAGASH, MAINE: 2006

I

MONDAY AFTERNOON

There is something in the northern Maine air that speaks of the first snowfall hours before it arrives. This is the same knowledge that birds find in those minutes before a rainstorm, or the tremor that rabbits feel in their paws before the quake. Snow has a way of talking, if you know how to listen. Billy Thunder, who was from downstate and therefore an *outsider*, heard it first that autumn.

"If this air had teeth, it would bite," Billy said, as if maybe he were talking to some of the guys at Bert's Lounge in Watertown. But he was standing alone at the upper end of the long and narrow Mattagash bridge, waiting by his mailbox for Orville Craft to arrive with that day's mail. Billy was expecting a shipment from Portland that would be marked DO NOT OPEN UNTIL CHRISTMAS on the outer brown wrapper. But he intended to open it immediately, maybe even smoke some of it.

A wind rose up from the river, caught the invisible current between the bridge's columns, and then swept out from under the ends, a wind ripe with winter. Billy zipped up his jacket, then reached into a pocket for his cigarettes. Being a native of distant Portland gave him the courage to say out loud what everyone else in town feels in their bones but rarely speaks. *Get ready for a long stretch of ice-cold white*.

No one knows when the first flakes of the year will fall. Sometimes, people are asleep in their warm beds when it happens. Other times, they are putting up firewood for the winter or feeding the dog or getting the mail. No one ever asks *why* it happens. They know that it *does* and that it *will*. When ice crystals in the upper atmosphere grow too heavy, they drop to the earth as snowflakes. If they fall in the night, snowflakes have only the sharp pinpoints of porch lights, those tiny sparks of human lives, to guide them down. But if they fall by day, then inside some warm Mattagash house or standing in a field of dead goldenrods or driving to the store, there is always one person who is first to say, "Look, it's snowing."

That Monday in October it was Billy Thunder, owner of the first mailbox above the one-way bridge, who would have the honor.

"Hurry up, Orville," Billy said. He was about to give up on that day's delivery when he saw the mail car, a blue Ford Taurus, poke its nose onto the opposite end of the bridge, three hundred feet from where Billy stood. At that same moment, Tommy Gifford flew by, so much wind left in his wake that Billy's jacket billowed, beating itself against his body. Tommy was in that black pickup he was so proud of, a truck that rode on four wheels large enough to carry a tractor.

Orville Craft had already driven his mail car a few feet onto the lower end of the bridge when Tommy roared onto the upper end. Orville kept his foot steady on the accelerator pedal. Bridge etiquette was simple. Every driver in town knew the rule well. Even the children in Mattagash knew it, as if they were born with it encoded in their DNA. *Whoever drives onto the bridge first has the right-of-way*. Because Orville was first, Tommy braked the pickup, threw it into reverse, and backed up. He sat waiting until the mail car drove off the upper end. Then the truck shot onto the bridge in a burst of acceleration. Seconds later, Tommy Gifford had crossed the river and disappeared down the road.

The first mailbox Orville had above the bridge was a new one, erected on a cedar post that past summer. Orville had grown used to seeing Billy Thunder hovering about at the end of the bridge like some kind of Fuller Brush salesman as he waited on the mail car. Tall, with straight, dark hair that grew an inch too far below the ears for most Mattagash men, Billy had a groomed appearance that indicated he hadn't done much heavy lifting in his life. He certainly hadn't done the kind of strenuous woods work that Mattagash males did to make a living. There was too much spring to Billy's step, his arm muscles resembling those that came from a gym, from lifting barbells rather than chainsaws. And the expression on his face spoke of a steady confidence and not the worried look that said prices for lumber might dip again and the bank would be coming to repossess the truck, the kind of worry that brought early wrinkles to a man's face. At twenty-eight years old, carefree and not married, Billy had the kind of personality that made the female species give him a second look when they thought their husbands weren't watching.

Orville was careful not to run over Billy's toes as he pulled up next to the box and put the Ford in park. He reached for the thin stack of letters on the seat beside him, the one with *Thunder #46* written on a piece of paper and tucked under the elastic band. He handed Billy his mail, another electric bill the boy had no intention of paying and several *Resident* and *Occupant* letters. Orville glanced down at the brown field bordering the river, at the tiny trailer sitting catty-corner to a grove of birch trees, their leaves yellow with autumn. It was more a makeshift camper than a trailer, but Billy Thunder had rented it his first day in town. On his second day, the mailbox had appeared, nailed to its skinny post. It was obvious that Billy Thunder was not one to sit around and wait for the Welcome Wagon.

"Have you done anything toward insulating yourself for the winter?" Orville asked. This was the loaded question that had been circulating the town for days.

"Yup," said Billy. "I bought a fifth of Jack Daniels. Hey, did you see that?" Billy was looking at a wet spot on the hood of Orville's car where something soft had hit, then vanished. "That looked like a fucking snowflake." With a cigarette firm between his lips, he used both hands to sort through the letters. He quit sorting when he felt a soft splat on the top of his hair. "Okay, that was definitely a snowflake. Fuck Almighty, it's still October."

"When was the last time you went to church?" Orville asked. "They *do* have churches in southern Maine, don't they, along with all them lobsters?"

Most of Mattagash would prefer to deny any ancestral connection to Billy Thunder, but since everyone in Mattagash *was* related somewhere back on the genealogical road, this wouldn't stand up in a court of law. Why, at a time when he should be looking for a sensible wife, Billy had jumped into a white 1966 Mustang convertible and driven eight hours north *looking for his ancestors*, as he put it, was good fodder for gossip. And fodder was always welcome in Mattagash, especially if it arrived in time to feed some of the ladies throughout the long winter.

"Nothing else?" Billy asked. He was shivering. "No package?" He watched as Orville turned and rummaged among the boxes on his backseat. "Hurry up, Orville. My balls are like ice cubes."

"If you stay in that camper all winter," Orville said, "they're likely to be snowballs, come spring."

Finding no package addressed to Billy Thunder, Orville turned back around in his seat and put the car in gear. Billy leaned down to the open window and looked into Orville's eyes.

"I bet you'll find it if you look again, Orville," he said. "I know you're a first-class mailman."

"You're kissing the wrong butt, Thunder," said Orville. "I'm not the man who sends the mail. I'm the man who delivers it."

Before Billy could reply, Orville hit the gas pedal and the mail car pulled away. In his rearview mirror, he saw Billy growing tinier, rings of smoke floating above his head as though they might be the gray ghosts of those ancestors he'd come searching for. One thing was obvious: Billy had as much Fennelson in him as he had Thunder. His mother had been born and raised in Mattagash but had disappeared downstate early in her life. She'd married a man named William Thunder, one that Mattagashers had never met and didn't care to, not with a name like that. There had long been talk in town of a Fennelson curse, an affliction carried in the family's genes that had plagued Fennelsons since the first ones arrived in the mid-nineteenth century. But after reasonable discussion over the years, most townsfolk had decided that the stupidity gene played a larger part in the curse than had fate. And now, here was a Fennelson descendant with plans to winter in a flimsy camper next to a windswept river. A betting club had started at the local café, just like the one they had each spring when folks bet on which April day the river will thaw and break free of its ice. Now they were gambling on the day Billy Thunder would either leave the camper voluntarily or an ambulance would back up to the door and take his frozen corpse away, a cigarette propped in its mouth.

As Orville drove from mailbox to mailbox, he kept watch for a large gathering of cars in the driveways of the more social houses. He had assumed there would be a surprise retirement party in the works somewhere. But the women must be getting better at planning their secret events. Or they were emailing each other, for Orville had not seen any signs of party subterfuge. He had just pulled up to Rita and Henry Plunkett's box, ready to deliver the pile of catalogues and magazines that Rita would have to stay up all night for years in order to read, when Billy Thunder zoomed by in the white Mustang. As usual, the car's canvas top was down and Billy was wearing earmuffs. Not long after Billy arrived in Mattagash, the mechanism that put the convertible's top up and down had broken, and now the canvas itself was caught fast in the gears and wouldn't budge. A few sensible men had offered to rip the canvas and raise the top manually, but Billy had refused. "You gotta be crazy," Billy had said. "This is a classic car. I'll drive with the top down until I can get it fixed." Certain that Billy Thunder was the crazy one, the whole town was holding its breath and waiting, what with the days turning so cold that even fur-covered animals were considering hibernation. And then, who but God would be able to find a *white* car in a snowstorm?

Except for a few newer homes that had sprung up on wooded back roads, most of the houses in Mattagash sat on each side of the main road as it followed the river. This meant most folks had a front window or a back window that could catch at least a small piece of river view, if not a big piece. And it meant Orville's job was all the more pleasant since every mailbox sat along the main road. Orville liked to think of his workday in two parts: the forty-five boxes *below* the bridge and the fifty-two boxes *above* the bridge. It was a nice way to break up the monotony of the day, and he had learned the technique from his father, Simon Craft, the previous mailman. Orville was almost fifty when he stopped delivering milk and started delivering letters. He saw in the job a great social act, the kind of work that joined and informed whole and distant communities, even if they didn't *want* to be joined or informed. In the sixteen years that he had been on the job, he had encountered only one significant thorn. And that's what Orville was thinking as he pulled up in front of #77, three miles above the Mattagash bridge. That, and the fact that it was, indeed, snowing. A few wet flakes were drifting down, disappearing as quickly as they landed.

This mailbox belonged to the Mattagash house with the best view of all, sitting atop a hill as it did, its windows able to see the river in both directions. This was Harold "Harry" Plunkett's house, part wood and part gray stone. Orville put the car in park and reached for the banded stack of mail that said *Plunkett #77*. He had expected the moose again, since he had gotten the moose for the past three years, ever since the feud first started. This was when Orville Craft refused Harry Plunkett's request for permission to fish at Craft Pond, which lay within easy sight of Orville's little get-away cabin. Since the cabin was a private place where Orville went to read the newspaper, he didn't want Harry intruding every time he had an urge for fresh trout. He figured Harry would understand, but he was wrong. And he realized this the day he drove up to #77 and discovered that Harry's traditional, silver-colored mailbox was gone. In its place was a mailbox shaped like a moose. The wooden antlers, firmly attached to the head with screws, served as the clamp that, when unclamped, would lower the moose's head and open the mailbox. It was into this creature that Orville Craft, as a proud and official mail carrier, was expected to place the United States mail. He had listened as Harry rattled on about how he had seen the moose mailbox at a craft fair in Quebec, Canada, and now he couldn't face life without it. That was the day Orville and Harry quit speaking.

To be exact, Orville quit speaking. For more than three years, he had done what his postal rule book insist he do. He had delivered letters *to a sound and acceptable mailbox, with no lewd words or drawings upon its surface*. But there was nothing in the book that said he had to have social conversations with his customers. So other than answering a quick postal query, Orville said nothing to Harry. It was the only form of ammunition a mail employee had, unless he grabbed a gun and started shooting. The whole town knew Orville Craft was too meek to go postal. Now, he had one week left to deliver the mail before he would retire. Five more days of Harold Plunkett.

Harry had to know this was Orville's last week. How could he live in Mattagash and not know? That was probably what had fueled him. At least Orville saw it that way as he sat in his mail car, holding a hand on the car's horn. A few seconds later, he saw Harry pulling on a denim jacket as he strolled toward the mailbox, taking his time, using that slow gait of his, knowing it would annoy Orville even more. Harry was still a good-looking man, his dark hair showing enough strands of gray to give him a splash of dignity, unless you saw him through the eyes of his mailman.

"What's all the noise about, Orville?" Harry asked. He was wearing a baseball cap that said *Jesus Loves You, But I Don't.* "You're gonna scare my moose."

Maybe Orville hadn't spoken much to Harry in three years, but for all those many days, he had practiced as a kind of mantra the things he would say once he retired.

"Oh, I bet you're wondering why I changed my mailbox," Harry said. He bobbed his head at the moose. "This morning I got to thinking. What's the use of owning such a fine-looking animal if I got to sit on my porch and look down at its backside? So I transmuted it. You know, transmute. To change in form, nature, or substance."

Orville felt anger so pure he envisioned being fired for running down a customer with the mail car on his last week before freedom. Harry had probably used a hacksaw and a welder to do the work, for now the moose's head pointed up the hill at Harry's front porch. Its ass, which had become the hinged door, pointed at Orville Craft. Harry Plunkett could have gone to a sensible craft fair in Caribou and bought something for his living room wall, maybe a canoe paddle that had a moose painted on it, art that was perfect for that long narrow space over the sofa. But no, he had gone to Quebec, where everyone is *French*.

"I'm not gonna stick mail into *that*," Orville said, the most words he'd spoken to Harry in three years.

"But aren't you the mailman?" Harry asked.

Orville had hated the moose for three years, its mocking dull eyes, its round, black nostrils. He despised everything about it since he'd come to know it well. While it did resemble the *real* moose Orville had seen drinking water from his pond or swimming the river in front of his house or eating up Meg's fresh garden lettuce, *real* moose did not have red flags glued to their sides. And now, five blessed days from retirement, the moose was mooning him, and that was more than Orville Craft could take.

With Harry watching, Orville spun the mail car around in the middle of the road. He felt certain there must be a rule against postmen doing police turns, but he didn't care. Three miles later, he flew across the one-way bridge, which was free of any oncoming vehicle. His and Meg's house sat not far from the bridge, but Orville didn't glance in to see if Meg was home yet from grocery shopping. Another five hundred feet past his own mailbox, Orville made a sharp right onto the gravel road that led up to Cell Phone Hill, the only spot in town high enough that cell phones could transmit. He put the car in park and then rummaged in the glove compartment for his cell phone. It was his daughter who had given him that skinny phone for his birthday. *All professional postal carriers should have cell phones, Daddy*, she had written on his birthday card.

Clicking the phone on, Orville punched the seven numbers he knew would cause a *real* phone to ring at the post office in neighboring St. Leonard. The office manager, Edwin Beecher, finally answered with his long and annoying "Heeeellloooo," as if he were the host of a popular game show. Orville explained what was happening at Harold Plunkett's mailbox. He listened for a minute as Ed shuffled through the rule book. Finally, Ed told Orville what he didn't want to hear. Harry's moose mailbox wasn't *violating any postal codes or restrictions, so as long as it's sound and acceptable with no lewd words or drawings.*

"Blah, blah," Orville said. Ed's voice was tiny, as if the post office itself existed down there in the coils and valleys of the cell phone.

"Come on, Orville, don't be so cantankerous. You only got this week left." Ed was still talking when Orville clicked the phone off.

The little mail car drove back down the gravel road that led up to Cell Phone Hill, taking its time now. But when Orville arrived back at Harry Plunkett's mailbox, Harry was still waiting, a few white snowflakes melting on his cap.

"I've been thinking while you were gone," said Harry. "I believe you're being cantankerous, Orville."

Without a word, Orville reached out, pulled down the moose's hindquarters, and stuffed the mail inside. Two bills and a personal letter. He had done it. He had delivered the mail come rain, come snow, come sleet or hail or *moose shit*. He put the car into drive, grinding the gears generously. His tires spit some gravel back at Harry as he drove away from the box. In his rearview mirror, he saw Harry run a jacket sleeve across the moose's back, as if petting it for a job well done.

2

MONDAY AFTERNOON AND EVENING

When Edna Plunkett crawled into her blue Toyota, she could smell snow in the afternoon air. The few flakes that had fallen earlier in the day hadn't amounted to more than wet spots wherever they hit. Now Edna wondered which morning it would be that the whole town would wake to find itself layered in white. With no other vehicle in sight, she had right-of-way on the bridge and so didn't bother to brake as she hit the lower end. The car crossed over a river so blue it hurt Edna to glance down at it. But that's what autumn did to colors in Mattagash. It brightened them, dazzling the onlookers. Mother Nature knew what she was doing all right. She was giving everyone some last splashes of red and orange and golden yellow before she gave them a solid blanket of white for months. *Maybe*, Edna thought, *autumn was nature's way of apologizing*.

She passed her brother Tommy's house and saw his dog sitting listless in front of its doghouse, the silver chain that held it catching sunlight. *Poor dog*, Edna thought, as she passed the sandwich board sign that sat on Florence Walker's front lawn. Edna noticed that the Word for the Week was *cantankerous*. Florence was an English teacher who had retired two years earlier but couldn't quit teaching. Below the word, Florence had written in neat letters: *stubborn; unwilling to cooperate*. Each week the new word began with a new letter of the alphabet. Mattagash had been from A to Z three times in the eighty-one weeks since Florence retired, from *anomaly* to *zinger*, from *atypical* to *zealous*, from *anathema* to *zenith*. Now they were back to C. Edna made a quick mental note of the word and its meaning, but she would have a full week to learn it. Let others in town ridicule the old teacher; Edna Plunkett appreciated the free education. She even wrote each word down in a secret notebook that she kept at the bottom of her sewing basket. Edna had plans for her future, and big words like *charismatic*, *daunting*, and *enigma* would come in handy.

At Mama Sal's house, Edna saw her mother standing next to the dead hollyhocks near the front porch. She felt her stomach tighten, the way it always did when she was about to discuss something important with her mother. She had hoped to gather some steam on her way to Mama Sal's front door. But there her mother was, entrenched as a post and wearing her pissed-off face. Edna cut the car's engine, grabbed her purse from the seat, and got out.

"Good thing Orville's about to retire," said Mama Sal. She was wearing the blue birthday sweater Edna's twins had given her. Her thick hair was pulled back into its usual gray ponytail. In the palm of her hand were a dozen dried hollyhock seeds and under her arm was that day's mail. "I got a good mind to start throwing pop bottles at the mail car." She shuffled the black seeds into a sweater pocket.

"Were you trying to flag him down again?" Edna asked. She had been told often that, of the two daughters, she was the one who most resembled Mama Sal. And this had always pleased Edna, even though her mother was tall and big-boned.

"He pretends he doesn't see me," Mama Sal said. "And me waving both my arms. All I want to know is why my disability check is late."

"It's against the rules to stop on his way back to the post office," said Edna. "You know how Orville loves his rule book."

As Mama Sal turned her aluminum walker toward the front door, Edna reached out and put a steadying hand on her mother's elbow. The walker had been the subject of much whispering in the family. Mama Sal bought it a decade earlier, the same month Edna's father died unexpectedly of a heart attack. A week after the funeral, Edna had driven Mama Sal to the first of many doctor appointments, followed by visits to a disability lawyer in Watertown. While the subject was taboo in that Mama Sal never brought it up, which meant no one else should either, Edna had seen the occasional document left lying on her mother's kitchen table. She had read words such as *lumbar back pain* and *inability to ambulate effectively*. Mama Sal occasionally referred to her condition more affectionately as "my damn back." Whatever mishap caused the injury in the first place remained unknown to her children. But the disability checks began arriving nonetheless, slender doves winging up monthly from Augusta. Over the years, Edna would drop by to find the walker having a good rest in the kitchen and Mama Sal upstairs taking a nap, even though they had long since moved her bedroom downstairs. Or the walker would be left at the door going down to the cellar and Mama Sal could be heard humming as she sorted through boxes of junk in the basement.

"Watch that top step now," Edna said, as Mama Sal maneuvered the walker's front legs up onto the porch.

Inside, on the kitchen counter, Edna noticed the box of medium-sized pumpkins she had dropped off in Mama Sal's garage the night before. She had to struggle to carry that box from the car to the garage. Now here it was, sitting in the kitchen, the pumpkins smiling over the rim. Edna looked at Mama Sal, who looked back.

"You had any company today?" Edna asked.

"I've known you to be a lot of things, lawyer, doctor, insurance agent, fire inspector, and minister," said Mama Sal. "So now you're a cop?"

Edna reached into the cupboard for a cup and poured some of the coffee that had most likely been in the pot since Mama Sal got up that morning. It poured like thin molasses. She watched as Mama Sal situated herself in the recliner by the window, that spot from which she watched the world go by.

"I was just asking," said Edna.

Mama Sal opened that day's *Bangor Daily News* and began reading. Edna pulled a chair away from the kitchen table and over to the recliner.

"I got something to tell you," she said, as Mama Sal flipped over to the obituaries. "Now, I don't want you to hit the ceiling, but I'm gonna ask Roderick for a divorce. The boys will be in high school soon. I think I might sign up for a class at the college. I'm still only thirty-seven years old."

Edna took a breath and waited. Mama Sal seemed to be listening well enough, especially since she folded up her *Bangor Daily* and Edna knew she hadn't looked at the comics yet, her favorite part. If all Mama Sal had done was hit the ceiling, Edna would have been satisfied. But she had gone further than that. She had hit *Edna*, a sharp quick scuff across the side of her daughter's head with the rolled-up newspaper.

"You're still trying to keep up to your sister's heels," said Mama Sal. "If Bertina was to shit blue, you'd be drinking ink all day. And now that she's back here in Mattagash, expecting handouts for herself and them Spanish-looking grandkids of mine, you been running over there every day like a headless chicken instead of staying home with your husband. Bertina's already had three divorces and you haven't had *one*. That's the problem, isn't it?"

Edna pushed her chair back and stood. She felt her eyes tearing up. But crying would only weaken her. She reached for her purse. At the kitchen door, she turned and looked back at Mama Sal. She could feel her bottom lip quiver, as it did when she was a child and felt so tiny in her mother's tall and grown-up presence.

"I guess pumpkins can walk," Edna said. When she slammed the door behind her, it was hard enough that Mama Sal's wind chimes chattered on the front porch.

When Edna pulled back into her own yard, it was already 2 p.m. and not the best time of day for any sensible Mattagash woman to go shopping. Since there were no department stores unless you headed south to Caribou or Presque Isle, important shopping for anything other than groceries was a three-hour round-trip. It would be evening before she returned, but she didn't care. Not on this day. That's when she noticed that Roderick's pickup truck was pulled in above the house. He must have come home for a cup of tea and something sweet, which he shouldn't be eating in the first place, not since the doctor had told him to lose fifty pounds.

Roderick was sitting at the kitchen table, half a chocolate cookie on a plate in front of him. When he saw Edna, he stopped chewing. It wasn't as if he'd starve to death if she were no longer there to cook his meals. He was obviously capable of foraging.

"So much for your diet," Edna said. Before she could say anything else, let alone "I want a divorce," her twelve-year-old twins burst into the kitchen in an identical dash to the fridge for sodas.

"Why are you guys not in school?" Edna asked.

"Basketball practice," one boy answered, as he grabbed the rest of Roderick's cookie. His brother was already on his way back to the front door.

"I hate to be a tattletale," Roderick said to Edna, "but Roddy slapped Ricky before you got home. What's your new rule? A dollar of allowance per slap?" The last twin stopped at the door and looked back at his mother.

"It was Ricky who slapped *me*," he said. "Daddy can't tell us apart." And then the twins were gone, in an identical burst of energy. Edna heard the front door slam and picture frames rattle on the wall in the living room. Since they had planned to name their first boy after his father, Edna and Roderick were bewildered when male twins came along. Unable to choose one namesake, they had finally named both boys after Roderick, in accordance to their birth order, and had simply divided the name between them: Rod Plunkett Jr. and Rick Plunkett Jr.

Edna watched until the twins had left the yard, identical legs cranking the pedals of their bikes. Then she went to the cupboard, lifted the plate that held up a stack of many plates, and took out a hundred dollar bill. She came back to the table and stood looking down at her husband.

"The boys will be in high school soon. It might not be a bad idea if we were to go our separate ways, at least for a little while."

Roderick stood up fast and reached an arm out to her. Edna leaned back, afraid to be slapped once more that day for telling the truth. But then Roderick raised his other arm and beckoned for her to step into them, to let him give her a hug. In all their years of marriage, Roderick had never hit her. Sometimes, Edna almost wished he would throw something. Bertina was always bragging about things her ex-husbands and lovers had hurled at her. "Latinos are very hot and passionate," Bertina said. "So are Italians." But on this day, Roderick was more scared than passionate.

"I'll clean up my act," he said, dropping his arms since Edna refused them. She went to the fridge and got out a can of lemonade. Roderick followed. "I'll wipe my shoes before I come into the house," he added, as if that thought had just flown into his mind and not because Edna had been nagging him for years. But it was so much more than muddy shoes on carpet. "And I'll take you every Sunday to the Chinese buffet in Watertown."

Edna closed the fridge door.

"I'll quit smoking this very minute. I know you been on me about that." He held up his right hand. "Hand to God, no more cigarettes."

"I took the hundred-dollar bill that we were gonna put into our savings account," Edna said. "Me and Ben Franklin are going shopping, and we're gonna spend every penny if it kills us."

Roderick followed her to the front door.

"Do you think you might be going through the change early?" he asked.

"Oh, I'm going through a change all right," Edna said.

Edna shopped all over the mall for things she didn't like and didn't need. A pair of cotton slacks, and winter on its way. A corkscrew with Elvis's head at the top when she hardly ever drank wine and she wasn't all that crazy about Elvis. A key chain, when she already had several the kids had given her for Christmases and birthdays. A throw pillow that didn't match the sofa. Lacy red socks she'd never wear.

But she bought some important stuff too. On her way home, she stopped at the craft shop in Caribou and selected oil paints, some brushes, and a large canvas. In high school, an art teacher told Edna that she had an artistic flair and should maybe even take lessons. But this was around the same time she met Roderick Plunkett, back from the Army, tall and muscular and wearing a starched uniform that had seen little action until he convinced

Edna to step into a Watertown motel room he'd rented for the night. That night now seemed a lifetime ago, and in a way, it was. It was Edna's lifetime that had passed, each year taking away more of the artistic girl who had dropped out her senior year to marry her boyfriend. Now, Edna was going to start a new life. Some people call it being born again. As Edna saw it, since she had been passed at the ripe age of seventeen from Mama Sal to Roderick, it was being born for the first time.

It was already evening when Edna saw the *Welcome to Mattagash* sign, with its big friendly moose. There had been a vote taken the year the sign was painted. The moose had won, with the loon coming in second, followed by the coyote in third place. The lobster, being a Down East notion far from ocean-less Mattagash, didn't even place. She drove past the sign and into a town that had grown quiet while she was gone. Edna had never before been shopping that late, all alone and that far away. There had been a soft panic mixed in with the good feelings, but she didn't let it enervate her one little bit. *Enervate: to deprive of strength, to weaken*. She drove past Amy Joy Lawler's house, the old McKinnon homestead and one of the first homes after the welcome sign. She drove past her own house, as if she didn't live there anymore. She could see a flickering light coming from the living room window and assumed Roderick and the twins were fastened to the TV for the night.

Headlights were already coming across the bridge, so Edna waited on her end for the vehicle to pass. It was her brother, Tommy Gifford, in his black pickup truck with those enormous tires. She heard Tommy toot once, a signal that he recognized her car, and so Edna tooted back. She pulled onto the bridge, glided the length of it, and memorized again the meaning for *cantankerous*. Only the downstairs light was on at Mama Sal's, in the room where her bed now was. Edna hoped she was saying her rosary beads and not watching the road like it was a movie. She felt a rush of freedom once she was past the house where she'd been born and raised. Ahead was Blanche's Café, already closed for the night, the windows dark and curtains drawn. Edna passed the moose that Roderick's uncle, Harry Plunkett, had installed as his mailbox. And then she passed Blanche Taylor herself, out doing her nightly run.

As Edna drove, wind blew dead leaves across the tarred road ahead of her. It was before the road ended that she saw the sign, *Mattagash Trailer Park*. There were so many retirees and old-timers living in the trailers there now that the local kids had nicknamed it Jurassic Park. Edna pulled up in front of Bertina's trailer, the oldest one in the park and the shabbiest too. She turned off the car and sat staring at the last trailer in the upper row of trailers, a one-bedroom that stood next to a clump of pine trees. It was empty now. The man who previously lived in it, a soil inspector from Bangor, had finished his work and disappeared back downstate. Ward Hooper. He had come late in the spring and rented the trailer, a home for the two months he would spend in Mattagash gathering and recording soil samples for the state. Edna first met him at Blanche's, the two of them sitting on stools and waiting for their lunch to arrive. He owned a white pickup truck, and he had asked Edna questions about herself as if the answers were important. *Have you always lived here? What do you think about the war in Iraq? Do you have children? What are the winters like this far north?* And even though it was *daunting* for her, she had answered. She had answered because Ward Hooper was so *charismatic*. She felt *euphoric* sitting there on that stool. It was almost as if, now that she had the big words to fit the big feelings, it hurt all the more. *Poignant: affecting the mind and emotions.*

This was the third time Edna had driven over to the trailer park for a visit. Mama Sal had been predicting that Bertina would spend her time lying on her Florida furniture and doing absolutely nothing now that she'd been forced to come back home for some R and R. But as far as Edna could tell, there wasn't much furniture to lie around on. During her first visit, she had been shocked to see in the living room nothing more than a ratty beanbag chair and a narrow sofa that looked more like an army cot. But that didn't stop Bertina from putting on airs, even if she got those airs on credit. "The shipping company is late delivering my *real* furniture," Bertina had declared six days earlier when she drove a rattling car up to Mama Sal's door, two dark-skinned girls fighting in the backseat. "I got crystal lamps and maple coffee tables *en route* from Tampa as I speak."

There were no lights on inside the trailer except for the back room the girls shared as a bedroom, two sleeping bags sprawled on the linoleum floor.

Edna went up the rickety steps and knocked on the door.

"Come on in, it's open." Bertina's voice.

Edna stepped into darkness and closed the door behind her. Across the room, Bertina's cigarette tip glowed orange.

"Is that you, Bertie?" Edna asked. "Why's it so dark in here?"

She heard a quick snap and then the room was flooded with lamplight. Edna could see Bertina now, half-swallowed by the beanbag chair, an ashtray filled with cigarette butts at her feet. Her straight brown hair, usually shiny and stylish, was now pulled back into a limp braid. Bertina had taken after their father, petite, with brown eyes instead of dark blue. Edna was plumper, the way Roderick said he liked her, and tall like Mama Sal.

"Come on over here," Bertina said, that same excitement in

her voice as those days when she'd brag about her high school dates, Edna still too young to think of boys. "I want you to see something."

Edna crossed the room and stood looking down at her sister.

"Close your eyes," said Bertina. When she stood, the beanbag chair sighed beneath her as it filled back out. She put both hands on Edna's shoulders and turned her to face the wall. "I mean it, close your eyes and keep them closed." Edna heard again the snap of a lamp switch.

"Okay, open them," said Bertina. Edna saw nothing but darkness.

"Why'd you put the lamp out?" she asked. She was staring at a pitch-black wall of the tiniest and seediest trailer in the park. What was so spectacular about that?

"Wait a sec and you'll see," Bertina whispered. And that's when the wall in front of Edna came alive with dozens of sparkling dots, tiny pinpoints of light. What she saw was impressive. It was, and she'd have to admit it, an *anomaly*. As her eyes adjusted to the darkness, Edna could see that it was a long, narrow painting hanging in a frame. An electrical cord ran from behind it and down to an outlet below.

"It's Venice, Italy," Bertina said. "I just got around to unpacking it." She reached out and touched a fingertip to the velvet surface. Edna watched as the thing rippled, its watery canals shimmering in the dark. She could see now that there were many buildings hugging the canals, each one bursting forth with a yellow light of its own. "I bought it at a gift shop in Tampa," Bertina added.

"It's interesting," said Edna. "Sort of *atypical*." She hoped Bertina would notice her use of the word.

"I couldn't leave Florida without bringing at least one piece of art with me," Bertina said. She had developed what Edna could only assume was a Florida accent, dragging out the ends of her sentences far longer than any Mattagasher would. "See them long, narrow boats?" She placed her fingernail against a gondola that had been lit from bow to stern. "That's what they use over there instead of cars."

The truth was that this electrical art really *was* unlike any Edna had seen. And art wasn't the only thing Bertina had to brag about. On Edna's first visit, she had been forced to look at a million photographs. There were shots of Bertina's orange tree in her sunny backyard, every leaf, every bug, every inch of bark. Then came fuzzy images of Bertina's in-ground swimming pool, which, along with the house and the backyard, she'd lost in the current divorce battle. Edna had even flipped through a dozen pictures of two peaked-nosed poodles, balls of hair around their ankles and rhinestone collars about their necks, poodles barking, running, sniffing, and, in one shot, even lifting their legs to pee on the orange tree.

"It looks like Bangor to me," Edna said. She hoped her voice held the disinterest she intended. "That looks like the mental institute where they kept poor Aunt Mildred." She pointed at a building with two domes, a host of firefly lights twinkling sadly from behind its windows.

"Aunt Mildred was bonkers," Bertina said as she snapped the light back on. She pulled the plug on the painting, and Venice, without the power generated by American electricity, shut itself down for the night.

When Edna got home a half hour later, she stood outside her house and stared up at the glittering stars. She thought again of Ward Hooper. Did he take up gliding as he planned to do, floating about the sky inside a wooden plane with no engine at all, no motor telling him what to do? A bluish flicker came from behind the living room window. Roderick and the boys would be watching television, as usual, Roderick stretched out on the sofa and the twins lying on the floor, on identical stomachs. She knew Roderick's breath would smell of fresh smoke when she leaned down to wake him. Staring at the light that came from her own home, Edna thought of all those Italian houses with miniature bulbs in their windows. Venice. Of course she knew it wasn't Bangor. And, of course, Aunt Mildred was bonkers. What had Roderick said, when the two of them had been forced by Mama Sal to take Aunt Mildred along to Bangor on their honeymoon, drop her off at the mental institute as if she was some kind of delivery package?

All her lights are on, but no one's home.

3

TUESDAY MORNING, AFTERNOON, AND EVENING

Before she died, Emily often came with him when Harry drove up to his favorite spot on the mountain. But Emily Plunkett was now another casualty of time. Harry got out of his pickup and stood looking at the grassy road, barely noticeable, that wound through the trees. Another twenty years and not even this light trace of the old road would be left. It had begun as a horse and wagon trail leading to Mattagash Brook, where a sporadic gathering of houses and people had once thrived in the wilderness. It was beyond the brook itself that his grandparents had built a home and raised a family. That was Foster and Mathilda Fennelson, and their homestead once stood in the midst of pines and white birches. That was before the old couple was forced to give up a way of life that was quickly disappearing. "What if you fell, Mama, so far from a hospital?" he had heard his mother ask Mathilda. "Daddy, with your bad heart, you should live nearer a doctor," she had said to Foster. So his grandparents had listened to the younger generation, had heeded the advice of those who no longer knew how to make soap by hand, how to shoe a horse, how to bury your own child in the family graveyard. His grandparents didn't have the words to say, "But what if I need to walk to the spring for a drink of water?" or "With my *good* heart, I should be nearer the sound of the ravens each morning."

They were brought out of the woods and down to Mattagash. The rest of their lives, the important part, the part that made them human, stayed behind in the old house. In town, they bounced from son to daughter until Foster, feeling useless, gave up the ghost one autumn morning. Mathilda then disappeared into a room at the St. Leonard Nursing Home, another old bee in a graying honeycomb of tiny cubicles and sad faces. Harry visited her there before she died, but since she no longer knew him, he stopped the visits.

Every time he went up on the mountain, Harry felt that deep loss of people and heritage. It was on the mountain that he often thought of Wallace McGee, the best soldier he'd ever known and now one of the many names on a long black wall near the White House. A man should be able to leave war behind once he's fought it and it's over. But it wasn't that easy. Civil War soldiers who couldn't adjust well after the war were said to have *soldier's heart.* In World War I, it was *shell shock.* In World War II and his father's war, Korea, it was *combat fatigue.* It took Vietnam and its aftermath for it to slowly turn into what it still is, *post-traumatic stress.* Harry had come to prefer *soldier's heart.* At least there was still something *human* left in it.

He turned away from the old road. It always hurt him inside each time he found the remnants of it. It was a road that made him think too deep and too long when his mind went walking down it, like those dangerous trails and paths through the steamy jungles of Vietnam. Unlike the freshness of the Mattagash woods, the Mekong Delta was a world of thick, green plants, a planet of muck—a *muck* that made noises as you pulled your boots up out of it. *Muck, muck, muck.* In those parts of the country where the canopy was double and even triple, the enemy hid in the terrain. They blended into it like snakes and spiders until they *became* it. It was a war of camouflage and concealment, where even the lizards swore at American soldiers, the Fuck You lizards with their *UckYou UckYou UckYou* taunts coming out of the invisible night. Those were the things that Wally McGee liked to read about so he could teach his fellow soldiers. Wally and his books. *Hey, Sarge, did you know that plant life in the jungle is in constant competition for sunlight? That's why it grows in layers and forms canopies in the first place.* Harry had seen it for what it was. *Everything in the jungle wants to live, Corporal. We sure want to live. But so does Charlie. And the jungle is on his team, not ours.* He felt he owed it to Emily and his ancestors to remember the old trail to Mattagash Brook. But he owed the jungle nothing.

Up through the treetops, Harry could see a patch of blue sky. The whole town was in a tizzy over snowflakes that had fallen the day before. But Harry knew they had a few more days before any sincere snow arrived. It would be an early snow, but snow didn't ask before it fell. When he reached the tree that had the plastic orange band tied around its trunk, he knew it marked the invisible line that separated his nephew Roderick Plunkett's land from Orville Craft's. He crossed the brook that was barely running water and onto land that had been Craft land for over a hundred years. Since it was quite possible some hunter from downstate was in the woods prematurely, trespassing and carrying a gun, Harry was wearing the red sweatshirt he'd ordered from a magazine. On the front were the words: *If you shoot me, City Slicker, you better kill me.* On the back was the rest of the message: *Otherwise, I'm getting up...* He liked the sweatshirt a lot, especially when he was at Blanche's Café and a city slicker was reading it, some guy in a new L. L. Bean hunting jacket, the kind that has a pocket for a cell phone.

A hundred yards in, through maples that still held their autumn-red leaves, Harry stepped out onto the trail Orville had bulldozed up the mountainside. It led to his cabin at the edge of Craft Pond, a pond so full of proud trout there might not be another like it in all of Maine. Harry stood for some time staring down into the dark waters that shimmered with light on the surface. In the branches above his head were the two gray jays that had followed him up the mountainside, hoping a sandwich might be hidden in his pocket. He could see the green roof of Orville's cabin above the clutch of birch trees to his right. But he wasn't worried that Orville might discover him there at Craft Pond. He knew Mattagash's finest mailman was busy going from mailbox to mailbox in the Ford Taurus.

On his way back down the mountainside, the gray jays still in pursuit, Harry noticed the sign nailed to the trunk of a maple. As he studied the words, he reached into his shirt pocket for his red timber chalk. Then he smiled, remembering that his chainsaw was close by, in the back of his pickup truck.

As Billy Thunder stood waiting for the mail car, he lit his third Winston of the day. Then he stuffed his hands into his jacket pockets, the cigarette held firmly in his teeth. Portland might smell of fish and seagull shit, but at least it had buildings tall enough to break a wind so cold your bones rattled when it hit you. He saw Orville's blue Ford reach the lower end of the bridge and roll slowly toward him. Billy waited as the car pulled to a stop and idled there, a parachute of exhaust rising from beyond its back bumper. He saw Orville taking his important time inside the car, inspecting a package, putting it back, inspecting another. Billy knew he was doing it to throw the weight of his government job around. He pulled a hand from his pocket and rapped on the window.

"Come on, Orville, for fuck's sake," Billy said, and there

went the swearing Winston again, bouncing up and down to his words. Whether the cigarette wanted to curse or not, in Billy Thunder's mouth, it had no choice. Mattagashers had witnessed hundreds of swearing Winstons since the day Billy drove the white Mustang past the welcome sign. "Do I have any fucking mail or not?" He watched as Orville hit the button that slid his window down.

"I've told you before, Thunder," said Orville. "You'll get your mail as fast as I can deliver it, like everyone else in town."

"Yeah, well, I'm not like everyone else in town," said Billy, accepting a thin stack of letters from Orville's hand. "Maybe you noticed?" He shuffled through the few envelopes. *Occupant. Sale. Resident. Occupant.* He heard Orville throw the little car in gear and was quick enough to toss his cigarette to the ground and get an arm in through the window before the car could pull away.

"I wouldn't do that if I were you," said Orville. "Otherwise, Tommy Gifford's dog is gonna have a surprise arm for supper."

"You got a lot of packages in there, Orville," Billy said. He removed his arm from the window when it was apparent Orville had put the car back into park. "It's a small, brown box."

Orville knew very well what those packages looked like. He had already delivered a dozen of them to Billy Thunder. The return name on the upper left corner was always *Elizabeth Miller, Portland, ME.* Orville once had even stretched the postal rules by asking Billy what was in those boxes. "They're from my girlfriend in Portland," Billy had told him. "Pictures of her naked as a newborn baby. And some condoms, so I don't catch something up here in the boondocks and take it home to her." Orville figured this statement was true, or it was not true. How to know with a guy like Thunder?

"I've been telling you for two weeks that I can't deliver what isn't mailed," Orville said.

Billy stood watching as the mail car sped up the road. When it braked at Tommy Gifford's mailbox, Tommy's chained-up dog let off a volley of sharp, angry barks. What was he going to do now? The Delgato boys had obviously shut off deliveries to him. They'd even stopped telephoning a week before with threats of what they were going to do to his kneecaps if he didn't send their share of the money back to Portland. Billy wasn't afraid of losing his kneecaps. What was the kneecap but a rest stop between the crotch and the foot? He could learn to walk as if his legs were wooden stilts, so long as he had money in his pockets for balance. Billy didn't even blame the boys for being angry. But Supply and Demand couldn't work if Supply quit speaking to Demand.

Maybe tomorrow, he thought. It had become his daily mantra. He wondered if he should go to Blanche's and spend money he didn't have on some hot food. His camper was now almost as cold inside as it was out. But how could he buy a bigger electric heater until another package arrived? He heard the toot of a car horn and turned to see Kenny Barker, his toothy grin filling up the bottom half of his face. Kenny wound his window down.

"Yo, Captain Kirk," he said. "How are things on the *Enterprise*?"

Billy put his hands back in his jacket pockets and crossed the road to talk to Kenny more privately. He already knew that ears grew on trees in Mattagash, and even moles had twenty-twenty vision.

"Check back tomorrow," Billy said.

"Aw, damn," said Kenny. "I shoulda kept getting my shit from that idiot in Watertown. It wasn't the best stuff, but he was a dependable idiot."

Billy shook his head. *Why do they do it?* he wondered. Why do customers who have been so loyal they eat from your hand like starving dogs turn so mean and spiteful?

"Did you just call me an idiot in a roundabout way?" Billy asked. All of Kenny's teeth disappeared at once.

"No," Kenny said. That desperate look appeared in his eyes, a look Billy recognized well and knew how to control.

"How do you think *I* feel?" Billy asked. "When I don't have merchandise to sell, I don't eat. I haven't been to Watertown on a date for two weeks. I haven't had a case of lover's nuts like this since grammar school. As a matter of fact, you're starting to look less ugly to me."

Kenny's window shot up. He gave Billy one last look before he hit the gas pedal. Billy watched as the car flew across the narrow bridge and was gone. He reached into his shirt pocket and pulled out his pack of Winstons. He counted twelve cigarettes. He looked down at the tarred road where he'd thrown the new one he lit up before Orville arrived, bearing nothing but cold wind and arrogance. He picked it up, shook the dirt from its filter, and slipped it into his pocket. It was a shame that a polished businessman like William Thunder would have to find work alongside unskilled laborers. But with no shipments arriving for the past fourteen days, the boys in Portland had obviously meant it when they said "*nada mas*." That they would trek north to find him, as they threatened in their last phone call, seemed unlikely. Billy doubted the Delgatos could find Bangor without the U.S. cavalry riding alongside with a canteen full of bourbon and a good road map. So how could they find tiny Mattagash, five more hours north? Still, he had no choice now but to go study the chalkboard at Blanche's, see if anyone in town needed a handyman.

Otherwise, it appeared Billy Thunder would have to stop eating, drinking, smoking, driving, and maybe even fucking.

When Orville arrived at the moose mailbox, Harry's truck was pulled into the driveway, Harry himself waiting next to the box. Orville found the packet with #77 on it and then whirred down his window. That's when Harry nodded at the wood blocks piled in the back of his truck.

"Nothing like getting up your winter wood, is there?" Harry asked. Orville quickly lowered the moose's rear end and deposited into its body that day's mail. "They say maple is a good firewood because it's dense and produces more coals."

Orville had not even glanced up at Harry. Instead, he pulled the car out of park and eased it back onto the road. Meg had warned him that morning. "Don't let Harry Plunkett get to you. If you went along with him as if it didn't bother you, you'd be taking all the sport out of it." Orville didn't see it that way, not when *he* was the sport. And besides, Meg wasn't the best judge in this situation. The Craft-Plunkett feud might have manifested itself in the form of a moose mailbox after Orville's refusal to let Harry fish at Craft Pond. But Orville was certain that the impetus—*impetus: that which incites; the stimulus*—had to do with a woman named Meg Hart Craft, who had once been blond by nature and had legs that seemed to go on forever under her summer dresses. Meg, whose high cheekbones had disappeared beneath a face most people would call pleasantly plump, whose long legs were now useful to carry around that extra seventy pounds and whose blond hair came from a little bottle with the word *Clairol* on it. Meg, who had learned to stare at a computer for hours as she played Hangman and Solitaire and some dumb game where a penguin in a tuxedo jumps over blocks of ice, all while she answered the instant messages that came winging from her sister down in Augusta. It had all started with Meg, at a high school dance forty-four years earlier.

Orville hit the gas pedal and headed off to his next stop, where Dorrie Mullins was awaiting her catalogs *du jour*.

It was after supper and Orville Craft was dressed in his regular green work pants, not the fancier ones he wore while delivering mail. It wasn't as if he donned a suit and tie when he went to work. But he felt he owed the government as well as his postal clients the courtesy of being a nattily dressed and presentable mail carrier. His shirts were well ironed and always a solid color, whether plain white or pale blue. No busy and distracting plaids for Orville, and certainly nothing with a silly slogan on it, such as the wordy shirts and caps Harry Plunkett often wore.

Meg, on the other hand, thought Orville worried too much about his appearance. She had fussed in the beginning since she was the one who had to starch and iron those shirts, as well as put that pleat down each leg of his solid gray or brown or black pants. "Your customers don't even see your pants," Meg had said. "And besides, who says the mailman has to be eye candy?"

On the other side of the marital coin, Orville himself had often wondered if Meg ever woke in the middle of the night, unable to sleep, if she ever lay there in bed beside her mailman husband and wished he was Harold Plunkett. Or, if she refused to go that far in her marriage bed, did she ever wonder what being married to Harry would be like? It was true that Harry was more of a character than a sensible man, like Orville Craft. The town saw in the former a seasoned storyteller, the kind the old-timers used to be, regaling folks with funny events that had happened generations ago, along with a bit of new polish. In Orville's book this was called bullshitting. But Harry had his fans; there was no doubt about that. And he had maintained a good physique over the years, always cutting his own firewood, always doing his own shoveling, even his own grocery shopping since he'd been a widower for a lot of years. By contrast, Orville paid for his firewood since it was cheap in Mattagash. And he paid for Tommy Gifford to plow his driveway on snow days. Meg did the grocery shopping for the two of them. Considering all this, Orville had developed what is known as a spare tire around his waistline and a certain slackness to the muscles in his arms and legs. It wasn't as if it took a weight lifter to hoist a letter from the car to a mailbox. And now he had only smaller packages to deliver, since UPS and FedEx were running the rubber off their tires daily, delivering to Mattagash all the junk that locals were ordering off the Internet. Orville didn't think he'd live to see it happen that the United States Post Office would be overtaken and passed by both UPS and FedEx trucks on the same day. But it had happened to him several times in the past year.

"I'm gonna take a little drive up to the cabin," he said to Meg. She was back on the computer in her sewing room, playing that same game where the penguin in a tuxedo jumps over blocks of ice to grab jewels. Her right hand on the mouse, Meg waved her left hand at Orville, as if to say she heard him.

Orville got on his four-wheeler and backed it out of its small shed. He was proud of his road up the mountain. And he was proud of the one-acre pond too, a small basin of blue water that surged up from an abundant underground spring. It was on Craft land, had always been on Craft land, and therefore everyone called it Craft Pond, even if the state and mapmakers didn't know it existed. Five years earlier, Orville had cleaned up the shores of the pond, pulling out and disposing of all the dead and fallen trees, the jagged and rotting stumps. He had stocked the pond himself with a few dozen sleek and beautiful baby trout. Two years later, he could walk the circumference while listening to the slap of fish hitting the surface of the water as they ate their daily quota of insects. He could see the early morning flashes of silver cutting swift arcs beneath the water. He had played a cosmic part in birthing this pond. That meant it was *his*.

Orville had made a fire in his stove and had a pan of water boiling for tea when he slipped the brochure out from under the sticks of rock maple that filled his woodbox. He put his glasses on and read the title aloud, softly, in case the birds and rabbits might hear him and start snickering. *Viagra. Is it for you?* He had picked the brochure out of the wastebasket at the post office, the day he'd stopped by as a civilian to buy a stamped envelope. With no one looking, he'd slipped it into his pocket and drove it home. After he sat on the swing and read the first two pages, he'd gone in to Meg's little sewing room and placed the brochure on the desk next to her computer mouse. Orville personally had not asked the question of Meg, since the brochure did it for him. *Viagra. Is it for you?* Meg didn't take time to read even the first line on page one before she gave him an answer. "No, Orville," she said. "It isn't for me. It isn't for me today and it won't be a year from now. In five years, when I'm seventy years old, the answer will still be no. And guess what, Orville? It's not for *you* either." And then she swiveled back around in her chair and made the penguin jump for a sparkling green emerald.

So Orville had hidden the brochure at his getaway cabin, a place Meg hated to visit for ten minutes, much less long enough to snoop. Now and then, when the mood hit him, he got the brochure out and read again how *Viagra relaxes the smooth muscle of the penis to allow increased blood flow and erection*. And how the U.S. Food and Drug Administration had approved Viagra for *erectile dysfunction*. There had been whispers about such things at Blanche's Café, wives sharing secrets when they didn't know their mailman was listening as he ate a piece of blueberry pie.

There seemed to be a few men in town who might thank the Food and Drug Administration if their wives would allow them. Booster Mullins, married to the eternally bullying Dorrie, was one, although Orville didn't know why anyone would want to have sex with Dorrie. There was Christopher Harris, who had moved up from Watertown when he married Gretchen Gifford. Phillip Craft was on the list. And Porter Hart, who was married to Meg's niece, Lillian.

But Orville didn't think he was dysfunctional at all. Was his four-wheeler dysfunctional if he didn't put the key in it and turn it on? A motor needs ignition. How could he be dysfunctional if Meg hadn't turned him on in over a decade? She didn't even try. And since Orville believed fully in his marriage vows, how could he know how well he might perform at the age of sixty-five, with or without Viagra? Of course, both he and Meg had been born, had grown up, and had married B.V.

Before Viagra.

Reading in his brochure about the little blue pill, Orville was reminded of that Greek god named Prometheus who went up to the sun and brought back fire to give to mortal man. But while it took only one person to swallow the pill, it took two to enjoy its benefits. And it appeared that Mrs. Craft would rather flirt with a bird wearing a tuxedo than her own husband. The pill would remain in a photo on page two of his brochure.

Orville poured hot water over his tea bag, and while it was steeping, he looked again at page one. It set the tone for the rest of the brochure, and it was Orville's favorite page. *Why VIAGRA? Because the children are gone and it's time to fall in love all over again. Because you can't spend all day Sunday reading the newspaper. Because that special look on your loved one's face is meant only for you.* This last line always saddened him. Meg's "special look" was strictly reserved for that penguin.

Orville put the brochure back under the sticks of firewood, and that's when it occurred to him. What was different about his road up the mountainside? There was something out of place, wasn't there? Something missing? Five minutes later, his cup of tea getting cold back at the cabin, Orville was sitting on his four-wheeler, staring at the spot where only sawdust remained of what had been a nice maple tree. The wooden sign he had nailed to it the day before, shortly after he'd discovered the transmuted moose, was now on the ground and leaning against a small fir. NO TRESPASSING TO CRAFT POND was still dark and bold, as Orville's marker had intended the words to be. But below them, in scraggly, piss-poor handwriting, someone had scrawled words with red timber chalk. *Guess who was here.*

Orville would never say the word aloud, but it's the one he thought of first.

Bastard.

Billy Thunder sat with his feet up on Buck Fennelson's hassock and waited for Buck to return from the kitchen with two beers. Life in the camper was getting more hazardous and now there was a cold in Billy's bones that he couldn't shake off. He had finally wrapped up in a small blanket he found lying on Buck's sofa, soft and warm, with dark blue dots in its design. Along with needing a bigger heater for the camper, if he didn't soon fix the Mustang's roof, he would turn into one of those ice sculptures he had seen at the winter carnival in Quebec City.

"What kind of job?" asked Buck, as he offered Billy a beer.

Billy had met Buck Fennelson his first week in town and had listened as Buck explained how they were fourth cousins. "Wait, maybe it's fifth," Buck had said, staring at the rug in Billy's camper as he thought hard. "But it could be sixth. We're related in at least three different ways, so maybe it's all of the above." Until he came to Mattagash, Billy hadn't realized he needed to know algebra to learn his family tree.

"Put it on the coffee table," Billy told him. "I'll drink it when my hands warm up."

"That blanket belongs to Frankie," Buck said and dropped onto the sofa beside Billy.

"Frankie won't mind, will he?"

"Naw," said Buck.

Billy didn't know who Frankie was, nor did he care. But now he wondered if Buck's new girlfriend had brought a kid with her when she arrived. He was going to ask but decided against it. Buck had enough problems as it was, one being his IQ. It was clear to even an outsider that Buck's brain had driven in first gear all its life. The whole town kept thinking the boy would shift one day, if not into third, then at least into a respectable second. But now, in his thirtieth year of life, it looked as if Buck was content to go it at his own speed.

"So, what kind of job is it?" Buck asked again. He popped the top off his beer.

"Lydia Hatch needs her firewood cut and piled," said Billy. "Do you know her? She sounded nice on the phone."

Buck took a drink of beer as he thought of Lydia Hatch.

"She ain't so nice in person," he said. "But then, she's got Owl to look after."

Billy now had the blanket up around his neck, which was also freezing. He pushed the tip of his nose down into the blue flannel and looked at Buck.

"Who's Owl?" he asked. He was starting to think that something about the blanket wasn't as it should be. He sniffed. What was it? Bleach?

"Owl's her grandson from downstate," said Buck. "That's his nickname." Buck allowed a fart to punctuate his last sentence, as if the fart were a period.

"Buck, the fumes in here are thick enough," Billy said. "What did you eat?"

Buck reached into his pocket for his can of Redman and flipped a chew under his lip.

"Mona's been cooking new stuff she finds on the Internet," Buck said. "She's in a club where they make recipes from different countries." Another fart arrived, this one louder and in bursts, more like an ellipses. "We just got to a place they call Brazil."

Mona. That would be the toothy girl Buck had met and fell instantly in love with at Bert's Lounge in Watertown during the Fourth of July weekend. At least, his bottom half fell in love. The top half was running on automatic pilot. Billy figured the romance would be over in a week or so, but in August he had seen Buck's green pickup go by, painfully loaded with everything from a washer and a dryer to a computer and a snow blower. That's when skinny Mona had moved into the tiny house Buck's mother left him in her will, the last mailbox at the end of the Mattagash road. Billy pushed his nose deeper into the blanket and inhaled. Not bleach but maybe some kind of ammonia? He noticed a movement in the corner, behind the color TV set that must have arrived with Mona since the only color Buck could afford was on his can of Redman. A dog lay sprawled on the floor there, sleeping soundly atop what had to be a dog pillow. The pillow had dark blue dots as its pattern, same as the blanket. Billy stared. Those weren't dots. They were small dog heads. This was the kind of pillow and blanket he had seen in pet shops. Buck beat him to the answer.

"That's Frankie," Buck said. "Mona's dog. He's been pissing on everything since he got here."

It was late afternoon before Jorge and Raul Delgato arrived at the Catholic cemetery on Ocean Avenue. Raul cruised the Cadillac Deville around the visitors' parking lot three times before he found enough empty spaces. It wasn't his car, but he knew that cousin Jorge liked to park it across two spots, crisscross, so no other vehicle could come close enough to dent the sides. A 2000 model, it already had a dozen respectable scratches and dings, but Jorge had always treated the car as if it had just that day rolled off the assembly line.

"Don't forget the candle," said Raul. He watched as Jorge eased his big body out of the passenger seat, a muffled grunt getting him onto his feet. Jorge worked his arms back and forth to straighten the sleeves of his black trench coat. It was always twisted under his ass whenever they went somewhere in the Cadillac. He reached into his coat pocket and pulled out the box of white utility candles, held them up for Raul to see.

"You should start wearing a corset, dude," said Raul. "You got tits now like a hooker." He leaned into the backseat and grabbed the brown package that was addressed to *William Thunder, Box 46, Mattagash, Maine.*

"Be nice," said Jorge, "and I'll let you play with them when it gets dark."

Raul took the brown package around to the trunk, which unlocked with an invisible click from his key chain. He put the box inside, next to the baseball bat, and covered it with a greasy towel.

"The post office closes in an hour," said Raul. "Let's make this quick."

The cousins headed for the closest entrance to the cemetery, just beyond the Visitor Parking sign. Two feet past the entrance archway, they stopped. Ahead lay hundreds of markers, headstones of all shapes and sizes, with avenues branching out into other parts of the cemetery, rows and rows, a battlefield for the dead.

"Fuck," said Jorge. "Are we at the right entrance? Where's the big angel with the big wings?"

"We should have asked Grandpa Delgato," said Raul.

They moved forward, past stone angels and praying saints, past many Madonnas and what looked like a cement donkey, maybe the same one Jesus had ridden into Jerusalem, now fossilized. They passed memorial markers to veterans, granite benches and circular flower beds, and still nothing looked familiar. They paused before an enormous pietà that made up the centerpiece of the cemetery, so huge it loomed over them. They stood staring at it in reverence, at Mary's bereaved face, at the lifeless body of the crucified son she held in her arms.

"I thought he was bigger than that," said Raul. "He's small for thirty-three."

Raul was first to make the sign of the cross and then Jorge. They moved on, turning north now and following a cobblestone path.

"There was a big angel with big gray wings, remember?" asked Jorge. "You could throw a stone from that angel to Grandma Delgato's grave."

"I don't see a big angel," said Raul. "Just them little ones."

"Where's a fucking map?" asked Jorge. "Even a mall has a fucking map."

"Don't swear," said Raul. "Maybe Grandma Delgato can hear you." He looked back over his shoulder, past the rows of headstones and plastic flowers, checking to see if perhaps the Virgin Mary had taken her eyes away from her dead boy to turn them angrily on the Delgatos.

"How can you find your loved one with no fucking map?"

"There should be a girl here," said Raul, "like at the movie theater. She could come with a flashlight and lead us to the right grave."

"I gotta sit down," said Jorge. "My feet are killing me."

"Dude, we gotta hurry," said Raul. "We need to say happy birthday to Grandma Delgato *and* mail the package, all in one hour."

Jorge selected a brownish bench with an inlay of roses as its design. He sank down on it and stretched out his feet, giving them a rest from the weight. He reached into his pocket and pulled out his flask, unscrewed the cap. Raul frowned.

"Shit, dude, that's not cool," he said. "We're almost at Grandma Delgato's grave."

"No kidding," said Jorge. He took a long pull from the flask, then put the cap back. "You show me where her grave is and I'll respect the fuck out of it."

Raul shaded his eyes from the afternoon sun as he scanned the headstones. It was a peach-colored stone with white, pearly flecks in it. He remembered that much. But where was it? It had been many years since the cousins had come to visit their grandmother. They had not always been on the best terms with her given that neither had been an altar boy. And now, both in their thirties, it was clear that any road to the priesthood was blocked with a big NO ENTRY sign.

But Grandpa Delgato, on his deathbed for the third time that year, had asked this last favor of his grandsons. "It's your grandmother's birthday, and this is the first year I can't go to her grave. Go there for me, I beg of you. Light a candle in her memory." He said this to Jorge an hour earlier, in his hospital room, when the cousins made the mistake of visiting him. Bad timing, that's what it had been. Riding down in the hospital elevator, they had every intention of going directly to the post office, and then to dinner, when Raul asked the awful question: *What if, this time, he really dies?*

"I can go ask someone inside the church," said Raul. "They'll look up her name."

"What's her *first* name?" asked Jorge. He looked at his cousin.

"Grandma," said Raul.

"Fuck, there must be a lot of Delgatos," said Jorge. "They been burying family members here since they got off the boat."

Raul sat down next to Jorge and reached for the flask. When he had drunk from it, he placed it on the bench between them. Otherwise, it had a good chance of disappearing back into Jorge's coat pocket. Sometimes, when Raul finally asked to see the flask again, it would be so light it carried only air.

"We can burn the candle here," said Raul. "And if we talk loud, maybe she can hear us." He watched as Jorge pulled the box of utility candles from his coat pocket and selected one. There were always a lot of things in the pockets of Jorge's trench coat besides the flask. Sunglasses. Gloves. Lifesavers. Condoms.

"Give me the matches," Jorge said and held out his hand. When all his cousin did was gaze at it, Jorge said, "You didn't bring the fucking matches, did you?"

Raul shook his head. "I figured you'd have a flame thrower in your pocket."

Jorge stared at a starling that had flown down to light on the top of a saint's head. The chiseled face looked familiar, one he'd seen many times in church as a boy. St. Isidore? St. Jude? Maybe St. Anthony. One of those guys. Catholic saints were like ex-girlfriends; it was difficult to keep track of who was who or who had done what. Jorge reached back into his coat and this time pulled out a pack of cigarettes. He knocked one out, put it into his mouth, and looked over at Raul.

"Gimme your lighter," he said.

"If I had my lighter," said Raul, "we could light the fucking candle."

Raul took a second long drink from the flask. He'd been rattled ever since they'd promised Grandpa Delgato to come to his wife's grave and wish her *Feliz Something*. Grandma Delgato had been famous in life for her yellow fly swatter, and Raul had felt its sting many times as a child. Sometimes, he was undeserving of the punishment, but even the innocent can forget to duck. And Grandma could swing wildly when she found something amiss in her house, such as the day her wedding ring had been stolen.

"What do you think he'll do when he gets the package?" asked Jorge. He had gone back to watching the starling, waiting to see if Isidore or Jude or Anthony might end up with an offering on the top of his head.

"I think he'll send us our money," said Raul. "Billy's no fool." He was holding the candle now, staring at its wick, as if maybe that would cause it to light, a trick candle like the ones on birthday cakes.

"He better send us our money," said Jorge. "Or we'll make room for him in Grandma Delgato's coffin, once we find it."

"Hey," said Raul. He was feeling an enlightenment, the kind humans often feel in graveyards, as if they are being watched by pietàs and saints and ghosts, and maybe even the Big Guy himself. "Wanna know something?"

"What, now you're ready to touch my tits?" said Jorge.

"Remember when Grandma Delgato died and all of us grandchildren were sent into the chapel, one by one, to tell her good-bye?"

Jorge remembered. Grandma Delgato had a sweet look on her face the first time he'd ever seen her smile. Maybe she was happy to be leaving her family behind, especially her grandsons. He found the flask and uncapped it. They would tell Grandpa Delgato the grave was lovely, covered with fresh flowers, and they had lit a whole box of candles. They would mail the package and go straight to Murray's Restaurant & Bar for a few drinks before they ordered their nightly steaks. All in all, it had been a good outing, a bit of exercise on a sunny autumn day with birds and flowers.

"Well, guess what?" said Raul. "I put the yellow fly swatter by her side, before they closed her coffin."

The starling lifted its wings and circled the statue's head, the sun catching its translucent spots. Jorge smiled as the bird flew upward, up over all the angels and Madonnas, all the saints and sinners, until it was gone.

4

WEDNESDAY MORNING AND AFTERNOON

During the night, a cold wind swept across northern Maine, a gift from the Canadian plains. Winter was now bearing down on the town in earnest. Unable to sleep, Edna stared up at the ceiling and thought about her future. When Roderick reached out and clamped off the alarm clock, it was four-thirty and the sky black, still two hours before it would break to daylight. She heard him rise in the darkness, his hands searching for his pants fallen from the chair, his woolen socks, his work shirt. She pretended to be asleep as she snuggled down so deep that guilt couldn't find her. Guilt had always ruined Edna's best-laid plans. Being a lumberjack was a tough job, no doubt about it. But Roderick had no interest in the real estate classes at the high school, or the beginning computer classes. Edna was the one who read the Continuing Education schedule every time it appeared in the local paper. There were even some gardening and nature classes that they could take together. It would give them something to talk about as a couple. Maybe she would feel more like a teammate and companion, not just a wife and mother. "Listen to this," Edna had said that past August, when the fall schedule was published. "'Shopping for Dinner in Your Own Backyard.' Don't that sound interesting?" But all she got from Roderick was, "Sure, if you're a goat." Still, she had not given up. She wanted to be certain she had tried to save her marriage before she walked away from it. "It's about edible plants that grow wild. And since they grow right in our backyard, that could save us dollars on our grocery bill." She thought that last part might jar Roderick toward an appreciation of botany. "You'll be picking shit that might kill me," was what he said. "If you put a mushroom on my plate, I wanna see the can it came in."

Edna had finally given up. The marriage was over, and she proved it by not packing Roderick's lunch that morning for the first time since she was laid up giving birth to the twins. As cupboard doors opened and closed in the kitchen below, she lay in bed and listened to the wind beating away outside. The noise in the kitchen was Roderick searching for the mustard, the bread, the bologna. Edna heard a frantic rattling as drawers slid open and then slammed shut. He must be looking for the candy bars. Ever since the doctor told Roderick to lose weight, she had hidden them in the canister that said *Rice*.

But what if Roderick was right? "It's your autumn depression," he said the night before as he set the alarm clock. "You get this way every year when the days shorten. I heard doctors talking about it on television. Some folks in Alaska even commit suicide." And he had made the sign of the cross, briskly, as though he were shooing flies. *Seasonal Affective Disorder*. Had he forgotten that Edna was sitting on the sofa and watching the program right along with him? Whether her mood was caused by SAD or not, Edna couldn't argue with him about one thing: she was not a happy woman.

By eight o'clock, the twins had disappeared on the rumbling school bus, and the cats had gone out into the fields in search of mice, and the morning quiet that Edna knew so well had settled about the kitchen like a fine snow. She was still in bed. What would Mama Sal say if she knew? Edna wished one of the twins would tattle to their grandmother, just to see what the backlash might bring. She wished they'd also tell Mama Sal how she hadn't bothered to fix breakfast for her sons, not to mention her husband. "That silver box sitting on the counter is called a toaster," Edna said, when first Ricky and then Roddy had come to lean in the jamb of her bedroom door in order to whine. "There's milk and orange juice in the fridge. And don't forget to let the cats out."

With the children gone and the cats hunting and Roderick not due home for hours, Edna stood at her kitchen sink and stared out the window. She was drinking coffee and thinking about the woman in Bangor who had shot and killed her husband as he slept. How bad does a marriage have to get? Edna doubted "Shopping for Dinner in Your Own Backyard" could have helped *that* couple. An awful thought bounced into her head, the way awful thoughts can sometimes do before a rational mind shoves them back out. "I wonder if poison mushrooms would show up in a police report?" The truth was that Edna couldn't hurt anyone, especially Roderick. For all his faults, she knew he loved her dearly. But for the past year, she couldn't find a love inside her heart to give back to him. Her marriage to Roderick had happened so fast. It was as if she went overnight from being a schoolgirl to a wife. Other girls in her class had thrown fun engagement parties with Pin the Tail on the Donkey games and then big weddings to follow. Lots of flowers and organdy and silk. Two days after Roderick proposed to her, Edna had bought a sensible blue skirt and jacket, with a white blouse. The next day, she and Roderick stood before a Justice of the Peace in Watertown, his wife and grown son as their witnesses. After cake and coffee at her mother's house, they untied the one tin can that someone had attached to the bumper of Roderick's car. But before they could pull away for a quick honeymoon trip to Bangor, Mama Sal had put Aunt Mildred's suitcase into the trunk and Aunt Mildred in the backseat. "They're expecting her at the nut house," Mama Sal had whispered. "She's talking again to Jesus and Christopher Columbus." Three days is a short time to change your life forever. There should be a halfway house for young girls who have been proposed to—not a mental institute, but a quiet place where they can sit alone and think before they jump and grab that gold ring of a wedding band. Aunt Mildred was Edna's father's sister, and Mama Sal had never liked her in-laws. No one in the family doubted that Mildred Gifford was of unsound mind. But it wasn't Edna's idea of a honeymoon trip.

Edna looked up at the clock that had been on her kitchen wall since the summer day she put it there, twenty years earlier, a wedding gift from some relative. Already past nine. Surely Bertina would be up by now.

Billy couldn't believe how fast the cold had arrived and with what seemed like very little warning. The old-timers in town were predicting an early winter, but they were basing this prediction on something the squirrels were doing and Billy couldn't see any science in that. He crawled out of his sleeping bag, which lay beneath three heavy blankets, and peered out the camper's window. A pale sun had ridden up from the horizon of trees beyond the bridge. No snow had fallen, but it might as well have. With snow on the ground, the day might even be warmer. At least he had borrowed a canvas tarp from Harry Plunkett to cover the Mustang. Harry promised he'd have time later in the week to work on the apparatus that raised the top.

Billy turned up the knob on his small electric heater and heard the coils rustling inside. He dressed fast and then dumped a package of hot chocolate mix into the one cup that came with the camper. Inside the miniature refrigerator that sat on the countertop, he found a carton of milk. It had been two weeks since he unplugged the refrigerator. Nothing would spoil inside the camper now, not even in daytime. He poured cold milk over the cocoa in his cup and put it in the microwave. He wished the camper had a real stove. A real stove would mean real heat emanating from its coiled burners.

The night before, Billy had bought his employee and himself a six-pack of Cokes and a box of donuts for a quick energy snack. He needed a pack of Winstons, so why not get Buck a can of Redman? Since he couldn't work bare-handed, he threw a pair of Monkey Face gloves on the counter. Over thirty dollars spent of the last fifty he had to his name, and the workday had yet to begin. But as field boss to the operation, Billy felt it was his responsibility to oversee expenses. True, this was money that could have gone toward a bigger and fancier heater, but Billy saw it as a sound investment in his future. He only owed the idiots down in Portland a few thousand bucks, give or take a couple hundred. With steady handyman work, he could pay them back in a few months and then things would return to normal. It wasn't his fault that he'd fallen behind on the payments. It was the fault of the women he dated in Watertown, all girls who insisted on eating supper at the Golden Dragon instead of getting a quick hotdog and a bag of chips at Rock's Diner. Girls who expected mixed drinks instead of beers, who smoked Canadian cigarettes and played the poker machine at Bert's Lounge. These were girls who knew how to have a good time. And they knew how to recognize the better ilk of men who had the means to show them that good time. It was Mr. Thunder's charisma that had set him back on his heels financially.

Billy turned the heater down to low. As he waited for Buck

to arrive, he decided to call Portland again, and again he had no choice but to speak to a machine. But this time, there was a bit more hope in the message he left.

"I got a day job now, so I can catch up on my back bill with you boys," Billy said, a professional lilt in his voice. "So go ahead and send me another Christmas package. No worries about me falling behind on my payments again." He listened as the machine clicked itself off, as if deliberately hanging up on him. If they'd trust him with one more shipment, he could make an even greater profit since his northern clientele was growing not just restless but impoverished.

When he saw Buck's old pickup driving down the path that led from the main road, Billy grabbed the grocery bag from the table. It would be good to crawl into Buck's warm truck for the ride over to their work site. But when he turned from locking the camper's door, he saw Buck standing by the Mustang, the pickup disappearing back up the path.

"Where's your truck going?" Billy asked.

Buck's face got that childlike look it always got when he felt like crying.

"Mona needed it," he said. "She's gotta take Frankie to the vet."

Billy wanted to curse Buck. They needed the truck and he had told him so the night before. Without it, they'd have to carry all those heavy blocks from where Tommy Gifford had dumped them on Lydia's lawn over to where she now wanted her wood stored for winter. He wanted to lambaste his employee, but how could he do that before Buck had even put on his work gloves?

All four windows up, the topless Mustang was on its way to Lydia Hatch's place. Buck had all but disappeared in the front seat, scrunched down as he was to avoid the cold wind coming at him over the top of the windshield. Billy was also crouched in his seat, his head high enough that he could see to steer. The

Mustang crossed the Mattagash bridge, where cold air assaulted it from the front, back, *and* sides. They met a few curious townspeople on the way, and all had ample time to get in a good stare since the Mustang was only traveling at fifteen miles an hour. But Billy figured less speed meant less wind chill.

Meg Craft was getting out of her warm car when the Mustang rolled past her house, looking like a boat that lost its sail.

"What in heaven's name?" Meg asked, only to realize that two men were inside the car. She could see the top of a head on the passenger side and a definite head behind the steering wheel. "It's that foolish boy from Portland with the foul mouth," Meg said, then went inside to call her niece Lillian.

At the old McKinnon homestead, Amy Joy Lawler was at her computer when she glanced up to see the white Mustang coming slowly down the road. It looked as if it was driving itself. She watched as it passed her house, its driver keeping a low eye on the road, his head barely noticeable above the steering wheel.

A quarter mile past the McKinnon house, the Mustang pulled into Lydia Hatch's yard and braked before it hit Lydia's dried lilac bush.

"Are we there yet?" asked Buck.

Billy turned off the ignition. He was still mad at Buck, but he was now colder than he was mad.

"Get your Redman out of the bag," said Billy, "and let's get to work before we freeze to death."

Billy didn't bother to knock on Lydia's door. It was still early, and she'd told him the night before exactly what the job would entail. They were to split into chunks of firewood the mountain of hardwood blocks Tommy had rolled off his truck above her house. Then, they were to carry the firewood over to the shed and stack it on the lower side. At ten o'clock, Billy was hoping that the old biddy might come out and offer them a hot chocolate or a bread crumb. He was wrong on both counts. Instead, she'd been keeping a close watch on their work from behind her kitchen curtain.

"Let's take a cigarette break," Billy said to Buck.

They leaned against the Mustang, Billy to smoke his cigarette and Buck to insert a fresh plug of tobacco beneath his lip. With the sweat of their morning work now growing cold beneath their jackets and shirts, Billy threw the Winston on the ground and stomped it out. He looked at Buck, whose face was pinched, as if some unseen force were drawing it inward.

"My stomach don't feel so good," Buck said. "We had Polynesian Sweet and Sour Fish for supper."

"Do you even know where Polynesia is?" asked Billy.

"No and I don't want to," said Buck, "not if that's how they cook their fish."

"Come on," said Billy. "We need a few minutes inside to warm up."

And this is what he told Lydia herself when she answered the door to his knock. Billy saw a quick flash of indecision.

"Otherwise," he said, "it may take longer than we figured."

"I guess you can sit a few minutes in the kitchen," Lydia said.

The kitchen was warm, with something good still baking in the oven. Buck sat on a chair, and Billy leaned against the counter. That's when he noticed a boy sitting at the table, his back to Billy as he drew on a sheet of paper. He looked to be about twelve years old. Atop the table were oil paints and colored pens.

"That's Owl," he heard Buck whisper as Lydia stepped into the kitchen and folded her arms. Billy waited. The smell of cake or cookies or whatever she had in the oven was making his mouth water.

"I hear you're related to the Fennelsons," said Lydia, giving him a good Mattagash look over.

"Yes, ma'am," said Billy. "I'm Abigail Fennelson's son." It was definitely a cake, maybe one of those marble kinds that had swirls in them. He wondered if she'd made a frosting for it or if she intended to leave it plain. Either way, it wouldn't matter.

"I was a Fitzgerald before I married a Hatch," Lydia said, as if Billy gave a flying fuck. "You'll soon learn to tell the Lace Curtain Irish here in town from the Shanty Irish. Good breeding gets passed on, and the Fitzgeralds were Lace Curtain Irish."

Owl stopped drawing and turned to look at his grandmother. That was when Billy understood the boy's nickname. The eyes didn't move. Instead, the head turned, taking the eyes with it. *Owl.* Lydia saw Billy staring.

"That's my grandson, Horace," she said. "Horace is a genius."

"No kidding," said Billy. If she offered him ice cream with the cake, he would decline, it being so damn cold outside and all. But maybe, in passing up the ice cream, he would be offered a second piece of warm cake. Buck was rigid in his chair, back straight, saying nothing. Billy figured his posture had something to do with Polynesia. Lydia had gone to Owl's chair and was now tousling the boy's straight yellow hair.

"All the Fitzgeralds have natural curls," said Lydia. "I've read that the poet John Keats had ringlets and so did the Lindbergh baby." She tried to wrap a strand of her grandson's hair around her index finger but no amount of twisting could create a curl. Billy looked at the spray of freckles across the bridge of the boy's nose, some light brown, others darker, some black as moles.

"I never met a genius before," Billy said. He wasn't even certain if this were true, nor did he care. On an average day, he would have pegged Owl as the village idiot. But on this day, he was cold and he wanted a piece of cake. And he needed to keep Lydia talking. If he could make friends with her, he and Buck might get work for the rest of the week. But there was no doubt, from his own nonprofessional observation, that Horace had fallen from the top of the half-wit tree. Or he had been thrown from his nest by the smarter owls.

"He's what they call a sa-VONT," said Lydia, raising her voice high on the last syllable. "You know, an artistic genius." She pulled a folder of papers out of a kitchen drawer and opened it. She gave the top sheet to Billy, who took it and stared down at the drawing before him. Blue and gray swirls, an eyeball here and there, what looked like an arm, a hand with two fingers. All the time he studied what he figured was some kind of animal body with a human head, he was aware that the pale face was turned toward him, the piercing owl eyes staring at him from beneath the straw hair. Lydia also stared, waiting.

Billy suspected an important response was needed for the occasion. He wanted to answer, and correctly, so that the cake, which smelled so damn good, would be his just reward. He heard Buck fidget on his chair, then cough lightly.

"Now I get it," Billy said. He released a great sigh of relief. "It's a clown riding an elephant. I can see the trunk and the tusks, and there's the clown's face and eyes."

Lydia Hatch grabbed the drawing, and so quickly Billy hardly realized what had happened. He looked at Horace. The owl eyes burned brightly as they stared back.

"No, it isn't," Lydia said. "It's a self-portrait." Before Billy could say anything, maybe mention how good that baking cake smelled or even apologize, Lydia Hatch opened the kitchen door and was waiting for her workers to leave. "Don't forget to pile the firewood along the lower side of the shed," she said.

Out in the backyard again, Buck was beside himself.

"You shouldn't have said anything but that it was beauty-ful and handed it back," he said. He was putting his gloves on one at a time, slow and easy like he always did.

"You don't understand," said Billy. "I *did* see a fucking clown riding an elephant."

Bertina was wearing a lavender housecoat over a thin nightgown. Edna had already taken her flannel pajamas down from her closet shelf, washed them, and now they were packed into her dresser drawer for the cold nights ahead. A thin nightgown belonged in Florida, not Mattagash.

"Roberta, my best friend from Tampa, gave me the funniest plaque as a going-away gift," Bertina said. She had her manicure set opened on the kitchen table. "As soon as my boxes arrive, I'm gonna put it up on the wall."

Edna was looking at Venice by daylight and wondering if all the folks in those Italian houses had gone off to work. It didn't look like much of anything went on in Venice during the day. The buildings were quiet and black, waiting for night and that invisible surge of electricity. Without those tiny lights, Venice wasn't much more than Mattagash, Maine.

"It says *divorce* in big letters at the top of the plaque," said Bertina. "In smaller letters below it says: *The legal alternative to axe murder*. Isn't that funny?"

Edna had no idea why she had left the breakfast dishes in the sink to drive straight back to Bertina's trailer. But there she was. She pulled one of the rickety chairs out from the oval table and sat down.

"I don't think divorce is funny," she said. She watched as Bertina patted her cuticles with cuticle remover, doing a careful, almost professional job on her nails. On the first visit, she had considered asking Bertina some big questions, such as why she was back in Mattagash and still not forty, about how her left eye, with those shades of bluish-purple showing through the pancake makeup, might have been a black eye a couple weeks earlier. But Bertina would consider that prying.

"Want me to do your nails?" Bertina asked.

Edna shook her head. She wished her fingernails weren't so short, the skin of her hands so rough. But she had always hated gardening gloves and never wore a pair when she planted seeds or weeded and pruned. And that past summer she had grown her biggest and best garden in years. Her hands always kept busy. There was the housework, the cooking, Monday washdays, and canning vegetables for the winter months. Edna had even been proud of her hands, knowing how useful they were to her and her family. But now, seeing them next to her sister's, she was aware of how she'd neglected them.

"A manicure is the first thing I do for myself on Wednesdays," said Bertina. "You should do something for yourself every day when you first wake up."

"But I always have to get up and pack Roderick his lunch," Edna said. "If I make it the night before, he complains that the sandwiches are soggy by lunchtime."

"You been packing Roderick's lunch all these years?" Bertina asked. "Shame on you." She reached under the table and Edna heard a snap. That's when she realized that Bertina had her feet in an electric foot massage. That's what the faint humming had been.

"But who else would do it?" Edna asked.

"A chimpanzee could pack its own lunch," said Bertina. She blew on a fingernail. "Course, that don't mean Roderick can."

"Don't be mean now," said Edna.

Bertina nodded at a small window, the only one in the trailer that framed the scraggly backyard. Edna saw dead weeds and grasses that grew up around the previous tenant's leftovers, which included a rusted swing set tilted to one side and a broken tricycle.

"See that yard? When spring comes, I'm gonna think of myself first and plant an orange tree."

"This far north, you can't get a watermelon to grow bigger than a cucumber," said Edna. "The cold stunts their growth."

"I don't care," Bertina said. "All that matters is that I thought of myself first when spring comes."

Edna wondered if her own growth were stunted by the cold. She remembered what Roderick said the night before, that she did this every year and that it was her autumn depression. But that wasn't true. She had never even considered asking Roderick for a divorce, much less asking Mama Sal's permission to do so. She thought of housewives in Alaska who at that very moment had opened a bottle of sleeping pills or fitted a noose around their necks or unwrapped a shiny razor blade, who were sitting in automobiles in frozen garages, cars that were turning misty gray inside as they filled with carbon monoxide.

"By the way, Mama Sal called," said Bertina. She was now snipping at the softened cuticles. "She said when you get here, I'm to send you home."

"How does she do it?" Edna asked. "She wasn't in her window when I drove by."

"If you want privacy from Mama Sal, you should buy a canoe." Bertina selected a different tool from the manicure kit. "She can't see the river from her chair."

Sunlight came in through Bertina's kitchen window and lit up the pretty bottles of nail polish, all waiting in a row for Bertina to select one. It was past ten o'clock, and Bertina was still doing something to please herself first. Edna wondered how life might have turned out if *she* had been the daughter to live in far-off Florida. Here in Mattagash, Mama Sal even inspected and often criticized Edna's garden. There were days she would come home from shopping to see little holes punched in the ground around her cucumber beds, little holes up and down the rows of carrots and beans, proof that Mama Sal had been there with her aluminum walker. In far-away Florida, Edna could have grown oranges in peace.

Bertina selected Cranberry Frost and loaded her brush with a thick burst of its polish. Edna watched as the black bristles swept cranberry across Bertina's nails. She wanted to change the subject before an argument came like a boomerang out of the past, as it often had done in their growing up years. Bertina always said Mama Sal favored Edna. But Edna had paid a price for that favoritism, hadn't she? It was Edna who looked out for Mama Sal, who drove her to Watertown to the doctor's office, who took her Christmas shopping, who picked up her pills at the drugstore. Moving away shouldn't mean disappearing.

"I think I'll give myself a facial," said Bertina. "You want one too?" In the autumn sunlight, her nails emerged cranberry red and she held them high as she blew on them with her warm Florida breath.

"But you just did your nails," Edna said. "You just did something for yourself already." She decided not to mention the foot massage.

"Really?" asked Bertina. "Well, watch me do something else."

The phone rang, a soft bleat that bounced about the tinny walls of the trailer. Bertina answered and Edna saw her frown.

"The kids get their breakfast at school, Mama Sal. So why should I get up at the crack of dawn and fry bacon?"

"Don't tell her I'm here," Edna whispered.

"She's not here," said Bertina. Her housecoat had fallen open, revealing the thin gown beneath, and beneath the gown the outline of a breast. Bertina had admitted to implants and a lift. Edna wondered how much new breasts would cost down in Florida. They were apparently items that one could keep in a divorce battle.

Bertina hung up the phone and reached for her cigarettes.

"What did she say?" Edna asked.

"She said you're suffering from autumn depression. And I'm to tell you to quit acting like a fool and go home."

Edna looked down at the brown mole on her hand. It seemed to be growing, like a mushroom, the malignant kind, the kind that could kill your hardworking, never-harm-a-flea husband. She looked over at all the frosted bottles of Florida nail polish. *Crimson Sky. Midnight Mauve. Purple Dare. Amber Autumn. Purely Pink.*

"You ever had an affair?" Edna asked. "You know, while you were still married to one of your husbands?"

Bertina arched both eyebrows in perfect disbelief.

"You have, really?" said Edna. "How did you not get caught?"

"I don't recall ever marrying an Einstein," said Bertina.

Edna was excited, as if maybe listening to Bertina's life experiences would be enough, would get her through SAD, through the long winter and into the spring sunshine. *Vicarious: to experience pleasure through another's experiences.*

"I think I'll have that facial after all," Edna said. "Then you can do my nails."

Three hours later, Billy had split enough of the hardwood blocks that his hands, arms, and lower back ached in unison. Buck's stomach had been acting up again and so Billy—head contractor, field boss, and fourth or fifth or sixth cousin—had done the most work in wielding the axe. Buck promised to make up for it by carrying and stacking the firewood himself. He had made a few trips, with many loads to go, when his culinary lifestyle caught up with him.

"You hear that?" he asked. Billy had been ignoring the growling sound, but now the growl had turned into a thump, the same *thump* a tapped watermelon emits if it's ripe.

"What's the problem now?" Billy asked. He stopped to wipe sweat from his brow, but if he stopped for long, he'd lose all the body warmth he was building up.

"I'm feeling a little cantankerous," said Buck.

Billy stared up at white clouds that were holding pink flecks of sunlight as they floated toward the mountain. He had always known that Florence Walker's grand plan to educate the masses would have a major flaw in it, and now that flaw had reared its ugly head. He looked back at Buck.

"You're feeling *nauseous* is what you're feeling, Buck," he said. Buck seemed relieved, as if nauseous wasn't as serious as cantankerous.

"I got past the fish from supper last night," said Buck, "so I must be dealing with breakfast now." He looked at Billy, who was waiting for an explanation.

"Mexican omelet," said Buck. "Did you know peppers ain't just green? They also come in red and yellow. But then, I never could hold my cheese and spices."

"Ignore it," said Billy. He glanced again at the sky. The day was disappearing fast. "We're almost done here."

Buck got that look on his face again that meant he would like to cry, but he went back to work. Five minutes later, he was staring hard at Billy.

"I better go find me a place behind the shed," he said.

"We got work to do," said Billy. "If we don't get the rest of this wood stacked by sunset, that old biddy won't pay us." He wanted to punch Buck. Why would any man, even a *fool man*, eat something called a "Mexican omelet" for breakfast, at the end of the road in northern Maine, cooked by a girl whose two eyes resembled those on a cod fish? And this was not to mention Polynesia. "Can't you hold it until we finish here?"

Buck reached around and pushed a gloved hand against his backside.

"I can feel the pressure," he said. It sounded like a news commentary, as if maybe Wolf Blitzer was embedded in his pants.

"Damn it, go on then," said Billy. "I'll finish this myself." He watched as Buck hurried past the shed and disappeared into the bushes above the riverbank.

Billy was wearing his earmuffs and had finished stacking the last pieces of firewood when Buck returned. He stood staring at the rows of neatly piled wood as he put his gloves back on. He'd been gone for an hour, doing God only knew what. Billy had no intentions of asking for details. It had taken him twice as long to finish, what with Buck in the bulrushes.

"You think she's gonna pay us good for this?" asked Buck.

"She said she'd pay what we're worth," Billy answered. He reached down on the ground behind the woodpile for his can of beer and knocked off the last of it, icy foam and all. He had felt no responsibility in alerting Buck to the fact that when he went to get his earmuffs from the Mustang, he'd found a six-pack of icy beer in the trunk, knowing American beer wouldn't go well with a Mexican omelet or Polynesian fish.

"Is that what she said?" asked Buck. "Then we're up shit creek without a paddle. Word's out around town that I'm not worth much."

Billy shoved his gloves into his jacket pocket. He spit on the ground next to where Buck's two big, burgundy boots with the yellow tips were parked.

"We were already up shit creek when you ate a Mexican omelet," said Billy.

As he headed for Lydia Hatch's front door, Billy wondered

what he might say in defense of himself if Lydia didn't think *he* was worth much either. He could hear Buck crunching along on the cold ground behind him, imagined the burgundy boots coming at him like two snowplows.

"You gonna use the Grateful Elvis on her?" Buck asked.

Billy smiled. He couldn't help himself. He wanted to remain aloof, wanted to hover over Buck Fennelson the way a foreman should, the way the Lace Curtain Irish—whatever the hell *that* was—probably hovered over the Shanty Irish. But he couldn't act anything but pleased to know he had another solid fan of his Grateful Elvis.

"Sure, if she deserves it," said Billy. "That's why I invented it."

Lydia Hatch stepped cautiously onto her front porch, the wind pressing her dress against the pudgy calves of her legs.

"Nice stack of wood," said Lydia, and Billy smiled.

"We sure worked our butts off," he said, throwing a small glance at Buck, who was stuffed inside his ski jacket. Lydia reached into her dress pocket and came out with a few rolled bills, which she handed to Billy.

"Good job," she said again. She turned back to the warmth of her house, anxious to be inside with Owl no doubt, where the two could stuff their faces with cake until the cows came home. Billy wasted no time in looking at the numbers in his hand. Three twenties. Sixty lousy dollars.

He did the math quickly. With the pair of gloves, the donuts, the Cokes, and tobacco—good thing he hadn't agreed to supply Buck with toilet paper—he'd be lucky to break even once he gave Buck a share. They had worked all day, and they had worked hard; at least Billy had while Buck was on his siesta.

"Miss Hatch?" Billy said. Lydia was about to close her door when she heard this. She turned, impatient.

"Yes?" she said. "What is it?"

Billy held the bills up. Then he did his Elvis impression, his lip curling, a lip with a mind of its own. The words came quickly and somewhat slurred, a trick that had taken him a lot of stoned nights to perfect.

"I just wanna say, FuckYouMa'amFuckYouVeryMuch," Billy told her.

"You're welcome," Lydia said and closed the door. He could see her silhouette inside the frosted glass as she stood immobile, thinking. Ever since he had invented the Grateful Elvis, five years earlier, he had seen this same reaction on a multitude of people. Billy knew what was going through her mind. *Did I hear what I think I heard, or did he actually say thank you?*

Buck was sitting on the porch, his puffy ski jacket shaking with laughter. Billy motioned for him to follow. There would be beers at Bert's Lounge in Watertown, and they wouldn't be so cold your lips hurt to drink them. The pitiful money he'd made would cover a small pizza too, and maybe a few songs on the jukebox. Buck caught up to him.

"You gonna pay me what I'm worth, Billy?" he asked.

Billy opened the door on the Mustang and heard it creak. The windshield seemed ready to crack and break if a feather wafted down on it. Winter hadn't yet started. What could December and January possibly be like?

"What do you think you're worth, Buck?" Billy asked.

"I worked hard, and them sticks were heavy," Buck said.

"You did work hard," Billy told him, "till the lava started pouring out of your ass."

Billy gave Buck one of the twenties and then pulled his last ten from his pocket. Thirty of the sixty dollars. He should deduct expenses, but he had no heart for it. Buck's face was a solid smile as he went around and cracked open the passenger door. Billy heard it creak with the cold, the way an arm is wrested behind a person to have it snap and break. As Buck settled into the front seat, the leather screamed beneath him. Billy got in and shut the door. He turned the key and heard nothing but a soft, painful *click*.

"You should have plugged it in," said Buck. "There's not much keeping it warm, given you got no roof." That wasn't it, but Billy had no intention of telling Buck that when he came to get his earmuffs and found the beer, he'd stayed to drink one while listening to the radio. And that meant he'd forgotten to turn off the ignition switch.

Billy sat there, saying nothing. He watched as the blue evening pushed in over the mountain range beyond the Mattagash River, as if the cold were a living thing, a thing with arms and hands and fingers, a thing that could come and get you if sat waiting for it. Maybe the cold was a clown riding an elephant. Billy tried the switch again, in case a miracle had occurred in the last sixty seconds.

Click.

"It ain't gonna start," said Buck. Billy slapped a hand against the steering wheel, but all it did was hurt his numb fingers. He looked at Buck.

"How'd you get so smart all of a sudden?"

Billy opened his door to a loud and painful squeal. It was as if the cold could get into iron and steel the way it got into human bones. They would get the blue tarp from the trunk and cover the car. Tomorrow, he would ask Tommy Gifford to come with his pickup and give the dead battery a boost. Tonight, he would hitch a ride to Watertown with someone who had a top to their automobile. And he would spend the night there, coming back the next day around noontime when the sun would be shining its best warmth. Watertown would mean hot food and some good beer, maybe a shot or two of tequila. And if there was a god, it would mean sleeping next to one of those young French girls who are always so warm when they open up their arms to the night.

5

THURSDAY MORNING

When Orville woke, he thought it was because his alarm clock had gone off, as it always did, at six thirty. By seven fifteen, he'd have eaten his breakfast and be out the door to the post office, ready to sort that day's mail for delivery. But the clock was sitting there quietly with that smug, illuminated look on its face. A couple minutes to six. Unable to fall back asleep, Orville stared up at the light Meg had installed over their bed years earlier, a rectangle of painted glass that hid the bulb above. Most Mattagash men who worked in the woods would be on the job for two or three hours by this time of morning. Those who drove the trucks were the earliest birds of all, usually roaring past Orville's house at two o'clock. He had heard them on those dark mornings when he'd risen to pee, heard the Jake brakes as they approached the bridge. Many of them didn't get home for their suppers until Orville had driven down from his cabin and put the four-wheeler back into its shed, around 7 p.m. Did he feel guilt? Sometimes. But then he'd remember what his father, Simon Craft, used to say. "See the pictures little boys are drawing in Mattagash? They're all trucks and logs and skidders. The parents are so proud they tack 'em to their refrigerators. Is it any wonder they're raising future lumberjacks who gotta get up hours before a mailman? Lumberjacks ain't *born*. In this town, they're *grown*."

And that's what Orville would remember, at two o'clock, when the first huge trucks went rattling by like trains, dragging their long bodies behind them. He'd peer out the lower window at yellow lights coming up the road, emerging from the darkness, and then hear the *whoosh* as the truck passed the house. Looking out the upper window, he'd see red taillights and hear the sound of Jake brakes. Then the truck would clatter over the bridge, on its way miles up a logging road where some poor half-asleep bugger was drinking the last of his coffee and waiting to crawl up onto his loader so he could load the truck with logs. And there Orville Craft would be, shaking his pecker dry and stuffing it into his shorts, seconds away from crawling back into that warm bed.

Meg didn't like to hear him call it a pecker. "It sounds vulgar and crude," she'd say, and that pinch of disgust would appear around her mouth muscles, an act that made her face look puckered. Back in their earlier years when they were still a threesome—a *ménage à trois* that included Meg, Orville, and his pecker—he would have been more careful with his wording. After all, he was often rewarded back then for listening to Meg's criticism and paying attention to her advice. He was delivering milk for the Watertown Dairy, before he began delivering letters and packages. Sometimes, on his route up through Mattagash, he'd pull the milk truck into his drive and flip it in park. He'd bound out of the seat and in a matter of a few long strides would be standing at his kitchen door. He'd open it slowly, noiselessly, although he knew the kids were safe in school in those old days and never a problem. That's when Meg would look up from whatever she was doing and see him standing there. And she'd smile as if she had not only missed him, but she *really* missed him in that husband-wife way. Maybe she'd be knitting or doing the dishes or folding clothes or cooking something for their supper, and there he'd be, standing in the kitchen in the middle of a workday.

She'd look up, that sweet look of surprise on her face, followed by the smile. And she'd stop whatever she was doing, she'd drop her knitting needles or half-washed plate or half-folded bath towel, half-mixed cake batter, and she'd come to him, put her arms around his neck, and that's when he'd touch her breasts beneath her dress. He'd undo her apron and let it fall on the floor. Let other men long for the days of nylon stockings and garter belts. Pointy high-heeled shoes. To Orville there was nothing sexier than a female wearing a dainty apron. "Let's go upstairs," he'd whisper. "Do you think we should?" she'd ask, and he knew it was her way of holding on to her modesty, of being a shy girl and letting the man in him take control. And he'd say "Yes, honey, I think we should."

Fifteen minutes later, he'd be back in the kitchen, tossing down a glass of water and Meg would be fixing her hair and making sure his shirt was straight and proper as she kissed him good-bye. That night at supper, the kids around the table, noisy and squabbling, their eyes would meet, his and Meg's, they'd meet halfway down that table of kids. And then their eyes would talk to each other. Their eyes would say things like "Remember today?" and "I love you." Sometimes, they would wake before the alarm clock, knowing the kids were still deep in their dreams. And Orville would turn her to him, would hear her coo and snuggle against his neck as he made quiet love to her, a love she accepted and even seemed to enjoy. Orville knew it was his for the taking since he was her husband, and that the one thing Meg wanted most in return during those early morning moments was not an orgasm, but that he not wake the children.

Nowadays, Meg Craft's eyes let her mouth speak instead, saying things like "Did you get my liter of Coke?" and "Don't forget to let the dog out when you leave" and "Please don't call it a pecker."

Penis. Organ. Member. Family Jewel. Phallus. Big Pete. What did it matter what you called it if you *never called it*?

The alarm clock began its modern bleat that Orville had come to despise, along with other modern things—like pantyhose for nylon stockings. He missed the alarm clock he'd had for years, the kind that had a silver crank on its back and two little knobs on its head, like ears, and when it went off, it rocked back and forth as if it was dancing for him, charming him out of his warm bed. He felt Meg stir as he pushed the off button on the digital clock to shut it up. He slid his legs out from under the covers and put his feet into the slippers waiting on the floor. He looked over at Meg's face, knowing that if he stared at her long enough, she'd sense it in that weird way human beings know things. The day was still dark, but he could see by the nightlight filtering in from the bathroom the shape of her nose, her mouth, her closed lashes. Meg twitched, as if feeling the weight of his eyes.

"Why don't you wear an apron anymore?" Orville asked, in those first words of the day that are so soft when spoken they arrive more like whispers. "You had a lot of them, all different colors. I remember one was a pale yellow and had a bluebird on the front, sitting on a brown twig."

Meg didn't even open her eyes for this.

"Orville, are you having a nervous breakdown?" she asked. "Where do you get those foolish notions?"

Orville felt a wave of emotion wash over him, as if his whole past life had come and gone in that one instant. Where was *he* when his life happened? What had he been doing for six and a half decades? He remembered a magazine article he'd read once, that if a man were an atheist he should put on his tombstone "All dressed up and nowhere to go." Now, Orville saw it differently. He was sixty-five years old, a good Christian man about to retire, and he too had nowhere to go. Nowhere but downhill, anyway. Or maybe uphill to Craft Pond. But how many fish can you catch? How many rides can you take on a four-wheeler before you have to stop and face mortality? He reached for his pants from the chair where he always put them. His shirt was draped over the chair's back. He grabbed socks from the sock drawer where Meg stuffed them on laundry day. He knew his shoes would be where he always left them, down in the kitchen, on the rug near the door.

"Don't forget to let the dog out," Meg said as Orville made his way downstairs.

He had two more days of his life to live as the town's mailman.

When Edna arrived at her mother's house, Mama Sal was waiting in the kitchen, the silver walker wrapped about her and the smell of breakfast bacon still in the air.

"So, where's that early snow everyone's been talking about?" Edna asked as she flung her purse on the counter.

"One of these days," said Mama Sal, "I'll give you the money so you can have that purse surgically removed from your arm."

Edna had already decided, given her plans for that afternoon, that she wouldn't let her mother spoil the day. She waited as Mama Sal took off her sweater and draped a towel about her neck. Then she stepped her walker up to the sink and put her head in under the faucet. Edna had already turned on the tap water and felt with her fingers that it wasn't too hot. She guided her mother's head under the running water.

"That water is too hot," said Mama Sal. "This is a human head you got here and not a potato you need to boil."

"Sorry," said Edna. She reached for the tap handle but did

nothing at all to move it over to *Cold*. "There, how's that?" she asked. She felt the stiffness in Mama Sal's body relax, as it always did.

"That's good," said Mama Sal. "I wish you'd learn the temperature I like."

Edna rolled her eyes for her own benefit and reached for the shampoo. She lathered up Mama Sal's head and then massaged the shampoo into the hair, kneading the scalp. She knew this was one of her mother's favorite things, having her hair washed and set in curlers. Yet Edna had to endure the criticisms every week.

"How's your back feeling today?" she asked. She was ready now to rinse. She put the tap over Mama Sal's hair and began washing away the suds.

"Still hurting," said Mama Sal. "I'd give anything to go down to the basement like I used to do. I gotta wait on Tommy now to carry up my box of Halloween decorations."

"I met him on the bridge early Monday evening," said Edna. "He tooted at me, which is more than I expected."

"That water's a tad hot for my taste," said Mama Sal. Edna moved the tap aside, but again did nothing to adjust the temperature. She positioned the faucet back over her mother's head and let the same water spray down. "Perfect," Mama Sal said. "I wish you'd learn my likes and dislikes."

"Has Tommy been by to visit you?" Edna asked. She'd much rather get Mama Sal's mind on Tommy and his estranged wife than on her relationship with Roderick or her visits to Bertina, which she knew had to be waiting in the wings.

"He rarely stops," said Mama Sal. Edna had squeezed excess water from the hair and now Mama Sal was toweling it dry. "We can thank that little girl he married for turning him against his family. And now where is she? Cutting hair in Watertown like she's a banker or something."

Edna smiled. What also upset Mama Sal about Tommy's divorce was that she'd lost her professional hairdresser, one who came to her house and did her hair for free every week. Now, she had to depend on Edna.

"Well, we tried to warn him before he married her," said Edna. "And because we were right, we're getting his cold shoulder."

Now Mama Sal had the towel wrapped around her head and fixed in place like she was an Egyptian queen. She put both hands on her walker and rocked herself around so that she was facing the kitchen table. Then she walkered her way over to the chair Edna had pulled out for her. She turned, backed up to the chair, and sank down. Edna's most comic twin, Roddy, the one Mama Sal seemed to favor for his sense of humor, liked to make the sound of a truck backing up whenever Mama Sal did this. The boys and Roderick could make sport *of* her and *with* her all day long, but Edna was doomed by birth to respectability.

"This is the danger in a child marrying," said Mama Sal. She had her lecture voice in place, and Edna knew a moral would be arriving soon. "At least your sister didn't bring any of those Latinos home. How's Roderick? That's one hardworking man."

Edna combed through the wet hair and selected a section on top for the first curler.

"I was thinking of giving him poison mushrooms for supper," said Edna, "but I changed my mind."

To her surprise, Mama Sal laughed one of her big laughs, the kind she reserved for Roderick and the twins.

"Roderick's got a stomach like a steel drum," said Mama Sal. "He loves food so much, he'd probably ask for seconds."

Edna found herself laughing too. It *was* pretty funny when she thought of it that way. She was five curlers along the top of her mother's head when Mama Sal said something she wasn't expecting.

"You're the only one of my three children to have a successful marriage," she said. "I'm proud of you."

Mama Sal said this last part as if maybe she'd been rehearsing it all day. She had never before told Edna she was proud of her for anything. And there had been so many times when she should have said it. There were days when Edna stood by the stove with school papers in her hand, a B that had once been a C, the occasional and unexpected A. And there were times when she brought drawings home with that scrawl across the top where Mrs. Bingham, the art teacher, had written, *This is wonderful work, Edna. You have the talent to move on to bigger things*. Or when Edna won the spelling bee in the sixth grade. Or when her pies and canned pickles were always first to be bought at any town fund-raiser. Never a word of praise and now here it was, all these chances down the road.

"I'm still gonna ask Roderick for a divorce," said Edna. She stepped two feet back, the comb in one hand, the curler she was about to put in Mama Sal's hair in the other. Mama Sal turned and looked at her, and Edna wanted to giggle at the sight. With those five curlers across the top of her head, she looked like a Mohawk Indian. But then Mama Sal surprised her.

"It's hurting my heart," she said. "Tommy is my only boy."

Edna knew by the tone of the words that this sadness was real. Tommy had been Mama Sal's pride, her golden boy. Edna came and put a hand on her mother's shoulder. They said nothing for some time as they listened to autumn wind in the porch chimes and watched cars going up and down the road. Florence Walker in her little brown Chevy. Sheriff Ray Monihan in his black sheriff car with the light on top. Dorrie Mullins in her purple Bronco. Meg Craft in her little gray Mazda. Henry Plunkett in his maroon pickup truck.

"Lives going back and forth, back and forth, every day," said Mama Sal. "And all we're doing is getting closer to our last ride."

It was almost a mother-daughter moment until Tommy's enormous black pickup went flying by, the huge tires turning like Ferris wheels under the cab, the engine so loud that the porch chimes seemed to pick up the noise and echo it back. And Edna could sense that the mother-daughter moment, maybe the first one ever, was officially over.

Harry Plunkett finished replacing the broken starter cord on Tommy Gifford's snowmobile, a Polaris 550 Supersport. It was a known fact that Tommy was hard on machines and women, and in that order. He had apparently developed a philosophy in kindergarten that he stuck to over the years. *If it ain't broke, break it.* Harry reached for the cup of coffee he'd put on the windowsill. It was in this garage that he'd opened his business two summers ago. Many of the jobs he got didn't take the greatest skill, just patience. But as Harry saw it, he was providing the town with a good service. Almost everyone owned a lawn mower or a snowmobile or a four-wheeler, and many folks had all of the above. Harry didn't charge city prices, but Plunkett's Small Engine Repair, as the sign on the garage door announced, helped supplement the monthly check he got from the Veteran's Administration.

Harry went inside the house to answer the telephone, thinking it might be his daughter, Angie. But it turned out to be another one of those anonymous, far-off voices wanting to send him a credit card. He'd hung up on the voice and was about to pour a fresh cup of coffee when he heard the sound of blaring music. He saw Billy Thunder cut the white Mustang into the yard, right next to Harry's pickup, and get out. Harry opened the front door.

"I'll be out in a minute," he said.

Billy nodded. He took off his earmuffs and gloves, which he

tossed onto the seat of the Mustang. He lit a cigarette. That was the biggest drawback of the convertible. You couldn't smoke as you drove, and it was the number-two reason Billy wanted the top fixed. Number one was that he was slowly freezing to death. He walked past Harry's pickup and stood below the garage, shielded from the wind as he smoked. That's when he noticed a few cars parked behind the building, some spotted with rust, others fender-less. Billy walked over to a 1974 Cutlass and kicked the block of hardwood that held up the right front wheel axle. He figured Harry must use the old cars for spare parts. Harry appeared behind him, pulling on his denim jacket. The T-shirt that disappeared beneath asked *Which Part of E=MC2 Don't You Understand?* Billy looked at the older man and smiled his downstate smile.

"I guess the biggest wear and tear on these tires is done by woodpeckers," Billy said. "How many cords do you get to the gallon?"

"See these boots?" Harry asked. He lifted one burgundy boot so Billy could better see the steel-enforced yellow toe. They were the same as Buck's boots, the kind lumberjacks wear to protect their feet from mishaps, yellow-tipped for visibility. "I get three good ass-kickings per pair and I've only used up two. Now, do you want me to look at that piece of shit you're driving or not?"

Billy seemed satisfied with that answer about mileage. He took his foot off the block of wood and followed Harry over to the Mustang. As they crossed the lawn again, Billy saw a sign hanging inside the garage door: AL GORE IS REALLY PRESIDENT.

"You sure like signs, don't you?" asked Billy. "T-shirts and hats. Don't you have anybody to talk to, Harry?"

Harry was about to say something sarcastic. "Even with the top up, a convertible isn't a thinking man's car." That's what he intended to say. Instead, an image of the old Vietnamese man flashed quickly into his mind, the *Papa-san*, bloody stumps where his arms and legs should have been, his eyes glazed with pain. He was lying in a sampan that the enemy had floated out from the riverbank, an attempt to trick the Americans, lure them into the open. Of all the many things Harry hated about Vietnam and being trapped there, it was the sampan searches he dreaded most. Hundreds of those small boats ran the Mekong Delta on a daily basis. It was how the locals made their living on the river, their sampans carrying a cargo of vegetables, fruits, and rice. But it was common knowledge that sampans sometimes carried other things. Sometimes, VC were lying flat on their bellies, packed like sardines beneath tarps and baskets of rice. And even the daylight hours weren't safe. If an American soldier moved that basket of dragon fruit, so pretty and oval-shaped with their pink and green spikes, would a barrage of bullets tear him apart? But for those sampans that floated the river by night, especially in hostile areas, the MO was simple: don't ask questions. Sampan at night. Just fire. "Shit, I think he's trying to talk to us, Sarge," Wally McGee had shouted, a second before Harry's men filled the boat full of bullets. Maybe it had been a blessing in the end. Maybe he would have begged them to kill him anyway. What old man, what *Papa-san*, wants to live like that? That's what Harry and the others told themselves for days, each of them grieving over the sight, over the frozen memory they would carry back to the United States of God Bless America on that air-conditioned plane, back into the peaceful towns and the shiny cities. Back to the faces in high school and college yearbooks of the boys they once were. Back to the families who welcomed them home but could never understand the men who had returned to them.

He's trying to talk to us, Sarge.

Don't you have anybody to talk to, Harry?

"When I push the switch under the dash, to send power to the pump, there's nothing but quiet," Billy was saying. "And now even the canvas is stuck. I'm afraid I'll rip it if I try to put it up manually. It's the original roof."

Harry walked around the car, giving it a close look and saying nothing. He was still trying to undo that picture of the bloody stumps, the pained eyes, the lips trying to work again, to share those last precious words. He'd almost forgotten about the *Papa-san*.

Billy watched, waiting. Harry said nothing.

"The trouble started when the thing that raises and lowers the top got a leak," Billy said. "So I took it to an expert in Boston. He replaced the left cylinder and it worked good for a while. But then the left side started going down slower than the right. Then it quit working altogether."

Harry Plunkett was only half listening. He could hear the sound of a northern raven from the trees along the riverbank, near where he kept his canoe tied up. He knew he had work to do and that he had a customer standing in front of him. He knew he was in Mattagash, Maine. He knew the man he had become, a widower about to turn sixty-three, father of one child and grandfather to two. But the sound of the Mattagash River, and of the raven, reminded him of another river, the sound of another bird, the silhouette of different trees, a different boat than a canoe. It reminded him of a different man. The river was any one of the dirty rivers and murky canals of the Mekong Delta on any given day or night. The patrol boat was a PBR. The bird was a Huey, a UH-1B helicopter gunship. The job on the river and in the air was to stop the flow of enemy troops, supplies, and arms into South Vietnam. And the man was Army Sergeant Harold Plunkett, still twenty-four years old until November. If he lived to see November. He was a man of few words in those days. Some nights, when silence fell like rain over the jungle, a menacing stillness that meant something bad was about to happen, he knew only two words: *Emily* and *home*.

"And with all due respect," said Billy, seemingly ready to run if

Harry lifted one of his boots, "this car is not a piece of shit. She's an American classic, and I've taken good care of her. I'm getting a little tired of the hicks in this backwoods town thinking she's just an old car."

Harry peered across the roofless car at Billy, as if remembering he had a customer. His mind and thoughts were back again. As he had done on all those black nights on the delta, nights when a leaf dropping in the jungle would make his heart race, he had taken himself away from a time and place. Over there, he had done this to save himself from the future. Nowadays, he did it to save himself from the past.

Harry Plunkett walked to the front of the Mustang. He released the latch to open the hood, then looked over at Billy.

"What's the wheelbase? A hundred and eight inches, right?"

"Shit, I don't know," said Billy. Harry lifted the hood.

"Nice," he said. "Detailed engine compartment and the valve covers and air cleaner are Ford Blue, just as they should be."

"Really?" said Billy. He glanced down at his car, as if seeing it for the first time.

Harry closed the hood and looked at Billy Thunder.

"The hydraulic mechanism, or what you call *the thing*, is what lowers and raises the top," he said. "It must have had a leak in it. Your expert down in Boston should've never replaced just one cylinder, or ram, but both of them. If I were you, I'd go back to zero and replace both cylinders. But, of course, I'm not a specialist. I'm an old hick from a backwoods town."

Billy thought fast. This was an upstaging, no doubt about it, and while he was fifty percent Mattagash, thanks to his mother, the part that *wasn't* Mattagash told him to take the scolding he had coming to him and keep his mouth shut.

"Where will I find cylinders for a 1966 Mustang up here?" Billy asked.

"Same place you'd find 'em for an Edsel or a Model-T," said Harry.

"Nowhere?"

"Nowhere," said Harry. "Find someone with a computer and enough brains to use it and get them to order you some. I'll put 'em in for you."

After Billy disappeared down the road in his Mustang, Harry had come inside the house and stood in the middle of the room. He didn't know what was happening, only that a wound had opened inside him and he knew it wasn't the physical one that had brought him home from Vietnam two months early. He looked around his kitchen, at the mug on the counter that the grandkids had given him for his birthday. *World's Greatest Grandpa.* The poster on his fridge had been taped there by his granddaughter during her last visit. He liked that little girl a lot. She reminded him of Emily in so many ways, the soft voice, the shiny dark hair, the sweet temperament. *Grandpa, today is the first day of the rest of your life.* Harry read the words again. The plaque over the fridge was one that Angie had sent last Christmas. *Why God Made Fathers.* She was only eleven when Emily died, and now she was almost thirty-seven. Her life was rooted in Portland, with a family of her own. Harry hadn't seen Angie or his grandkids in over a year. Mattagash wasn't their idea of a vacation hot spot. After his daughter left home, it had been just Harry Plunkett in the small house, trying to keep up family appearances.

His eyes moved slowly around the room, but Harry's mind was moving too, remembering the T-shirts and hats he had piled in his closet. *A Hangover Is The Wrath Of Grapes. Shut Up And Paddle. Procrastinate Now.* And his favorite fishing hat: *When In Doubt,*

Trust The Trout. He could have answered Billy Thunder's question. After all, here was a young man who had driven a broken car north to Mattagash and put his finger on a broken spot in Harry's soul, a place no one else in town had thought to look. Harry could have said, "Listen, it's not that I don't have somebody to talk to; it's that the somebody I *want* to talk to is no longer here." It had taken him twelve long years of thrashing the blankets off at night, of waking up and shouting, "Who's there?" to the shadows of an armchair in the corner, with Emily waking to talk him back to sleep. Twelve years before he felt he could tell the woman he loved about the horrors of Vietnam, about the men he had lost, about Wally McGee, his best soldier. And when that moment finally came, it came too late. She'd been to a doctor. Soft, little Emily. When you're a man known for his bravery as Harry was—hell, the goddamn military had given him a Purple Heart—that would be the time to act, to save your wife. But Harry soon discovered that he couldn't do anything. He couldn't grab an M60 and start mowing down every shadow that moved. He couldn't plan an ambush. He couldn't even hide. Emily had died before he could speak to her of the faces and voices who were waking him at night, haunting him. And now, Emily was among them.

Harold Plunkett stood alone in his small house on the banks of the Mattagash River, a house in which every window looked out upon water and trees and road, a house that could see the enemy coming from a long way off, a house he had built when he came home from Vietnam and married Emily Mason. And that's when all the words on all the hats, the T-shirts, the signs, the posters, and the mugs, all the words flew out of drawers and bounced off walls and closet shelves. *Sixty Is Not Old If You're A Tree. Rehab Is For Quitters. If All The World's A Stage...I Want Better Lighting. If You Shoot Me, City Slicker...You Better Kill Me.*

Harry stood alone in the middle of his kitchen and said no

words at all. Why should he, when there was no one there to hear him? He stood and thought about the ocean of words he'd been sailing upon for years, an ocean in which he was now drowning. So many words, and yet now, with the afternoon sun beginning to touch the river, making it shimmer, he could think of only one small word. So he said it aloud.

"Emily," he whispered.

6

THURSDAY AFTERNOON AND EVENING

A pale sun rode in and out of cloud patches as Orville hit the bridge. He always felt airborne at times like that—nothing above him but sky, nothing below but river. In the sky over the mountain to the north, he noticed a string of Canada geese cutting a wide V in the sky, some of the last stragglers to head south. Orville had been hearing their distant honkings late at night when he let the dog out before bedtime. The geese knew what was coming, that's why they had a plan. Orville saw Sheriff Ray Monihan approaching the opposite end of the bridge in his black sheriff's car. But Orville had the right-of-way, given the First Come–First Served philosophy of one-way bridges, and that also applied to lawmen unless it was an emergency. Ray pulled to the side and waited. Orville nodded hello as he came off the bridge and slid the mail car up close to Billy Plunkett's box. No Billy in visible sight, and that was a good thing since Orville was already late in his deliveries.

By the time he slowed for Blanche's mailbox, he noticed that she had a nice crowd of cars in her yard and it was not yet two o'clock. But some of the women in town liked to gather at Blanche's in the afternoon. Orville often saw Meg's gray Mazda in among the herd, a fact he did not like or approve of but had no control over. Meg did what Meg saw fit. And on top of this, everywhere he looked, he saw cars made by Japanese and Germans, the country's two biggest enemies during World War II. Somehow, that seemed discrepant to Orville Craft. *Discrepant: not compatible with facts*. He also noticed on this day that among the female-driven cars at Blanche's was the topless white Mustang. This was not a surprise, considering that Billy Thunder's lifestyle bordered on the kind led by matrons and English royalty.

Orville had put Blanche's mail inside her box and clamped the door shut when he heard a thump on his trunk. He looked into his rearview mirror to see Billy Thunder on his way up to Orville's window.

"Hey, Mr. Mailman," said Billy. "Did you happen to have a little box for me today?"

"As a matter of fact," said Orville, "I *did* deliver a small box. You'd better get home, Thunder, before someone steals it."

Before Orville could say anything else—even if he had intended to, and he didn't—Billy Thunder made a dash for the Mustang. As Orville watched, Billy shifted the car into first gear and then gunned it. The tires caught tar, and the Mustang screamed out of the yard and up onto the main road. Billy hadn't even bothered to put on his earmuffs.

There was no sign of Harry. The moose was alone. Orville was actually disappointed. He put the car in park and pretended to flick through some advertisements that lay beside him on the seat. He had two more times to deliver mail to #77, and he wanted to let Harry know something was up. Make him nervous. Harry's pickup was parked near the garage. Orville didn't think Harry was the type of man to take an afternoon nap. Where was he? Now Orville was the nervous one. He had lived all his life in the same town as Harry Plunkett and yet knew little about him. Harry had come home wounded from Vietnam and decorated to the hilt. That was back when the whole country was going to hell in a hand basket. College students were taking drugs instead of tests. Professors were running around with hair down to their shoulders, tripping over their bell-bottoms, higher than kites. Orville remembered that the *Watertown Weekly* had run a story about Harry's unit being ambushed and how two of his soldiers had died. The town of Mattagash had thrown a welcome home party for their hero. The only person not to show up was Sergeant Harold Plunkett. There were those who said he went fishing. Others said he was home, both doors locked and a gun at his side. Wherever he was, the party had been a huge success.

Before he drove off, Orville looked at the moose mailbox.

"Tomorrow, buddy," he said. "Get ready to rumble."

Edna had kept the items hidden in the trunk of her car since her shopping spree. Now the easel was set up in the dining room and the canvas in place when she heard Roderick drive into the yard. She had made a pot of beef stew earlier, before she drove over to wash Mama Sal's hair, and it was still warm on the stove. She hadn't expected Roderick home for lunch, but then, she hadn't packed it for him again that morning. Why couldn't he go to Blanche's like the single men who had no women to feed them?

Mama Sal knew why. She had called ten minutes before Roderick's pickup pulled into the yard and didn't even bother with *hello*. "I hope you've got a hot biscuit and a slice of ham to put on the table for your hungry husband," Mama Sal said. Edna felt the same courage she often did when a telephone line stretched four miles between her and her mother, not to mention the bridge.

"Why can't he pack his own lunch? He's a grown man." There was a brief silence on the other end of the line, one that said Mama Sal didn't approve of even the meekest confrontation.

"Your husband is out working to pay the bills," Mama Sal finally said. "That's *his* job. *Your* job is to feed him." And then she'd hung up. Edna had turned on the oven, and when it was hot enough, she slid a pan of Pillsbury biscuits inside. Now here was Roderick, ten minutes after the phone call and, like a well-wound clock, driving into the yard. This was proof that he'd stopped at his mother-in-law's to tattle on his wife and then listen as Edna got a scolding over the phone.

Roderick wiped his feet at the door. Edna could hear the loud scraping of his boots and knew he wanted her to hear.

"I'm home," he announced.

"There's a pan of biscuits in the oven," Edna said. "When you hear a bell ring, they're ready."

She was opening her green paint when Roderick came into the dining room. She could feel him standing behind her shoulder, breathing heavy from that extra fifty pounds, not to mention the smoking. He was watching her work, maybe wondering if he should tattle this to Mama Sal too. It was as if Roderick thought Mama Sal had some kind of mystical power. Like a fortune-teller in a turban, she could reveal the future to him if he gave her enough facts and information.

"What's this?" he asked. Edna didn't bother to turn and look at him. She began patting the canvas with pats of bright green paint.

"What's it look like?"

"When did you decide to take up painting?"

She could sense him leaning in for a better look—Mama Sal's spy.

"Hear that little bell going off in the kitchen?" Edna asked. "That means your biscuits are ready. If I were you, and if I wanted a biscuit, I'd take them out of the oven before they burn. Turn the burner on beneath the beef stew and it'll be warm in no time. There's a box of donuts on the counter."

She went back to her work, patting more green across the canvas where she wanted some trees to grow. Roderick had hovered a few more seconds, watching her paint, before he gave up. She could hear him now in the kitchen, swearing softly as he burned his finger on the hot pan of biscuits and rattling the silverware as he found a spoon and a knife in the drawer. Edna knew this was his way of whining about having to get his own lunch. Fifteen minutes later, he was back in the dining room, a toothpick hanging from his mouth and staring at Edna's work.

"Whose pickup is that?" Roderick asked and pointed at the white outline of a truck that had appeared on Edna's canvas while he ate. "White's not a smart color for snow country."

"It's nobody's pickup," said Edna. "If you invent something in your head, it doesn't have to belong to anyone." Before she knew it, he'd be wanting to drive the white pickup on her canvas over to the town office so he could register it.

"You get good enough at them things," Roderick said, "maybe you can sell them over the computer."

"Maybe," said Edna. *Them things*. How could she ever talk to him? She had seen television shows about how artists lead lonely lives. And here she was, less than an hour into her first creation. Roderick moved forward to plant a kiss on her face, but Edna leaned down to derail it. She picked up her new book, *Easy Steps to Basic Painting*, and opened it to any page, pretending to read. That's when Roderick turned and left the room. She heard again the sound of footsteps on the porch and the truck door opening and closing, a man reversing himself, rewinding his life. Edna listened to the sound of his pickup pulling out of the yard, a dark blue truck nothing like the white one that had driven out of her subconscious mind and parked on her canvas. She hadn't expected to draw it, but there it was, as if maybe she could bring him back to Mattagash if she painted his truck, a kind of artistic voodoo.

When Edna heard the bus brake, she looked up at the clock. Almost three. The twins were home from school. Roddy broke through the door first, letting it slam back and hit Ricky.

"Hey, watch it!" said Ricky. "Or I'll kick your goddamn butt."

"You catch it, you can kick it," said Roddy. "And you can even kiss it."

Edna decided to ignore the rule she had set, a dollar a curse from the allowance. Otherwise, the twins would be in the dining room asking all sorts of questions. She heard the fridge door opening and bottles clinking about inside. Now the cupboard door opened, the one where she kept bags of cookies and potato chips. She heard it slam. The silverware drawer opened next. When it also slammed, forks and knives and spoons clinked painfully. She waited for the pantry doors, where she kept the peanut butter and jelly, knowing the twins would want their sandwiches. And there went the pantry doors. It was as if her life had become that of spectator in a house filled with noises, the sounds of human lives being lived with or without her. In a few hours would come the sound of Roderick's blue pickup turning back into the yard, his door shutting, his boots on the front porch, and then the door opening. *I'm home*.

Edna wiped her brush on the cotton rag she'd found under the sink, then doused it in a glass jar filled with turpentine. She looked at her work and smiled. It was not a bad job for her first try. There it was, a white pickup truck driving away from the viewer, headed down the road. Behind the steering wheel was the back of the driver's head, his neck and shoulders. It was a man wearing a light blue shirt, with most of his brown hair hidden beneath a baseball cap. A man leaving town in the heart of autumn, without looking back. On each side of the truck, the land was on fire, and that's where Edna had had the most fun, painting orange and yellow and red blobs on all her trees, leaving bits of the bright green to peek through in places. She felt a power in what she had created. She could even destroy it, could paint over it. Or she could turn the truck around, put a smile on the man's face, maybe even figure out how to paint the blinker as if it were blinking, and the truck driving into her yard. But what good would it do? For one thing, it wouldn't be true. This first painting she had done was the last glimpse she'd had of Ward Hooper that day he drove away from Mattagash, his job in soil conservation over. So why kid herself?

Orville had done his deliveries for the day and had stopped off at Blanche's for his piece of blueberry pie, a tradition since he began his job as mailman. Florence Walker was there, having the daily special with some old woman Orville didn't know. He had always wondered if Florence, a spinster, might have some kind of dark secret that even Mattagash couldn't get out of her. Meg thought he was imagining things. "Just because a woman don't stand out at her mailbox in a housecoat and flirt with you over a book of stamps don't mean she's *that way*," Meg had said. Maybe, but one other thing was certain. Orville would miss the town flirts, even if they did hold him up some days and keep him running behind schedule. There were two widows under sixty and three divorcees along his route, the latter sometimes leaning into his delivery window so that he could catch a glimpse of white cleavage before he put a book of stamps in an outstretched hand, a hand that now had a birthstone ring where a wedding band had once been.

"Harry hasn't come in for lunch," Blanche said as she gave Orville his cup of tea. "Have you seen him?"

The whole town knew about Harry's moose mailbox, and Orville had no doubt they were making sport of him behind his back. Maybe Harry Plunkett got their attention and respect, but it was Orville who got them their mail on time.

"Nope," he said.

"Strange," said Blanche. "That's not like him."

Orville finished off his piece of pie.

"One more day," he said to Blanche as he paid his check. "Then I'm a free man."

Orville was almost to the one-way bridge when he saw what looked like a man standing in the middle of the road, waving his arms.

"Damn," Orville said, although he hated to swear within the mail car itself when he was still on the job. He knew who it was. Box #46. Billy Thunder. Orville slowed the car and pulled to the side of the road. It was either that or flatten the boy squirrel-flat by driving over him.

Billy came around to the driver's window and stood there waiting. Orville could tell by his face that Billy wasn't there to compliment the United States Postal Service. He hesitated before he put his window down.

"What is it, Thunder?"

"You think you're funny, don't you?" asked Billy. Orville tried to answer this honestly.

"I've been known to tell a joke now and then," he said. "But I'm no Will Rogers."

"What kind of joke is this?" asked Billy. He pulled a small sample box of dishwasher detergent from his pocket.

"That looks like the detergent sample I put in your mailbox today," said Orville. "I put one in every mailbox. If you don't want it, Thunder, throw it away."

"This is war, Orville," said Billy. "You don't fuck with a man who's down on his luck." He slammed the sample box back into the car. It hit the steering and bounced into the passenger seat. Orville wasn't happy about the box either. He resented it when companies sent out sleazy samples to the multitude, all those *Residents* and *Occupants*, hoping to addict them to a new product. Postal carriers shouldn't be turned into pimps by rich cartels sitting behind corporate desks.

"A customer's luck is between them and their god," said Orville. "I deliver the mail, and sometimes packages are among it."

Billy stood watching as Orville's mail car crossed the bridge. He was thinking about revenge the way he often thought of sex, a thing you can sink down into and lose yourself in for hours. How do you break a man who doesn't have a heart beating beneath his shirt? Where's the Achilles' heel on a mailman? That's when Billy remembered the gossip at Blanche's, on one of those days Orville had stopped for his blueberry pie, eaten it, and then left so people could talk about him. It had started out as a secret that Meg told her niece Lillian, who shared it with the four members of her rug-braiding class, who all swore before God they'd never tell. Now it was all over town.

Five minutes later, Billy was inside his rental camper, sorting through his stash of Valiums and sleeping pills, all beautiful *supply* that had fit so nicely with *demand* at the Portland Nursing Home. This was the place where his mother had once nodded off in the afternoon sun, oblivious to the woman she had been for the past fifty-two years of her life, one of the youngest cases of Alzheimer's her doctor had ever treated. She was oblivious to her children as well, including her youngest child, William Thunder Jr. *Billy*. He had been her favorite, her pet. At least that's what his siblings claimed. Now, what did it matter? That's what Billy asked himself all those nights he couldn't sleep, nights when wind coming off the river had rocked the camper until he thought it might be airborne, might hit the water and float like a silver boat all the way to the Bay of Fundy. What did it all matter to anyone now who had been the pet and who hadn't? The last time he'd seen his mother alive, a few months earlier, she was standing in the long green hallway at the nursing home, bewildered as a child. When Billy put his hand on her arm, she glanced up at his face, that blank look he was noticing more and more in her eyes. "Can you tell me who I am?" she had asked her son.

But before this, when Billy was still visiting her and still believing that she would recover, that whatever was wrong in her brain would untangle itself, all those snarled and malfunctioning areas, he had seen in the social atmosphere around him a good place to peddle a few wares. Someone's grandmother might need sleeping pills that her doctor wouldn't prescribe. Someone's great-aunt, a Valium. And there were the wrinkled old guys who were courting the wrinkled old women. He never sold them more than 50 milligrams for fear they'd be poking holes through wooden doors and puncturing the tires on their wheelchairs. But thanks to Billy, the Portland Nursing Home, at least for a time, had its share of eighty-year-old men waving from doorways as sexy young nurses passed by, both female *and* male.

Then, Billy lost his mother for good. After that last visit, when he took her by the arm and led her back to her room, he had told her everything his heart could handle. "Your name is Abigail Fennelson Thunder," he said, his voice low so as not to frighten her. "You're fifty-two years old, and you have three children. I'm the youngest, your son, Billy." Before he could say anything else, one of the attendants arrived with a supper tray. As Billy turned at the bedroom door and looked back, she was looking at him too, as if maybe somewhere in her tormented brain she remembered the baseball games, the birthday cakes, the scraped knees, the schoolbooks, the Christmas presents. Then she looked down at her plate, excited to see creamed potatoes.

Billy had gone home and made big plans, dreams where he would come into the kitchen and find her cooking dinner. He would put his arms around her, surprising her, and she'd turn and smile at him, remembering he was her son. He would save enough money to find a place for them to live, maybe even enough money to hire a nurse. He was still planning when he got the phone call no person who loves another person wants to get. His mother had suffered a stroke. Billy remembered the doctor's words in bits and pieces. *Severe and long-standing high blood pressure. Hypertensive bleeding within the brain*. It was as if her body knew the truth, even if her mind no longer did. Her body knew what was coming, all those blank and frightening years that lay ahead, bewildered days and fog-filled nights. And so her body had taken her back, had taken her home before the other illness could.

And it was somewhat true that Billy had driven up to Mattagash because it was where she was born and raised. With his father also gone, he had no one left but a brother who didn't return his phone calls. And a sister who didn't return his phone calls. And maybe it was true that he'd made most of those phone calls asking for money. His mother had always believed in him, and his heart had never left her side. So he *did* feel closer to her in Mattagash. But if it ever came up in a court of law, he had really gone to Mattagash for more reasons than searching for the Fennelson family ancestry. He had some pressing issues in

Portland, one being all those bad checks that had bounced higher than basketballs, especially the one he had given his girlfriend. The stack of unpaid parking tickets didn't worry him as much as the bouncing checks. If he could sell enough pot, if he could get back his good business sense that he lost for a time, he could cover the checks, pay off the boys who sent those brown boxes, and maybe even marry the girlfriend.

But for now, *right now*, it was payback time. Billy opened the cap on the bottle of pills, each one a brilliant blue, and knocked a couple into his hand.

The Delgatos were in the sports aisle at Walmart. Raul had visited his mother in Boston the previous weekend and forgot the baseball bat at a bar in Little Italy. Now he and Jorge were shopping for a new one. They had a business meeting set with an acquaintance later that night, in an empty parking lot out by the airport.

"The ball bounces harder off aluminum than wood," said Jorge, which is what he said every time Raul suggested, nostalgically, that they buy a wooden bat. "Plus, they don't break at the handle like a wooden bat can."

The model of bat had not come quickly to the cousins, although they had decided upon Easton as the manufacturer. The bat used by the Little League team the cousins had played on as kids had been an Easton. Jorge felt that keeping this tradition alive would bring them good luck. That the Portland Peanuts had never won a game was an irrelevant statistic.

The cousins had shopped long and hard on their first visit to the sports aisle. Easton offered a smorgasbord of bats. The Hammer, the Stealth, the Rampage, and the Cyclone models were contenders at first. But there was something formidable about the Typhoon, something sailors probably knew well. Jorge loved its ultra-thin black handle, its white middle section, and then the word itself written across the extended barrel in angry black letters. Dark blue and black, colors that were difficult to see at night in an alley, were also the colors of a storm that could wipe out everything in its path. They had selected the 32-inch, instead of the 31-inch, after Raul made an aerodynamic observation that rated alongside *Why do curve balls curve?* and *How does drag affect the speed of a pitch?*

"If you swing at someone and they run," said Raul, "that extra inch might make the difference."

The Typhoon had been the Delgatos' weapon of choice ever since they'd spent almost a year in the slammer for an armed robbery charge. Actually, it was *Raul* who had done the time, since the gun was registered to him. A burglary gone bad had persuaded the Delgatos to change their MO. Actually, it was Raul who decided they should do this, after a lawyer finally got him out of jail once the star witness recanted. That Jorge had discussed the case with this witness could never be proven, but the witness—he was also the victim, a seventy-year-old convenience store clerk—woke up one morning with amnesia. When Raul stepped back into the Portland sunshine and saw Jorge waiting for him in a 1995 Cadillac Deville, an ancestor to the 2000 model, he had lit a cigarette and said, "No more guns. If you want me to be your partner, we find a new way."

In the seedy bars on the waterfront, the Delgatos soon became known as "The Typhoon Cousins." Jorge enjoyed leaning down to a negligent business associate in a bar and whispering in his ear, "The last word you're gonna see tonight is *typhoon*." A philosophy had emerged. If you leave a Smith & Wesson gun in a bar, you will be out some money and possibly even your freedom.

But who registers an Easton Typhoon? And then, should they get caught again for robbery or assault, they didn't know of anyone in Portland who had done extra time for packing a baseball bat.

Jorge checked the sales tag to see if bats had gone up in the past year. Only $49.99 before tax. Where could you get a loaded gun for that amount of money?

"Think they've ever seen a Typhoon up in Waddamash?" Jorge asked. As he warmed up, he imagined the watermelon of Billy Thunder's head exploding on contact.

"Mattagash," said Raul. "You swing pretty good for a heavy man."

"Grab a ball and pitch to me," Jorge said. He gripped the cushioned handle of the Typhoon as he rocked back and forth on his feet, finding that perfect stance. Smiling, Raul selected a new softball from off the shelf, a Diamond Flyer, sun yellow with red stitching. He paced thirty feet up the aisle before he turned. As he began his windup, Jorge peered up into the rafters at Walmart and pointed to an invisible center field, as Babe Ruth had supposedly called a 1932 hit into the bleachers at Wrigley Field. Raul brought his elbows back, lifted his right leg, and threw the yellow ball down the aisle at a leisurely speed. The crack of cork against aluminum startled him. It seemed to startle Jorge too, as if he hadn't known his own strength. The cousins watched as the Flyer flew like a small yellow sun over home appliances and Barbie dolls, over towels and indoor furniture, tableware and linens, until it disappeared from their sight.

"Fuck, dude," said Raul, as the sound of shattering glass echoed through the aisles. A woman's scream rose up from lighting fixtures. "I thought you were going to bunt."

Harry dreamed of his father again, a man who had come home in a coffin from a place called Bloody Ridge, a man he hardly remembered. But there he was, still young and boyish. He seemed more like a son now than a father. "I have something for you," Leonard Plunkett whispered. "I brought something back from Korea." When he opened his hand, Harry saw that it clutched the Purple Heart. Leonard Plunkett had to die for the medal that his son lived to receive, a posthumous gift from the military. The country wasn't proud of Harry's war. But he had paid the price for it anyway, along with his fellow soldiers and the innocent Vietnamese women and children, and men so old they had no teeth and no heart left to fight. "Take it, son," said his father. And that's when Harry tried to stop his own hand, tried to tell his unconscious mind that it was a trick. *Don't take it!* But his hand reached out anyway and touched the ribbon. This was when it always happened, when his fingers touched the medal itself, that his father's hand changed into the hand of a skeleton, just bone, the skin rotted away. As always, Harry struggled to wake up, but there was the fleshless face, the eye sockets black as coals. It was *him*, reaching again for the pant leg of those Army-issued fatigues. It was the first man he'd ever killed, a nameless gook intent on never letting Harry forget him. The others, the ones that followed, they no longer bothered him. But this one, this first one, was slow to die. Over the years, and as he'd done that day in the jungle when Harry stood over him, ready to fire the bullet that would finish him off, his eyes had pleaded with the American soldier who was about to kill him. He reached out and grabbed the back of Harry's pant leg as the gun exploded. All these years later, and through the vehicle of dreams, Harry knew what the eyes were trying to tell him. *I am a man, like you. I have a woman I love. I have children in my future.* My *family will mourn me. Can we stop this, you and me?* But he would have killed Harry too, had it been the other way around.

Harry recoiled from the dream skeleton. He fought the blankets on top of him but knew he was still asleep. He knew the pattern well by now. He was still asleep because *she* hadn't come yet to stop the nightmare. And sure enough, there she was. Emily. Her smile was what he would remember on his deathbed, when his time came. Emily's smile was the most gentle thing, not taking up any more space than was needed. *It's all right, Harry,* that's what her smile said. *I know now what you went through.* *Go back to sleep.*

Harry opened his eyes. He heard wind rocking the chair on his back porch. Tears ran freely down his face. It's an amazing thing in a man's life when he comes to a realization, when he recognizes that the places which breed horror can also breed love. Otherwise, how could Emily arrive each time, just behind the black eye sockets and the bony fingers? *We are what we dream,* Harry told himself.

7

FRIDAY MORNING

Wind rocked the hanging sign that said *Blanche's Café*, swinging it back and forth on silver chains. Around the front steps, dead leaves had pooled into orange and yellow piles, with a few red maples here and there for effect. Blanche's cat sat licking its front paws as if maybe it had eaten something good from the autumn fields. Harry liked the sound of the bell when he first opened the door at Blanche's. It was an old-fashioned sound you didn't hear much anymore. It was good to know there were still places where a bell rang when a person stepped inside, a bell like a pleasant voice, saying, *Well, look who's here. What can I do for you?*

He was the first customer, as usual, and right on time for the first order of eggs, the first pancakes, and the first strips of bacon from the griddle. He took off his denim jacket and hung it on the deer antlers by the front door. He pulled out one of the four stools at the little service bar.

"Where were you yesterday?" Blanche asked as she poured him the first cup of coffee. "I saved a meatloaf special for you until I finally had to sell it. You're not going to Watertown to eat behind my back, are you?"

"Yesterday was the first day of the rest of my life," Harry said. "So I took the day off." Blanche gave him that appreciative frown she always did when Harry said something witty.

"Even Orville didn't know where you were," she said. "You missed out on a day to torment him and now it's Friday, his last day."

"I don't need to be present to torment Orville," said Harry. "My moose does it for me."

"Tell me something," said Blanche. "I mean, we all know Orville thinks the Lord didn't rest on the seventh day. He used it to create mailmen instead. But other than that, why him?"

"He's like that mountain," said Harry. "He's there."

Blanche went to the refrigerator and opened it. She took out a carton of eggs. Harry watched as she bent to grab a roll of paper towels from a bottom shelf. Her long brown hair was pulled back again in a ponytail. Her jeans weren't too tight, the way some women in town wore them. Instead, they looked comfortable. And that was the operative word for Blanche too, and how most people felt around her. Comfortable. She still had a nice body, but then Blanche was a runner. She put in six miles every day, either in the early hours as dawn crept over the town, or at night, under the shine of moon and stars. Harry often saw her running, absorbed in her own thoughts, her legs thinking for themselves as they ate up the road in front of her. In the summer she wore tank tops and shorts. In the winter, she'd be in sweats and a jacket. Sometimes, if it was night and the road dark, Harry would follow slowly behind in his truck as she ran, his two headlights lighting the way for her. He figured that owning a business couldn't be easy on Blanche. She and her husband had been divorced for so many years now that he had another grown family somewhere downstate. She was a decade or so behind Harry in years, so he estimated her age to be a year or two over fifty. He didn't remember her from school. He was a senior in those days and she was lost somewhere down in the lower, anonymous grades of grammar school. She would have been a young girl in 1966, the year he shipped out to Fort Lewis, Washington, that halfway house for the insane asylum that had once been a little country called Vietnam. By the time Harry returned and he and Emily got married, Blanche was already living downstate. It had been a year earlier that something in the air called her home, and now Blanche's Café was a favorite gathering place.

Blanche slid a plate of eggs and bacon in front of Harry. She reached for silverware and a napkin.

"Were you staring at my butt again?" she asked.

Harry didn't know how to respond to Blanche most of the time. She was as outspoken and confident as Emily had been soft-spoken and shy. But that she had a nice butt had been the hushed topic of many male comments at the café.

Harry cut into the first egg with his fork.

"Is there a charge for staring?" he asked.

"Guess what? I missed you yesterday," said Blanche. "Maybe it's time you made your move. We're not getting any younger. Especially *you*."

The bell over the door rang and Harry looked up to see Tommy Gifford and Bobby Fennelson. They pulled out stools next to Harry's and reached for menus. They sat staring at the words as if maybe the writing had changed over the past year and some new dish was about to jump out and surprise them. Blanche put an empty cup in front of Bobby and poured him a coffee.

"Coke," said Tommy. "No ice. Eggs and bacon."

Bobby put down his menu.

"How the fuck can you drink a Coke for breakfast?" he asked. "This early in the day, that's like drinking motor oil."

"My mouth, *my* taste buds, *my* breakfast," said Tommy.

"Girls, please," said Harry. "Do we have to listen to this every morning?"

The red wall phone rang and Blanche answered it.

"Yes, Ray, salmon loaf and mashed potatoes," she said. "Yes, it's chocolate pudding. Sure, I'll save a plate for you." Blanche hung up the phone.

"Some kids broke a few beer bottles at the town dump," she said. "The sheriff's been doing extra duty out there, hoping to catch whoever it was."

"Those were probably *my* beer bottles," said Bobby.

"No town in America has a safer dump," said Tommy.

Blanche went back to the kitchen, and Harry heard the sound of eggs cracking. He was still trying to sort out his thoughts. She *had* said it, and he had heard her very well. *I missed you yesterday*. He had no idea she felt that way about him. Had he grown blind, living alone as he did?

"Hey, Harry, tell us a war story," said Bobby.

"Yeah, Harry, how many of them slant-eyed bastards did you kill?"

Harry grinned. It was always his first response when anyone asked him about Vietnam, as if the grin gave him time to think. He threw a ten-dollar bill onto the counter next to his plate.

"Apparently not enough of them," Harry said.

Orville was disappointed that Billy Thunder and his swearing Winston weren't waiting for him at the end of the bridge. He had in his hand the very brown box that the young man had been so anxious about, a package with those four smug words, *Elizabeth Miller, Portland, Maine*, as its entire return address. Orville had planned a cat-and-mouse game with Billy, pretending there was no package before finding it in the backseat just as the boy was about to hyperventilate. He looked down at the flimsy camper in its clutch of birch trees on the flat, but the roofless Mustang was gone. How much more agony could Billy Thunder endure? And with snow predicted any day now, what was he going to do? He'd need a shovel, not just for the road down from the bridge to the camper, but to shovel snow off the Mustang's seats. Orville put the brown parcel into the mailbox. He had fifty-two more houses to go, and then he would be a regular citizen of the town.

At Blanche's Café, Orville glanced over and counted five cars in the yard. The place would be almost empty by the time he got done, around three, depending on whether the populace detained him. He wouldn't mind a last flirt with his divorcees, since a peek at cleavage was out of the question, it being the season of sweaters and jackets. And he wouldn't mind that sad, come-hither smile from his widows. It was the Sal Giffords, with their junkyard-dog personalities, that Orville dreaded. But so far, it had been smooth sailing, with a few of his clients even leaving him a note of retirement congratulations in their mailboxes. He was now more certain than ever that a retirement party was in the works. But at which house? These high-tech times were difficult to read. Some days, as he delivered the mail—Orville refused to let Meg refer to it as *snail mail*—he could almost hear the Internet messages flying over his head like carrier pigeons.

As Orville arrived at the house with the panoramic view of the river, he saw Harry Plunkett waiting by his mailbox. Orville slowed the car, letting his right hand reach out to touch the newspaper that lay on the seat beside him. Patience. That's what he'd been telling himself for three years.

Harry was smiling as Orville pulled up to the box.

"Last day, Orville?" he asked.

Orville said nothing as he pulled out the packet that held Harry's bills, along with a few flyers. In a matter of minutes, he'd be at the last mailbox on his route, Buck Fennelson's house.

When he turned around and drove back, he'd no longer be the official mail carrier.

"Did I see you talking to my moose yesterday?" Harry asked. "He's from Quebec. He doesn't understand English."

Orville unclamped the rear-end door and stuffed the letters inside. He pushed the hinged door back up and heard it snap shut. He said nothing as he steered the car back onto the road. He drove toward the trailer park with its nine silver boxes waiting like a purple martin birdhouse, minus the droppings. Then, it was straight on to Buck's house at the end of the road and Orville Craft's last stamp, last envelope, last red flag, last mailbox. But it was also the beginning of all-out war with Harry Plunkett, one he knew might last forever. And like those haggard soldiers of wars past, Orville Craft would stay in this one for the duration.

By noon, Billy and Buck had finished splitting all of Amy Joy Lawler's firewood. By one o'clock, they had stacked the wood neatly in even tiers by her back door. All morning long as Billy chopped and stacked, he had tried to think of other beverages that could quench the human thirst better than a cold beer, even during frigid weather. Billy did have that case of Jack Daniels at the camper. But while Jack might warm a person up, he doesn't take away the kind of thirst that comes with a hard day's work. What made all this thinking troublesome was that Blanche didn't sell beer, Mattagash being a dry town.

While Billy had been inwardly philosophizing as he worked, Buck had been outwardly whistling. As soon as he finished one song, he'd quickly start another, none of them songs Billy had ever heard. When each new song began, he had to resist asking

Buck to shut up. It was as if the two of them were on a chain gang, singing Negro work songs and picking cotton. But at least Buck's stomach wasn't singing, so Billy let him be. When they finished the job, Billy accepted the hundred and twenty dollars Amy Joy gave them—not bad for four hours of work.

"I can get Mona a birthday present now," said Buck.

"What are you buying her?" Billy asked as he handed Buck sixty dollars.

"A box of white wine," said Buck.

Billy opened the door to the Mustang and heard it creak. At least there was no sign of snow, as there had been the past few days. The sky was now bright blue and the sun carried enough yellow in it to look believable. The day before, Billy had stopped by Kenny Barker's camp on the banks of the Mattagash River. Kenny had a computer and so he helped Billy search around on the Internet until they found not just a classic car site, but a classic *Mustang* site. Billy made Kenny a deal. If Kenny would use his Visa card to pay for the hydraulic mechanism Harry Plunkett needed to fix the Mustang's top, he'd not only get his money back, but he'd also get a hell of a discount on the next shipment Billy got from Portland. So Kenny had smelled a reefer burning and clicked *Order Now* on some website out in Arizona.

"Wanna ride to St. Leonard with me?" Billy asked. "I'm dying for a beer."

"Well, ah," Buck said. He stared at the roofless Mustang, thinking.

"It's your fault Mona has the pickup again," said Billy. "Come on, get in."

Buck did so reluctantly, his rubber work boots squeaking and his nylon ski jacket swishing as he swung his arms. He pulled the car door shut and pushed himself down in the passenger seat. Finally, he lay with his head pressed against Billy's leg.

"Now don't do anything wild while you're down there," Billy

warned. "I happen to prefer women. Unless, of course, you're good at it."

"Damn you, Billy," said Buck, his face flushing.

Billy put on his earmuffs and gloves and turned the key. The engine purred.

"Pilot to copilot," said Billy. "We got ignition."

Eight miles later, they were pulling into the grocery store in St. Leonard. Billy parked the Mustang next to the gas pump that said *Regular*. Buck sat up in the front seat and looked all around, as if he had no idea where the car had landed, the Sea of Tranquility, maybe. Billy got out and shook his arms to put some warmth back in them. He slapped both hands against his frozen cheeks, hoping to stir the blood there, get it circulating. He reached for the gas cap and unscrewed it. It was the original cap, with the raised and galloping mustang in its center, but the threads were corroded from usage. He would order a vintage one once he got his financial life back in order. He put the nozzle into the tank and started the pump. Buck got out of the car and stood watching the numbers flicking, indicating gallons and dollars. His face was red with cold.

"I think I'll take Mona out to eat on her birthday," Buck said. "Someplace warm. How come you don't have a steady girlfriend, Bill?"

Billy left the pump in the tank and reached into his shirt pocket for his pack of Winstons.

"When it comes to women," he said, "I believe in catch and release."

"I wonder how it knows," Buck said. He was still staring at the rolling numbers, his face full of wonder.

"Knows what?" asked Billy.

"How does it know when it's done?"

Billy stared at him. Sometimes, he didn't know for certain if

Buck was fooling around or if he was sincerely stupid. He pushed up his jacket sleeve and found his watch. Two o'clock.

"We need to get back to Blanche's before Orville stops in for his pie."

Inside the store, Billy pulled off his earmuffs and let them dangle around his neck. He went first to the aisle where pet foods were kept and selected a small bag of dog food and a rawhide bone. He grabbed a six-pack of Buds from the cooler and made his way to the cash, where the fresh packs of Winstons waited.

"Let me give you some free financial advice," Billy said to the sleepy-eyed girl who was clerking. "Start selling *Playboy*."

"Know what I've been thinking, Bill?" Buck asked when Billy came out carrying the cigarettes and beer and dog food. "We could go into business together. We could call ourselves Billy and Buck."

Billy forced a smile. It sounded like an old vaudeville act, tuberculoid and down on its luck. But if Billy's luck didn't improve, that's exactly what they'd be. *Billy & Buck*.

"Get aboard ship, Luke Skywalker," said Billy. "I'm gonna buy you a piece of pie."

8

FRIDAY AFTERNOON

On his way back from Buck Fennelson's mailbox, Orville drove slowly. He wanted to remember the way the road followed the river, with houses strung along each side. He wanted to savor it in a way he hadn't done for thirteen years. He knew the old logic that lay behind the plan, why the first settlers had built along the river. It had little to do with a pretty view and much to do with practicality. That river used to be a well-used road, a means to visit friends and family who lived on either side of it and along its banks. It was there for a man to canoe down to St. Leonard and Watertown for supplies and necessary business, before poling back upstream. The earliest coffins had been taken by canoe downriver for burial in St. Leonard churchyards, back before Mattagash established its own graveyards. And then, the river was the only way lumberjacks could get all those logs, millions of feet of lumber, from the woods camps to the mills waiting downstream. Having lost all that to time and technology, the river now seemed almost cosmetic, as if it had been ordered from L. L. Bean and shipped to Mattagash by FedEx.

He would miss that daily drive along the river. Was he doing the right thing to retire? When had he decided it was the best choice at this stage of his life? Now, on his last day, Orville couldn't remember. It was what everyone wanted, wasn't it, to retire so they can spend time with the family, play golf, go fishing, travel? The truth was that Orville Craft no longer had a family to spend time with, unless you counted his wife, who was rarely home. His children were married and gone, building their own families and lives elsewhere. Orville had never played a game of golf in his life and even though he had forbidden Harry Plunkett to fish at Craft Pond, thus adding fuel to their feud, he wasn't all that crazy about fishing. All he really had was his four-wheeler and his little cabin. If only he still had Meg's interest in those things. Better yet, if only he had her interest in *him*, the husband who still loved her. And that's the thought that had awakened him so many nights, nights that turned into predawns and the roar of logging trucks flying by, bleary-eyed drivers hitting the Jake brakes before crossing the bridge. Would Meg have been more satisfied if she'd married Harold Plunkett? Orville couldn't compete with someone as charismatic as Harry, not when he felt threatened by a computerized penguin in a tuxedo.

Orville drove slowly past the nine silver mailboxes at the trailer park. He drove past Lauren Harrison's house, the younger of his two widows, and thought again of the tanned summer cleavage that always tumbled toward him when Lauren leaned down to take her mail from his hand. Was he doing the right thing? Or was he retiring early because of Harry Plunkett's moose? Could it be possible? Ed Beecher had said to him, "I wish you'd reconsider this retirement thing, Orville. You're not pretty to look at, but you're a damn reliable mailman." Even Meg had questioned him about it. "Folks don't retire to the pasture these days unless they want to go or they're pushed," Meg had said. "You're not the type of person who can sit idle. You might have a nervous breakdown if you're not busy."

Had it been the moose? Had it finally worn him down? Its two flared nostrils, those silly antlers screwed to the top of its head, that thrusting nose that had mocked Orville for three long years. Until the nose turned into the ass. He touched the newspaper lying on the seat beside him, felt the bulk beneath it. Awful thoughts kept free falling into his head. Could the moose be a substitute for his own unhappy marriage? His own uneventful life? Was it that Harry Plunkett had come home from the war a decorated hero clutching the Purple Heart, when Orville didn't have the courage to drive his four-wheeler over twenty miles an hour? Even his feet hadn't met the challenge, being flat and therefore not good enough for those long marches the Army required, especially in wartime. So he had been classified 4-F, as if that F stood for *failure*.

Orville knew one fact for certain, and he had accepted it. He was on a combat mission. And when that mission was over, no post office from here to wacky California would give him a job. He slowed the Ford as he rounded the curve. There was Harry's house, straight ahead. Maybe he should have brought a gun instead. He could stick it into the moose and pull the trigger, blow its guts out. But he had decided on the hammer, the lesser of two evils—and hopefully a misdemeanor in the state of Maine. He had kept his cool all week. That was the best way—use the element of surprise. He slid his hand under the newspaper and felt the cold, metallic claws. He kept his eyes on Harry's front door as he pulled up next to the box. He didn't want to be interrupted should Harry burst out of his house and run to the moose's rescue. And this was when Orville Craft realized that the element of surprise had backfired on him, for *he* was the one surprised. The moose was gone. In its place was the same sensible silver box Harry Plunkett used to have *before* he bought the moose. Orville stared at the mailbox, a small cobweb still attached to its red flag, a regulation mailbox that had not done a single thing to insult him.

Edna was having a coffee at her kitchen table when the phone rang. She answered, hoping it wasn't Mama Sal. It was worse. It was Dorrie Mullins.

"They're peeping again," said Dorrie, and Edna felt quick tension in her stomach.

"Who might you be talking about?" she asked.

"The twins," said Dorrie. "I caught 'em looking in the bedroom window last night at my granddaughter. She's only thirteen and now she's hysterical. You been warned twice already, Edna. You need to do something about them boys."

"And how do you know it was *my* boys looking in the window?" Edna asked. She had never liked Dorrie Mullins, a bully of a woman.

"How do I know it was the twins?" Dorrie asked. "Well, let's see. There were two heads, with two faces, and the two faces were identical. *You* do the math."

Edna was still sitting at the table an hour later, a cup of cold coffee in front of her, when the front door opened. Roderick was home from his doctor's appointment in Watertown. He came into the kitchen carrying a plastic sack in his hand. When he saw her at the table, doing nothing but staring at that cup of coffee, she could tell by his eyes he was already on the defensive.

"Turning cold out there again," he said. "Probably snow any day now."

Edna watched as he took off his winter coat and draped it over the back of a kitchen stool. The collar of a red shirt peeked above the gray woolen sweater Mama Sal had knit for him, love and admiration in every stitch. Edna knew how to knit, but her patience ran out for anything bigger than a mitten or a sock.

That's why Mama Sal had knit the sweater, to set a good example. If Edna found the talent one day to knit Roderick a sweater, Mama Sal would knit him a pulp truck.

"I'm back from the doctor's," Roderick said, as if Edna hadn't figured that out. She saw him look over at the stove, the empty burners where there should have been pots hissing and spitting, potatoes and carrots and a chunk of meat boiling.

"Dorrie Mullins called," said Edna. "The twins are peeping again."

"Heck," said Roderick. "I wish I had a dollar for every window I peeped into when I was a boy. It's natural. They'll outgrow it."

He put the plastic sack on the counter, then tossed his P. J. Irvine Company hat at a chair near the window. Edna watched it fly like a Frisbee, hit the seat, and careen off. It fell to the floor, visor-up. If she didn't get it now and put it where his eyes could see it, he'd make a racket searching for it in the morning.

"I bought some more nicotine patches," Roderick said and nodded at the plastic bag. "I run out of my last supply."

Edna took the coffee cup to the sink and rinsed it under the faucet. She knew Roderick was watching her. She could almost hear him forming the words he would later tell Mama Sal. *She must have sit there all day in front of that cup. That's what she was doing when I left for my doctor's appointment.*

"I got something to tell you," Edna said. "You might as well hear it from me before you hear it from the town gossips. I had an affair." She turned and looked at Roderick.

For a moment, she saw herself through his eyes, her short hair beginning to speak of a gray strand here and there, wearing her old jeans and a rose-colored blouse that brought out the blue of her eyes. Everyone knew that the color rose was Edna's signature color. She was big-boned and pretty, at least Roderick thought so. Now here she was, three years from forty and yet feeling as if she had lived several lifetimes in Mattagash, and all of them as Roderick

Plunkett's wife. What would it be like to be a secretary for a little company that cared about its employees, with a good-looking boss who flirted with the girls in the office? Or what if she had become a lawyer? She would have made a great stewardess even though she'd never been on an airplane in her life. *Would you like coffee or tea? How about a pillow for your head? Peanuts anyone?* But all Edna really wanted to be was happy. Could a stay-at-home artist find personal joy between fixing supper and doing the laundry? Artists, at least the famous ones, seemed to have lots of affairs in between drinking themselves to death and even cutting off an ear. That little bald man, Pablo Picasso, had been like a bull in the cow pen according to one documentary Edna had watched. And the younger the cows, the better the old bull liked it.

Roderick was still waiting, knowing the way a deer knows that those headlights are coming right at him and maybe they're going to hurt.

"What kind of affair?" he asked. Edna felt her eyes water. She wanted to slap him.

"It was a love affair, Roderick, for crying out loud," she said. "I cheated on you. I broke our marriage vows. This past summer. He was here working for the state. Soil. I tried to end it, but I don't think I can. He loves me, and I suppose I love him too. I may have to move downstate to be with him. The boys can go to school down there if I can find one that will take them. I want a divorce. There, I said it."

It had spilled out, one thought pushing the next ahead of it, anything and everything she could confess. What was making her do this? Was she really suffering from a lack of sun? Were there women in Alaska who would love to trade places with her that very second?

"Walking out on your marriage for another man," Roderick said. "That's like switching horses in midstream."

"Horses," she said. "How romantic."

One thing was certain. If Roderick Plunkett and Ward Hooper were horses, Roderick wouldn't be the stud.

"Mind if I ask his name?" Roderick said, his voice too small now for such a big body.

"Ward," said Edna. "You don't need to know his last name."

Roderick nodded, as if to say he understood. What's in a last name, anyway? He ran a hand through his hair, his fingers undoing the ridges made by his cap. He turned and looked out the window as Billy Thunder's topless Mustang flew by, headed toward the bridge and the heart of town. He looked back at his wife.

"Doctor says my blood pressure is down," he said.

Billy Thunder sat next to Buck on one of the four wooden stools at Blanche's. When the bell over the door rang out, he glanced up to see Orville Craft. Orville took the stool at the end of the counter, leaving one empty between him and the two men.

"Last day, Orville?" Billy asked. He saw Blanche cutting a slice of blueberry pie and fitting it onto a plate. "Let me pay for that piece of pie, Blanche," said Billy. "And anything this man is drinking."

"There's no need," said Orville, but Billy held up a hand in protest. He pointed a finger at his bill and watched as Blanche added the price of the pie and a cup of tea.

"A little retirement present for my mailman," Billy said.

"Thanks, Thunder," said Orville. He even appreciated the token now that there seemed to be no sign of a retirement party anywhere in town. How could Orville have known when he first began delivering the mail thirteen years earlier that his only retirement gift would come from a foul-mouthed rooster from Portland?

"By the way, Thunder," Orville said, as Blanche put his cup of hot tea next to the piece of pie. "You got one of them little boxes you been waiting for." He took up his fork and cut away the first bite.

Billy sat watching him eat. *You got one of them little boxes you been waiting for.* What did he take Billy Thunder for? A moron who would rush home again, his tires spitting up rocks and leaves, only to find a sample tube of toothpaste waiting for him? Billy wished now he'd gone for 100 milligrams instead of 75. Keep it stiff until spring. That would teach Orville Craft to mess with a man's emotions. He looked down at the piece of pie, knowing he had to act fast or it would soon be gone. Buck was leaning over now to watch Orville eat, as though it were a new Olympic event. When Orville stopped to put milk in his tea, Billy turned on his stool and peered out the window.

"Wow, did Harry Plunkett just hit your mail car?" Billy asked.

Orville dropped his fork and pushed back his stool. In a matter of seconds, he was at the window, peering out at the cars in the driveway. Billy quickly lifted the top crust of Orville's pie and tossed the bits of ground-up blue pill onto the blueberries. He had already considered that the food in Orville's stomach might diminish the effects of the pill. That's why he had chopped a quarter hunk off that second pill and added it, brought the dosage up to 75 milligrams. He estimated it would take effect in thirty minutes. With the tip of his finger, he stirred the pieces of Viagra into the filling and put the crust back in place. He was wiping his fingers on a paper napkin when Orville returned to his stool.

"You need eyeglasses, Thunder," said Orville.

Billy threw some money onto the counter to pay his bill.

"Now that you're retired, Orville, you need to take life easy," he said. "Stop and smell the cannabis." He looked at Orville and grinned. Orville decided to ignore the grin, given it came from downstate. "Don't take any hostages," Billy added, patting Orville on the back. Then he was out the door, Buck Fennelson following at his heels like a well-trained dog.

Five minutes after finishing his last workday piece of pie, Orville Craft had come home to find Meg typing away at her computer as she talked on the phone. He paused in the doorway to her sewing room after saying *I'm home, Meg*, seeing her wave a hand in the air as if to say *I hear you, Orville*. He stared at her back as she chatted up some friend and clicked keys, all at the same time. He now felt foolish that before he came inside the house he had glanced behind the garage to see if any cars were hidden there. So there would be no retirement party? The piece of pie from Billy Thunder would be his only gift, the only festivity to mark this important rite of passage?

Orville went on up the stairs to their bedroom, as he always did after work, and slipped off his work clothes. He hung the neatly creased pants on a coat hanger and topped them with the pale blue shirt and tie. He selected a pair of green pants and one of the green shirts that Meg had folded clean and put into his dresser drawer. There was an irony, he knew, in the fact that his clean and always neat *after-work* clothes were the very types that most Mattagash men used as *work* clothes. But theirs would end up splattered with oil or axle grease or spruce gum, grime from the floors of garages or dust wafting up from a woods road. Orville's clothes rarely needed detergent in the wash, and Meg had often commented that she was lucky to have married into one of the few white-collar families in town.

Orville stood again outside the door to Meg's sewing room. He often wondered why she didn't call it her *computer room*. The computer had replaced the sewing machine ten years earlier. He figured the reason might be that Meg would have to admit she hadn't sewn anything since the girls were in grammar school. He waited, hoping she might say, "How's it feel to be retired? Do you want to sit and talk about it?" But she was still on the phone, her right hand still clicking and clacking. He went out to the garage and started up his four-wheeler. Instead of heading straight up the mountain road to his cabin, as he always did, he decided to give her one more chance. So he rode the buggy across the autumn lawn and past her window. Inside, Meg turned away from her computer to look out at him, that same pinch of disgust in the muscles around her mouth. He saw her point at the phone attached to her ear, telling him in hand signals that she couldn't hear for his racket. Orville turned the handle on his four-wheeler, giving its engine full speed, and tore off across the backyard and onto the road leading up to his cabin.

He had split a block of dry cedar for kindling and then checked the mousetrap under the bed before he noticed the tingling sensation. At first he thought he might be having a heart attack, that even chopping a block of wood was too much work for a former white-collar employee. But then reason hit him. The heart isn't located below the belt.

In thirty seconds, Orville had roared the four-wheeler to life. All he could think of on the bumpy ride down the mountainside was that yellow apron Meg used to wear, the strings tied into a sexy bow at her back, the apron with a bluebird sitting on a twig. He thought of how those strings would undo themselves in his hand, surrender themselves, him being a man and all. Orville thought of the yellow apron.

Twilight was moving in, shadow-slow, and a light was now on in Meg's sewing room as Orville roared the four-wheeler back into the garage. He turned the engine off, taking his time, yet fully aware of the swelling against the crotch of his pants. This was unlike the old days when he used to pull the milk truck into the yard, flip it into park, and bound from the passenger seat, hoping to find Meg standing in the kitchen, that female blush coming to her face and neck when her eyes met his. Now, he was no longer a postal employee, responsible for bundles of letters. He was a retired man, age sixty-five. He had *one* package to deliver, and it was addressed to Meg Craft.

Again Orville was standing in the doorway, staring at his wife's back, which was now more familiar to him than her face. It was that blasted computer who saw Meg's face for hours each day.

"Who lit the fire in *your* pants?" she asked, not bothering to turn in her chair. "I've never seen you drive that four-wheeler so fast."

"Where's that yellow apron you used to wear?" Orville asked, his voice calm and steady. He watched as Meg shook her head.

"I knew you were on the verge, Orville," she said, "what with this retirement thing. But I didn't think you'd go crazy unless the post office gave you permission." She clicked a few times with her mouse and Orville saw shiny pots and pans appear on the screen, prices listed below each one.

"It had a bluebird on it, Meggie Lou," said Orville, "with its claws hooked around a brown twig."

Meg's chair swiveled slowly around. *Meggie Lou* was the sexy name Orville used for his wife. A lot of blue moons had passed since she'd heard him call her that, back in those days when the kids were in school and he'd stop by the house, his milk truck idling outside, all the glass bottles clinking in their crates as they waited for him. Meg looked at Orville's face first, then down to the generous bulge in his pants.

"What's wrong with your pecker?" she asked, cautious.

"You shouldn't use the word *pecker*," said Orville. "You said it was crude language, remember? And there you are, using it in front of your penguin."

"Oh... my... god," Meg said. She let go of the mouse and put her mouse hand up to her mouth. "You finally did it. You took one of them stupid pills."

Orville stepped deeper into the room.

"I never took any such pill," he said and felt a pride he hadn't known since he and Meg were first married and he had been given permission to feel romantic whenever the urge hit him. Orville reached for her hand and pulled her gently up from the chair. Meg looked like she might pass out, so he put his arm around her. He nuzzled her neck then, remembering how she liked this warm-breath nuzzling in the old days, the kind of foreplay that made her start cooing, little dove-like noises he longed to hear once again before he died. Meg didn't coo now, however. She shoved him back against the wall, hard enough that the framed picture of Jesus holding a wooly lamb crashed to the floor behind him.

"Now look what you did to Jesus!" Meg cried.

Orville took her face in his hands and tilted it up toward his. He leaned in and kissed her lightly on the lips.

"I love you," he whispered. The tingling had now grown to a magnitude he had only read about in his brochure. He unbelted and unzipped his green work pants. He stepped out of them, still mindful of the creases, and lay them aside. His boxer shorts were next.

"Let me dial 9-1-1," Meg pleaded. "You're having a nervous breakdown."

"I wouldn't call *this* a breakdown," said Orville.

Penis. Organ. Member. Family jewel. Phallus. Big Pete. Pecker. Maybe Meg had been right. Maybe he needed to give it a better and more dignified name. In the rush of excitement and pleasure that was now pulsing over him in warm waves, the name Dwight came into his mind. That was his grandfather's name, and it was a good, strong New England name. *Dwight.*

"Come with me," said Orville, his voice now low and he hoped seductive in that old way, that way husbands and wives know in the beginning of their marriage. Those were the days when just the feel of her breasts flattening against his chest in a good-bye hug could cause any number of organs to stir. "Come on, sweetheart," he said. And it seemed that one word was enough to do it. At least, he saw Meg smile, that slow and lazy *old* smile, the one that meant she was happy to be his wife, his companion, happy to let him take her hand and lead her up the stairs.

When Meg finished undressing, Orville was already naked and in bed.

"You won't believe what foolish thought just went through my mind," Meg said. She reached her hand out and put two fingers on his lips, let him kiss them. He'd forgotten what her breasts looked like, outside the truss of that Cross Your Heart bra she always wore. They were whiter than he remembered and now spilling down like soft loaves of bread, and he loved the sight of them, knowing he must look older and whiter to her too. He hoped she wasn't going to say something to break the spell. In the past, after she had gone through the change, she had told him unsavory things, and he knew she did so to deter any notions of romance he might be harboring. Mostly, she described her symptoms, using words like "dryness" or "moistness," and once, even "yeast," as though Meg might be talking of making a cake instead of love.

Orville pulled her forward, felt the warm breasts now touching the skin of his chest, burning him with memory and love.

"What, sweetheart?" Orville asked, his words soft. "What went through your mind?" He knew this wasn't like the old days. He knew by the intensity surging in him that Dwight was more of a doer than a thinker, cut from the same cloth as George W. Bush, the country's president for whom Orville had voted twice.

Dwight intended to get in there and stay the course until the job was done.

"I was wondering when the kids would get home from school," Meg said. And as Orville lifted himself gently above her, he wasn't sure if what he saw in her eyes was not so much passion as the kind of glistening that occurs when one is about to cry.

9

FRIDAY EVENING

Billy tore open the bag of dog food. In a plastic container, he poured three cups of the dried nuggets. He found the half doughnut he couldn't finish at breakfast and slipped it into his jacket pocket. Then he walked to Tommy Gifford's house, which sat one mailbox up from his. He knew Tommy wouldn't be home. He had seen the black pickup with the huge tires crossing the bridge as he ate his supper. At the drive leading up to the faded A-frame, he saw the dog, a black and brown medium-sized breed of what looked to be part collie and part shepherd. It was sprawled, as usual, inside its crooked doghouse, the black nose hanging out in case a scent wafted by.

"Hey, boy," said Billy. "It's me." At the sound of his voice, the dog tore out of its house, dragging the clanking chain behind. The overhead runner, a steel cable stretching from Tommy's house to a tree twenty feet away, allowed it to get within three feet of Billy before the chain caught. Billy threw the piece of doughnut onto the ground and watched as it disappeared in two quick bites. When he pulled the cover off the plastic container, the dog stood on its hind legs, tail wagging, straining to reach the food. As it ate, Billy knelt beside it, stroking its back. He noticed that the water pan next to the doghouse had turned over and was now empty. He picked it up and knocked away the dead leaves.

He filled the pan with water from an outside spigot he had found a few days earlier, at the back of the house.

"Here you go, boy," Billy said. "You're thirsty, aren't you?" He wondered what was going to happen when winter arrived and water would be frozen even at noon. Hearing a human voice, hearing words that were soft and kind, the dog whined and lay down at Billy's feet. Billy reached into his coat pocket and pulled out the rawhide bone he had bought. "Ever seen one of these?"

The dog jumped and caught the bone in its mouth. It ran to the doghouse, the chain clanking behind. Hearing the chain always reminded Billy of a play he'd once taken part in, back in the eighth grade, *A Christmas Carol*, in which he'd played the ghost of Marley, the miserly partner who had returned to haunt Scrooge by dragging chains weighted down with cash boxes and keys, deeds and ledgers. Billy was only in his chains a few minutes before he felt something break inside his spirit, something the bones know about freedom and dignity, whether human or animal. That's why, the first time he saw Tommy Gifford's dog, a couple weeks after listening to its angry barks and mournful howls, he felt a true pity for it.

A leash lay curled on the front porch, its leather handle faded. Billy picked it up and tested it for strength. When he knew it was workable, he knelt beside the dog, talking to it in soft tones. The animal dropped the rawhide bone and thumped out of its house. It stood on hind legs, tail frantic with wagging, its paws on Billy's chest.

"You want to walk, don't you?" Billy said.

He undid the chain from the dog's collar and snapped the leash loop in its place. He turned toward the road and the dog rushed ahead, pulling and straining against the leash, wanting to break free, something it did now only in dreams, in those places where dogs go when they sleep, fields large enough that their legs peddle and their spirits soar, that place where forgotten dogs can fly.

Billy walked the dog along the river, through the stand of birches with their rattling yellow leaves, a place where no one would think to look for them. For thirty minutes, the river wind had beaten at him, chilly and wet, until he knew he must take the dog home and head off somewhere warm. Back at the A-frame and the crooked doghouse, the dog whined and tried to follow him. Billy went back once, then twice, to kneel and bury his face in the soft fur. He again offered the dog the rawhide bone and watched as it pulled an end into its mouth and began to chew.

"I'll be back tomorrow," Billy promised.

It was only when he saw his mailbox looming up ahead that Billy remembered that day's mail. Already at work cutting Amy Joy Lawler's wood when Orville made his rounds, he had forgotten to check the box. After work, he'd been busy getting beer, gas, and dog food. Then he had to hurry to Blanche's to slip the Viagra into Orville's pie, all before coming home to leftover spaghetti for his supper. So that was the day he gave up? That was when he finally admitted that his dealings with the Portland office were over? He opened the mailbox door, expecting nothing but those pesky flyers, some smelling of perfume, others promising fortunes in contest prizes. And that's when he saw it. The box was the perfect size and weight and had the same lovely address on its return label. *Elizabeth Miller, Portland, ME.*

Back in the camper, Billy put the box on the table and turned the electric heater on high. He reached for the Jack Daniels he kept on the counter and took a strong hit from the bottle's mouth. He wanted to savor the feeling, the notion that he'd soon be back in business, back in social demand, and back in the money. The Portland boys had obviously decided to give him a second chance. He felt a certain pride that the Delgatos still believed in their Man in the North Country, in his ability to sell ice cubes to Eskimos. He wouldn't let them down this time. This time, he would charge even more for the goods, but the goods were worth it. And in charging more, he'd pay the cousins off sooner than they expected. He cut the binding tape as he had done so many times. Then he sliced a lid across the top of the box, which he opened. He stood for a few seconds, peering down at the contents. All the fire of the booze seemed to fall through his body, taking that joyous rush of adrenaline with it. He reached into the box and lifted from it a finger, the cloth around its severed base a bloody red. Morons. This was supposed to scare him? A fake finger made of rubber, the kind kids use for Halloween pranks? Couldn't the assholes have found a *real* digit, even if they had to donate one of their own? He imagined them buying the rubber finger at some novelty shop in Portland, poring over a display of fake fingers and toes, taking an hour to select the right one. That's when he saw the piece of paper in the bottom of the box. He took it out and unfolded it. *Le muerte visitará*. Death will visit. Billy crumpled the paper in his fist. Fools. Didn't they know that the noun *death* is feminine, not masculine? True, they were born and raised in Maine, full-blooded Americans by the name of George and Ralph Delgato. But they seemed to feel their Puerto Rican heritage, given to them by genuine Puerto Rico–born parents, would elevate them greatly among the functioning nightlife and small-time narcotics trade in the seedy Portland bars that stretched along the waterfront. Therefore, they had become *Jorge* and *Raul*, the *Delgato cousins*.

"*La muerte, idiotas*," Billy muttered. He might have had two years of high school Spanish, but weren't these two dummies born to people who *spoke the fucking language*? He imagined the two of them, big square thugs that they were, chewing on the erasers of their pencils as they wrote the note. *Hey, George... I mean, Jorge, how do you write the word* death *in Spanish?*

Billy flipped the top back onto the box and put it on the floor by the side of his bed. He picked up the phone and dialed that number he knew so well. When the machine clicked on and he heard Jorge grunt that brief, "Yo, leave a message," Billy did as the machine asked.

"Hey, morons!" Billy shouted into the receiver. "Hey, you big, ugly, hairy, stupid, fucking Spics! Guess what? You're never gonna see your money!"

Murray's Restaurant & Bar was almost empty. It was two hours before they would order their steaks for the night, with the stuffed and smothered baked potatoes, and the salads loaded with oil and vinegar. But it didn't matter. They had a lot of planning to do, and they had always believed in several pre-dinner drinks.

"I told you we should have used a real finger," said Jorge. "This ain't a TV show, for fuck's sake. We should have let him know we mean business."

Raul used his swizzle stick to click at the ice cubes in his drink.

"I thought it would work," he said. He had been the queasy one all through their growing-up years. He had been the one who passed out when Jorge's nose started spurting blood that day in the fourth grade when they had the fistfight on the playground. "Besides, where would we find a real finger?"

"Are you kidding?" asked Jorge. "Look around. There are fingers everywhere. See that old man in the corner table? Ten fingers. Look at the bartender. Ten fingers."

"Okay, so now we'll send him a real finger," said Raul. "We

can go down to the waterfront tonight. Wait for a sailor to stagger out of a bar."

"Too late," said Jorge. The waitress brought them a basket of nachos with a bowl of salsa. Jorge cracked a chip and dipped it.

"Don't pass out now, Raul," he said. "This is only salsa." He grinned as he ate the chip. Nothing Raul had ever done in his life would be forgotten, except the good things.

"But you haven't killed anyone before," said Raul. "Not completely."

"I was never this pissed off before," said Jorge. "We're out a lot of money. And besides that, he insulted our heritage. He called us Spics."

"Oh," said Raul. "I thought you were mad because he said you were hairy."

Jorge stopped chewing and looked at his cousin.

"He said we were *both* hairy," said Jorge.

"But I'm not hairy," said Raul. "When you take off your shirt, Jorge, you're like a teddy bear."

"You're a Delgato," said Jorge. "Of course you got hair on your chest. Fuck, I bet Grandma Delgato had more than we do."

"Ever wonder why I never take off my shirt at the swimming pool?" asked Raul. "I even swim with it on?"

Jorge's grin was slow and he enjoyed the way this knowledge was settling on him.

"You mean your chest is all smooth and shiny?"

"Maybe not shiny."

"What does it matter? He called us Spics. Big, ugly, hairy, stupid Spics."

"You might be big and hairy, but you're not ugly," said Raul.

"And you're not...." Jorge stopped. He had gone far enough.

"Still," said Raul. "I don't like the idea of killing someone. You could go to jail for life."

"*We*, Raul," said Jorge. "*We* could go to jail for life. You'd be an accomplice."

"It would be better not to completely kill him," said Raul. It was true that even a bowl of salsa sometimes unnerved him, especially when Jorge was eating it as he double-dipped the chips and some of the salsa stayed on his chin, as did droplets of blood when Jorge cut himself shaving, which was every time he shaved.

"I won't know until I start," said Jorge. "But I know one thing. I don't intend to stop until I hear something crack." He pulled a map of Maine from the bottomless pocket of the trench coat, unfolded it, and spread it open on the table. He pointed to Mattagash, at the northernmost peak, at the end of a solitary road through green bumps and blue circles that Raul guessed would be mountains and lakes.

"Wow, dude," said Raul. He tapped his finger at a place on the map. "There's Bangor, and it's not even halfway up the fucking state. I never been as far north as Bangor. Have you?"

"Who would go to Bangor?" asked Jorge. "Stephen King maybe, that's it."

"So why are *we* going?" Raul started the journey from Bangor to Mattagash with his finger moving north on I-95, passing Millinocket and coming to a halt at Houlton, where the interstate ended. From then on, it was scraggly Route One.

"We're not going to Bangor," said Jorge. "We're going to Waddamash."

"Mattagash," said Raul. He was the one who had addressed all those boxes from a nonexistent woman named Elizabeth Miller. He even knew the zip code by heart. "It doesn't even look like there are places to eat."

"We'll bring cigarettes and booze in the trunk," said Jorge. "And candy bars, in case we get in a blizzard."

Raul found the word *Caribou*, a couple hours south of

Mattagash. He'd seen a documentary on caribou once. Even the females grow antlers.

"No fucking way," said Raul.

After thirty minutes of steady and intense lovemaking, Orville and Meg Craft were still lying in their bed, heads on individual pillows, staring up at the light fixture on the ceiling.

"I see cobwebs," said Meg. "I need to dust that fixture."

Orville said nothing.

"And I think the fixture itself is crooked," Meg added. "I'll straighten it tomorrow."

Orville moved the toes on his right foot and felt the sheet above them avalanche into small furrows.

"I can't for the life of me remember when I bought that fixture," said Meg. "I should replace it. I'm getting sick of the flowers on it."

Through the bedroom window, Orville saw the top branches of his white birch bending in the wind. A blue jay lifted its wings and rose on the current. Now he couldn't help it. He cast his eyes down the length of his body and saw the stiff cairn holding up the sheet above it, like the supporting pole in a tent. It was plain good luck that Meg hadn't got out her electric blanket yet for the winter months ahead. Orville didn't want to think of third degree burns, not to mention a possible electrocution.

"I think my mother might have bought that light fixture for my birthday," Meg said now. "Back in the 1970s."

"Oh, for heaven's sake, Meg," said Orville. "Will you stop the nervous chattering? That's not going to make it go away."

Meg lifted herself on an elbow and stared down at the sheeted hump that was still announcing itself proudly.

"Then what *will?*" she asked. "And please don't look at *me*. I've done my duty and then some."

"I don't know," said Orville, and it was the truth. He hadn't felt this kind of vigor and duration since the days when he sat on the edge of his boyhood bed with a girlie magazine in his free left hand. Not even in the earliest years of his marriage could he go full-throttle for almost an hour without a bead of sweat for his efforts. And if Meg had been agreeable, he'd be going for round three about now, that's how ready he still felt. But she hadn't been agreeable. "I vowed to support my husband until death do us part," Meg had said, when their second session was finally over. "But I didn't know it would be death from *this*."

"I wish you'd go ahead and admit it," Meg was saying now. "You know darn well you took one of them pills, Orville. You've had that brochure up at your cabin for months."

"On my mother's soul, I never took a pill," Orville said. Why couldn't she give him due credit? This was the Real McCoy talking to them from beneath the sheet.

The blue jay returned to the top of the birch, a sunflower seed in its beak. Orville watched as the bird held the seed in its claws and quickly cracked it with its beak. Afternoon sun touched on its feathers, turning them blue as sky. Blue as blueberries.

Blueberry pie.

That's when the film of his brief stop at Blanche's replayed, winding backward first, then playing forward. Billy Thunder was two stools away from him. So how did he put a pill in Orville's pie?

Meg sat up and slid her legs out of bed.

"Well, I can't lay around all afternoon staring at it," she said. "I got work to do."

"I didn't take a pill," said Orville. "But someone gave me one." He had taken a bite of the blueberry pie and stopped to put milk in his tea. Then the film played far enough ahead that Orville had his answer. *Wow, did Harry Plunkett just hit your mail car? You need eyeglasses, Thunder.*

"Why, you underhanded, no-good, scheming fool," said Orville, looking down now at the peak beneath the top sheet, pointed like a dunce cap. "I ought to wring your neck."

"Heavenly god," Meg said. "Now he's talking to it."

Orville sat up on his side of the bed and found that the movement was painful. It was like being given a pitchfork and having no hay to pitch, much less a barn to hang the thing in when the workday was done.

"It was Billy Thunder did it," he said. He had a good mind to fill a small box with a steaming pile of dog poop, write *Elizabeth Miller, Portland, ME*, at the top left corner, and mail it to Billy Thunder. Let him stick his fingers in *that*. But then a thought rushed through Orville's mind. Should you punish the man who has given you the best hard-on of your life or reward him? "He put one of them pills in my blueberry pie."

Meg had pulled on her slacks.

"Of all the nerve," she said. "There should be a law. People should get the death sentence for doing that." She reached for her bra, slid her arms over the two large cups and past the straps. She quickly and expertly did the clasp. She turned to look at Orville.

"How long will it last?" she asked.

"I don't know," he said, his voice now wistful. He had believed, if only for a short time, that even as a retired mailman he was still one hell of a man.

"Well, what does the brochure say?" Meg was getting that impatient tone to her voice.

"I never read the last page," Orville admitted. "I figured if you wouldn't let me buy any, I didn't need to know about after-effects."

Meg pulled on her sweatshirt that said *World's Sexiest Grandma*, the one Debby's kids had given her for her birthday. She slid her feet into her loafers.

"I'll have to get on the computer and find out," she said. Orville felt his heart sink if nothing else. Had she forgotten so quickly how good it had been?

"You're gonna ask the penguin?"

"Don't be a fool," said Meg. "I'm gonna Google it."

"No you're not!" said Orville. He didn't know what that meant, only that it sounded painful. Meg gave him that look again, the one that made the muscles around her mouth pinch up.

"Maybe you shouldn't retire," Meg said.

Five minutes later, Orville was standing behind Meg's shoulder, wearing the corduroy robe that Debby's kids had bought for *his* birthday—*World's Sexiest Grandpa*—and doing his best to keep the front of it closed as Meg surfed the web. In no time, with a few *clicks* and *clacks*, she had the answer.

"For most men," Meg read, her glasses on the tip of her nose so that she could see the words, "a minimum dose of 50 milligrams will ensure and maintain a firm and lasting erection for up to four hours."

For the second time that day, Meg's mouse hand flew up to cover her mouth. Orville coughed softly.

"Knowing Thunder," he said, "he probably gave me a bigger dose. You know, for the joke in it."

Silence rocked the house. Wind sliced into the pewter chimes on the front porch and they tinkled like leaves on a quaking aspen. Those were the trees Orville liked to listen to best, those days when he sat alone at his cabin and read the first sexy page of his brochure. *Why VIAGRA? Because the children are gone and it's time to fall in love all over again. Because that special look on your loved one's face is meant only for you.*

Meg turned and looked at Orville. On her face was a desperation the likes of which he hadn't seen since their first date, that day at the 1962 Maine State Fair, when Orville finally convinced her to step inside the tent for a close-up glimpse at Lobster Boy.

~

Edna stared at the finished painting, her first work of art. The driver of the white pickup truck now had his left elbow resting out his window, relaxed, his right hand on the steering wheel. Roderick believed in driving with two hands. "It's dangerous to drive single-handed like that," he'd tell Edna whenever she used a free hand to dig in her purse or open a stick of chewing gum. "What if a tire blew and you had to stop fast?" Edna had allowed the man in her painting to drive with one hand. She had made his light blue shirt a darker blue, and she had taken away the baseball cap. She wanted him to feel comfortable as he drove, free. What had started out as a single man with those first strokes of the brush and hours at the canvas was now two people, a *couple*, driving away from their creator, maybe leaving town for good. The female companion sat in the passenger seat, the back of her head turned as if she were gazing out her window at the autumn leaves. Her hair was short and brown. The blouse she wore, what could be seen of it above the seat of the pickup, was rose colored. In the bed of the truck itself, Edna had painted a brown suitcase, so plump it must be stuffed with enough clothing to last a long time. A lifetime, maybe. So, had the woman packed in a hurry? Had the man come to rescue her? Was the couple in a rush? Edna didn't know yet what elements to use that might imply *speed* to the onlooker. If she had let them leave in a boat, the way people in southern Maine might leave a seaside town, she could have painted small white wakes breaking behind, seagulls rising up in surprise, wind whipping at their hair and clothing. *Tension*, that's what the art book said this element was called. But how do you show speed in a lumber town at the end of a two-lane road? Maybe she could paint a trace of panic on each of the faces. But all that could be seen of the couple were the backs of their heads since Edna didn't know how to paint faces yet. She decided, being their creator, that they were leaving on their own terms. They were two people headed down the tarred road before the snows came. There must have been just future ahead of them, since neither bothered to turn and look back.

Roddy came down the stairs from his bedroom and stood behind his mother's shoulder as he stared at the painting.

"Where are you going, Mama?" Roddy asked, and it caught Edna off-guard. "You taking a vacation?"

Edna was glad he was standing behind her, unable to see her face. Was she so transparent that a twelve-year-old boy could read her symbolism, even if her husband couldn't?

"Why aren't you in your room?" she asked. "Your punishment isn't up yet."

Now Ricky appeared and stood gawking at the painting. He was eating a raw hot dog.

"Is that you in the pickup, Mama?" Ricky asked. "Who's that man driving? That ain't Daddy."

"So, what do I have here?" Edna said. She dropped her paintbrush into the bottle of turpentine beneath her chair. "Two identical art critics?"

"Ricky's eating a cow dick," said Roddy.

"Roddy *is* a cow dick," Ricky said back. In response, Roddy slapped his brother's hand. Edna watched as the hotdog landed on the pages of her new art book that lay opened on the floor. *Easy Steps to Basic Painting*.

"Get back to your bedroom right now!" she shouted. But the

boys had already scampered toward the stairs, Ricky in hot pursuit of Roddy. "And if I get one more peeping call, you're both going to reform school!"

Edna heard the bedroom door slam. A loud crash was followed by a stream of swearwords. She looked back at the painting. Until she learned how to create the element of *speed*, perhaps she should let that short, brown hair grow a bit longer, and maybe turn it blond. And she should make that signature rose-colored blouse disappear into a sensible green.

When Harry saw that it was eight o'clock, he turned off the television and reached for his jacket. He was sick of watching TV news in the evenings. It had become a different box since the days when Walter Cronkite's face peered out at America in black and white while his mouth told of important things that were taking place in the country and around the world. Nowadays, celebrities and athletes and puffed-up pundits ruled the airways. History had been Harold Plunkett's favorite subject in school, but he hadn't watched the TV news much before he enlisted in the military. He was too busy watching Emily Mason, how graceful she was when she walked, the pretty smile, the dark shine of her hair. He knew when he first saw her, at a craft fair in St. Leonard, that he was going to marry her. Emily promised to wait for him so Harry volunteered before he would be drafted anyway, thinking the United States Army was a way to see the world while he helped stop the spread of Communism to American shores. He wasn't in the war zone long before he and other soldiers saw firsthand what was happening. It was a corporate war, shiny as hell, but Sgt. Harold Plunkett fought it anyway. In 1968, he had come home alive, a proud owner of the Purple Heart. For a lot of years, before she finally stopped asking, Emily wondered what he had done with that prestigious medal. But Harry never told her. He had believed, once upon a time, that Vietnam had been worth something, had taught everyone a lesson not easily forgotten. Otherwise, his fellow soldiers, young men like Corporal Wallace McGee, had died in vain. But now the country was plunged into yet another war, this one in Iraq and Afghanistan, a war even more corporate and shiny than Vietnam.

Harry had driven past Sal Gifford's house when he saw her. She was in sweats and a jacket, a bonnet on her head. He slowed the pickup to a crawl as he came within twenty feet of her. He dimmed the lights and saw Blanche wave a gloved hand, indicating that she knew he was there. He followed along behind as she ran, lighting the way, although she had told him she knew the road so well after months of running on it that she never worried about falling. "Once you know about the pothole in front of Sal Gifford's house and the frost heave past the old school, the rest is smooth sailing," Blanche had said the first night he found himself following her as she ran.

The sky was loaded with bright stars. Free of the light pollution over heavily populated areas, it always sparkled on those nights of moon and stars and planets. It reminded Harry of a planetarium he had once visited with Angie, as if it were something built by man and not part of the natural universe. Below the stars, down on Earth, colored leaves lay splattered along the roadsides like blotches of paint. Harry saw them scatter in the wake as Blanche's running shoes passed over them. Sometimes, driving on a tranquil night like this, Harry Plunkett was reminded of how mortal he was. In Vietnam, he didn't need to be reminded. Mortality slept with him in those months as he waited for his tour to end. It woke with him each morning, ate with him, fought at his side. Mortality was just another foot soldier praying to go home.

They passed the sign that said DUMP, at the mouth of the road that led to it. They passed Florence Walker's sign with its same word, *cantankerous*, until Monday morning when a word beginning with D would replace it. Then Tommy Gifford's house, where the chained dog barked loudly. From there it was a straight run toward the bridge. Blanche didn't bother to look down at the camper on the flat where Billy Thunder's small, yellow light burned against the night, but Harry noticed it and smiled. He liked Billy Thunder. When the ordered parts came for the Mustang, he'd do a good job of fixing the roof. Maybe Billy would *freeze* all winter as he drove his convertible around Mattagash, but it was unlikely he'd *freeze to death.*

On the straight road across the bridge, Blanche opened her stride, almost gliding. Harry still followed at a respectable distance. At the lower end of the bridge, on the right, was Hair Today, where Verna Craft had opened a hair and nails salon. The Protestant church sat on the left, next to the graveyard. That's where Emily was now buried, along with both of Harry's parents. On his father's grave was the bronze veteran's plaque that told of his death in Korea, with the 9th Infantry. His father's war was the first major clash of good versus evil for an America that was still listening to its news on radios. It was the Free World standing up to Communism, as the Cold War turned into a sizzling hot potato. War is all in the *words*, Harry knew now. In late August of 1951, the Republic of Korea's 7th Division captured Bloody Ridge, those three interlocking hills southwest of the Punchbowl. Their triumph was short-lived, for the next day the North Koreans took the ridge back in a violent counterattack. And that's when the 9th Infantry was ordered to scale it. A molehill, really. It was a battle that lasted ten days, until, finally, the North Koreans abandoned the place. Of the many killed on both sides during the intense and bloody combat, Sgt. Leonard Plunkett was one, a few days shy of his twenty-ninth birthday. He would come home in a box, but "the conflict" would wage on for another two years. Now, wedged between the sheer magnitude of World War II and the nightmare that was to follow in Vietnam, Korea had become the forgotten stepchild. So what had the loss of his father's life been about in the end? The Demilitarized Zone was still there, with a crazed dictator peering out at the world from behind a treasure trove of missiles and bombs.

When his mother died, Harry placed his father's Purple Heart inside the coffin with her.

The last thing Edna should have done that night was drive to Bertina's trailer. But when you're an artist and you've just finished your first work of art, what good is it if you have no one to share the excitement? She couldn't show Mama Sal, who would only criticize her for wasting valuable time, not to mention paint. And Roderick would ask a hundred details about her white pickup truck. He wouldn't ask important questions like, "Is that your lover behind the wheel, Edna?" Instead, he'd be asking things like if the pickup truck came from Walt's Chevy Sales in Watertown. How many miles to the gallon? And he'd be sure to sign off with how people shouldn't drive with one hand on the wheel.

Edna lifted the painting from the backseat carefully, since some of the paint was still wet. She intended to give it a name soon, something pretty, maybe like the bottles of nail polish Bertina had. *Crimson Sky*. *Purple Dare*. *Amber Autumn*. Maybe she would call it something romantic like *Seasonal Escape*. She almost forgot to knock on the trailer's door. Most of Mattagash didn't knock when they visited each other. But Bertina had let it be known that she considered this custom uncivilized. "If you walked into a home in Tampa without knocking first, someone would pump a bullet between your eyes."

Bertina's voice was distant, coming from the bedroom maybe, but it definitely gave Edna permission to enter. She leaned the painting against a leg of the kitchen table and took off her coat. She saw that Bertina's bedroom door was open, her television set flickering images off the walls, its sound turned down.

"Who is it?" Bertina asked.

"It's me," said Edna. She heard the sound of a mattress creaking. Bertina appeared in the bedroom doorway, her hair mussed, her eyes swollen as if she'd been sleeping too hard, maybe even crying. She was in a pair of cotton pajamas, pale blue, that looked as if they'd been on her body since that morning. She went into the tiny kitchen and stood before the narrow refrigerator, which was green, same as the narrow stove. Across the refrigerator's door was a huge dent, one that had come with it, free of charge.

"You okay?" asked Edna, and Bertina nodded. She pulled out a can of beer and popped its top.

"Want one?"

Edna shook her head. She could feel her excitement rising now, waiting for Bertina to turn and notice the painting. But Bertina stood there in the kitchen, staring at the bottles of nail polish still on the table. She stood there as if she couldn't remember whose kitchen it was or how she had ended up there. Edna wondered if getting married and divorced a lot of times can do that to a person, can catch them in the middle of a thought so fast they can't remember who they're married to or where they live, which kitchen they're standing in. Maybe they no longer even know *who they are*, especially those women who keep changing last names with every new marriage.

"I got something to show you," said Edna. "It's my first attempt." She lifted the painting onto the kitchen table. The light would be better there, and Bertina wouldn't have to take a single step forward to look at it. Bertina looked at the painting now, dreamlike, the way she had the bottles of nail polish.

"The right bumper is crooked," Bertina said.

Edna studied the truck. The bumper was, indeed, a bit lower on the right than on the left.

"I guess that's my style," said Edna, remembering something she'd read from her new art book. "You know. Unrealistic spatial proportions."

Bertina stepped closer to the painting and leaned down for a better view.

"Well, what do you think?" asked Edna

"Why are they driving away?"

"I'm not sure," said Edna. She felt her artistic nature with all its "raw power, stamina, and resilience," as the book said, beginning to fail her. Any second now, the artist in her would be waving a white flag. "I guess they're leaving because they want to." She stared at the truck. It could almost be a wedding car if she had painted a string of cans tied to its bumper.

"Oh," said Bertina.

"Well?" asked Edna.

"I think you should paint a license plate on your truck," said Bertina. "Otherwise, I hope you know how to paint a cop car."

Edna's eyes moistened with tears. She hated *tearing up*, as Mama Sal called it. It wasn't a natural talent but a fault.

"I'm kidding you," Bertina said and put an arm around Edna. "This is a wonderful job you've done, Eddie. You've got real talent, you know that? I could never paint something this good in a million years."

Edna let the artist in her go ahead and cry. She wasn't sure at that moment what had moved her more. Was it what Bertina had said about the painting? Or was it because her big sister now had a loving arm around her shoulders, hugging her? And she had called her "Eddie," the childhood nickname that Edna used to hate for its boyish sound. Now, hearing it again and feeling that arm that didn't belong to Roderick or the twins, she was overcome with emotion. In that single moment, Edna knew for certain that she really *was* an artist, for a true artist cries over small poetic things that most people find stupid.

"Come on," said Bertina. She took the painting and leaned it tenderly against the wall. Edna saw respect too in the gesture. "Get yourself a beer. This calls for a celebration. My little sister is a genius."

As Harry followed Blanche, he passed other homes where other Mattagash lives were unfurling inside. At Orville's house, just before Cell Phone Hill, he noticed the mail car parked in the front yard. Now that the car itself was retired, no longer a vehicle employed by the government but just another Ford Motors product, its demeanor appeared somehow less snotty. He passed Cell Phone Hill and then Sheriff Ray Monihan's house. Harry saw Ray inside, remote control in hand and sitting in front of his television set. Black-and-white images were flickering off the mirror that hung on the wall behind the sheriff's head. Harry figured the images were reruns of the old *Andy Griffith Show*. Ray was a fan of the man from Mayberry, the "sheriff without a gun."

The pickup truck rolled past Porter and Lillian Hart's house. The old brick school was next. Since Mattagash's young blood had moved away and enrollment numbers couldn't justify the expense, the school had been closed for years. It was now used for town functions and storage. It was Ed Lawler, the school's first principal, who had gone into his office one night and put a gun to his head. Teachers and school kids swore that the principal's ghost still walked the empty halls. The young might be moving away, but at least the ghosts were staying in town.

There was a time Harry could drive through Mattagash and see whole families lounging in front of their TVs or sitting around the kitchen table playing a board game. Or maybe they were sprawling in chairs on their front porches, adults talking up the events of the day while the kids played and swatted blackflies. But all he saw now were lights burning in single rooms where a man or woman or child sat alone, staring face-to-face at their best new friend, the computer. The pickup rolled past Lydia Hatch's house and Harry wondered if anyone had taught Owl to use a computer. It might do the kid some good, give him a bit of freedom from Lydia. Even geniuses need to escape now and then.

The first house a visitor would see as they passed the welcome sign with its moose in the artwork was Blanche Tyler's own small home. "From my bedroom window," Blanche once told Harry, "I can see the moose smiling on the welcome sign." Harry put on his blinker, even though blinkers were rarely used in Mattagash since everyone knew where everyone else lived. As Blanche reached her mailbox, Harry drove past and pulled into the driveway. He got out of the truck. The sound of his door closing echoed back from the river. Blanche pulled the bonnet off and her hair came cascading down onto her neck and shoulders, an avalanche of hair. She leaned against the hood of the truck, still breathing hard.

"So, what brings you out on a starry night?" she asked.

Harry said nothing. He turned and looked down the road to where the *Welcome to Mattagash* sign sat atop its two thick posts.

He remembered the day when the women's committee had put up the very first sign, a smaller one. That had to be fifty years ago. The whole town had turned out with picnic baskets and bottles of pop for the unveiling. That night, someone made a bonfire in the field across the road from the sign. Everyone stayed late for a hot dog roast until the youngsters grew tired from playing tag and kick-the-can. Then, slowly, folks said good night to each other and drifted off to their homes, leaving behind only glowing embers, fireflies, and stars. Harry's mother had been one of those people.

"Tell me something," said Harry. "How does a man who's about to turn sixty-three years old *make a move*, as you put it?"

Blanche took in a deep breath of air, head back, filling her nostrils with it. Then she exhaled deeply. Harry had seen her do that before too, once a run was over. She had told him it was good to breathe deep, that it relaxed tension in the muscles. He already knew so much about Blanche by stopping by the café each day, especially those little things that, once you string them together, make up the important part of a person's life.

"I guess he'd do it the same way a man in his twenties would," Blanche said.

Harry nodded. He kicked at the front tire of his truck. He put both hands in his jacket pockets, his fingers feeling the chill of night.

"We could go to a movie," Harry said. "But our elbows will probably rub other elbows while we eat popcorn and our feet will stick to the floor."

"I hate sticky floors," Blanche said.

"We could drive up Cell Phone Hill and look at the stars," said Harry. "The frogs are all gone, but we could listen to the cell phones peeping."

Blanche smiled.

"Nothing like the sound of cell phones on a starry night," she said.

"You're not going to help me, are you?" Harry asked.

"Nope," said Blanche. She turned then and put her hands against the hood of his truck, began her after-the-run stretching exercises, flexing first the muscles of one leg, then the other. Harry saw a car pass the welcome sign and head toward the guts of town, its two yellow headlights cutting the way.

"We can go to my place," he said. "I'm a pretty good cook if you don't expect something fancy. We can watch a movie, then maybe sit on my back patio and let the moon rise over the river. You'll need a warm coat, maybe even a glass of wine. I gotta tell you, it's been a lot of years since I've been on a date."

"Just so you know," said Blanche, "the hooks are now at the *front* of the bra."

10

SATURDAY MORNING AND AFTERNOON

Roderick had left for his day's work, as usual, just before dawn. He'd been working Saturdays for extra money. He still thought the way the old-timers did, that you worked six days and then, like God, you rested on the seventh. "Folks today are lazy," Roderick liked to say as he drank his morning coffee and put on his work gloves. "Before you know it, the forty-hour week is going to be ten hours long." Again, Edna had stayed in bed and listened to the banging of cupboard doors down in the kitchen. He was still searching for where she had hidden the candy bars. She knew he'd never look in the canister that said *Rice*. Maybe she could put other words on her canisters, words like *Divorce* and *Alimony* and *Help*. He had finally given up, for she heard the pickup spin out of the driveway. She listened as the sound of it was swallowed up by yet another day of work, another day of life.

It was almost lunchtime and she was halfway through her second cup of coffee when Edna decided to do it. She'd been thinking about it for days and now it was jump or get away from the ledge. She opened the phone book and flipped to the back pages where she often scribbled phone numbers. There it was, scrawled under the letters *WH*. She had called information days earlier and asked for the number. Ward Hooper. The operator had found the name quickly. After all, Bangor isn't New York. How many pages of Hoopers did she have to search? "I have only one Ward Hooper," she had said, using that clipped voice operators use to let callers know how important and how busy they are. "On Clairmont Drive." And before Edna could respond, even to lie, before she could say with her best business voice, "Yes, Clairmont Drive, that's the one," she heard an automated voice giving her the number. The operator was already gone, clipping a fingernail maybe, out in Texas or over in India, wherever operators lived these days. Or maybe she had dropped dead to know that Edna was going to telephone another man behind her husband's back. Edna had written the seven digits down, but as soon as the last number became ink on the page, she had chickened out.

Now she was ready. She listened as the phone rang twice before a man's voice answered. She wondered if he would be home. It was a Saturday, after all. If he'd taken up gliding as he planned, maybe he was out soaring soundlessly over the Bangor Mall and the huge statue of Paul Bunyan, and even the mental institute where poor Aunt Mildred had stayed. But it was his voice. She had not spoken to him since early July, the day he left Mattagash, but she had not forgotten the kindness in that voice, for it was indeed a *charismatic* voice. And again she felt the words Florence Walker had taught her coming to the rescue, giving her emotions a name. She felt *daunted*, and yet *euphoric*. She felt so *poignant* that there could be no doubt this phone call was *affecting the mind and emotions*.

"Ward, it's me. It's Edna," she said. "I'm calling from Mattagash to say hello and inquire how you're doing." She heard movement over the line, that kind of shuffling people do with a phone as they think, a sense of expectancy. A dog began to bark and sounds of excitement came out of the earpiece of Edna's phone. She heard him say, "Queenie, quiet down." There was a *thunk* as the receiver was put down. In the background, muffled voices filled the air. Soon, he was back.

"I'm sorry," he said. "The mailman just delivered the mail. Who did you say you are?"

Edna felt the *poignant* starting to melt. *Daunted* began to outweigh *euphoric*. She took a deep breath and tried again.

"Edna Plunkett," she said. "From Mattagash. Remember how we used to sit at Blanche's Café and talk about how I have twin boys and a daughter and I don't think we should bomb any country, and how you're going to take up gliding one day?" She heard the surge of recognition, felt his mind reeling until it caught the memory.

"Yes, of course," Ward said then. "How are you, Edna? How are things up in Mattagash?"

She had wondered for weeks how she would tell him, how she would bring up the subject without seeming too pushy. *I'm about to get a divorce* didn't seem like the best way. It would sound forward and needy.

"Well, they've been better," said Edna. "I'm suffering from Seasonal Affective Disorder and it's put me in a tailspin." She shifted her weight on the kitchen chair, her back tensing, her legs feeling like they might fall asleep, even during so important a phone call. "I was wondering if you might be coming back to take some more soil samples."

She heard another awkward pause coming at her like an invisible slap in the face, another silence too long.

"Well, the samples I took last summer turned out fine," Ward said then. "No need to take any more, but I sure did enjoy my time up there. You have a very friendly town."

"Did you take up gliding?" There were a hundred things she might have asked at Blanche's Café as the two of them waited for their food to arrive. Things like "Are you married, Ward

Hooper?" But he had never mentioned a family, a wife, a son, a daughter, a home, a garden, not even a parakeet. He had never even mentioned owning a personal car so all she knew of him was that official state vehicle he drove, the white pickup truck. She had assumed this meant he possessed none of the above, except maybe a car. It never occurred to her that he might not speak of these things because he considered them personal, considered them his own, in that protective way unless someone with a big mouth full of nosy questions wrested them away from him.

"Ward, is that Sheila?" It was a woman's voice, one that seeped past the man on the phone and leaked into all those little dark holes in the mouthpiece. "Remind her that your birthday party is tomorrow night. She'd better not forget to pick up the cake, and she'd better not be late."

"It's someone from that town up north where I worked this summer," Ward said, and Edna had to catch herself. She wanted to say, "It's not just someone, Ward Hooper. It's Edna."

"I'm sorry for the interruption," Ward was saying now into the phone. "Edna, right? This is so nice of you to call me. No, the soil samples turned out fine, and the studies will be mailed to the state when they're complete. I'm sure someone at the department will see that a copy of the report is mailed to Mattagash, if you folks would like one."

And that's when Edna began to understand. When someone is kind, truly kind, they don't sit and talk so much about themselves, especially at a quaint little place like Blanche's Café. They don't say *I got a wife whose voice is so musical you'd swear she was a movie star, and my daughter, Sheila, is often late and sometimes forgetful, but she's a great kid, and oh yes, did I mention that I live on Clairmont Drive or that our dog Queenie barks every day at the mailman?* You don't do any of these things if you are the sort of person who is *empathetic, able to understand the feelings, thoughts, and attitudes of others.* Instead, you see the need in *them*, you see the longing in those thoughts, the sadness in those attitudes, the hurt behind those feelings. So you talk to them. You say things like *So, you have twin sons? I bet that's a workload.* Or, *What do you think about the war in Iraq? Think we belong there?* Or you even ask about the only environment a person really understands, the only town, the only *soil* they've known. You ask, *Are the blackflies always this bad in the summers? Does it snow a lot in the winters?* This is what you do when you're empathetic.

"That's great news," Edna said now. The woman seemed to have gone away and the mailman must have continued on down Clairmont Drive, and maybe Queenie went to eat some dog food. "The folks here have been wondering so I'll let them know. We're sure gonna look forward to that report."

She hoped he didn't hear that tiny gasp in her voice. It was the same little intake of air Edna had learned to do as a child, when Mama Sal would be looming big over her. It seemed if you could take in a bit of air, all to yourself without anyone noticing it, your own secret, it would be a good way not to cry. In thirty-plus years, Edna had perfected the technique.

"Thank you for calling, Edna," Ward Hooper said now. "Please tell everyone hello for me. I hope I see you all again one day."

"I will," said Edna. "And tell your wife hello for us."

She lay the phone down on the table next to her coffee cup. Her SAD was back, big time. She could feel the weight of it pressing down on her shoulders and neck as if it were a ton of fresh snow, pushing any happiness out of her. After Ward Hooper left town, it was as if her life went back to being just a life again, with all the sparks gone out of it. A life unplugged. Venice without electricity. What about that excited chill she got seeing his white pickup parked at Blanche's? That's when she sat outside in her car, using her compact mirror to dab on some lipstick. Then that sparkling pause at the front door when the brass knob seemed about to burn her hand, that surprised expression on her face when Ward glanced up to see who made the bell ring. That "Oh, *you're* here, Ward Hooper?" look that she had practiced over the months he was in town and now, now that the look was as good as it could get, she had no more use for it.

It was eleven o'clock and Billy Thunder was sound asleep when he heard his phone ring. With no odds jobs to be found around town that day, hard as he had solicited for them, he had nothing to do but sleep in, buried beneath several blankets. He lay on the narrow bed listening as his answering machine clicked on. "This is Thunder. You know what to do, so do it or hang up the phone." Then came his Grateful Elvis. "FuckYouNowFuckYouVeryMuch." Billy heard the sound of heavy breathing, a sense of living energy on the other end of the phone line. He could tell that it was the older and fatter one, George Delgato, or *Jorge*, as he called himself. Jorge always paused a long time before he said anything, even when Billy *did* answer the phone. It was part of his swagger, a way of doing business that said, "I'm so important I'm not in any hurry at all."

Billy leaned over and peered down at the incoming number that always turned up as if by magic on his telephone. He knew the Portland number by heart, but this wasn't a Portland number. All it said was *Out of Area* in the plastic window box. Billy waited, staring at the telephone as if it might tell him who was holding the receiver on the other end of the line. If it were the Delgatos, surely they were still in Portland, driving that big ugly Caddy from bar to bar, their stomachs riding ahead of them like air bags, acting like mafia big shots and waiting for night to fall so they could chow down on steaks at Murray's Restaurant & Bar. But why hadn't Raul's phone number announced itself as usual? There was a *click* now. Whoever was calling had hung up. Billy picked up the phone and punched the little star and then 6 and 9. He got an automated voice. *We're sorry but the last incoming call cannot be...* He hung up. Before any kind of panic could set in, Billy laughed so that he could hear for himself there was nothing but calm in his voice. Those two idiots had a hard time finding Murray's once they'd hit the Bacardi bottle, which started around noontime. They were screwing with his head, wanting him to think they were on their way north. Good move. It almost worked too. *Le muerte visitará.* Death will visit.

Billy lay back on his bed and shut his eyes.

"*Patearé asno de muerte*," he said. *I'll kick death's ass.*

And this was when the sadness came creeping in, his younger life coming to haunt him, to remind him of how bad his present life was turning out. There had been a time—had it been in his freshman or sophomore year of high school?—that he had been the golden boy. He was good with math, good with languages, good with art and history, good with geography. His brother and sister still seemed to love him. He had first pick of girls in his class and was good at baseball, better at basketball. So when had his future risen up like a snake and turned to bite him? How did it happen that he was now in Mattagash, Maine, in a camper that would look like a soup can if someone wrapped a Campbell's label around it, with business associates who often had to close down shop for a stint at the local penitentiary? He thought of the girlfriend he had left behind in Portland. Her name wasn't Elizabeth Miller at all, but Phoebe Perkins. She was a waitress at Murray's Restaurant & Bar, and she believed for certain that Billy Thunder was the best idea to ever stroll into her life. When he left Portland to avoid those bouncing checks and maybe establish a new business arm in a remote and deprived area, Billy hadn't even stopped at the restaurant to say good-bye. The last he had seen of Phoebe was when she slid away from him in bed, at her apartment on Baker Street, had showered, had dressed in her pink uniform that all the waitresses wore at Murray's, and had kissed him good-bye as he lay half-asleep. His mother would have said that Phoebe was a good girl. Maybe that's why Billy believed somewhere down in the parts of his heart that were still good, still running on conscience, that Phoebe Perkins deserved someone better than a small-time drug dealer recently let go from the home office. He should have told her that he was leaving town for a while, until things cooled off. The problem was, that *last* check he wrote and the one with the most numbers on it, a check for *one thousand dollars and zero cents*, was written to someone named Phoebe Perkins. Billy had postdated it and was certain he could eventually make it good. So Phoebe had put the check on her dresser and had cashed one of her own. She counted a thousand dollars worth of bills into Billy's hand. Ten Ben Franklins. He needed that money to pay off a loan from the Delgato cousins so that they would keep him on the work force as their best salesman. You have to spend money sometimes to make money. Everyone knows that. When the Delgatos demanded their thousand back, that's when Billy had written the check to Phoebe. So while he was at it, he wrote a few more, one to Mason's Grocery for $300, and one to Everette's Construction Company for $500, and one to Lori's Lawn Supplies for $200. Mason trusted him just enough, Everette was someone he knew from back in high school, and Lori was an older woman who had the hots for him. That would be enough to give Phoebe back cash money for the grand he'd borrowed. He would tell her to tear up the check he'd written to her, now that his bank account had become a hotbed, with checks bouncing like Mexican jumping beans. But then

Billy couldn't stop writing bad checks. The phone company got one, the water company, the electric company. His brother got a $100 check for his birthday and his sister the same, although their birthdays were months away. *Splurge on your special day!* Billy had written next to his signed name. He wrote checks to people he hardly knew. One was for $75 for the oldest waitress on the floor at Murray's, a generous tip because she was over sixty and should be at home watering flowers instead of working so hard to make a living. So the bank wanted him too, along with Mason, Everette, Lori, and the others. Billy felt like that pastry he had read about as a kid, the gingerbread man, with everyone in town chasing after him, wanting to sink their teeth into his ass.

Still, everything could have been fixed somehow, with enough time and money, except for one thing. When he'd gotten that money from Mason and Everette and Lori, the thousand bucks that would repay Phoebe and stop her from depositing a check that would only bounce to the moon and back, Billy hadn't given her the money. He had gone down to the local poker game in the brown two-story building on the corner of Frisk and Renfrow, the best damn poker game in town, with the intentions of making that thousand dollars double, maybe even triple. As he rang the doorbell on the second floor where the game was held, he imagined himself strolling into Murray's the next day, using that slow, sexy walk he knew he had. He'd wait until Phoebe could pour herself a glass of Coke and take her ten-minute break, sitting across the table from him and staring at him like he really was someone important and worthwhile. He knew what he'd say to her, dragging it out before he finally produced the money. *Here's a thousand bucks to cover the check I wrote you, Phoebe, because it's gonna bounce. And here's another five hundred for trusting me. Buy yourself something pretty.* But instead of saying any of those things to her, Billy had hurriedly packed up and left town. He did this because it had taken him less than two hours to lose every penny of the thousand bucks.

But he still had hope at that point. The Delgato cousins—big, stupid, ugly idiots—had been paid back their thousand and so still liked and respected Billy enough to support his interests in expanding the company northward. "Where the fuck is Maggatash?" George had asked, when Billy first told them of his plans. The white Mustang was already packed with his suitcase and his mother's old scrapbook of family photos with plenty of Mattagash ancestors peering out at the modern world with tight-lipped smiles. "Mattagash is at the end of the road, north of Caribou," Billy had told George, or *Jorge*, and watched as he chewed his steak. Jorge probably thought that if a car drove north as far as Bangor, it would fall off the edge of the world. "Think you'll have good sales so far up in the sticks?" asked Ralph, or *Raul*. And Billy replied fast and sure, "Absolutely. They're starving up there for good supplies." He watched as Raul chewed his own steak. They were steak and baked potato men, and they washed it all down with Bacardi, and it was a mortal shame that someone like Billy Thunder worked for those two idiots in the first place. But Billy had jumped from a cliff and no matter how hard he flailed his arms, he couldn't seem to do anything but keep falling. Somewhere down below, he knew, was the bottom, with all those jagged rocks waiting like teeth for him to hit. One day, when his ship came in, Billy would be his own boss, running a legitimate business of some kind and Phoebe would be the girl he would settle down with, once he'd known a lot more women first. And so the Delgatos supplied him well. And Billy made sure everything was nicely hidden down in the coils of that classic convertible before he struck out for the outpost known as Mattagash.

And for a time, after he got settled in, Billy was actually gaining ground, could see some blue sky above the cliff, even if it was illegal blue sky. He figured he could work all summer, pay Phoebe back, give her an extra grand for the trouble he'd caused, and even have a nice nest egg for himself. So, what went wrong? That's what he asked himself each day when he woke up past noon with a tongue that felt like someone had laid carpet on it during the night, his head aching, his heart talking to him before he could shut it up. What went wrong? He could blame it on the pretty French girls in Watertown and their demands to be wined and dined until the roosters crowed. He could blame it on Texas Hold 'em, the only poker game he could find and one built more on good luck than good skills. Whatever he might blame it on, Billy had slowly stopped sending money back to the Delgatos. They believed his phone calls at first, his reasons why. Dentist. Mechanic. Uncle Sam. Aunt Someone. And stupid as they were, they kept sending him the small brown box with *Elizabeth Miller, Portland, Maine*, on the outside wrapper. How many boxes was he now behind? Four? Five? He no longer remembered, but he was certain Jorge Delgato, big dumb George, missed every penny as he chewed his steak and stared across his baked potato at Raul.

But what hurt Billy the most, what stirred his heart in those waking hours, was Phoebe. He hated his own cowardice in how he had treated her. When he thought of Phoebe, he remembered her in the small ways, the important ways. He thought of how she washed her uniform by hand, leaning over the small sink in her apartment. "Because I can save money this way," Phoebe told him, the first time he asked why she didn't use the machine in the apartment laundry room that ate quarters for a living. He remembered the pantyhose hanging to dry on the shower rod in the narrow bathroom, the shape of Phoebe's legs still in them. He remembered her curled asleep on the sofa, knees drawn up to her chest, the stray cat she had rescued from one of the restaurant's trashcans nestled by her feet, which were probably aching even in her dreams. Being a waitress is a tough life. But loving Billy Thunder had turned out to be even tougher.

Billy knew his eyes had teared up, for he felt a strong emotion wash over him, part loneliness and part shame. The ringing phone startled him. The Delgatos again? He listened as the message played. *This is Thunder. You know what to do.* Then the Grateful Elvis. When he heard hysterical laughter being recorded, he didn't bother to sit up and look at the incoming number. He reached for the phone.

"Jesus, Buck," he said. "You've heard it a hundred times."

For a few seconds, Billy listened to noises that might be considered guffaws on the other end of the line. No one would ever appreciate and enjoy his Grateful Elvis more than Buck Fennelson, his fourth or fifth or sixth cousin. But now the guffaws seemed to blend into what might be taken for sobs. And that's when he knew that while the Grateful Elvis was still cracking Buck Fennelson up, something else was making him cry.

"Mona left me," Buck finally said.

11

SATURDAY EVENING

Orville and Meg Craft sat at their dining room table, a candle flickering between them. On each of their plates was a generous serving of Chinese Pie, that mixture of hamburger, mashed potatoes, and creamed corn beloved by Mattagash cooks. It was really shepherd's pie with the addition of corn. But somewhere along the culinary path, it had become known as Chinese Pie. Orville couldn't remember the last time Meg had done that, set the dining room table and opened a bottle of wine. Most often, they ate in the kitchen where they could watch the small TV over the sink, rarely speaking except to ask each other to pass the butter or the salt. Sometimes, Meg took her plate into the sewing room and ate there while she sent emails and read messages. But tonight she had even selected two of the wine glasses out of her china cabinet, a place so forbidden to Orville and the children that they never dared open its door. This supper then, this site of bread-breaking, would be the best atmosphere to deliver the speech he had ready for her.

Sitting alone at his cabin that morning and watching more of the migrating geese disappear over his pond, Orville had spent a lot of time thinking about what he would say. Then he had gone to Blanche's Café with the idea of talking *man to man* with Billy Thunder. But it hadn't been the right time at Blanche's. Billy was already at a table with Buck Fennelson and the whole room was full of eyes and ears. Now, however, was certainly the right time to talk to Meg. He would not wait until they finished the homemade chocolate pudding she'd whipped up, despite how much he loved it. When was the last time Meg had given him chocolate pudding that didn't come in a little plastic tub with a seal over its top? He was ready with his speech. *Meg Craft, I'm your husband. I don't want to hear about dryness, and I certainly don't want to hear about yeast. So, go to the drugstore in Watertown and buy whatever it is you women need once you reach a certain age. You get it, and you meet me in our marital bedroom at least once a month. I don't think that's asking too much.*

He would talk later to Billy Thunder in some private place, maybe even down at that tin can where he was living until December killed him. Orville was a changed man and it had nothing to do with retirement. It had to do with the electricity of life, that sweet current that pulses through the young but disappears when older humans need it most. Husbands and wives, even those who are not yet seniors, are supposed to take up gardening, bird-watching, ceramics, golf, travel, knitting, stamp collecting, tropical fish. Orville had read a hundred magazine articles and listened to all the radio talk shows on Sunday mornings at the cabin. Never had anyone said, "Listen, life is short. Pretend your body is still in its twenties. Jump for the brass ring. Swing for those bleachers. Dive into the deep end of the pool. Act like a fool if you must, but at least *live*." He would remember that October day until it came his time to die, the day he delivered his last letter, the day of the blueberry pie, and then home from the mountaintop to Meg. The things that flash before a man's life as he dies are made of moments like that.

"I'd like to say something," Meg said then. She passed him a spoon for his pudding. The pudding was creamy and thick, the way Meg's mother had learned to make it from her own mother, melting genuine squares of chocolate. It was *real* pudding and the cream on top had been whipped by hand. Orville put the spoon down after a couple bites. He looked at Meg, waited.

"I think we need to get some more of them pills, and we need to pick a special time, even if it's just twice a month," Meg said. "Husband and wife time."

Twice a month. Orville felt jubilant. *Jubilant: full of delight and joyous abandonment.* He looked at the woman he had married so many years earlier. How did she know how he felt since they rarely talked?

Two times every thirty days.

"I know you're too shy to buy them yourself," Meg continued, "so I can ask Lillian to get an extra prescription. She's letting Porter take them now, did you know?" No, he didn't, but he *had* overheard at Blanche's that Booster Mullins, Christopher Harris, and Phillip Craft had all been given sanctions from their wives.

Orville felt relief floating up inside him as if it were a balloon, relief that he wouldn't have to speak to Billy Thunder about anything personal, let alone a subject as private as Viagra. And it was a relief that Meg still loved and wanted him after all, despite his paunch and his white legs and his thinning hair.

Meg went to the kitchen then and came back with the coffee pot and two cups.

"Of course, I'd never discuss this with Lillian unless you gave me the okay," she said. She poured him a cup of coffee and then slid her fancy milk creamer toward his reaching hand. It was the one her mother had given them as a wedding gift, the crystal creamer coming with a crystal sugar bowl. Meg had used the set for the small gathering at the house after her mother's funeral and, later, her father's funeral. And she had used them for Debby's wedding reception which had also been held at home, when their oldest daughter married. But Orville couldn't remember seeing the creamer in service other than those three times. Instead, it held court next to the sugar bowl, both safe behind the glass door of the china cabinet and looking quite superior to the regular dishes the family used daily. That's when Orville noticed that the plate on which he'd been eating was one of Meg's fancy plates, with a bouquet of red roses in the center and a gold trim circling the outer edge. Before he could comment on how nice the dishes looked or say anything at all, such as *Sure, Meg, go ahead and get some pills from Lillian*, she produced the crystal sugar bowl. She put it down gently and close enough that Orville's spoon could reach it without any effort.

"Sugar?" Meg asked.

At Buck's house, there was now no sign that Mona had ever been there. No tropical foods were being baked inside green banana leaves in the oven, no female sweater draped over the sofa, no computer, no movie magazines, and no Frankie the dog lying on a blue blanket. *How could people disappear so fast?* Billy thought as he walked around the small house, examining the empty spaces. He wondered now if Phoebe Perkins had done the same thing when Billy had taken his belongings and disappeared north in the white Mustang. Had she stood stunned and bewildered, realizing for the first time how painful and lonely an empty space can be?

Buck seemed as hurt over the fact that he didn't know who owned the pickup truck that had carried Mona away as he was with her departure. Apparently, she had arrived with her sister and backed the vehicle up to Buck's small house. She had emptied it of her things, telling him nothing more than that she no longer loved him.

"It was a Ford," said Buck. "Probably a 2004. Silver, with white letters on the tires. Black toolbox in the back of it. It was damn near bigger than my house."

Billy was only half listening, knowing that this interest in the truck was really in *who owned it*. For it was *who owned it* who had stolen Princess Mona from him.

"Too bad she took her snow blower," said Billy. "That would've come in handy this winter."

Buck didn't smile at this. He had collapsed down into the sofa as if he'd never again have the energy to lift himself out of it. Billy was trying to find the right thing to say, the best words of comfort. But he was too overwhelmed with how he himself had left Phoebe. At least Buck had been there to witness Mona's departure. He didn't come home late from work, tired of life and a shitty job, to unlock his door and walk into an ambush. Billy stared at the two framed photographs sitting atop Buck's TV. One was of his parents, dead now for some years. The other was of Buck himself, pale-faced and needy, the sad eyes looking out at the world as if pleading for someone to come to his rescue. Billy assumed it was taken during Buck's last year of school, his sophomore year, before he dropped out for good. He picked up the photo and slid his finger across the loose dust on its glass. Teachers didn't like Buck much, he'd told Billy some weeks back, because he wasn't too smart. Buck was unlacing his purple boots with the yellow tips. He looked up at Billy.

"It's all part of the Fennelson Curse," said Buck. "Mona leaving me like she did."

Billy nodded, as if agreeing. Dorrie Mullins had told him about the curse during a lunchtime at Blanche's. Dorrie had almost *married into it*, as she said, but since she didn't want to live her life with a rabbit's foot dangling from her rearview mirror, she had broken off a high school engagement to Terrence Fennelson, who later fell off the St. Leonard water tower where he'd climbed for a closer look at the moon. According to Dorrie, the Fennelson family had for generations fallen from rooftops, trees, Ferris wheels, and horseback. They'd been hit by trucks, hail balls, horseshoes, and shotgun pellets. It seemed to Billy that *meteorite* was the only item missing from the list.

"Maybe this isn't a curse at all," said Billy. "Maybe it's a blessing."

Buck took a handkerchief out of his hip pocket and blew his nose. His eyes had turned red and watery.

"Ah, man, Bucko, I'm sorry," said Billy, and he meant it.

As Buck pushed the handkerchief back into his pocket, he nodded at a manila envelope that was lying on the coffee table.

"She left that," Buck said, "before she drove off in that silver Ford pickup with the fancy tires. I wish I knew who owned it. Whoever it is has some money to throw around if he can buy himself a fancy truck like that. It had a sunroof."

Billy saw by the name on the manila envelope that it came from a doctor's office in Watertown. Inside were the results for a pregnancy test for a *Ms. Mona Ferguson. Positive. Twenty weeks. Name of Father: Mr. Arthur Benton Fennelson.*

Buck.

Billy looked fast at Buck. He was perched on the sofa's edge like some kind of dazed gargoyle, waiting.

"Guess I passed the test," said Buck. He was half proud. Billy's mind was running, trying to do some quick math. Buck had met her when, around the first of July? Billy remembered because he was a reluctant witness to the event. It was the Fourth of July celebration at Burt's Lounge. They were sitting outside at one of the tables with an umbrella over it when Mona went sashaying past. Buck's eyes and heart had followed her all the way to the door of the ladies room. An hour later, he asked her to dance. Two hours later, he was so in love that nothing Billy could say would snap him out of it. Four weeks after that night, Buck's old green pickup had crossed the bridge, loaded to the gills with everything Mona could grab and carry, including the snow blower. *Fourth of July*. It was now the middle of October. Three and a half months. That was fourteen weeks. He looked at Buck. Should he tell him he probably flunked this test too?

"I guess we can add paternity suit to stuff the Fennelsons have been hit with," said Billy. Instead of laughing, Buck nodded.

"Damn curse," he said. He scratched the top of his head.

Billy had been in Mattagash long enough to know most people believed that maybe his maternal ancestors, the Fennelsons, weren't so much jinxed by the fast hand of fate as by slow-wittedness. But he was also discovering that for every slow-witted Fennelson, there were a dozen fast-witted ones. And that was a damn good ratio. He put the envelope back on the coffee table. He had to visualize it first, a plump-faced boy, an urchin wearing Buck's hand-me-down coat and purple boots with yellow tips, a moon-faced child who would give Horace "Owl" Hatch a run for his money. *Little Buck*.

"If this is true," said Billy, "if this isn't one of Mona's lies, then you're going to make one hell of a good father."

Buck beamed instantly, as if he'd been thinking of how much fun it would be to own a small child, someone to play games with, watch cartoon marathons with, eat Cheerios with each morning.

"I figure I will too," Buck said.

"But you got some important questions to ask Mona first," Billy added. "You don't need to pay child support for years if it's not your baby."

"I wouldn't like that," Buck admitted. "Especially since I can barely pay for *me*."

"Exactly," said Billy. "We'll get you a test, Bucko. It's called a DNA test."

"I hate tests," said Buck.

"I know you do," Billy said. "But I bet you'll pass this one with flying colors. And the next time you meet a girl you love, you're going to keep condoms in your pocket."

"I like tests where you can pick the answer," Buck said. "You know, like maybe it's A or B or C. Sometimes, it's even D."

"Dr. Thunder has prescribed some medicine, cousin of mine," Billy said and stood up. He reached for Buck's coat and tossed it over to him.

"I like it when you call me cousin," said Buck. "You know, like family."

Billy & Buck. The Vaudeville Show.

"And the medicine is supper at the Golden Dragon," said Billy. What was money for but spending? "Followed by some shots of tequila at Bert's Lounge. I can already smell the perfume on those good-looking waitresses."

That's when Buck's face smiled again, a forgiving face, a face filled with enough kindness to override all the regret. Billy knew the Buck Fennelsons of the world. He'd gone to school with some of them, had seen them teased and beaten at recess, had seen them standing alone at school dances wearing pants an inch too short for their legs. He'd seen them waiting to get picked for baseball, waiting for someone to motion them over at lunchtime, waiting at the end of the line at movie theaters. Sometimes, he'd been part of the teasing, other times he'd been the rescue.

"They got little pieces of meat on sticks at the Dragon," said Buck.

"Yes, they do," said Billy. "Now zip up your coat."

Edna felt her artistic nature telling her she had to go *somewhere*. She felt as if she were living life now in the third person. Maybe she was hanging on a wall somewhere in Venice, trapped inside a painting as Italians peered into her lighted windows. She had her purse slung over her left arm and her keys in her right hand, ready to run, hand on the doorknob, and yet she hesitated. That pull of motherly and wifely instinct made her linger upstairs so that she could listen to what was taking place downstairs. Once she was certain that Roderick and the boys would be okay without her there, she would leave quietly. She had told them good-bye down in the basement room that she and Roderick had fixed up enough to call a rec room. There was a used pool table down there and an older television set that worked well enough. Feeling guilt for not having catered to them for the past few days, she had popped two bags of popcorn. "You have fun visiting Bertina," Roderick had said. "Don't worry none. I'll be here babysitting. You go and express yourself all you want." He was up to something, no doubt about it. Edna imagined Mama Sal counseling him. *Pretend you're interested in that artistic shit she's going through, and she'll soon forget all about it.* He had never offered to babysit before, so something was stirring.

Edna tiptoed back across the living room floor, her footfalls soundless on the carpet, until she stood at the top of the stairs.

"You're ugly," she heard Roddy say. "Your face looks like a monkey's ass." This was followed by a slap.

"You're identical twins." Roderick's voice. "If one of you is ugly, then you're both ugly."

"Everyone says we look like *you*, Daddy." That was Ricky. Edna was the only one who could tell their voices apart.

"Monkey's ass," Roddy said again, and something hit the wall with a thump. Edna hoped it wasn't her knitting basket, which she always left at the end of the sofa. After the thump came a crack, maybe the plastic trash can by the back door. Where was her babysitter? What was Roderick *doing*?

"Don't throw stuff that'll break," she heard him say.

Edna had seen a painting in her art book that spoke to her soul, even though the artist didn't seem much more skilled than she was. It was called *The Scream* and was painted by a man who lived in Norway. That's how Edna felt, that she was silently screaming. She crossed the room again, but instead of heading out the door and into the chilly night, she turned toward the staircase and her own bedroom. She would crawl into bed, maybe read quietly with the two cats curled into balls at her feet. Even artistic souls must tire of the roller-coaster ride, those peaks of pure emotion often followed by valleys of despair and endless cocktail parties. Surely they seek a safe place now and then, a spot that shuts out the din of genius, not to mention family members.

Edna washed her face with Noxzema and water, and then brushed her teeth. She pulled on her flannel pajamas. She would buy a few sets of flannels for Bertina and the girls as early Christmas presents. She slid under the covers and then reached for her new art book. She flicked through pages until she came to *The Scream*. With the shade of her lamp tilted, she could better read. *Through his powerful and haunting paintings, Edvard Munch often depicts dangerously seductive* fin de siècle *women, all isolated characters in barren landscapes*. Edna pulled open the drawer of her nightstand and took out the tablet that held all her favorite vocabulary words. She scribbled *fin de siècle* on a blank page. She would look it up the next day, maybe ask Florence Walker its meaning. She wondered if she herself might be one of those isolated women in a barren landscape. After all, Mattagash wasn't exactly Paris, France. It wasn't even Paris, *Maine*.

The cats appeared and wound themselves into tight balls on the end of her bed. In no time, they were asleep. Edna knew they would wake in an hour or so, stretch, lick their paws, and then pad downstairs where one of the boys would let them out for a late-night pee. The cats, with their indifferent stares, seemed to have life figured out. If only they would share the secret, Edna thought, as she put the book away and snapped out her light. Maybe the answer lay in not expecting too much for oneself. The cats didn't dream of mice in another town, for instance. Or a better grade of milk. The cats didn't switch horses in midstream. They took what they saw in front of them and curled up next to it. Sometimes, they even purred.

Billy had driven Buck home after a night of Chinese food and a few good drinks. The evening out on the town had cheered Buck up no end. "We'll get this all worked out with Mona," Billy had told him. "Don't you worry none." Buck seemed relieved, maybe even happy again. He stood at his door and waved as Billy drove the Mustang out of the yard. They'd taken Buck's pickup to Watertown now that it was no longer high-jacked by Mona, and now Billy hoped to get the Mustang home and covered before the night brought more cold. Besides, he had an important appointment.

It was 9 p.m., as agreed upon. The Mustang was back in its place above the camper and Billy was waiting at the end of the bridge. Finally, he saw the small gray car coming slowly toward him, weaving a bit, as if the driver were nervous. Prior to a sale, most of his customers drove as if they had a sign taped to their back bumper. ARREST ME. I AM ABOUT TO BUY DRUGS. The car crossed the bridge and then pulled onto the hard gravel at the side of the road where Billy stood. He waited until the window rolled down and the hand came out. He shook the bottle and heard the blue pills rattling inside. He liked to do that, shake the pills, make a noise, let the customer know who was boss. Then, satisfied, he placed the bottle into the outstretched hand.

"Before I take any money, I have to tell you a few things about these pills," Billy said, his voice important. "I feel it's my responsibility."

He heard his customer put the car in park, letting it idle. Billy nodded. He looked up the road and saw nothing coming but the night. There were no yellow headlights to be seen for half a mile. He looked to the other end of the bridge. All clear.

"It took a long time for me to find a company that sells bogus stuff," he said. "But I did my homework and I found one. A lot of people were complaining about them online, saying their pills weren't real. That's because they have no *sildenafil citrate* in them. I know those are big words, but it's the *sildenafil citrate* that makes Viagra work in the first place. You understand so far?"

Meg Craft leaned out her car window and looked up at Billy.

"Verna says they never hurt Phillip," said Meg. "And Phil's been taking them for two months. Gretchen Harris has no complaints. Dorrie Mullins neither. I've heard nothing but good reports from your customers."

Billy nodded, pleased to hear this.

"Still," he said, "I told the other girls what I'm telling you now. It may look real, same kind of pill, same packaging, but there are risks in buying counterfeit Viagra." He sounded like a lecturing professor. "When this stuff is bought over the Internet, there's no way of telling what you're getting. It's often made in factories in Asia with no quality control. In other words, it might even be contaminated."

"I'll take my chances," said Meg. "If Orville gets sick, I'll nurse him back to health. We got good insurance, and the hospital is only thirty miles away."

"Man," said Billy. "Bad case, huh?" He was always sympathetic to his clients, no matter what their needs.

"*You* should know," said Meg. She gave him a frosty look, then retracted it. It was her pride, or it was Orville twice a month.

"It's not approved or regulated by the FDA," Billy added, as if Meg were signing a contract. "And it's illegal to sell it in the United States."

"If I go to jail, I go to jail," said Meg.

"The real stuff costs anywhere from eight to twelve dollars a pill," said Billy. "I'm gonna have to charge you top dollar to make any profit. Twelve dollars for twelve pills is a hundred forty-four dollars."

"These will last six months," said Meg. "Surely he'll give up after that." She handed the money out her window to Billy, who pocketed it without counting.

"Thanks," said Billy. "I got a friend printing up an article I found in the *New England Journal of Medicine*, how Viagra won't work for three out of ten men. Guess your bad luck was to marry one of those men. I'll have it ready in a couple days. You can give it to him to read if he starts asking questions. Twenty dollars a copy."

"Brilliant," said Meg, and Billy could tell that despite her initial misgivings, Meg had warmed to him.

He lit a cigarette and stood in the cold to smoke it as he watched Meg's disappearing taillights. Billy had discovered a new market in Mattagash and was thankful for it, given his Portland connections had been severed. He had found a new niche simply because most men, and certainly Mattagash men, won't talk to doctors much less each other about private things, not like the girls do. Men don't compare notes. Hell, if the men had pulled a trick like this on the women, it would be all over in three phone calls and two instant messages.

The half-moon rode over the river, reflecting silver and white. A chilled wind. A heaven bursting with stars. And that's why Billy thought of his mother again. What had she always told him before the sickness carried her memory of him away? "One day,

Bill, you're gonna find your way again. One day, son, that good heart is gonna lead you home."

Blanche snuggled against Harry's arm, her head resting in the crook of it. He felt the weight of her body pushed against him, so unlike Emily's in their last months together. Lying at his side during her illness, Emily was like a wish, something fragile that he might damage if he wasn't careful. In the last days, before she finally died, even touching her face with his lips had seemed to hurt her. Finally, and although Emily would never ask it, he had started sleeping in the chair beside her bed, his hand resting near hers. He had almost forgotten what it felt like to hold a woman who could *be* held. Blanche had those runner's legs, and she seemed to need someone to embrace her, as Harry did. After dinner, when he asked if she wanted to sit out on the chilly patio and watch the stars, she had smiled and said, "Don't you have a warmer place we can go?" She had put her arms around his neck and pulled him closer, kissing his face and then his lips. What surprised Harry was how they seemed to fit so easily, Blanche's body into his body, her thoughts into his head. And they had gone into his bedroom and he had pulled the blinds and turned to see her taking off her jeans, her sweater, her bra, her panties, as if undressing in front of him was the most natural thing in the world. She had turned to him, fully naked and unashamed. Making love to her was as easy and right as he could hope for, and when it was over, he knew what it was he had been feeling in his heart for a lot of months. All those mornings when he came to the café for breakfast, the first customer to make the bell ring, she would step up to the counter where he was sitting on one of the four stools. And a wave of comfort always washed over him then. He never doubted she would be there, a pot of coffee in her hand and wisps of hair already beginning to fall at the sides of her face. And there were those nights when he followed her in his pickup as she ran along the twisting road, tired from a full day's work and yet still able to hit that fast stride across the bridge. Blanche, running beneath the stars. Dependability. Comfort. Companionship. And *love*. Something he never thought he'd feel again for a woman other than Emily. But Harry knew now that love was a soldier. It can invade the human heart. Build canopies through jungles. Scale castle walls. Cross moats. Love can probably walk on water.

"Harry?" Blanche asked. "You ever do anything in your life that you're sorry for?"

"Every day," he said. He leaned over and pressed his lips to her face. She smelled clean, the way a river smells in the spring. When summer came, he would take her in his canoe all the way to Mattagash Falls. They could fill a basket with food. Maybe take sleeping bags. Spend a night under the stars.

"Seriously," said Blanche. "I mean something really important. You got any big regrets?"

Harry curved his arm upward so that his hand could touch her hair. He made small circles, caressing her temples with the tips of his fingers.

"I can't remember," he said. It wasn't true. He had always regretted being unable to tell Emily of his nightmares before she became too ill to listen. Those last days between them were too important, with other things to talk about, like how Harry could raise their eleven-year-old daughter on his own. Emily had wanted to leave as much of herself behind as possible. That way, Angie would know where to look for her mother when she was grown and had questions. When Emily knew for certain that her time was brief, she had begun scribbling in a red journal.

Harry had never read it. He found it in the bottom drawer of their bedroom dresser a year after she died. When Angie turned twenty-one, Harry gave her the journal. Then he went back into the bedroom and cleaned the rest of Emily's clothing from closets and drawers, put it all in boxes, and drove it down to the community center. He figured the time had come, for Angie's sake if not his own. *It hurts, Daddy, to see all her things still in place, as if she's coming back one day.* That past summer, it had been twenty-six years since Emily disappeared from the world. Angie would be thirty-seven on her next birthday.

"I wish I'd been better at the divorce," Blanche said, and Harry was grateful to have her there beside him. He knew most men would find it difficult to understand, maybe even believe, but she was the first woman he'd made love to since Emily died. "I let the kids see too much fighting before I finally threw in the towel." She turned over on her side, lining her body against his, her arm thrown against his chest.

"You're a human being," said Harry. "And you know what they say about us humans. We make mistakes. But if we're smart, we learn from them."

He had learned, hadn't he? He often asked himself this question on those sleepless nights, those nights of the terrified faces, the hollowed eyes peering at him from the shadows of the bedroom, the voices whispering him awake. Corporal Wallace McGee from Philadelphia was a frequent visitor. Wally had looked up to Sergeant Harold Plunkett, his superior, even though Harry was only twenty-four himself, three months shy of his next birthday. Wally was twenty-two and the platoon's point man. His fellow soldiers knew he was cautious in finding trip wires and booby traps, and that meant they might live to go home again. It was a night before the boat would go out on morning patrol, a sticky night in June of 1968. Wally had been distant all that day, barely speaking. Harry knew his mind was on a place beyond the Mekong Delta, that place a man either sees or he doesn't. "Something wrong, Corporal?" he had asked. And that's when Wally McGee had turned to him and said, "Sarge, do you believe that when your time is up, it's up?" And Harry had laughed. He didn't want any of his men giving in to this sense of defeat, especially a good man like Wally. "I believe in mistakes," said Harry, "and being in the wrong place at the wrong time." But Wally wasn't dissuaded by this. "I need to tell you something, Sarge," he said. "In case anything happens to me." And so Harry had looked at the boy and said, "Get that nonsense out of your head, Corporal. Keep your mind on seeing that girlfriend again, that pretty one you told me about." Harry was about to add that he understood, to confess that there were nights when thoughts of Emily were so strong he almost couldn't sleep, couldn't talk, couldn't even breathe. Emily, and a spot along the Mattagash River where the fucking birches grew thick and the kingfishers fished and the sun shone yellow on a clear blue water with no poisonous snakes, no floating sampans loaded with VC. But before Harry could say any of that stuff, Wally McGee had made his own confession. "That's just it, Sarge," Wally said. "There *is* no girl. There's never gonna be one. When I enlisted, there was this guy I met at basic. I don't know how he knew what I was feeling inside, but he did. He helped me to understand why I didn't care if I ever dated a girl again in my life." And that's when Sergeant Harold Plunkett had told Corporal Wallace McGee to shut the fuck up. That's even how he said it. "Shut the fuck up, Corporal. It's all bullshit anyway. Hell, you're the best man I got. How can you sit there and tell me you're a queer?" And that's when Wally McGee had punched Harry's arm, all grins. "Shit, you believed that stuff, Sarge? Man, you are some gullible. Hey, I got a sampan dealership in Philly I want to sell you." Then Wally had picked up his rifle and started cleaning it. As Harry watched, all of that manhood he admired in the young corporal was back. It was back and filling up any weak places that had allowed him to speak his heart. And Harry could see that Wally McGee had perfected this role, this act, this protective cover he had put up around himself. At least, Harry could see it *now*. But he didn't see it that night as the jungle closed in around them and the river ran dark and shimmering under a full moon. All he wanted then was to go home to Emily. And he wanted to believe that strong and masculine young men like Corporal Wallace McGee were what they presented to the world, just as Harry wanted to believe that the United States of America was what *it* presented to the world. It was all about democracy, and he still believed that when the helicopter, that metallic Freedom Bird, lifted him up out of the muck, the blood and the feces, the sweat of fear, and soared him over the dead and dying bodies below. He was lifted out of the insanity with a hole in his side that would eventually heal and a bigger one in his soul that would never heal. What did he regret most in his life, Blanche had asked him, what act? That he didn't know how to comfort Corporal Wallace McGee. That he was too scared to give up any of his own manhood at that fragile moment in time. He had wanted to tell Emily about what happened as morning was breaking some forty summers ago, at a spot halfway around the globe. He wanted to tell her all about Wally and what the boy had done as dawn crept over the jungle, bringing with it the dark, moving shapes of small men who blended into the trees, men with arms that could look like unmoving branches, fingers like vines, eyes like fireflies. Men who became the jungle because it was their mother. He wanted to tell Emily this so that maybe Wally would disappear from the nightmares that lived inside Harry's head.

"Hey, you, what are you thinking?" he heard Blanche ask.

Her body had melted into his, soft and warm. She was part of him now.

"Oh, nothing," Harry answered.

Tommy Gifford's dog lifted its nose into the air and sniffed, using those thousands more receptors than humans have for smell, using the keen olfactory sense its ancestors had given it down through the ages. The wind was bringing the dog an important message. Its brain was picking up the smells in layers until it had an answer as to what was nearby. Cologne. Body sweat. Cigarette smoke. That's when he knew for certain that the man was standing at the end of the bridge again. The dog's life was now mostly smell. For the first year, he had truly believed that each human being who appeared would be the one who would untie the rope. That was the year of the fast-wagging tail and happy eyes. Gradually, when the humans only tossed their table scraps on the ground beside his doghouse, a few stopping to pat him on the head, he grew to understand that these visits were not about him, not about his heart anyway. They were about his stomach and keeping him alive. The tail became cautious in the second year, wagging slowly as the eyes looked for a sign that maybe that day would be different. Someone would undo the rope and he would be free to run. In the third year, the dog had given up on the humans. But at night, cramped inside his house, mosquitoes vying for a spot beneath the hairs on his rump, he still dreamed of running. He would scale the bank along the creek, then burst out across that open field he had seen once, the day his rope broke and he made a run for freedom. But they had caught him and brought him back. The rope was replaced by a steel chain and the reality of *running*, that notion of using the legs to propel the body forward, seeped into the dog's subconscious mind and became the stuff that dreams are made on. This is why, when the man first stopped to touch him and later feed him, it meant little to the dog. Only when the man undid the chain and walked him, let him feel his legs moving again, did the dog sense a change in its heart. He began to believe, as dogs are quite able to do, that he would soon be free. Each time he saw the man walking toward him, he felt his tail wagging as it did in the old way. That's when the dog would stand on its back legs, learning happiness again.

"Look what I got for you, boy," said Billy. He reached into his pocket and pulled out a doggy bag from the Golden Dragon. In it were some chunks of meat left over from the spare ribs he and Buck couldn't finish, along with a few greasy bones. As Billy stood, watching the dog gulp down the pieces of meat, he was overwhelmed with sadness, and it was not just for the dog, but for his own captive way of life that was dragging him along, the chain pulling him closer to the edge of that cliff.

The half-moon had now risen well above the camel hump in the mountain behind the river. What Mattagash didn't see as it slept was a midnight blue Cadillac Deville that paused before the welcome sign, its yellow lights staring at the lettering as the occupants of the car commented on the artwork.

"It's like a big cow," said Raul Delgato.

"It's a moose, are you fucking blind?" asked Jorge Delgato.

Nature lesson over, the Cadillac moved on toward the belly of town, carrying with it the Delgato cousins of Portland, Maine. It drove slowly past Blanche's house. Next was Lydia Hatch's, where her grandson Owl lay asleep across the end of Lydia's bed, his cowlick pushed against the pillow, a wet thumb thrust into his mouth. It passed the old McKinnon homestead where Amy Joy Lawler was deep into her dreams. The old school was next, and then the Hart house, and Sheriff Ray's ranch-style. It rolled past Cell Phone Hill, which glistened with frost, and then Roderick and Edna's house, where even the twins were asleep in their identical bunks. At Orville and Meg's house, the retired mail car was pulled up close to the front porch.

The Cadillac and its yellow headlights paused at the lower end of the one-way bridge, as if the Caddy itself was uncertain about crossing such a narrow structure. Then the midnight blue car went forward slowly, its front tires inching up onto the bridge and following its two streams of light as it made its way across, not seeing or even thinking of the rushing river below. Its back tires came off the upper end of the bridge and the car sped up a bit, as if relief were pushing the gas pedal. Maybe this is why Jorge and Raul Delgato didn't see the darkened mailbox with *Thunder #46* written on it. Nor did they bother to look down on the flat by the river. If they had, they would have seen a small window of light shining forth from Billy Thunder's camper, the only light still on in Mattagash. What they were looking for in each passing yard was the classic white Mustang, hoping it might be parked in some driveway, its uniqueness announcing itself to the world.

Neither man felt the eyes of Tommy's chained dog or saw its warm breath coming in cloudy puffs from the doghouse as it watched from the end of its tether. The car rolled past the mailbox that had *Gifford #47* painted on its side. It then slowed for Florence Walker's sandwich board sign, pulling to a stop and idling, the gray exhaust fanning out from the muffler as the Delgato cousins studied the Word for the Week.

"That's a good word," said Jorge. He lifted the fifth of Bacardi from between his legs and drank from it, a quick snort. Then he reached into his pocket for a pack of cigarettes and beat one out.

He looked over at Raul, who was still studying the definition on the sign.

"For fuck's sake," said Jorge. "Stubborn. Unwilling to cooperate. What part of it don't you get?" Two years older and two years smarter is how Jorge saw his relationship with his cousin.

"You're the one who is cantankerous," said Raul. "You promised me there would be no gun. The Typhoon Cousins, remember?"

"We're too far from civilization not to have a gun," said Jorge. He reached beneath his seat and pulled out a Beretta 92FS, with a silencer attached to the threaded barrel. They were four hours into the journey up to Mattagash before he had revealed to Raul that the Beretta was riding with them.

"What if Thunder's not alone?" Raul asked, and saw his cousin shrug off the thought.

"I got plenty of bullets," said Jorge.

Raul shook his head, but at least this gun was registered to Jorge himself. It was Raul who had gone to jail over the last registered gun, and that had been for a mere robbery. He put the car back in gear and it went on, pausing at the sign that said *Dump*. Jorge nodded at the gravel road running behind the sign.

"Pull in here so I can take a piss," he said.

"But what if someone sees us?" asked Raul.

"Do you see anyone around, even a Big Foot?" asked Jorge. "There's more fucking traffic on Mars."

Raul put his blinker on, indicating a right turn. Jorge stared over at his cousin's face.

"A fucking blinker?" he asked. "Do you think that moose on the sign is following us?"

"It's just habit," said Raul.

The Cadillac rolled slowly down Dump Road, over gravel that crunched beneath its tires. Glistening spruce and pines grew close to the roadside, hugging the ditches with their branches which moved in the wind. Beyond and above the trees, the night was filled with pinpoints of flickering stars and the white half-moon.

"Dude, this is one spooky place," said Raul. He wished now they had put the Typhoon baseball bat in the front seat and not in the trunk. And maybe the Beretta wasn't such a bad idea.

"Pull over right here," Jorge said, and pointed to a wide berth in the road. "Or get ready to be sprayed."

Raul quickly pulled the car to the side of the road and put it in park. He reached for his own cigarette and lit it. His lighter snapped shut in the darkness with a heavy *click*, as if a trapdoor had closed. He looked over at Jorge, who was searching for the door handle.

"What if we don't find him?" Raul asked. Jorge stopped patting the side of his door and looked back at his cousin. As Raul drew on his cigarette, Jorge saw his features well, the tight jawline, the eyes, saw that his cousin was actually afraid. He smiled.

"Spoken like a true city boy," said Jorge. "We could find a fucking pimple in a town this small. That Mustang is a sitting duck. It's your fault we didn't get up here before dark." He went back at the door, groping about until he found the handle. The door opened and light flooded the car. Raul watched as Jorge moved his heavy body forward in the seat so that he could lean over enough to get his right leg out. He rested there, his breathing strained.

"Dude, you need to go on a fucking diet," said Raul. "Not yet forty and you walk like Grandpa Delgato."

With a great grunt, Jorge lifted himself from the car. He shook his arms to straighten his trench coat, then turned and gazed back into the car at his cousin.

"If an Amtrak train comes along, be sure to get out of its way," said Jorge, and slammed the door. Raul smiled. He reached for the bottle Jorge had left on the seat. It would be a good story to tell in the bars back in Portland, how they even crossed a fucking one-way bridge after they saw a moose on a welcome sign. He got out of the car, the bottle still in his hand. Jorge was standing a few feet away, his back to him. Raul heard the sound of pants unzipping and then a heavy stream of urine being released. No one would want to be sprayed by Jorge Delgato. That would be like being sprayed with a fire hose. Maybe even pissed on a by a moose. He took a long hit off the bottle before recapping it. Above his head, the sky over Mattagash was flickering with stars.

"What the fuck is that?" he asked. He heard Jorge zipping up his pants.

"What the fuck is what?" Jorge asked.

"That long white thing," said Raul, and pointed up into the mass of thick stars over his head. Jorge looked up too, and for a few chilly seconds, the Delgato cousins pondered the marvel of the Milky Way.

"It looks like a big ribbon," said Jorge.

"Maybe pollution," said Raul.

"Global warming," said Jorge.

"Like acid rain and shit," said Raul.

It was right then, as Jorge started to deliver one of the many jokes he always had for his cousin, that he knew something had gone wrong in his chest. He brought a hand up to his heart and felt the pressure of it beating beneath his coat. Panicked, he reached his other arm toward Raul, beckoning to him, hoping to tell him with a gesture what his mouth could not speak. He would not say what he had planned to say seconds earlier. *How the fuck would you know what acid rain is? You got lost in Caribou, Maine*. It was true. They had driven around the small so-called "city" of Caribou for an hour, trying to find the one road that led north to Mattagash. Annoyed, and even hungrier, they had finally pulled into Miller's Restaurant and availed themselves of a couple steaks, a baked potato each, and the endless salad bar. And they had enjoyed the pretty waitresses, flirting with them until closing time and the restaurant doors shut behind them. Raul had wanted to get a motel room and sleep it off. But Jorge, being older and wiser, felt that striking at night would be the best tactic. Visit Billy Thunder when he least expected them. *How the fuck would you know what acid rain is? You got lost in Caribou.* Jorge was still reaching his hand, gesturing to Raul. *Help* is all Jorge Delgato wanted to say now.

Raul saw the outstretched hand. "No fucking way," he said. "You been drinking all the way up here. It's almost gone, dude. Let me have another hit first." Raul turned his back on his cousin. Bacardi bottle in his hand, he again stood looking upward, his eyes trying to trace the Milky Way across the sky to its end. "It's like a long white scarf," Raul said. "Like Grandma Delgato used to wear to confession."

Raul heard the deadly thump against the side of the car as Jorge's body struck full force and then pitched backward, two hundred and forty pounds of dead weight. He dropped the bottle in the road and raced around the front of the Cadillac, reaching out both hands, desperate to help his cousin. But Jorge, or George Delgato as his birth certificate stated, was now flat on his back, both eyes open and staring up at the Milky Way, staring into that heaven of stars so big and shiny in Mattagash. Raul dropped to his knees beside his cousin and reached for his wrist. He knew people in movies felt for a pulse, but he didn't really know what a pulse was supposed to feel like. *Fast*, like someone knocking on an apartment door, the police maybe? Or *slow*? Like raindrops dripping from the eaves of your girlfriend's house, irritating the hell out of you, especially if you're there to hide from the police. Or is it the heart you listen to first? He leaned closer then and put an ear to Jorge's chest. Nothing, no rumbling heartbeat, no steady heartbeat, nothing. Raul scrambled back across the gravel road in front of the car, feeling with his hands until he touched the Bacardi bottle. He quickly brought it over to his cousin and put the lip of the bottle to Jorge's mouth.

"Drink this, Jorge," Raul whispered, his voice close to a whimper. He had seen this done in films too, but usually it was because someone was freezing to death in Alaska, after a plane crash. Or they were having a leg amputated in a Civil War film. The rum ran down the sides of Jorge's cold and unmoving mouth. "You bastard, this better not be a joke."

But Raul knew it was no joke. He had heard the thud of the body against the car, the awful grunt when Jorge hit the frozen ground. Raul reached into his pocket and pulled out his cell phone. He banged out the numbers, *9-1-1*, all three luminous and shining like the stars overhead, glittering and magical in the black of night. But all he heard was the dull tone that told him no reception. He put the phone back in his pocket and leaned close to Jorge's face, listening for a sign of life. Nothing. He tried again to feel a pulse, *fast*, *slow*, *medium*, any kind of pulse. He stood, letting his cousin's cold hand drop back to his chest. He hurried around the car and slid again into the driver's seat. He pushed the switch for the headlights and both beams shot forward into the night. Trees glistened in the gleam, the frost sparkling. Raul jumped out of the car and looked frantically for the light of a house, a trailer, a cabin, a camp, a hut, a tent, a cave, wherever these hicks must live. Only stars stared back at him, and that half-moon, now so white it seemed made of paper and nailed to the sky. Ahead, at the side of the road, a sign stood out in the swatch of light from the headlights. *Dead End*.

Raul went back and knelt beside his cousin. This time, he put his face against Jorge's cheek, felt with his own warm and living skin how quickly the body grows cold once it gives itself up to death. This thought frightened him instantly, causing him to pull back with a gasp, almost a loathing. And then he felt ashamed. This was his cousin. But already a stiffness had come into Jorge's body, changing it as death claimed the body for its own. He tried lifting Jorge, maybe get him up and into the backseat of the car. But even if Jorge Delgato had been alive and helping, Raul would have difficulty getting his hefty cousin to sit up, much less stand. He felt beads of perspiration forming on his forehead, growing instantly cold. He could drive back the way they'd come until he found a house with a light on, even if that was all the way to Caribou. He could knock on someone's door and rouse them from sleep. He could tell them, "My cousin had a heart attack. Call an ambulance." He could do that. Yes, that's what he would do. He took one of Jorge's large hands into his own, trying to warm it, even though a part of him was repulsed by the weight of death, its heaviness. He had only touched one dead person, his Grandma Delgato in her casket, that day he put the yellow fly swatter by her side, and even that had been an accident. He would never forget the chalky blue lips, the white of her hands that lay buried in a mound of prayer beads.

Raul drank again from the bottle as he sat there on the gravel road and did what Jorge had always encouraged him to do. He used his brain.

"He's already dead," Raul said, speaking softly, as if maybe the stars could hear, or the winter animals that had settled deep into the trees and brush for the night. "The police will come with the ambulance. They'll ask what we're doing here. They'll run a check on me. And now I got that fucking Beretta that maybe Jorge registered in his name and maybe he didn't. Maybe it's even registered to a *Raul* Delgato. And what will Billy Thunder tell them?"

Raul drank more of the rum and when a dog began to bark, a distant yelp that rang along the riverbank, he wondered if it might be a wolf. Or worse yet, a wolf that was now informing an entire pack of wolves that a man from the city was sitting flat on his ass in the middle of a dead-end road that led to a dump. Wolves talk to each other. They would drag him past the dump and into the thick trees. Maybe someone, some mountain man with shaggy hair and yellow teeth, would find his bleached bones in the spring. He leaned over Jorge again, this time forcing his hand to go deep into the shirt pocket. Only cigarettes. In the coat pocket was where Jorge kept his wallet. Everyone who knew Jorge Delgato knew this fact, for Jorge was too fat to sit on a wallet if it was in his hip pocket. Raul pulled the wallet out fast, as if something might bite his hand if it lingered, and slipped it inside his own coat pocket. With no identification on the body, it would give him time to get out of that awful place, get back to the warm lights of Portland where he could think more clearly. *Use your brain for once, Raul. That's why God put one inside your head, even if it's not a very big one.* He could hear Jorge's voice, his constant nagging. But now he was thinking fast and more like Jorge. He couldn't stay there and wait for the police to come. Jorge would know that and would understand. Raul looked up into the heaven of blinking stars, distant and cold. He wondered if Jorge was already up there with God and the Blessed Virgin. True, he walked slow on earth, being a fat man, but surely the soul is weightless, fast as a runner. Surely, Jorge would be putting his make on the Virgin Mary by now. He liked to brag about that, with the others gathered around to listen, admiring him. "First thing I'll do when I get to heaven is make sure everyone has a good reason to start calling her just *Mary*." But maybe, maybe it was Grandma Delgato who met Jorge at the Pearly Gates, and she was beating him all over the head and neck right then with that yellow fly swatter she used on her grandsons every time they got into trouble.

"Jorge, are you up there?" Raul asked the heavens. "Can you

hear me, dude?" Autumn wind beat down the gravel road and the branches of the roadside trees seemed to reach in, wanting to touch him. "I gotta leave you, Cuz," Raul said. "I got no choice."

The only reply was another bark of the distant dog, an answer that came riding on more cold wind, a wind that made Raul shiver in the chill of its bite. Jorge would leave *him*, no doubt about that, if it were the other way around. Shit, Jorge would leave if Raul were still alive and breathing and hanging onto his cousin's pant leg, begging him to stay. Jorge would head for a breakfast steak at Miller's and another glimpse of the pretty Caribou waitresses. Jorge always thought of himself first. He had let Raul take the rap how many times now since they were boys in grammar school? Even when he stole Grandma Delgato's wedding ring and pawned it in grade seven, he had blamed it on Raul. And Raul had taken the blame, being younger and wanting his cousin's acceptance. Raul Delgato had felt the yellow fly swatter all one day and into the next over that wedding ring. And what about the three times Raul had spent in jail, the first because it was *his* checkbook Jorge had taken and written out all those bogus checks. And the second because it was Jorge who dared him to use the Typhoon on the ATM machine outside the Portland bank. "You're like a scared girl, Raul. Grandma Delgato has bigger balls than you do. Come on, no one is watching you." How could Raul know that a camera was watching him? And the third time, at the convenience store, the one owned by that old man with bushy, white eyebrows, a man as old as Grandpa Delgato, an old man crying and praying, his hands held high as Raul emptied the cash register—*that* time, the gun was registered to a Ralph Delgato and not a George Delgato. And then, two days earlier, who had to pay for the broken lamps at Walmart, when it was Jorge who batted the fucking softball toward Lightning Fixtures in the first place? The more Raul sat at his dead cousin's side, the more he remembered the yellow fly swatter and the angrier he became.

"Fuck you, dude," said Raul.

Tommy Gifford's dog was the only living thing that saw the Cadillac arrive, and it was the only living thing that saw it leave, when the red taillights cautiously approached the glistening one-way bridge, crossed slowly, and then disappeared past the moose on the sign, until eventually the sound of its engine died away.

12

SUNDAY MORNING

Edna was awake before Roderick. She lay in bed, feeling the weight and warmth of the cat that was sleeping on top of her feet. Mr. Whiskers. On top of Roderick's feet was Mrs. Paws. Just as she had her favorite cat and Roderick had his, so the cats had their favorite person. Had the humans decided on a favorite cat first, or was it that the cats had already picked a favorite human? It was this special attention from Mr. Whiskers that always prompted Edna to give him his bowl of food first in the mornings. She heard Roderick pulling himself out of sleep and toward the waking world. It was his morning to sleep in, often staying in bed until eight o'clock. Those were the mornings she'd slip out of bed, put the TV on with the sports news, and then go downstairs to make pancakes and coffee. Then she'd bring breakfast upstairs on a tray. "What did I do to deserve this?" Roderick would ask, pushing the pillow up behind his back, taking the fork she offered, then tearing into the pancakes and syrup.

There had been good mornings, hadn't there, in the past? And wasn't the divorce rate in America high enough already without Edna adding to it? She'd read the statistics in a magazine at her dentist's office. For first marriages, it's 41 percent. For second marriages, it's 60 percent, and for third, it's 73 percent. No wonder Bertina wasn't getting any better at matrimony. The percentages were against her. And then, four states don't even report divorce rates and one was California. Surely, if California threw *their* numbers into the lot, the percentages would blow up. Hollywood was out there somewhere.

Edna heard Roderick do that Sunday morning grunt that always woke him up, followed by a peddling with his feet that sent Mrs. Paws into a tizzy. The cat jumped then from the bed, padded across the room and out the door. Roderick turned over to look at Edna, folded his pillow, and tucked it under his head for support.

"Morning," he said. "You been awake long?"

"Not long," said Edna.

"What're you thinking?" He said this almost cautiously, having been told too often and too honestly over the past few days exactly what her thoughts were.

"Oh, I don't know," said Edna. "Lots of things."

"Well, I'll tell you what I been thinking," said Roderick. "That maybe you and me could go on a second honeymoon. We never really had a first one, not with your Aunt Mildred with us. Maybe we could go somewhere down along the ocean."

Edna thought about that. The ocean. It was a thing she knew nothing about, unless it was something she read or saw on television. She had always imagined that the ocean was like a big dog, rolling over, licking and lapping. A dog that could turn and bite if you weren't careful.

"I don't know," she said. "Tommy says there are towns down on the ocean where everyone paints their house white and their shutters black. The whole town." She wondered what color house Ward Hooper lived in. Was it white with black shutters? But then, Bangor was a safe distance from the ocean.

Roderick let this thought play through his mind.

"You sure it's not Russia he's talking about?" he asked. "Where the communists live?"

"He says they call it Downeast," said Edna. "He trucks through there now and then. But maybe he's pulling my leg."

"I'm glad I don't live on the ocean," said Roderick. "At least a river lets you do what you want to."

Edna smiled. When he said things like that, it helped her remember why it was she had fallen in love with Roderick Plunkett, tall and slim in his army uniform. It was his good heart and his solid way of thinking, even if it wasn't a fancy way of thinking.

"I bet seagulls shit on white houses as easy as the colored ones," Roderick added.

She wished he had stopped with the river line.

"I'll think about a trip," Edna said. "But I can't promise anything."

"Okay, honey," said Roderick. He reached out and touched her arm.

"Want some pancakes in bed?" Edna asked.

Harry had been hearing the distant sounds of northern ravens all morning, the grating *pruk-pruk-pruk*. There seemed to be a whole flock of them, their excited calls rolling in from across the river and down from the hill behind his house. The dawn had come alive with ravens, as if born on their wings. But Harry was still asleep, and this outward sound, this concept from the waking world, reminded him of other birds, another time. That's when he heard the voice. Not all nightmares happen at night. Harry knew this well. They happen when the conscious mind lets down its guard, lowers the drawbridge over the moat. That's the place where sorrow lives, deep in that castle of the subconscious. It lives there with guilt and hate and love and the ability to kill another human being as easily as save him.

He heard it clearly, that young and energized voice, so excited to learn more about the world they were destroying by the second. *The Crow Pheasant is a glossy black bird, somewhat clumsy, that inhabits forests where it can stalk and hide. Hey, Sarge, that sounds like us. We're clumsy, and we stalk and hide.* That was the first time they'd heard the orchestra sound filling the night, echoing through the jungle. "What the hell is that?" Wilson, from St. Louis, had wanted to know. "Holy shit, it sounds like a marching band." And Wally McGee had gotten out one of his nature books. *Man, listen to this. Two birds will often synchronize their call, coop coop coop, and soon the jungle is an orchestra of sounds. That's what we're hearing, Wilson. A whole bunch of Crow Pheasants. God, I hope this stuff we're dumping on the jungle doesn't kill everything that's alive.*

So, this morning it was Agent Orange? He never knew what Wally might want to talk about until he arrived in Harry's dreams. Corporal Wallace McGee was the most outspoken soldier, the one who asked the right questions, even if he never got any answers. *What the hell are they dropping, Sarge?* Now, almost forty years after he left Vietnam for good, Sergeant Harold Plunkett knew the answers. Because the Ho Chi Minh Trail was nothing more than a tunnel through the jungle, the military came up with an ingenious plan to destroy those canopies of plants and shrubs that enemy troops were hiding beneath. The idea was to wipe out the ground cover, so they could pick off the enemy from the air and reduce the chance of ambush on the ground. And yet, they didn't know what it was they were dropping on the jungle. Agent Orange was a defoliant, a chemical stored in canisters with orange stripes, thus the name. Planes flying overhead dropped the poison and American soldiers walked blindly into it. Hardest hit were troops on the ground, sometimes being sprayed with the stuff while they were in the field. The U.S. Army even tried to blame the first signs of illness on the people of Vietnam themselves.

They must be up to some nasty tricks, those slant-eyed bastards. It killed the jungle all right, but it also killed birds and animals and fish. Back in 1968, Wally McGee had already guessed this would happen. His Philadelphia father was a chemist. *The vegetation is dead. Cattle and fish are floating belly-up in the river. This is dioxin, Sarge.* But the military gave its assurance, its word. There was no need to worry. Agent Orange wasn't harmful to humans. So the soldiers drank the water, they walked through the dust, they wore it on their clothes for weeks at a time.

Harry heard the ravens again, a flock of them, distant and excited. Maybe they saw a carcass on the roadside. Ravens tell other ravens where the food is. They invite each other over all the time. *Pruk-pruk-pruk.* He knew sweat was forming on his forehead. His subconscious mind was telling his conscious mind this fact, was informing it. *Coop-coop-coop.* He was falling upward to the sound of the ravens, coming closer to waking. He even knew at this point that Blanche was asleep in bed beside him. But his mind was still in that other place where not even ravens can follow. *Some things heal with time, Corporal. Here are facts you don't know, you being gone for all these years. The mangrove forests are almost like they were before we dropped all that shit on them. They're different, but they're thriving. And the Crow Pheasant is back again, hiding and stalking. Can you believe how strong nature is? Did you know she wants to live that much? Why can't people come back like forests, Wally? Why do people have to stay dead?*

When Harry opened his eyes, he heard the ravens along the trees now on this side of the river. Maybe a coyote killed a deer during the night. There was always something dying so that something else could live. He glanced around the bedroom, a quick search as he always did. Then he looked over at Blanche, who was staring up at him, her eyes sleepy and loving. Harry took a deep breath. This time it was Agent Orange and the Crow

Pheasant. Sometimes, it was the old *Papa-san*, his eyes glossy with pain. Other times, it was the village of faces they had come upon during one patrol, everything dead—women, children, even the dogs and chickens. Sometimes, it was the jungle itself, its dark and murky mysteries, its lush and green surprises, the sounds of plants and creatures within it growing, living, dying, feeding off each other, fighting for those thin strands of sunlight. Who knew, when the dreams came, what they might bring? Sometimes, it was that first VC Harry killed, a month after he was deployed to Vietnam. For a lot of years, the nightmares and flashbacks had become so rare that Sergeant Harold Plunkett thought he might be free of them at last. But in the past few days, they were coming back with more and more frequency, and Wally seemed to be the one bringing them, as if he were carrying them in a knapsack on his back. Like Ed Lawler's ghost over at the old school, Corporal Wally McGee was getting around. He was back in uniform and stalking through the jungle of Harry's subconscious mind. *Don't you have anyone to talk to?* Billy Thunder had asked that day he came to get the Mustang fixed. Well, Harry had a lot of people.

He felt Blanche move next to him, pushing her body closer, letting it curve into his. She was now a part of him that he'd been missing for so long. He felt her fingers touching his face, tracing the line of his cheekbone.

"Who's Wally?" she asked. "Who's the corporal you were talking to?"

Harry felt the weight of his body drawing him downward. Mekong Delta. June 1968. A sticky night that was building toward a muggy dawn. *Shit, you believed that stuff, Sarge? Hey, I got a sampan dealership in Philly I want to sell you.*

Harry looked down at Blanche.

"Did you promise to make breakfast at your house?" he asked. "Or was that one of those night-before lies?"

Billy slept with the dog at his side. Sun was now leaking through the window of the camper, so he threw one arm over his eyes to keep it out. It was far too early for him to get up, what with no job and no reason beyond coffee. He and the dog had had a busy night. First of all, Billy figured Tommy Gifford wouldn't think to look for the animal until he tossed his supper scraps on the ground. And maybe not even then. Billy could return the dog long before that. It wasn't really stealing; it was only borrowing. And when it didn't bark at everything that moved, Tommy would appreciate that. So Billy had taken the dog the night before, on his way back from meeting Meg on the bridge. He brought it into his camper and then poured himself a glass of Jack Daniels. When his glass was empty, he had poured another. And why the hell not on a Saturday night? While the dog lay on the bed chewing on a new rawhide bone, Billy sat at the table and took out a yellow legal pad. He found a pen. Before he started to write, he finished the Jack and poured himself a third glass. No ice. He liked his Jack like his women, straight-up and honest. And who was counting if he had a couple more shots as he wrote a letter to Tommy Gifford?

With sun now coming in at him from all angles of the camper's windows, Billy gave up and opened his eyes. The letter for Tommy was still on the table, and he smiled, remembering how drunk he was the night before when he wrote it. He would tear it up before he returned the dog to its chain. Sober, he realized there was no place in his life for a pet. He had no home of his own and no steady job. He lay then with the dog beside him on the narrow bed, its paws on his chest. When it whined, Billy reached for a folded blanket on the foot of his bed and covered it. The animal's body heat felt good against his side. He pulled his arm in closer, hugging the dog to him. He felt it relax. Billy was good with animals because he could think like them. He knew they had deep emotions. When he first saw the dog chained in Tommy's yard, he imagined himself in its place. And that's how he *knew* how the dog felt. He knew that after a time, as the years passed, the dog began to see the chain as a part of its body, an extension that had grown there, another tail, another mystery of life for it to ponder. And that's when Billy had written the letter, drunk on Jack and sentimental as a girl.

Dear Tommy Gifford. Thank you for the table scraps and for the doghouse with a leak in its roof. This note is to tell you that I am leaving. I would have liked to be the pick of the litter, the pup that got a good family. Call me crazy, but I think the legs I was born with were meant to run. Please don't come looking for me. And please get a stuffed dog if all you want is something to tie to your house.

In school, when Billy was still bright with promise, his English teacher encouraged him to write poems and stories. That seemed like several lifetimes ago now, and that was too many lifetimes for someone still not thirty years old. After Billy brushed his teeth, he would tear up the letter. He would get the dog back to Tommy's in a matter of minutes. And he would come back to the camper for a good long nap. It was far too early to take on the world.

It was on his way back from church that Sheriff Ray Monihan Sr. decided to turn right on Dump Road and follow it to its end, see if any mischief had taken place there during the night. It had been a busy week, ever since the full harvest moon that past Friday night. People went a little crazy under the full moon, and a harvest moon was an extra dollop of nuttiness. But even with no moon, the dump had become a hot spot where habitual drinkers liked to stop and toss out their bottles. At first this worked fine since the Women's Committee held a monthly bottle drive and appreciated the windfall. But then some of the younger boys, ruffians like the Plunkett twins, started hanging out there afternoons after school. Their favorite trick was to stand empty beer bottles up on rocks and throw stones to break them. Even those dark-skinned Florida granddaughters of Sal Gifford would turn up to break bottles right along with the boys. As town sheriff, Ray Monihan had warned the youngsters, but, being youngsters, they'd ignored him. And that wasn't the only disrespect. Behind his back they called him "sheriff without a cell phone." This was because Andy Griffith had been called "sheriff without a gun" on Ray's favorite television show. Sometimes, Ray would find *Mayberry Sheriff* written in the dust of his car door or across the trunk, by a finger belonging to some prankster.

Ray was looking up at the blue sky that seemed to be held up by the tips of evergreens and wondering if it might snow *that* night when he saw something large and dark lying in the road in front of him. It looked a lot like a body. Maybe a large man. His first thought was that it was another prank. They'd played a lot of tricks on him that past summer alone, as if he were Barney Fife or something. There had been a woman's purse sitting in the road so Ray stopped the sheriff's car and got out to retrieve it. When he was six feet from it, the purse bounded into the woods. Ray could hear the giggles and grunts, along with branches and twigs snapping, as the scalawags ran for cover. Tying a rope to a purse and baiting passersby. Ray's own generation knew that trick and yet he'd fallen for it several times over the past few years, once with a hammer and again with a brown teddy bear. His biggest scare had been a practical joke that still steamed him when he thought back to it. He had come upon what looked like a child in a blue dress lying dead in the road, struck by some heartless hit-and-run driver. Ray had braked the car so fast he felt his dentures move forward in his mouth. Racing to the victim's side, he discovered it was only somebody's old walking doll plastered with red ketchup.

So, on that cold Sunday morning of bright blue sky, Ray supposed that what looked like a large body lying on the road meant that the kids had graduated to bigger jokes. They probably used an old pair of their father's work pants, a worn-out coat, some straw, and a lot of imagination. Instead of anger, he felt a certain pride that Mattagash youth could be so creative, for it certainly *did* look like a real body. Ray slowed the car to a crawl. Pulling alongside the motionless heap, he braked and opened his door for a closer examination. And that's when Sheriff Ray Monihan realized that what looked like the dead body of a big man was, in fact, *the dead body of a big man*. The face and hands were the only exposed flesh and they were grayish-blue, as if a layer of tinted glass covered the skin. The eyes were open and staring upward, the eyeballs like frosted marbles.

Ray Monihan shut the door to his car and leaned back in his seat. He had to calm himself so he could think. Had Andy Griffith ever come upon a dead body? No, he hadn't. Even that bungling fool Barney Fife hadn't, and that's because Mayberry wasn't the kind of place that would *allow* dead bodies. Andy never even got called to a home where an elderly man or woman had expired, as Ray Monihan had. Nobody seemed to age in Mayberry, much less die.

Ray slowly opened the car door so he could get a better look, make sure he saw what he thought he saw. Grayish-blue skin, marble eyes, big man over two hundred pounds, black overcoat, black shoes. This time he noticed a Bacardi bottle that lay a few feet away, the morning sun reflecting from its green glass. Ray shut the door again. He felt his breath grating inside his chest, that feeling of hyperventilation coming on.

"Stay calm," Ray told himself. He knew he had to call an ambulance as his first move. But even if he wasn't the sheriff without a cell phone, even if he *owned* one, he would still have to drive to Cell Phone Hill to get it to work since Mattagash had no reception for cell phones. His house was on the other side of the bridge. He didn't want to leave the body alone to drive home and make the call. Find a nearby house with a telephone!

Ray Monihan drove forward fifty feet so as not to run over the body and kill it again. Then he spun his car around in the road, a genuine cop turn. He wouldn't use the blue light, let alone the siren. If he did, all of Mattagash would jump into their cars and pickups and follow him, wanting to know what the trouble was. A thought occurred to him. What if the body was grayish-blue but *alive*? All the more reason to keep things quiet until he could get a Watertown ambulance to come roaring up Dump Road with its red light blaring. Then and only then would he call the Watertown Police Department for reinforcements. After all, Watertown had had a dozen dead bodies already, not to mention a couple of flashers. Other than the natural deaths of a few elderly folk, this was Ray Monihan's first genuine 10-54. *Possible dead body*. In truth, Ray knew that the man lying in the road was a *definite dead body*. But he didn't know the code for that.

The sheriff's car cut a wide arc around the body and then sped off. At the mouth of Dump Road, Ray braked, wondering at which house he could stop to make a call. It would have to be one whose owner was small-mouthed enough to keep a 10-54 to himself. That's when he saw Orville Craft's car coming. It was just passing Henry Plunkett's house and looking like it was out of a job now that Orville was retired. Ray put the sheriff's car in park. He jumped out, waving both arms.

Orville had felt a loneliness all morning, it being Sunday. There was never mail to deliver on a Sunday, and still, each Sunday he would feel that itch to get back on the job. Monday always came around with its letters and packages and stamps. He always had Monday to count on in the past, but now Monday didn't belong to him anymore. What had he been thinking of that he retired sooner than he had to? Why didn't he wait until, bony and half-blind, unable to see the white line in the road ahead of him, the villagers had come with torches and pitchforks to force him out of the job as mailman?

So Orville had finished his breakfast and, nothing but time on his hands, decided to take a ride. Meg had been reading a magazine and giving him sweet looks over the top of it, and he was thinking what a lucky man he was after all, until the loneliness hit him. "Why don't you go for a drive," Meg said. "It'll do you good. I'm cozy right here on the sofa." So he had gone, past all the mailboxes that he could identify blindfolded just by the sound of their opening doors. He didn't mind the regulation-shaped boxes along the road that had been made pretty. There was Rita Plunkett's, with a painted red cardinal sitting among white cherry blossoms. Verna's, with its lighthouse scene from the ocean. Gretchen's had all those painted violets winding around its borders. And no one in town had quite figured out what was on Lydia Hatch's box since she had turned Owl loose on it with a brush and a can of paint. Some days, Orville saw birds and flowers, other days spiders and snakes. But most were plain silver mailboxes with plain red flags, and that was enough. What he had learned about mailboxes was that a bill from J. C. Penney or a notice from the bank went inside the fancy ones as easily as into the plain old silver ones.

Orville had driven past the widows and divorcees he'd no longer have as clients. He turned at Buck Fennelson's house before he ran out of tarred road. On his way back, he passed the trailer park. He passed Harry Plunkett's house, where it sat high on the bank of the river, paying no mind to the mailbox that no longer concerned him. He passed Blanche's Cafe, which was busy with its usual after-church breakfast crowd. He passed Rita and Henry's house, and that's when he saw Sheriff Ray Monihan standing at the mouth of Dump Road. Ray was wearing his official sheriff's jacket and waving both arms like he was Raggedy Andy.

Orville pulled his car over and put it in park. He slid his window down. Ray came around the car and peered in at him.

"Keep calm," said Ray. "For God's sake, don't panic."

"Okay," said Orville. "What is it?"

"Keep your wits about you," said Ray.

"Well, I don't have a reason to lose them," said Orville. "Do I?"

Ray took a deep breath.

"There's a dead body lying on Dump Road," he said. "A big man I've never seen before. You need to go telephone an ambulance. But don't let anyone else know until we get that body out of here."

The tingling Orville felt now was on the nape of his neck. He saw Ray Monihan step back from the mail car, only it wasn't a mail car anymore. It was just *a car*, and that's something else Orville had felt on his morning drive. He could sense the pride gone out of his vehicle, as if, like an aging horse that knows it can no longer pull the cart, it's ready for the bullet. He threw the car into gear and clamped down hard on the accelerator pedal. Employed once again, the Ford Taurus tore off from the sign that said *Dump Road* faster than Orville intended it to. It flew past *cantankerous* and took the curve before the bridge in what would be considered dangerous driving by anyone over thirteen. Orville hoped with all his heart that, this early on a Sunday, no other vehicle would be approaching the other end of the bridge. To hell with bridge protocol, for Orville doubted he could stop at that speed. But the bridge was clear, and he crossed so fast the rails were a blur.

His own house was the logical place to make the call, given it sat not far below the bridge. He hoped Meg was asleep on the sofa, using a lazy Sunday to finish her magazine. He didn't want to think the worst of Meg, especially not then—*twice a month, two times in thirty days*—but he was afraid she'd get on the phone to her niece Lillian about the emergency call Orville had just made for an ambulance. And Lillian would call Rita. Who would call Verna. Who would call Dorrie. Who would then get on her direct line to Fox News. By this time, the body would be given a name and even a reason for being dead. He slowed the car when he saw his own mailbox up ahead. A small red car sat in their driveway, one that belonged to none other than Meg's niece. Even if he could trust Meg and Lillian to be mum for an hour, they were probably on the computer right then, shopping for frying pans and necklaces, and taking up the one phone line into the house. Then Orville remembered his cell phone, still safely in his glove compartment, and the fact that Cell Phone Hill was less than a quarter mile past his house. Orville hit the gas and hoped Meg didn't bother to look out and see his car flying by.

It was still too early for any lovers or adulterers, thieves and scoundrels, or folks running for elected office to be up on Cell Phone Hill, so Orville had the place to himself. He parked in the circular space at the top, then rummaged in the glove compartment until he found his cell phone. He beeped it on and was relieved to see that it was still charged. He had only used the phone a few times, such as when he had to call Edwin Beecher about a postal question. Did Ray Monihan tell him to dial 9-1-1? No, he hadn't. He told him to dial the ambulance directly. Orville thought fast and figured that Ray hadn't wanted those women with police scanners listening in on this important call. No problem, he would dial the Watertown Ambulance Service directly, and at the next town meeting, he would mention again how it might be time that Mattagash got its own ambulance. What was the number? He had stored it in his speed-dial feature after Ray Monihan suggested he do so, given that Orville came across all sorts of emergencies and near-emergencies while on his deliveries, from a genuine car wreck to cows running amok and chickens roosting in a mailbox.

Orville stared down at the cell phone in his hand, at the nine numbers that represented speed dial. There had been a little memory device he had used in picking those numbers for certain people, a personal attachment to each that made sense. For instance, he'd chosen the number one for his home phone since that meant Meg. And he'd chosen number two for Marcy since she was his second child. But now he couldn't remember who the rest of the numbers were for. Marcy had warned him about this when she gave him the cell phone for his birthday. "Write the names next to the numbers on the card so you can remember them," she said. "It's not about age, Daddy. We're all forgetful."

Orville studied the numbers from three to nine. On a whim he pushed eight, listened to the phone ring twice, and frowned as Debby answered. She was his firstborn, and he never wanted to call her on his cell phone since she now lived in Arizona and his low-rate calling plan only worked on his home phone. Why did he even put Debby in there in the first place? Probably because if Marcy happened to mention to Debby that she was on her father's speed dial, it would hurt Debby's feelings to learn that *she* was not. Orville hung up on Debby. He pushed four, although he was quite certain it was not a number he had assigned to the ambulance service. After a couple rings he heard Ernie Fisk say, "Fisk's Garage, this is Ernie, can you hold a second?" Ernie put him on hold. Good. Orville clicked off the connection. The number three stared up at him, teasing him. Sure, Orville could call someone and ask them to look the number up. Or he could go ahead and dial 9-1-1 and set the scanners to buzzing all over northern Maine. But something in him born of his ancestor's genes, those stubborn old Mattagash genes, made Orville want his speed dial to work, damn it. He knew he had to hurry. Not that the dead body was going anywhere, but Ray Monihan might, such as up to heaven from a heart attack.

Instead of pushing three, Orville decided to eliminate one more number first, giving him better odds. He pushed six, just to be sure it was the request line at the country music radio station in Watertown.

"WWTR, for the best country music in northern Maine," said a woman's voice. "What's your request, please?"

Orville looked around, making sure no one had arrived on the hill to hear him.

"Can you play that song by Faith Hill?" he asked. "It's called 'Breathe.'" It wasn't so much that he liked the song, even though he requested it twice a week. He just liked saying Faith Hill's name from the top of Cell Phone Hill.

Orville hung up and stared at the three, the five, the seven, the nine. Now he was certain of nothing. Could it be possible that the two was not Marcy? He punched the two and Marcy answered on the first ring.

"Sorry, honey," said Orville. "I dialed the wrong number."

"See, Daddy, I told you to write down the names of—"

Orville pushed End and left Marcy in midsentence. What good was speed dial if it took so damn long? He pushed seven and heard Frank Finley answer at the St. Leonard Fire Station.

"Frank, it's Orville," he said. "Sorry, I dialed the wrong number. I'm trying to call the Watertown ambulance. It's an emergency. I'll talk to you later." He hung up. If he had told Frank Finley there was a dead body lying on Dump Road, Frank would've started up the dusty fire truck and knocked down a couple mailboxes on his way to Mattagash. The brake linings on a fire truck should be reserved for a fire.

Orville looked back down at the list of numbers. He had three, five, and nine left. He studied them, and then picked the five.

"Taylor's Lumber Company," someone said. Probably Lester Taylor's son who worked for his father. When he and Meg built a back porch on the house that past summer, all their supplies had come from Taylor's. "We're not here to take your call right now, so please leave a message at the beep."

Orville clicked off the connection. He stared cautiously at the nine and the three before pushing the nine. It rang once before Orville remembered that nine was Hair Today, the salon owned by Verna Craft where Dorrie Mullins worked as receptionist. Horrified, as if the phone had actually burned his hand, he pushed End. It was bad enough he had to talk to Dorrie once a month, when he made an appointment for his regular trim. Then he remembered that it was Sunday. The salon would be closed.

One number left. As his finger was about to push three, which he now knew for certain would cause a phone to ring at the ambulance service in Watertown, Orville's own cell phone bleated. It surprised him so that he threw the skinny thing onto the floor of his car. Maybe the dead body itself was now ringing him up. "Hey, Bud, where's that ambulance?"

The phone rang four more times before Orville managed to find it, down there among the floor mats and knobs and levers. He pushed the Receive button.

"Hello?" he said.

"Orville, did you just call Hair Today?" Dorrie Mullins herself.

"No," Orville lied. He hung up and pushed the three before Dorrie could make his cell phone ring again. He listened to two bleats before Ray Monihan Jr. answered, with that girlish voice of his.

"Blanche's Café," said Ray Ray. "Can I help you?"

Blanche's. When had he put that number in speed dial? It wasn't like he called ahead to have his blueberry pie waiting at the end of a workday. Regardless, he now had Ray Ray on the phone, and Ray Ray was even more excitable than his father.

"Hello there, Ray Junior, this is Orville Craft," he said. "How are you this morning?"

"Crazy," said Ray Ray. "We just finished the breakfast rush."

"Is Blanche there?"

"She's off today," said Ray Ray. "I'm busy here, Orville. Talk fast."

"Ray Ray, listen to me," said Orville. "I'm on official business, on your father's orders. I need you to look up the Watertown Ambulance phone number for me. Can you do that?"

"Wait a minute," said Ray Ray, very impatient. He must have put the phone down on the counter, for Orville heard the clatter of dishes in the background. A woman laughed loudly. He figured it was one of the two waitresses who worked the Sunday after-church breakfast rush. Then Ray Ray was back.

"I can't find the phone book," he said. "I'll have to call you back. But Daddy knows the number by heart."

"I know, but he had to stay with the dead body," said Orville. Then he winced.

"What dead body?" asked Ray Ray.

"Get me the fucking number," said Orville.

"Did you just *swear*?" Ray Ray asked.

Orville clicked off the phone and closed his eyes. Not even on the baseball team or in the locker room during his high school years had he ever used that word. He slid his window down an inch and let in cold air, the kind that clears your nostrils just to breathe it. His phone bleated again, and again Orville jumped. It was such a whining, sniveling sound, nothing like an old-fashioned phone. It sounded in pain, maybe because it was so skinny and thin. Malnourished. Anorexic, even. *Thank God for Ray Ray* was what Orville was thinking when he said hello and heard Dorrie's voice.

"Did you just hang up on me *again*?" Dorrie was using her annoyed tone.

"No," Orville lied a second time. He could be easily unnerved by Dorrie. When they were kids in school, she had the largest scab from her smallpox shot of the entire class.

"Then why did your number come up twice on this phone?" Dorrie asked. "Besides, we're closed. I dropped by to pick up some shampoo. What did you want?"

Orville sighed. Technology had not been invented for the likes of Dorrie Mullins, she who was credited with first bringing *feng shui* to Mattagash. With eyes on the back of her head and equipped internally with radar, Dorrie didn't need any help from science.

"I wanted you to not call me back, Dorrie," said Orville. "That's why I hung up before you answered."

"So you *did* hang up on me," said Dorrie. "Be sarcastic all you want, Orville, but this phone's been ringing off the hook for the past five minutes and it's all your fault. Getting everyone in town all riled up over a body."

"And what body would that be, Dorrie?" Orville asked.

"The one Ray Monihan found lying dead in the middle of Dump Road," said Dorrie. "Thanks to me, the ambulance is on its way."

Orville felt despair creeping in as he sat there in his car, a skinny apparatus stuck to his ear, alone up on Cell Phone Hill. From up there, he could look down at the world. He could even see the spire of the Protestant church where he and Meg had gotten married, and where both his parents now lay buried in the graveyard behind. Meg's parents were buried there too. He could see the old school with its red bricks and its black-shingled roof. He could even see the small building that was now Hair Today, with its lavender sign out front that held the salon's full name. *Hair Today, Curls Tomorrow*. He imagined Dorrie inside, resting on her plump elbows as if they were pillows as she talked on the phone. Why Booster got a prescription for Viagra was another of those mysterious ways under which God often worked. Saltpeter would be Orville's choice.

"It was Frank Finley who called me first," Dorrie was saying now. "He wanted to know why you needed an emergency ambulance. So I called the sheriff's house and there was no answer. So I tried Gretchen's number, and Gretchen said you went tearing off the bridge like you were Paul Revere. Then I called Meg and she has no idea where you are, but she did get a call from Debby down in Arizona that you were trying to reach her. But Debby couldn't call you back 'cause your cell phone's been busy. So I called Rita Plunkett and asked her to do a drive-through. Rita found Ray Monihan standing by the sign to Dump Road. He told Rita she couldn't go up there because she might run over a dead body and that *you* had gone to call an ambulance."

Orville had almost gone to sleep, lulled by cold air seeping in the crack of his window and meeting up with warm air coming from the car's heater. He was also lulled by the lullaby of Dorrie's droning voice. This was his own fault. He had to hint to Frank Finley that something big and dramatic was afloat in the morning air, didn't he? He had to brag, giving in to that ages-old battle between the fire station and the post office, they with their shiny, yellow coats and loud, red truck and important-looking hats. Miles and miles of hose. Those tall boots. That ladder. The occasional Dalmatian if someone happened to buy one as a pet. How can stamps and envelopes and a pen hooked to the counter by a chain compete with all that?

It had been his own bragging that did him in.

"Big mouth," Orville said, forgetting that the cell phone was grafted to his ear.

"What did you call me?" Dorrie asked.

At the mouth of the road leading up to Cell Phone Hill, Orville braked to see if any traffic might be coming and there certainly *was* traffic. He sat and waited while the St. Leonard fire truck went flying by, its red light blaring and its siren wailing. Driving the truck was its usual driver, John Rainey, one of St. Leonard's volunteers. On the back of the truck was Frank Finley himself, hanging on to the ladder and wearing that shiny, yellow slicker his wife had bought him for Christmas.

Faith Hill was singing the last chorus of "Breathe" as Orville crossed the bridge. At the sign that said *Dump Road*, he saw that a dozen cars were parked pell-mell along the roadside. Ray Monihan's car was driven lengthwise across the mouth of the road, blocking traffic, its blue light swirling around inside the glass bubble on top. Ray was leaning against the hood, looking all hands-and-feet nervous. Spectators were out of their vehicles and standing around in the road, talking to Ray or smoking cigarettes. Orville pulled over and parked where he would be least seen. He picked up his cell phone again and glanced down at the numbers on it. He took a deep breath and pushed number one. When Meg answered the phone, he would assure her that he was all right.

He would tell her using that male voice he brought out for family emergencies—a baritone but calm so as not to frighten her—that he would be home *once the dead body has been removed.* He heard someone answering at the other end of that invisible wire.

"Watertown Ambulance," said a female voice. "Is this an emergency?"

"People!" Sheriff Ray Monihan shouted, his hands cupping his mouth. "Please listen. I'm going back to wait by the body until the ambulance comes. I'll take Frank Finley and the fire truck with me. I want the rest of you to stay here like well-behaved citizens." When Ray got into his car, a disgruntled roar went up from the spectators. They had waited ten minutes and felt that was enough time for any well-behaved citizens. As Ray's car turned and headed back up Dump Road, its blue light flashing, a couple dozen cars were following him.

The dead body hadn't gone anywhere, and it was most definitely dead when Ray leaned over it, cautiously, and gave it a good look. He had already run a crime-scene ribbon across the road, tying one of the yellow plastic ends to a spruce on the left side of the road and a leafless aspen on the right. That's when he realized that he should take some photographs. Where was his camera? On his kitchen counter, that's where. Ray Ray had borrowed it to take pictures of a chipmunk that was coming to their bird feeder. He watched as Frank Finley backed the dusty fire truck up to the yellow ribbon, an attempt to hold back the spectators and keep the crime scene pristine.

"Come on, Ray, we won't touch him," said Bobby Fennelson.

"Maybe we can identify him," said a tall, willowy man Ray had never seen before.

"Hell, I can't even identify *you*," said Ray. He blamed this on the fact that too many sons-of-bitches were moving to Mattagash, buying up land on the river and populating the woods with camps and noisy four-wheelers.

"Does he have a wallet?" asked Rita Plunkett. "His license will have his name on it." With each question and comment, they pressed forward as a group, some whispering, others talking loudly. Ray heard a radio playing somewhere.

"Stay back, folks, this is official business," he said. On the words "official business," the yellow ribbon broke and one end went curling back to the leafless aspen. Before Sheriff Monihan could issue another useless order, people had crowded around the body and were gazing down at it. Gasps were heard. Verna Craft began to cry. Sounds rose up of more cars coming, gravel spitting beneath tires in a hurry. One engine sounded like a loud mosquito as Ray Ray's little red VW Bug screamed to a halt behind Tommy Gifford's truck with its gigantic tires.

"Step back so I can guard the body!" Sheriff Monihan shouted now. But no one seemed to be listening to him. If Dorrie called the ambulance only ten minutes earlier, it would be another half hour before it arrived. How could he contain a mob for that long?

Orville Craft stepped up to the line of people circling the body. He had planned to go home, disappointment in his pockets, but that need to *see* brought him back. A quick look and he'd be on his way, beat the traffic jam that was sure to occur.

"Who is he?" someone asked. And that began a new refrain that rippled through the crowd with more people offering their opinions.

"He looks like a hoodlum," said Phillip Craft.

"Do you think it was murder?" asked Mickey Hart.

"There's no sign of foul play," said Ray. He felt better now, calmer, the sight of the dead man wearing off as others were now repulsed by it.

"He could be a terrorist," said Dorrie Mullins. She was staring down at the body with great solemnity, one of the few women who was able to scrutinize it without any crying or screaming, or even fainting, as Verna Craft had just done.

"By the looks of that rum bottle," said Ray Monihan, "I suspect the only thing this man terrorized was his own teetotaling mother."

"That's Bacardi," said Tommy and before Ray could say anything, Tommy Gifford had leaned down and picked up Exhibit B, the body itself being Exhibit A.

"Give me that!" Ray grabbed for the bottle, but Tommy passed it to Kenny, who passed it to Ray Ray, who passed it to Rita, who passed it to the tall, willowy man who, when he'd had a good look, finally passed it to Frank Finley.

"Here," said Frank, and gave the bottle to Sheriff Monihan.

"Gosh darn it," said Ray. "How many fingerprints do you suppose this bottle has on it now? That makes all of you accessories after the fact. Is there anyone left who hasn't touched this bottle who would like to?"

"I haven't touched it," said Orville.

"Orville, I was joking," said Ray. He took the bottle by its top, holding it with two fingers as he placed it in the trunk of his car.

"Want me to load him into the fire truck?" asked Frank. "Just till the ambulance gets here?" He gave Ray Monihan a hungry look that told Ray all he needed to know. Frank the fireman wanted the body, as Orville the postman had wanted it. But Ray the sheriff was going to hang on tight to his first dead man.

13

SUNDAY, HIGH NOON

Harry and Blanche had enjoyed a late breakfast, this time with Harry sitting at her kitchen table, rather than on one of the four café stools. He kissed her good-bye at the front door.

"I'll see you tonight," he said.

As he backed out of the drive, Harry waved and saw Blanche wave back. Then he gave the truck some gas and headed for the bridge, on his way home to the house that sat high on the hill.

When Orville Craft reached the mouth of Dump Road, he turned left, in the direction of the bridge. He hoped Meg wouldn't be too disappointed when she heard how her husband had sat like a cuckold on the top of Cell Phone Hill. Orville had no doubt that the events of this day would be told over the years, a story passed down from generation to generation, like a fragile egg. And that's what was on his mind, that and the general feeling of despair that seemed to follow him around since he retired.

Harry Plunkett passed Cell Phone Hill and then Orville and Meg Craft's little blue house.

Orville Craft passed Tommy Gifford's house with its chained dog and then glanced down to see Billy Thunder's car sitting beneath a blue tarp, next to his camper by the river.

Harry Plunkett's front tires hit the lower end of the Mattagash bridge as Orville Craft's front tires hit the upper end. Perhaps if a camera had been filming the event, using photo finish as is done at horse races and car races, a technique to tell which horse's head or which front bumper was first, there would have been a definite answer as to *who* had the right-of-way that day. But there were no such cameras. There weren't even witnesses since they were all up on Dump Road staring down at a dead man.

To Harry, it appeared that his tires had hit the bridge first and therefore he had the right-of-way. The same thing appeared true to Orville, about his own tires and his own inalienable rights. The maroon pickup truck rolled slowly across the bridge toward the blue car that was rolling as well. When no more than ten feet separated the vehicles, they both stopped.

Harry sat behind the wheel of his truck, staring at Orville, who was staring back. When Orville tooted, Harry tooted back. Orville tooted two more times, to which Harry answered with two toots of his own. Orville put his car in park. He got out and slammed the door. He would be teased about speed dial to eternity. And he was certain the story of his being fed a blue pill by Billy Thunder was all over town. To have these insults topped by Harry Plunkett forcing him to back off the bridge was too much to ask any man. He approached Harry's window, which Harry promptly wound down.

"Is something wrong with your reverse?" Harry asked.

"Back up," said Orville. "I was on the bridge first."

"No, you weren't," said Harry.

"Listen, Plunkett," said Orville. "This is more serious than you realize. The Watertown ambulance is about to come flying up to this bridge any second now. Ray Monihan found a dead body on Dump Road this morning. Some tourist."

Harry figured this was true, or it wasn't.

"Then you'd better back up," he said, "so the ambulance can get through."

"I'm not going to do it," said Orville, and he was pleased to hear that his voice sounded as if he meant it. Maybe this was what Billy Thunder's best gift to him had been. He was a man again, the head of his house, a husband. *Twice a month. Two times in thirty days.* "You're breaking the law."

"No, I'm not," said Harry. "I was on the bridge first."

"No, you weren't," said Orville.

They were blasted with the sound of a horn and Harry looked into his rearview mirror to see Buck Fennelson's old green pickup waiting to cross the bridge. Harry leaned out his window.

"Orville won't back up!" Harry yelled.

Another car was approaching the bridge behind Buck's truck, and Harry saw that it was his nephew, Roderick Plunkett.

"Back up, Orville!" shouted Buck.

Orville strode back to his car, got in, and turned off the engine. As if his hand couldn't help it, he laid it on the horn and let the thing blast for several seconds. Then he again got out of the car. He dangled his keys in the air so Harry could see them before he turned and flung the keys off the bridge.

Harry, Buck, and Roderick watched in amazement as the keys reached their apex, sun catching the pretty silver, before they dropped below sight and into the river below. Then Orville got back into his car and slammed the door. Harry didn't know what to say. This wasn't the mailman he knew. He had actually been ready to tell Buck and Roderick to back up, so he could too. He had been about to let Orville win this one. But Orville had just stepped on his good intentions.

Harry pulled his own keys from the ignition and slipped them into his jacket pocket. He opened the door to his pickup and slid out. He walked over to Orville's car and tapped on the glass.

But when Orville hit the window button, nothing happened. No keys meant no ignition, and no ignition meant no window going down. Orville peered out through the glass at Harry.

"What is *wrong* with you?" asked Harry.

"What's wrong with *you*? Back up so we can both go home."

"Well, you'll have to get a ride," said Harry. "You threw your keys in the river."

"That would be my problem, wouldn't it?" said Orville. As Harry watched, he hit the lock button and locked his door. At least those still worked.

Harry stood staring down at Orville Craft and thinking. Buck appeared at his side.

"Can't we push him off the bridge?" asked Buck.

"Not if he keeps it in park," Harry answered, "and his foot on the brake."

"How about a tow truck from the other end?" asked Roderick.

"That could work," said Harry. "Maybe Tommy Gifford's pickup could do it."

Orville was listening to all this and wondering why he had thrown his keys into the river, why he hadn't backed up before anyone saw the gridlock on the bridge. He could be home with Meg, using up one of those two monthly guarantees to help him over the blues he was feeling. Harry was right. What was wrong with him? He saw Myrtle Hart's car pulling onto the upper end of the bridge and rolling slowly toward him. Myrtle stopped a couple feet from Orville's bumper, put the car in park, and got out.

"What's going on here?" she asked.

"Orville threw his keys off the bridge," said Buck.

Myrtle tapped on the glass of Orville's car.

"Are you okay, Orville?" she asked.

"He can't put his window down," said Harry. "He's a product of our modern age."

"Tell Plunkett to back up so we can all be on our way," Orville shouted out at Myrtle, who turned and looked at Harry.

"Back up, Harry," said Myrtle. "You're being childish."

"I was on the bridge first," said Harry.

In his mirror, Orville saw more cars pulling up behind Myrtle's.

"What's going on?" he heard someone ask.

"Orville Craft threw his keys into the river," said Buck.

"Orville won't back up," said Myrtle.

How does it happen, Orville wondered, that a man can be driving home to his wife one minute, and the next he's trapped on a one-way bridge, keyless, an object of ridicule? But maybe this latest pitfall would turn things around for him. Surely, growing cold and hungry, bored with the sight of a wounded and bleeding mailman, a retired one at that, the rabble would then turn on Harry Plunkett. That's when he saw Harry reach into his jacket pocket, pull out his own keys, and toss them over the side of the bridge. Orville watched, entranced, as the keys flew high into the air, turning ass over end, until they fell toward the river below. He felt locked inside a slow motion dream and not a real-life Mexican standoff on the Mattagash bridge. In his rear mirror he saw irritated faces peering at him from behind windshields. Why were people so angry these days? Angry and in a hurry. What had happened to the world that there now existed something called *road rage*? Had there been *horse rage* or maybe *wagon rage* in Grandfather Craft's day? No, of course there hadn't. It was as if the whole planet was now on some kind of speed pill.

Myrtle tapped on Orville's window.

"Do you want me to get Meg?" she asked. Orville dreaded to even think of this happening. He hadn't considered Meg, had he, when he hurled his keys over the railing of the bridge? Harry caught the look on Orville's face.

"That's a good idea," Harry said. "Go get Meg. Just walk on

across the bridge and you'll be at her house in less than two minutes. Won't she, Orville?"

Orville felt the small car growing dizzy around him. Sure, Harry Plunkett would love to get Meg Hart out there on the bridge to see her husband humiliated. That was the source of the trouble between them in the first place, the teasing, the jealousy. Orville had stolen Meg at the school dance just as Harry Plunkett was about to make his move on her. Meg was the spoils of war. Go get Meg, indeed.

Myrtle gave Orville a sharp look before she headed off, walking, across the bridge.

"You're really gonna get it now," said Harry.

Orville felt as if he might cry. How did he get into this mess? A mixture of things. First the impending retirement, then the transmuted moose mailbox, then the Viagra, then the *real* retirement, then Meg's amazing promise, then the dead body, then speed dial. Looking back, it was a wonder he was as calm as he had been until Myrtle went to squeal on him. That's when he saw the purple Bronco belonging to Dorrie Mullins pulling up behind the line of cars that had accumulated behind him, at the upper end of the bridge.

Orville clicked the lock that would lock *all* the doors on the car.

Dorrie came up alongside Orville's car and peered in at him, as if maybe he were an exotic animal trapped in glass.

"Move it," said Dorrie. "And move it now."

Orville imagined his little car being lifted up in her hands, another of those stories where human beings find amazing strength in times of stress. Or maybe she would use *feng shui* on him, what her husband had been calling *feng shit*, ever since Dorrie began moving his favorite chair around the living room in search of better *chi*. She would hurl Orville over the bridge, and he would land upside down in the river, able to peer out his window and see his keys lying next to some fish before he drowned. He put his head back against the seat and closed his eyes.

"Orville, wake up." It was Ray Monihan peering at him now through the glass. When news arrived of the standoff on the bridge, Ray had left the body up on Dump Road with Frank Finley riding shotgun over it. He wasn't worried since Frank couldn't go anywhere with it if the bridge was blocked. "The ambulance is gonna need to get through."

Orville cracked his door open an inch.

"Make Harry back up," he said. "I was on the bridge first." Then he shut his door again and locked it.

Ray turned to Harry, who shook his head. Bets were now being placed by Roderick and the others as to who would back up first. That Meg might be on her way to the bridge had made the game more interesting.

Ray went around Orville's car to the passenger door. He heard the clicking sound that meant Orville had unlocked it, so he opened the door and got in. Orville clicked the lock back on as Ray settled into his seat.

"What's going on here?" Ray asked.

Orville hunched his shoulders.

"I don't know," he answered honestly. "I guess I ran out of self-control."

The sheriff nodded. There was nothing more pathetic than a man in that position.

"This thing with you and Harry," said Ray. "What's the cause of it anyway?"

"It started in 1962," said Orville. He could hear the painful wail of the ambulance now. It must be close to the house where he and Meg had lived peaceably for so long. "Harry was going to ask Meg to dance, but I beat him to it."

Ray looked over at Orville, studied his face.

"Harry Plunkett wanted to dance with Meg?"

Orville nodded.

"We were at the graduation dance at school," he said. "It was the year both Meg and Harry graduated. Someone put 'The Mashed Potato Song' on the record player, and Harry started walking toward Meg, you know, to make his move. That's when I stepped in and asked Meg to dance with me instead."

"Is there really a Mashed Potato dance?" Ray asked.

"Sure there is," said Orville. "First, you grind one foot down on the floor, like you might be putting out a cigarette butt and trying to pull it back toward you at the same time. Then, you step down on the other foot and do it all over again." Ray said nothing for a few seconds. He was thinking back to his own school dances. He wished the school was still up and running, like the old days. He listened to the sound of the siren getting closer. Harry and Meg? He couldn't see it. Nor could he imagine Harry Plunkett doing something called the Mashed Potato. A waltz, maybe. Possibly the twist.

"And then," Orville continued, "I wouldn't let him fish at my pond and you know how Harry likes to fish."

"There's trout all over northern Maine," said Ray. "Lakes and rivers chock-full. Harry don't need to fish in your pond."

The ambulance roared up to the end of the bridge and screeched to a halt. The driver had turned off his siren now, seeing that the bridge was impassable.

"But my pond is stocked," said Orville. "Big trout begging for the hook. And it's *my* pond and Harry's got it in for me over Meg."

"Well, the ambulance is here," said Ray. "You gonna back up?"

"Sorry, Ray," said Orville. "Besides, my keys are in the river."

Ray got out of the car and heard the door lock behind him. He walked over to Harry's pickup.

"Any chance you might back up?" asked Ray.

"There's already five hundred dollars in the pot," said Harry. "I can't do it, Ray. These guys work hard for their money."

Ray nodded that he understood. He saw the driver of the ambulance now making his way past the line-up of vehicles on the bridge, headed for the middle. Dorrie came up from the rear and tapped Ray on the shoulder.

"You need to get everyone to back up, one at a time, and then get the tow truck to pull these two cantankerous fools off the bridge," said Dorrie.

"I'll handle this in my own way," said Ray.

"Are you the sheriff?" the ambulance driver asked. He had someone else with him, one of those important-looking medics, all anxious to give mouth-to-mouth.

"My guy is deader than a doornail," said Ray. He was thinking fast. "We got us a plugged bridge here, as you can see. I'm gonna have to walk the body across to the ambulance. You got one of them stretchers you can lend us?"

"Are you insane?" asked Dorrie. "Pull Orville and Harry off the bridge."

"Dorrie, I'm the sheriff in this town," said Ray, "and I'll make the decisions."

"You're only the sheriff until our next town meeting," said Dorrie.

"I need five or six strong men!" Ray yelled to the crowd and saw Tommy Gifford and Buck Fennelson step forward from the lower end of the bridge. Phillip Craft and Kenny Barker and Mickey Hart moved in from the upper end.

Meg Craft came running past the pickups and cars until she reached the middle of the bridge. She looked at Harry, who was leaning against his truck, drinking a soft drink. Then she looked at Ray.

"Where's Orville?" she asked.

"In there," said Ray. Orville waved when Meg saw him. She went over to the car and rapped on the window.

"Orville, have you gone wacky?" she asked.

Buck and Phillip arrived with a stretcher, and Ray motioned them to take it on across the bridge.

"My car is parked over there," Ray said. "And Tommy's got his pickup. You can put the stretcher in the back of the pickup and ride with me."

Ray looked then for the driver of the Watertown ambulance and saw him talking up Little Lucy, who was now twenty-two and probably the prettiest girl in Mattagash. All curves and blue eyes. Ray went over to the driver.

"Wait for us," he said. "We'll be back in twenty minutes with the body. We gotta walk it a quarter of a mile."

Orville wished he could turn on the radio, block out conversation that might cause him to buckle. It was time to make a stand or leave town forever. But Meg banging on his window and urging him to give up was not helping matters. If he could turn on his radio and if his cell phone worked from the bridge, he'd press number six and get the country station to play Faith Hill again. He imagined Faith singing and that helped him concentrate. *I can feel you breathe, washing over me*. Meg was pounding on his glass now.

"Damn it, Orville, this has gone on long enough," she said. "Back this car up."

"I don't have any keys," Orville shouted out at her.

"What?" asked Meg. "What happened to your keys?"

"He threw them in the river," said Harry. "They're probably lying right next to where I threw mine."

Meg turned on Harry now.

"You," she said. "This is your fault, always teasing him. Why don't you grow up, Harry Plunkett?"

Orville smiled. Meg taking up for him like that, and against Harry, the man she might have married if Orville hadn't been able to do the Mashed Potato so well.

"I was on the bridge first," said Harry.

"Who cares who was first?" said Meg. "You're not teenage boys, for heaven's sake." She looked back at Orville and pointed her finger at him. "You're in big trouble, mister." She turned and went back past Harry Plunkett's truck and the dozen other vehicles, along with the ambulance, that were now piled up and waiting at the lower end of the bridge. Orville watched her elbows getting smaller until she disappeared into the crowd.

Billy Thunder had been sleeping in as usual until the thought of a late breakfast at Blanche's pulled him awake. He had showered in the cold and cramped bathroom, then blow-dried his hair so that it wouldn't freeze to his head. Pulling on the winter jacket Buck had given him, he grabbed his pack of cigarettes and stepped outside. He was about to pull the tarp off the Mustang and fire it up until he heard voices coming from the bridge.

"What the hell?" Billy said. Cars and pickups and people lined the entire length, as well as the road leading up to each end. Half of them were facing the lower end of the bridge and half were facing the upper end. It must be an accident of some kind. In the middle of the bridge, Orville Craft's car sat staring at Harry Plunkett's pickup truck. Billy left the Mustang sitting where it was. In less than a minute, he had climbed the hill and was now pushing his way to the center of the bridge.

"Got a cigarette, Billy?" someone asked, and he looked to see one of Roderick's twins. Roddy or Ricky, he had no idea.

"You're too young to smoke," said Billy. He saw Harry

Plunkett leaning against his truck, drinking a soft drink. Orville Craft peered out from inside his locked car as Billy walked past.

"What's going on?" Billy asked Little Lucy, who was talking to a guy wearing a white uniform. Billy hoped to ask Lucy out on a date soon, but he figured her mother, Big Lucy, would want a top on the Mustang before she let her daughter go.

"The sheriff found a dead body on Dump Road," said Little Lucy. "This guy has come to get it with the ambulance. But Orville and Harry met midway, and neither one will back up. So the sheriff and some of the guys went to get the body on a stretcher."

"Whoa," said Billy. "I slept through all that?"

"Here they come!" Lillian Hart shouted.

The sheriff's car was leading the five volunteer pallbearers who carried, shoulder-high, the stretcher with the dead body. The body itself was covered with a blue tarp Tommy Gifford had been using to protect his canoe. Bringing up the important rear and moving slowly so the walking men could set their own pace was the red fire truck with Frank Finley hanging on to the back ladder. A naughty finger had scrawled *Frank Sucks Hose* in the dust of the front door panel. The delegation rounded the small curve that led to the bridge. Seeing the strange sight, Tommy Gifford's chained dog went crazy barking at the end of its tether. Ray Monihan stopped his car, put it in park, and got out.

"People, move back so we can pass!" Ray shouted. The spectators, men and women and children, pushed back to the railings of the bridge and created a pathway.

"He's getting heavy, Ray," said Phillip Craft.

"This boy didn't miss too many meals," said Tommy. He grunted as he got a better hold on his side of the stretcher.

When Harry saw the pallbearers, he got into his pickup and closed the door. He'd seen enough dead bodies. The crowd could have this one. So he sat and read that week's paper as the men carried the stretcher onto the narrow bridge. They walked it past gawking faces and wide eyes and hands that reached out here and there to touch the blue tarp, ensuring that the story they told their grandchildren one day would be all the more historic. When the pallbearers reached Orville's car and Harry's pickup, the vehicles had taken up most of the passageway. They eased the stretcher over toward the upper railing so they could pass. Ray was ahead, moving people out, shooing them back. Curious, Orville leaned forward in his seat to watch.

"Hold still for a second," said Dorrie Mullins, who had appeared with a video camera held up to one eye. Then, "Turn him a little to the left."

"Put that camera away!" the sheriff yelled.

And that's when Roddy, or maybe it was Ricky, grabbed the end of the blue tarp and yanked it off the dead body. George Delgato, better known as *Jorge*, emerged in all his glory, the blue-gray skin, the eyes like frosted marbles, the gray-white lips. Dorrie stopped filming. There were gasps. Screams erupted. Billy Thunder could only stare at the rigid corpse, his own face expressionless.

There would be a debate for years as to what happened next and why. Some said that if Roddy Plunkett—or maybe it was his twin, Ricky—hadn't pulled off the tarp, it wouldn't have happened in the first place, since that one action put Buck Fennelson face to face with a dead man. That's when Buck panicked and dropped his hold on the stretcher, up at the important front end. Others accused Dorrie Mullins who, filming as she was, accidentally tripped Kenny Barker. There were even those who said it was Orville Craft's fault. When Mickey Hart put a hand onto the hood of the mail car to steady himself, Orville feared it might scratch his paint job. So he had tooted the horn, startling Mickey. *Whoever* caused it to happen didn't matter as much as *what* they caused to happen. Once Buck dropped his hold on the upper end and Kenny Barker, who was in line behind Buck, tripped and went reeling to his knees on the bridge, the whole team lost its equilibrium. They veered dangerously to the right and George Delgato's body, being big and heavy, pulled them off-balance. Given all these factors, there was no place the body could go but over the railing of the bridge and into the river.

For a few frozen seconds, as if waiting in unison for the splash that finally *did* come from below, no one spoke. Then, as if thinking the thought *en masse*, everyone rushed to the lower side of the bridge and looked down. George Delgato's body did, indeed, float for a few seconds until the strong river current pulled it under, the flap of the black trench coat finally disappearing beneath the surface.

14

SUNDAY AFTERNOON, 2:00 TO 5:00 P.M.

For over two hours, Ray Monihan and his un-deputized manpower searched for but could not find the body of George Delgato. Their canoes motored the circumference of the island where the river liked to carry dead logs and ice floes in the spring, and the occasional city trash thrown away by tourists. Ray and his men then followed the river three miles down to the Mattagash town sign, the one with the moose on it, a moose that seemed to see and know all things. But no body. As if anxious to get out of town, Jorge Delgato had gone undercover. The Watertown Police Department had been called, since it appeared that the dead body was no longer under Mattagash jurisdiction but was now a matter for the state police. A group of St. Leonard men were already in canoes and boats, loaded with nets and searching the river downward, where they were met by men in canoes and boats from Watertown, searching upward.

Sheriff Ray Monihan had lost his dead body. And by the time he got back to the Mattagash bridge, where the crowd had grown more impatient by the minute, he had lost control of the spectators. Some folks were still braving the outdoor cold, a *plein air* gathering. Others, mostly women, waited in their autos, motors on and heaters running. Orville Craft was still in his car, all the doors locked. Harry was sitting on the tailgate of his pickup truck, showing a magic trick to the boys who had gathered around him. Orville had listened to the excitement of the kids as Harry made a coin disappear into his elbow, then tied a knot in a rope without removing his hands from either end. Once, Harry even counted eleven fingers on his hands as the boys stared, fascinated. *He only has ten fingers, you little fools*, Orville thought. Then he was forced to watch as Harry made a match disappear inside a handkerchief.

Ray Monihan had already sighed so many times that day, ever since he found the body, that he had no energy for another one. But he certainly felt like sighing when he saw all the angry faces waiting for him to do something about the gridlock. And to make matters worse, Frank Finley was on the wrong side of the river with the St. Leonard fire truck.

"What if a house catches on fire?" Frank asked, three times in one minute.

"Call Watertown and tell them to cover for you," Ray said, as Frank followed him onto the bridge. There had been one fire in five years and it had to do with cheese bursting to flame atop some nachos in Verna Craft's oven. But Frank Finley was on call in his sleep.

Dorrie met the sheriff first.

"It's so cold out here it could snow," said Dorrie. "People want to go home and have a warm supper."

"Then go home, Dorrie, and have your supper by all means," said Ray. "Your vehicle is on the same side of the river as your house."

Ray made his way to the middle of the bridge where he stopped and leaned down to Orville's window. He rapped on the glass.

"Any chance you're ready to back up?" Ray asked. "I can get Tommy to pull you with his truck."

"No, but I'm ready to go ahead," said Orville. "He can push me if he wants."

"Doesn't Orville have to go to the bathroom?" Roddy Plunkett asked the sheriff.

"Maybe he's wearing Depends," said Ricky.

"What about flipping a coin?" asked Ray. "You can pick first for heads or tails."

"I don't like the fifty-fifty odds," said Orville. It was true. Where Harry was concerned, luck seemed to pile up on *his* side.

Ray found Harry sitting on the tailgate of his pickup truck. He didn't know who was the more stubborn of the two, just that they were both being very cantankerous. Before Ray could say anything, Harry looked up at him and grinned.

"The pot is now at twelve hundred bucks, Ray," he said. "The only ones betting on Orville are the women, and that's cause Dorrie sent word to Blanche."

That's when Harry saw her, the cascading hair, the sure walk she had. Blanche was wearing a green winter jacket and gloves and her faded jeans, slowly making her way across the bridge, past cars and trucks and people, until she reached Harry.

"I had no idea so much could happen while I was taking a bubble bath," said Blanche. She looked over at Orville, who nodded hello from inside his car.

"I might have to break our date tonight," Harry told Blanche.

"So, what's the story?" she asked.

"I was on the bridge first," said Harry. "But Orville won't back up."

Blanche went past Harry's pickup and over to Orville's car. She leaned down to his window.

"Hi, Blanche," said Orville. He had always liked Blanche. She made the best blueberry pie north of Bangor.

"Hi, Orville. You're not going to back up?"

"No," said Orville. "I can't do it, Blanche."

"I understand," said Blanche. "You gotta do what you gotta do."

She went back over to Harry.

"Are you going to back up?" Blanche asked. Harry shook his head.

"If I'm not at your place by 8 p.m., consider the date canceled, okay?"

"Okay," said Blanche. "Guess it'll be a rain check."

Harry smiled. This was one of the reasons he knew he could love Blanche Tyler. She thought like him. They both knew Dorrie Mullins was standing a few feet away, waiting for a victory that would never come. He watched as the green jacket disappeared back into the cars and faces at the lower end of the bridge.

"Okay, people, I want you to get into your vehicles," Ray was now instructing the crowd. "Then, one at a time and in an orderly fashion, I want you to back off the bridge. You can leave your autos in the field or at a friend's house. I'll give anyone a ride home if they live *above* the bridge. And I'll voucher you can find a friend to drive you home if you live *below* the bridge. Let's let these two men work this out."

A wave of protest shot across the bridge, coming from both ends and meeting in the middle. Even Orville was shocked. He had expected they would all back up so Tommy Gifford could come with his huge tires and pull Orville off the bridge. Harry would win.

Bobby Fennelson approached Ray, who was now in the process of instructing drivers to be careful as they reversed their vehicles.

"Don't back on anyone's toes, try not to bump into the bridge, and don't take any wooden nickels," Ray told them, hoping some levity might help.

"I wanna drive my truck home tonight," said Bobby. He was wearing his black cowboy hat. There was always more swagger in Bobby when he wore the Stetson than when he wore his sensible P. J. Irvine cap with the visor. "Now get those two old fuckers off the bridge, Ray."

"You're gonna have a heart attack, Bobby, if you don't slow down," said Ray.

"Listen to me," said Bobby. "Maybe Andy Griffith would've left two guys on a bridge to work stuff out. But he lived in Mayberry, and that ain't a real town, Ray. This is Mattagash. People have real needs here."

Sheriff Ray Monihan saw Dorrie approaching cars, talking to the drivers, and realized that she was in the midst of forming a protest group. So he let his traffic directing be for the moment and strode back to where he'd parked the sheriff car. In less than a minute, he was standing again in the middle of the bridge.

"I said to go home," Ray told his constituents. These were the people who voted every two years as to who should be the town's sheriff. Ray knew it was possible that the box next to *his* name would never see another X marked on it. "This situation will be resolved by morning."

Sheriff Ray Monihan raised his revolver and held it in the air over his head. Even Harry was surprised.

"I'm the sheriff without a cell phone, remember?" said Ray. "I'm not the sheriff without a gun."

Bobby Fennelson kicked the back tire of Orville's car.

"Ray, you are so full of shit," he said. "You don't have the balls to—" A bullet whizzed four feet above Bobby's cowboy hat. Ray figured it would probably come to earth somewhere near the camel hump on the back mountain. But for once there was silence, a stunned silence, but silence nonetheless. Then, Bobby straightened his cowboy hat.

"I guess I'll walk home and put a pizza in the oven," he said.

"See you tomorrow," said Ray.

Bobby Fennelson walked on across the bridge and off the lower end, headed in the direction of his house.

"He's not such a hothead," said Ray, "once you explain things to him."

As Harry and Orville watched, the crowd retreated, like an army recoiling itself. One by one, car engines roared to life. Frank Finley parked the fire truck in the field and hitched a ride back to St. Leonard with the ambulance driver. Little Lucy walked across the bridge and used Gretchen's car to drive home. Gretchen, in turn, used Lucy's car. Neighbor rode or walked with neighbor. Finally, there was just Ray and Harry and Orville left.

"I hope you two are off this bridge by the time Dorrie becomes sheriff," Ray said.

With everyone gone but his nemesis, that being a word Orville had learned from Florence fifteen weeks earlier, he saw no reason to remain in the car. He reached for his gloves and got out. Harry was back in his truck now and reading the rest of the weekly paper. Orville stood looking out over the bridge, breathing in the river air, and thinking how quiet the world had grown. In grandfather Dwight Craft's day, all communication would have shut down if the ferryboat hadn't been operating. Orville supposed someone could stand on one side of the bank and shout across the river news of a death or a baby being born. Or if a man had a canoe and an important need to cross the river, that could happen. But it would be a slow communication. Nowadays, those emails and instant messages jumped that river as if it were tinier than a mud puddle. That's when Orville heard Billy Thunder firing up the Mustang down on the flat by the birch trees.

The Mustang's tires hit the upper end of the bridge and the car rolled toward Orville's back bumper, where it stopped. Billy got out and slammed the door. He was wearing the earmuffs, which he took off. The bulky ski suit he borrowed from Buck lay folded on the passenger seat, as if Buck were still in it. In the backseat lay the personal items Billy could pack in a hurry. He walked over and stood next to Orville.

"Okay, I think understand this," said Billy. "I think it has to do with being as stubborn as our ancestors. But I need to get across this bridge. You and Harry can drive right back on once you let me pass. No one will ever know."

"Is this another one of Harry's magic tricks?" asked Orville.

"It's a family emergency down in Portland," Billy said, and it was not even a full lie. That the Delgatos had been in town looking for him the night before was obvious, and it was something he had never believed would happen. Raul must be back in Portland by now. If the cops knocked on his door, would he tell them about the brown boxes shipped north?

"I guess you weren't told," said Orville. "The keys to my car are in the river."

"Fuck," said Billy. He walked over to Harry's truck and rapped on the window. Harry cranked his window down.

"Don't even ask," said Harry.

And that's when they heard the commotion. Harry turned in his seat to look at the lower end of the bridge. Meg Craft was carrying a cake and followed by a half dozen women. Myrtle. Gretchen. Edna. Even Blanche was with them. In their arms were sacks and bags and plastic containers. Cars were now arriving again at the upper end of the bridge and more women were getting out, all carrying items. Little Lucy, Big Lucy, Verna. Meg's niece, Lillian, carried two folded blankets. Big Lucy had a lawn chair. In unison, the group began to sing.

"For he's a jolly good fellow, for he's a jolly good fellow."

"Oh shit," said Billy. "Here comes Orville's retirement party."

Harry shook his head. There were two things he had promised

himself he'd never be ambushed by again. The first was the Viet Cong, and the second was a group of women carrying a cake.

"See ya," said Billy, and hurried past Orville, who was grinning. Billy jumped into the Mustang, not bothering to open the door this time. He backed off the bridge as Tommy Gifford was pulling into his yard. Billy was thinking of going back to the camper to wait it out, just him and Miss October, when for some inexplicable reason, he drove the Mustang over to Tommy's house. The chained dog let off its usual volley of barks, especially when it saw Billy getting out of the Mustang. Tommy jumped down from his chariot-on-wheels, his feet hitting the ground hard. There had been another of those bets going around Blanche's Café, what month it would be that Tommy broke an ankle. The stakes rose when he won five grand with a lottery ticket and was now drinking more than usual.

"Shut the fuck up!" Tommy yelled at the dog, which was getting crazier by the second, yanking on its chain and trying to reach Billy. Tommy picked up a rock and hurled it at the animal. The dog disappeared, whimpering, to the other end of its chain. It sat on its haunches and watched.

"Want a beer?" Tommy asked.

"Sure," said Billy. Tommy reached up into his truck and pulled down a six-pack, passed it to Billy. Then he slid his rifle out from behind the seat.

"Let me take care of my dog first," said Tommy. "That's what I was about to do this morning until Ray found that body." He cracked open the rifle and pushed a bullet into the chamber. Billy looked first at the rifle, then over at the dog. It lowered its head and lay down to stare back at them.

"What do you mean?" Billy asked, but he knew.

"I ain't losing another night's sleep over my ex-wife's dog," said Tommy. "And I'm sick of people complaining about the barking."

He snapped the rifle shut. "Have yourself a beer. I'm gonna take him to the gravel pit behind the house. I'll be right back."

Billy wasn't sure what his move should be. Getting all teary-eyed over a mongrel, a mutt, wouldn't set well with someone like Tommy Gifford. The dog was cowering now as Tommy approached, as much afraid of him as it was of the gun he carried. Tommy was undoing the chain when Billy reached from behind and grabbed it.

"Hey, Tommy, I might as well take him off your hands," said Billy. "I mean, there's just me and Miss October living in the camper, now that Miss August and Miss September moved out. I could use some company." The dog, having Billy and his scent so close, jumped from its position and put both paws on Billy's chest, its tail wagging. Tommy watched this.

"He don't usually go to people," said Tommy.

"He's probably smelling that dog I dated Saturday night," said Billy.

Tommy smiled, but his eyes were thinking and Billy could read them well.

"What'll you give me for him?" Tommy asked. A poker game, if Billy ever saw one, and Billy knew poker. He knew the game so well he'd lost thousands of dollars to it.

"What do I have that you want?" asked Billy. He was thinking of pills maybe, if he could coax Kenny Barker to give him a few hits of speed. Maybe a bag of weed? He'd have to use the fake Viagra money to buy some pot from the guy in Watertown who'd been selling it until Billy put up his own shingle. A case of beer? He could afford that. And he'd throw Miss October into the pot as well, even though he had to drive all the way to Watertown to buy a *Playboy*. But before he could offer any of those things to Tommy Gifford, he knew what was going to happen. The dog was now licking Billy's hands, its tail wagging furiously, its nose sniffing at his jacket pocket as if maybe a treat were hidden there.

"Looks like you two are old friends," Tommy said, and he smiled again. He turned and stared now at Billy's car. *Wimbledon white. The running horse stamped on the back of each seat. The extruded aluminum grille. Ford-blue valve covers and air cleaner. Fog lights.*

Billy's 1966 classic Ford Mustang.

"You gotta be kidding," Billy said.

"I'll take that piece of shit for the dog," said Tommy. "That's my only deal."

"Ah, Tommy, come on, man," said Billy. "You're asking for my heart here."

"Hell, you probably wouldn't get shit for that car on eBay," said Tommy. "It needs a lot of work."

"But this is a *dog*," said Billy. "And I'd get at least ten grand."

"Yeah, I know," said Tommy. "I was fucking with you. Besides, I got a bullet in my gun with this dog's name on it. You know how many nights of sleep I lost?"

Rifle under his arm, Tommy grabbed the dog's chain and yanked the animal away from Billy. He lifted it by the collar and pulled it to its feet.

"Get up and walk," Tommy said to the dog.

"The dog and fifteen hundred dollars, and the car is yours," said Billy. Surely Tommy had that much cash still in play from the lottery ticket. He would send a thousand back to Phoebe, the money he owed her. The rest would be enough to hold him over for a week while he got things packed. Then he'd catch a bus back to Portland. A Mustang was a fine thing, but it had no heart beating inside it.

Tommy smiled. He cradled the rifle under one arm, then popped the top off his beer.

The party had lasted for an hour, with no one mentioning the dead body. For the sake of festivity, they had let it go, literally, downstream. Orville couldn't remember when he had been more proud of Meg. She had put her earlier anger aside to carry out the surprise she had been planning for weeks. All the invitation cards had been given out by hand, person to person, so that Orville wouldn't be putting them in mailboxes around town and realizing that something was afoot. *We request the pleasure of your company at a surprise retirement party for Orville Craft, at the home of Meg and Orville Craft. No gifts, but please bring a salad or pastry or casserole. Sunday at 4 p.m.* How could Meg have known as she wrote out the invitations that the address for the party should have been *Middle of the Mattagash Bridge*. As plates with sandwiches and cake were passed around, along with thermoses of hot tea and coffee, she had told Orville *why* she had the change of heart. "Because I got home and looked around our house," said Meg. "I saw the photos of our kids on the bookshelf, grown and gone. I saw the photos of our loved ones no longer with us. I thought of what it would be like to go into that room and look at *your* picture and know you were never coming home, just as the widows on your route must feel about their husbands. So I grabbed the cake and told Lillian to bring some blankets." And Orville had thanked her, and he had eaten a sandwich and drank hot tea, which warmed him. And he ate a slice of the retirement cake with its blue plastic car sitting on the top, a plastic mail man standing next to it.

Billy Thunder even returned to eat two sandwiches and brought with him a dog on a leash. Sheriff Ray Monihan and his only son, Ray Ray, attended the party, whining up to the end of the bridge in Ray Ray's little red Bug. Phillip Craft, who was

Orville's third cousin, also came. Orville didn't even mind when he saw Blanche take Harry a sandwich and a cup of coffee. He had studied Harry's face for signs of breaking but saw none. He didn't let this rattle him. Instead, he enjoyed his guests, their puffs of warm breath forming words on the cold air as they talked. There was a sense of excitement, of winter coming, of the harvest past with its full moon. This would have been how their ancestors visited and talked, all those years before they had even electricity to distract them. Then, shivering, the women had packed up the plastic plates, the paper napkins, and the red balloons, the thermoses of tea and coffee. By the time the bridge was empty again, save for Orville and Harry, evening was moving in and bringing with it a blue twilight.

After an hour of silence between them, and with no more action on the bridge, Harry sensed Orville was getting restless. He was staring over the top of his steering wheel at the pickup truck. Harry knew Orville was getting restless because that's how *he* was feeling too. And he was far more used to sitting in wait, in steaming rain and temperatures so high Orville couldn't imagine them, mosquitoes bigger than he'd ever seen before.

Harry got out of his truck and slammed the door. He leaned back against the bridge rail, resting his butt on it. He stared down the Mattagash River to where the current was cutting V's around the island. He heard Orville's door open and slam.

"How are you holding up?" Harry asked. It had been six hours. In the beginning, he had given the finicky mailman two hours at most. When Meg had appeared with cake, Harry was certain the standoff would end when the party did. He had apparently underestimated the man.

"Fine," said Orville. "You?"

"I'm enjoying myself," said Harry.

A long string of Canada geese was cutting a wedge over the river, leaving behind the sounds of excited honking.

"I've never seen so many Canada geese as this year," said Orville.

"They can afford to migrate again," said Harry, "now that the Canadian dollar has gone up."

Orville smiled. "Pretty soon, they'll be on their way back north."

"And before we know it," said Harry, "it'll be time to pick the first fiddleheads."

Orville had been trying to pretend that he wasn't missing a hot supper right then. The cold sandwich from his party would hold him only so long. Fiddleheads. They were ferns that grew wild in the spring, in those places along the river and creeks that were moist and shady. Cooked in a pot of potatoes and loaded with butter was the best way to fix them. He could almost smell the unique aroma they gave off when Meg boiled the first mess each spring.

"I know a place where fiddleheads grow so thick they hurt your eyes," Harry said now. Orville felt his stomach respond with a tumble. His own special place was a half-mile down the riverbank from where he and Meg lived, where the old Harrison farm once thrived. But often, Orville would get there too late, only to see size twelve boot prints in the mud, as if the Missing Link also loved fiddleheads. He assumed feet that big must belong to Roderick Plunkett. Whoever it was, he left Orville with sparse pickings.

"Is it near the old Harrison farm?" he asked.

Harry shook his head.

"Roderick always picks that place clean," said Harry. "I'm talking about a place that the old-timers might have found and picked a hundred fifty years ago. Fiddleheads the size of half dollars."

Neither man spoke as they stood side by side on the bridge and listened to the tail end of the geese, the birds themselves fading to pencil dots in the sky as the honks evaporated on air and twilight.

"I like them cooked with a piece of pork," said Harry. "Then served with homemade biscuits and butter."

"It's not gonna work, Plunkett," said Orville.

15

SUNDAY NIGHT, 7:00 TO 10:00 P.M.

His shoulder pressed against the driver's door, Harry tried to nap during the time he might have caught the world news, had he been home. But it was becoming a chore to tune in these days. The world seemed to be exploding, the ways to kill each other sped up. Harry knew now what he didn't know back in 1968, that the propaganda for war was getting slicker. It was all about finding the best words to rile up the masses. What had once been *Remember the Alamo* had morphed into *Remember the Maine*, which had morphed into *Remember Pearl Harbor*. There was Uncle Sam with his *I Want You!* plea behind that pointed finger. *Loose Lips Sink Ships*. *Till We Meet Again*, *Buy War Bonds*. Then, as proof that it could get even worse, the United States of America had finally arrived at simplistic and arrogant words like *Shock and Awe*, words you might hear at a keg party thrown by college frat boys.

Harry heard Orville's car door open and then close.

To keep warm, Orville paced the bridge. He could barely see the silhouette of the island now that evening was coming in to claim the land. Ray had not found the body there, even though the island liked to catch things that floated downriver. That's where Orville and Simon Craft had occasionally gone fishing, on those rare days his father found time. On one fishing trip, a crayfish had bitten Orville's toe, scaring him enough that he dropped his rod into the river. The old man laughed so hard it made Orville forget about being embarrassed and he laughed too. That memory stayed with him, one of the few good times he'd had with his father.

A pickup truck approached the lower end of the bridge, yellow headlights on. Roderick Plunkett's truck. It stopped at the *Bridge Out* sign that Ray Monihan had put in place and idled there. A door opened and Edna got out. Her purse was slung over one arm and she was wearing a rose-colored winter coat. Then Roderick turned his truck around and it became red taillights. As Edna walked past Harry's pickup, she glanced in and smiled. Harry was asleep behind the wheel, his lips slightly parted. When she reached Orville, she stopped.

"Lots of excitement today," said Edna.

"You can say that again," said Orville.

For a few silent moments, they stood near the railing, looking downriver.

"Well, I better be going," Edna said. "Myrtle left the keys to her car under the mat. I'm gonna use it to visit my sister."

"Sorry for plugging up the bridge," said Orville.

"That's okay," said Edna. "I haven't been standing out here on the bridge since before I was married. It's a nice trip down Memory Lane."

Orville watched as she disappeared off the upper end of the bridge. He heard Harry opening the door to his pickup. The door slammed and the echo came back at them after it bounced from the waters around the island, that same spot where Orville had been hearing the laughter, still in echo, from that day the crayfish bit his toe.

Harry pulled on his gloves. He came to where Orville was leaning back against the railing.

"How's it going?" Orville asked. "Did you have a snooze?"

"We should have kept the leftover cake," said Harry. He wondered if, while he napped, Orville had gone to the bathroom, urinating over the bridge's rail and into the dark river below. He figured Orville Craft was too finicky to pee in public, even in front of another man, and was hoping the Craft bladder might be the factor that ended the gridlock.

"I've been thinking," said Harry. The air, cold and thin, was leaking beneath his denim jacket.

"Not much else to do on this bridge," said Orville.

"I didn't buy you a retirement present."

"That's okay," said Orville. He wondered what was up.

"But I got something for you," Harry said. "Wait here. Don't get in your car and back off the bridge or anything."

Orville watched as Harry went back to his pickup, opened the door, and took out a flashlight. He closed the door, then leaned over the side of the truck's body. Orville saw him fumble for something that was lying beneath what looked like a towel or an old shirt. Before Orville could decipher what it was, Harry had it under an arm and was on his way back to the railing. As Orville stood watching, Harry let the light shine across his retirement gift. The moose mailbox.

"I didn't have time to wrap it," said Harry. "Want me to get you a hammer? I got one in my truck."

Orville was staring down at the moose's face as he had stared at it for so many days of his professional life. He saw a sadness now in the animal's eyes, as if it longed for the forest, that place where it could use its great sturdy legs, that tail for swishing deer flies, the hooves that leave cloven marks along mountain paths.

"No, I guess not," said Orville. He had his own hammer anyway, now in the trunk of his car.

"Throw it over the bridge then," said Harry. "Get it out of your system."

The moose stared up at Orville. He felt a bit foolish now that he'd let it upset him every workday for three years. Meg had been right. It was just a metal box with antlers and clamps.

"I'll pass," said Orville. He watched as Harry put the mailbox back in his truck.

The cold crept in. Harry and Orville stood side by side then and stared down to where the last of the twilight was disappearing, to where the outlines of black trees were still silhouetted on the mountain behind the river. It was the same old mountain they'd known as boys, with that camel hump perched on its back. The moon appeared above the horizon, less than a half-moon now, C-shaped and white.

"The new moon is next week," said Harry. "But I like the full moon. You can see the night better."

"Me too," said Orville. Several times, under a full moon, he had driven his four-wheeler up the mountain to his cabin, headlights off, only owls and stars watching.

Harry took a toothpick out of his shirt pocket and put it into his mouth. The moon over Vietnam was, to Sergeant Harry Plunkett, a killing moon. He couldn't imagine it was the same moon Emily gazed up at, half a globe away. The moon over Vietnam was an alien moon, just as that country with its strange birds and snakes and monkeys, was an alien planet. It was as if The Little People could even see at night. They could crawl out of rocks and trees and vines, then melt back into them. They could rise up instantly from a pile of leaves and take on the shape of a human holding a gun. They could smell American cologne on a downwind, yards away from the face that wore it. *The Little People*, that's what they sometimes called the gooks, as if they were only clever elves playing pranks. Leprechauns with slanted eyes, stalking the jungle for that pot of gold. Their eyes were born to that world. You could hate them, as Harry and the other soldiers did to survive, but you had to admire them too. They were farmers and peasants, poorly equipped and often hungry. They'd sacrifice their own women and children, strap their slender bodies with booby traps, offer them up to The Cause if they had to. Those were the rules of that foreign place, that strange planet. How do you fight Victor Charles, considering all that? To survive, Harry forced himself to believe that the moon shining over Vietnam was not Emily's moon back in Mattagash.

"I've been thinking," Orville said. "I was wondering what our lives would be like if you and Meg had gotten together that night of the dance."

Harry had been thinking too. A year after he left Vietnam, a man would walk upon the moon's surface and it would become just another piece of real estate. But this new comment from Orville came at him fast. Meg? Orville must mean his own wife, Margaret Hart Craft. This must be some kind of verbal trick, something Orville thought up during that three-year war with Harry's moose.

"What dance?" Harry asked, cautious.

"Your graduation dance at the school," said Orville. "Back when you and Meg graduated, 'The Mashed Potato Song' started playing and you got up and were headed straight for Meg, to ask her to dance." Orville remembered that Meg was wearing a blue prom dress and had a carnation tied around her wrist. Her hair was curled on the top of her head like small loaves of bread. French curls, the girls called them. In her high heels she was taller than Orville by an inch. He thought she was the most beautiful girl at the prom. "But I cut you off and asked Meg to dance first."

Harry was trying to remember if he had even *gone* to his graduation dance. Yes, he had, but he had no date that night. He had preferred to go alone rather than be stuck with some silly girl he didn't care much for in the first place. He would have asked Sandra Henley, since she was smart and fun, but she had started dating a boy from St. Leonard. So Harry and a few of the guys had spent most of that night behind the gym drinking too much beer and chasing it with tequila. But they had popped in and out all evening, sometimes to listen to music being played on the record player, other times to grab another plate of food. He'd been sick that night for the first time, drunk on Jose Cuervo and puking off his mother's front porch.

"I was going to ask Meg to dance?" Harry said. He knew for certain he would never do such a thing. Meg was nice enough, but she was too tall and loud for him. And if there was one dance Harry Plunkett wouldn't be dancing, it would be something called The Mashed Potato.

"The front of the stage was decorated with pine boughs," Orville said. "Meg was standing by the punch bowl, at the table under the basket hoop at the back of the gym. There were blue and white streamers wrapped around both hoops."

As Orville described that night, Harry remembered it. The school was still new and bustling. Blue and white had been their class colors. The fir boughs pinned along the front of the stage smelled fresh from the forest. The table with the punch bowl and snacks was placed at the back of the gym so that blackflies and June bugs fluttering through the open front doors would have to travel to get to the food. What had been their class motto? *Finished, Yet Beginning*, the cardboard letters covered in aluminum foil and pinned to the curtain on the stage. Behind the food table was the back door exit.

"What did I do when you cut me off?" asked Harry.

"You just kept going," said Orville. "You hit the exit door and never looked back."

Harry smiled, knowing Orville couldn't see him. He'd probably come inside to use the bathroom. Then he had taken the shorter route back to where the guys were gathered behind the gym with a cooler of beer. He was probably half drunk by then. But not drunk enough that he'd ask Meg Hart to dance.

"So that's why you been such a prick all these years?" Harry asked. He turned to look at Orville then and could see his features well enough, with light from the half-moon and now a sky filling up with stars. "What does Meg say about this?"

"She didn't see you coming," said Orville. "But I think she likes it when I tease her about cutting you off *at the pass*."

Harry thought about dancing with Meg. Would he feel like a blue and white streamer, whirled and twirled and dipped until all the stretch was gone out of him? Worse yet, would he be mashed like a potato before it was over? Even Meg's hairdos back then were menacing. Should he tell Orville Craft the truth?

"That was a nice pond behind your cabin," said Harry, which *was* the truth, "until you turned it into Disneyland."

Orville allowed himself some well-deserved satisfaction. He had told Ray Monihan this and Ray had doubted it. *There's trout all over northern Maine. Harry don't need to fish in your pond.*

"I need to start thinning out those trout," said Orville. "Either that or put them all on a diet. Feel free to help me out."

"Okay," said Harry. "I'll make a visit when the season's back."

A cold wind rolled off the end of the bridge, a whistling kind of wind that caught its sound in the girders below.

"I think I'll take a nap," said Orville. "I'm glad I got those two blankets."

When Edna arrived, Bertina was sitting in her beanbag chair and smoking a cigarette. Since no imaginary furniture had arrived from Florida, her lamp still sat on the floor, its yellow bulb bathing the room in deep amber. It was the kind of bulb Edna used as a porch light.

"You should have come to the bridge today," Edna said. She threw her purse on the sofa and sat next to it. "There was so much excitement, I don't know where to start."

"I had enough excitement for one lifetime," said Bertina.

Juanita, the youngest of the nieces, appeared from out of her bedroom. She came to Bertina and leaned down over the beanbag chair to hug her mother.

"Night, Mama," said Juanita.

Bertina pushed her daughter's dark hair back from her face. Valencia appeared next in the doorway, wearing what looked like baby doll pajamas.

"Good night, Mama," she said.

"Honey, put one of my sweaters on over those jammies," said Bertina. "You must be cold."

The girls said good night to Edna and disappeared into their bedroom. Edna felt guilt now. She could have taken them shopping since they'd moved to Mattagash, given them some money to splurge.

"Why didn't you plug in Venice?" she asked. The velvet painting was unlit, all the buildings black with night. From what she'd heard about Italians, they didn't go to bed that early. Some of them partied all night long.

"A bulb burned out," said Bertina. "Apparently, it's like a set of Christmas lights. When one goes out, they all go."

Edna looked at the outline of a gondola. Venice had shut down, like one of those blackouts that happen in places like New York City and everyone sleeps in subways and staircases and on rooftops, and nine months later a lot of babies are born.

"Did you hear about the dead body?" she asked.

"I lived in Miami," said Bertina. "You have to step over dead bodies just to take out the trash."

"Well, it's big news up here," said Edna. "Roderick says whoever the man was, he was a Hispanic." She let this news settle like dust. Bertina was putting her cigarette out, the brown afghan falling from her lap. She stopped stubbing and looked over at Edna, studied her face.

"Oh, I get it," said Bertina. "Hispanic? So it's all over town that he's my ex-husband? Well, you can tell Roderick and Mama Sal and all the big-mouthed bitches in this town that my ex-husbands are alive and well. Unfortunately."

"No one has said that," said Edna. "Only that he was a Hispanic." This was a lie. It *was* all over town that possibly, possibly and maybe even likely, that dead body had once been married to Bertina Castellano del Arroyo, which was the name Bertina had used on the most recent birthday and Christmas cards sent home to Mattagash. If it was just gossip, it would soon disappear, nothing to anchor it. Edna figured gossip was like a leftover party balloon. It rises into the sky and hovers there. Maybe it even bounces against the floor of heaven.

"Oh, I don't care," said Bertina. "Let them gossip."

"I didn't mean to upset you," said Edna. "I came to talk to you."

"You want advice on how to get a divorce," said Bertina. "I've been ignoring your hints. I don't need Mama Sal on my case any more than she is now."

Edna was about to protest, to tell her sister that she'd come to call off the dogs of divorce. There were percentages floating about in the universe that had convinced her she should stay in the safe nest of her marriage. Otherwise, she might end up living in a house on the ocean that she could paint only white. But before she could say anything, the phone rang. Bertina reached out and grabbed the receiver. She leaned toward Edna, the phone cradled against her breast so the caller wouldn't hear.

"Do you think I like living here like this?" Bertina asked, her voice a whisper. "Well, I don't. And I'll tell you the truth for a change. It was Ricardo who walked out on *me*. Now I'll give you some advice, since you been asking for it. Happiness is like them plants you been yapping about. Sometimes it's growing right in your own backyard and you don't even know it."

Edna couldn't speak, even if she wanted to. If she had hoped to gloat, waiting for this day to arrive as she lived for years in Bertina's shadow, this would be the time to do it. Instead, she took Bertina's hand and lifted the fingers with their perfectly painted nails up to her lips, left a warm kiss there.

Bertina smiled. Then she put the phone to her ear.

"She's on her way home, Mama Sal," Bertina said. "You can go off-duty now."

If he had been given a choice, Billy Thunder would have called for the secret meeting to be held at Buck's house. There was no reason for women to be driving to the end of the tarred road that evening. A few vehicles pulled up in Buck's yard would go unnoticed. But given the deadlock on the bridge, and given he wanted Orville Craft to be at the meeting, Billy soon saw the genius in holding it right out in public. If anyone did come to the bridge that late, it would appear that a few men had stopped to chat in the open air and smoke a cigarette, if they were smoking men. So when he had the change of heart inside his camper, the dog staring at him and wagging its tail, he had made the four phone calls that needed to be made. He told the men only that it was of utmost importance that they be on the middle of the bridge at 9 p.m. sharp. And they were not to tell their wives. Nine o'clock was late for a working man on a Sunday night and Billy knew it. But he had no choice. Once the bridge became free again, he was heading south. He knew Buck would drive him as far as Watertown in the morning. From Watertown he could catch a Greyhound to Portland, even if it took him three months to get there. He assumed a company named Greyhound would sell him a ticket for his dog. If not, he'd rent a car, and even return it when he got to Portland.

Billy left the dog chewing on what was left of its rawhide bone. Then he made his way up the grass road to the bridge. At Orville's car, he rapped on the window.

"There's a meeting in three minutes," said Billy. "You need to be there."

Orville, who had been sleeping in the backseat, warm beneath the blankets Meg's niece had brought him, got out of the car. He straightened his jacket and slacks.

"What's this about, Thunder?" he asked.

"The others will be here soon," Billy said. "I'll tell you then."

Billy went over to Harry's pickup and knocked on the window. Harry wound it down.

"I'm holding a meeting in two minutes," said Billy. "Got an issue that needs to be resolved with some of the guys."

"This would be the place to resolve an issue," said Harry.

"Do you mind if it's private?"

"Nope," said Harry. "I'll listen to the owls."

Billy nodded. He liked Harry Plunkett and wished he had gotten to know him better. If he hadn't been leaving town in the morning, if he had been staying on in Mattagash, he was pretty sure he and Harry might even become buddies.

Porter Hart was the first to arrive, parking his vehicle at the lower end of the bridge since he and Lillian lived not far from the old school, a few houses up from the welcome sign.

"What's going on?" Porter asked.

"Some kind of meeting," Orville said.

"Wasn't the full moon last week?" asked Porter. "This whole town has gone to hell in a hand basket."

The others arrived right on time and from both ends of the bridge. Booster Mullins, married to Dorrie. Christopher Harris, originally from Watertown and married to Gretchen. Phillip Craft, married to Verna, who owned the Hair Today salon and fainted several times a year. And Porter Hart, married to Meg's niece, Lillian.

"What the hell is this about?" asked Booster.

Billy flicked his cigarette butt out over the railing of the bridge. He hoped he was making the right decision by inviting these men to a meeting. If not, and they turned on him, he would meet up with George Delgato somewhere downstream.

"I do something now and then that I'm not proud of," he said, "when I need some money in my pocket." He hadn't realized until then that a lot of emotion was riding behind his words. Maybe it was connected to those memories of his mother that were coming to him lately.

"We all need money," said Porter Hart.

"I'm gonna tell you men the truth," said Billy.

"We'll freeze to death if you don't do it soon," said Booster.

"It's about your wives," said Billy. Seeing Chris Harris's strained face, he added, "No, not that. They're all too old for me. No offense."

"Thunder, for crying out loud," said Orville. "What is it?"

"You're not selling them stuff, are you?" asked Phillip Craft. He had heard rumors of Billy Thunder's business clients.

"Sort of," said Billy.

"Holy shit," said Booster Mullins. "Is Dorrie smoking pot?"

Billy smiled, knowing the best thing for Mattagash would be if Dorrie Mullins got stoned now and then.

"I'm selling them these," Billy said and pulled a bottle of the bad Viagra out of his jacket pocket. "This is Viagra that don't work. It's made in some shitty factory in the Philippines. I started selling these pills when I heard some ladies talking in a bar back in Portland. They were all pretty unhappy that they were getting nailed a few times a month by their old men. One of them said she wished there were fake pills she could slip into her husband's bottle and that she'd pay good money for them. So that's how I come up with this idea. I got on the Internet and sure enough, a lot of people were complaining about bad pills they bought from an Asian company. So I placed an order to that same company."

The men were listening hard, trying to understand.

"What's this got to do with us?" asked Booster. Then, as if a single thought passed over them at once, they understood. Perhaps they were remembering the last time they had taken the little blue pill and nothing big happened.

"Damn," said Christopher.

"Son of a bitch," said Booster.

"But," said Orville.

"Meg just bought her first supply last night," Billy said and wished Orville's face hadn't gone so sad.

"Are you gonna keep selling them?" asked Phillip.

Billy shook his head.

"That's why I'm telling you," he said. "But you guys have to start thinking for yourselves. The reason your wives are smarter than all of you has nothing to do with brains. It has to do with sociability."

"What?" asked Christopher.

"Sociability," said Booster, "the tendency to associate or mingle with companions." It had been on Florence's sign that past summer.

"They gather at Blanche's almost every day," Billy said. "They telephone each other. They send emails and instant messages right over the tops of your heads. They're a well-organized unit, and unless you men come together as a thinking man's army, they're gonna whip you at every turn in the road."

"What do we do?" asked Orville.

"For starters," said Billy, "you can get the real thing from me and switch the bad pills with good ones. Your women will think you're back to operating all on your own. And since I already made good money from your wives, I'm gonna leave you guys with a big supply of real pills. For free. And then I'm outta the pill business for good."

"It's a deal," said Phillip.

"Damn right," said Christopher.

"Now what's the word to remember?" Billy asked.

"Sociability." Even Orville spoke the word, now that he was finally part of a group. Bonded males. Billy saw them smile, one at a time, until all five men were happy again. They were peers, compadres, homeboys, soldiers in the same war, teammates, associates. Hell, they were the Boys on the Bridge.

As Edna drove Myrtle's car back down the road, she thought of all those pretty dresses and pants and blouses that could be bought for a dollar or two at the Good Shepard store in Watertown. Next week, she'd buy an entire box full, all usable clothing, and she'd drive it over to Bertina's girls. She passed Harry Plunkett's pretty little house up on its hill and remembered how Emily was always the first to set her flowers out in the spring. When she passed the sign that said *Dump Road*, she shuddered to think that a dead body had been lying there all night. She passed Florence Walker's house and wondered what the D word would be the next day when the town woke up. No one knew how Florence managed it, but those vocabulary words seemed to turn up all by themselves, bright and early on Monday mornings. Once, Edna had asked Florence, "When do you put up the new word?" And Florence had answered, "When the time is right."

Edna parked Myrtle's car on the grassy edge of the road, where so many other vehicles were waiting like lost dogs for the bridge to clear and their owners to come fetch them. She put the keys back under the floor mat and got out. The stars over Mattagash were bright pinpoints, sparkling white, so much smaller than the swirling yellow stars Van Gogh had painted. But then, no stars were ever that yellow except in Van Gogh's own mind. Edna didn't want to be the kind of artist who has to go crazy for the sake of art. Maybe Pablo Picasso and others had lots of affairs and left their families, but she didn't have to do the same. Instead, she'd be the modest kind, like Grandma Moses. Things were changing, and she could feel that change in the air, like snow. Just before Christmas, the days would start to grow longer again. The earth would tip back toward that yellow sun, and as it did, it would pull her SAD with it. Before she knew it, the calendar in her kitchen would be turned to May, and the mountain behind her house would be loaded with wild cherry buds. Summer would come next, all buttery yellow and grass green. The dog days would be back in August. In October, all over again, the leaves would burst to autumn colors and everyone would be guessing what day the first snow might come. She and Roderick didn't have to drive to the ocean, to that place called Downeast, for a second honeymoon. They could stay right there in Mattagash, in their own comfortable home. Come spring, she would paint the house. She was already tired of the pale green. And she would plant so many flowers that everyone would come to admire them, tons of flowers like the French artist Claude Monet had in his garden. She would set up her easel in the midst of daisies and hollyhocks and sunflowers. People would visit and ask questions about the flowers. And she would say things that she learned from her book. She'd say, "My work, like Monet's, indicates that there is a reciprocal relationship between gardening and painting." She had looked up the word *reciprocal* and written it down in her notebook of words. *That which is given or done in return*. It seemed to Edna that maybe marriage is like Monet and his garden. It's reciprocal.

She walked slowly across the bridge. This was the same old bridge she used to walk with Roderick years ago, when she was on her way home from school and he'd be following along just to breathe the same air she was breathing. At the other end of the bridge, she saw Roderick's pickup idling there as it waited. She had called him from Bertina's to ask if he would please come get her. He hadn't complained, even though he would usually be in bed by then, getting ready for dawn and another workday. She would get up in the morning and make his sandwiches, put a piece of low-calorie candy in his lunch pail and maybe one of those little notes she used to tuck in, back in the old days, down under the banana and the chocolate donut. *I love you. Be careful at work today. Your wife, Edna.* On the ride home, she would tell him the truth. She would say, "Ward Hooper was a nice man who worked for the soil department. There was nothing between us but talks. I'm sorry, Roderick. I don't know what got into me." And Roderick would breathe easy to hear these words as he drove them home, both hands safely on the steering wheel. It was all about words anyway, Edna knew. It was how humans used them, and which ones they chose.

In the middle of the bridge, Edna paused long enough to tell Harry and Orville good night, to stay warm, and to not let the bedbugs bite. Then she walked on across the bridge, the river far below her unseen and powerful, surging itself toward the sea.

16

SUNDAY NIGHT, 11:00 P.M.

It was when the darkness was working its way toward dawn, with laces of pink slowly forming on the horizon, the jungle stirring. They were moving out, getting the patrol boat filled with supplies. Wally McGee was distant, as if listening for something no one else could hear, not even the jungle. Harry had turned to tell Private Barry Wilson, the tall kid from St. Louis, to turn off his transistor. Eric Burden and the Animals were barely audible, singing "We Gotta Get Outta This Place." But barely audible was too loud in the jungle. "Put it away, Wilson," Harry said, as a barrage of automatic weapons cut the dawn wide open. "Ambush!" he heard Wally shout. They were shooting from behind any tree, rock, or shadow that would hide them. Harry was thinking, "How did they *do* that? How do they appear without sound, as if out of mist and air?" And that's when he realized he'd been hit in his lower right leg. He saw blood exploding up over the top of his boot. And now Private Wilson, a kid who wanted to go home and become a lawyer, was bleeding from his mouth and nose. He still held the transistor in his hand, as if he were surprised to see it there. Blood poured from beneath his helmet as his legs collapsed and he went down. "Medic!" Harry was shouting, as he and Wally McGee tried to cover Wilson's body. They were pinned down on the riverbank as their flank men filled the trees with gunfire, doing their best to drive the enemy back. Harry pulled his shirt off and Wally did the same. Ferguson, a twenty-year-old medic from Texas, already had two bamboo poles and with the shirts, they made a litter, got Wilson on it. *We gotta get out of this place.* Harry was thinking, *He's just a goddamn kid who wants to listen to a rock song. What's he doing bleeding to death in this jungle?* Ferguson and Greer, the black kid from Los Angeles, were now crouched, ready to pull the stretcher carrying Wilson back toward the clearing where a helicopter could land for him. And that's when Harry saw the grenade, sailing on air like a small and harmless toy. It struck the dirt and rolled to within four feet of the litter where Wilson lay bleeding yet still alive, where Harry and Ferguson and Greer and McGee all stared at it. Harry could almost feel their thoughts coming to meet his, as if war gives men the ability to communicate the way insects do, without speech. *Shit, that's a frag. Five-second fuse.* How does a man decide it's the time he will die? Is five seconds enough to think it out clearly? Are ten? Would an hour be better, or a day? War doesn't think that way. Harry heard Wally shout, "Move out!" Then it was all slow motion, that wild world of colored birds and flowers, of jungle rot and death, a liquidy motion as Wally threw his body up and forward, onto the grenade. What Harry remembered most about the explosion was not the spray of blood or bits of bone and shrapnel, but the shock wave that followed it, one that seemed to push through the bones of his own body. Wally was still alive. Greer had pushed Wilson's dead body off the stretcher, the private's eyes staring upward as if still thinking that helicopter would save him. "One less lawyer," Greer said, knowing it would have made Wilson laugh. Tears were running down his face. Wilson was going to be Greer's best man at his wedding. Harry crawled over to Wally's side. Ferguson and Greer dragged the litter behind Wilson's body and lay there as the flank men poured more bullets at the VC. Ferguson pulled out a morphine needle and shot it into Wally's arm, but Harry knew it didn't matter. And that's when he felt it, the sorrow for lost words between humans, lost life, lost love. He pulled Wally's body into his arms and sat cradling it. He wanted the boy to know he wasn't going to die alone. Maybe it was too little, too late, but it was all Harry had in his possession there in the jungle, three seconds before a second bullet ripped into his side. Now, it was Sergeant Harry Plunkett that Ferguson and Greer were getting onto the litter made of shirts, one Harry's and the other Wally's. Ferguson and Greer were pulling him backward now, out of the barrage of fire, away from Corporal Wally McGee and Private Barry Wilson, whose small transistor lay on the ground near his feet. They'd take care of the injured and dying first, and come back for the dead next. How do they do it? That's what else Harry was thinking, as Ferguson pumped morphine into him and started the plasma. How do young men who were at the movies one day in Oklahoma City, or at a beach in Florida whistling at the pretty college girls, or skiing on some quiet mountain in Vermont, how do they become heroes overnight, heroes in an alien world? Harry would mourn for Corporal McGee and Private Wilson forever, and they were just two of the men he lost. And so the bird, a UH-1B helicopter gunship, a *Huey*, that flying symbol of the war itself, had lifted him up and carried him over the dead bodies and marble eyes as it sprayed the jungle below with rounds of mortar. When Harry woke from the nightmare that was real, he was in a hospital in Cam Rahn Bay. The bullet wound in his leg was painful but superficial. The wound in his side would take three more months at Walter Reed Hospital to heal. Then he was sent back to Mattagash where he could begin again that simple and uncomplicated life he'd left behind. But he felt like an imposter. It wasn't his skin anymore that he was living inside. It was a suit, a uniform that still belonged to the U.S. Army. And he had brought something else back from Vietnam, a whole new vocabulary of words and no opportunity to use them. It was as if he'd been away studying Anglo Saxon or Medieval German. The army taught him a new language. *Boom Boom Girl. Jesus Nut. Hooch. Beehive Round. Uncle Ho.* The military had words and letters for everything, especially those things most difficult to deal with, since letters and words could conceal the awful truth. *Body count. KIA. Body bag.* Even the grenade that killed Wally McGee was more than a *frag*. It was also a *lemon*, a *pineapple*, and a *baseball*, at least to the guys on the ground. To the gods in the Pentagon and at 1600 Pennsylvania Avenue and those other high places where gods live, it was an M-26A1, an Offensive Fragmentation hand grenade with a five-second fuse.

Harry came home speechless to a world that was quickly filling up with words. In a matter of years, billions of emails a day would be fluttering about the planet. Over two million every second, and 90 percent of them would be useless spam. Hundreds of television stations. Billboard signs and text messages. And yet, in all those words, among all that clutter, Harry was still searching for the truth.

Shock and awe.

If you shoot me, you better kill me... otherwise, I'm getting up.

Sergeant Harry Plunkett came home to a fact of life so unpleasant that he lived years before admitting it to himself, that never again, not even making love to Emily or waiting at the hospital as Angie was born or fishing the best spots along the river, never again would he ever, *could he ever*, feel so intensely alive as he had in the midst of that death jungle, in the heart of that heartless war. He had lived aware of every cell in his body, electrified, prickling in anticipation of anything that moved or breathed. He could hear his own heart beating and he had rejoiced at the sound of it. Mortality was the best drug on the market.

Harry woke quickly, snapping from the dream as if someone had shaken him. He looked around, fighting to remember where he was. Then he knew. Mattagash. On the bridge. Inside his truck, which was now freezing cold. Shivering, he sat waiting for his heart to stop racing, waiting for forty years to fall back into the past where it belonged. He took a deep, cold breath, then another. That's when he heard rapping, a soft *rat-a-tat-tat*, like a toy machine gun. Orville Craft was at his window. Harry rolled it down.

"Hey, neighbor," said Orville.

"You're still here?" asked Harry. His words became puffs of vapor, even inside the pickup.

"Guess so," said Orville. He sounded almost chipper. "Eleven hours now, but who's counting?"

"I didn't think you'd last this long," said Harry.

"I didn't either," said Orville.

"What's it gonna take?" asked Harry.

"I don't know," said Orville. He was struck with an image of the two of them living on the bridge forever, friends and loved ones bringing them food and clothing, until they eventually grew into the steel itself like two aging rust spots.

"Have you thought about what's gonna happen in three and a half hours?" asked Harry. "Danny Broussard's truck is gonna come screaming onto this bridge."

"Danny's a go-getter," said Orville, "always gets that first load of the day." It was Danny's yellow headlights he saw first those predawn mornings when he'd fumble to the bathroom to pee, Meg still snoring in their bed. Then the logging truck would fly past the house and become red taillights as Danny hit the Jake brakes before he crossed the bridge. He missed that warm bed. He missed Meg.

"He'll be half asleep," said Harry, "and not expecting a mouse on this bridge, let alone two vehicles. No way will he see that little sign Ray put up. Of course, he won't be loaded yet, but that Kenworth weighs about twenty tons empty."

"It'll do some serious damage all right," said Orville. "But it'll do it to you first, since you're on the lower end of the bridge."

"Yeah, I already thought of that," said Harry. "Well, I guess it'll be quick for both of us."

"I came to tell you that I found a candy bar in the glove compartment," Orville said. "You want half?"

"Sure," said Harry. He was starving. He reached for the half-bar that Orville held out to him and then hesitated. What if Orville had filled it with laxatives or something? Or worse yet, Viagra crumbs, as Billy had done to *him*? Harry imagined himself leaving the pickup right where it was and sprinting to Blanche's.

"Go ahead," said Orville. "It's safe. Here, I'll give you my half."

"Thanks," said Harry. He had to smile. Where had Orville Craft been hiding a sense of humor all these years? As Harry ate the sweet chocolate, he saw that Billy Thunder's light was still on, down in his little camper, which was likely much warmer than Harry's pickup. It was as if the whole town had gone to bed and left them on the bridge, even Blanche and Meg, as if everyone might be tired of the silly battle between them.

Harry felt the cold in his toes and fingers so he got out of the truck. He needed to move, to build up some warmth in his body. Orville was wearing a bulkier coat now, over the lighter coat he had worn earlier in the evening. How had this wimp turned into Robert Peary, headed for Antarctica? He was standing at the railing, looking down at what would be a river if he could see it. The only light, other than the half-moon and a thick smattering of stars, was the yellow light from Billy's camper.

Harry blew on the tips of his fingers. He reached in his jacket pockets for his gloves. He could smell snow in the air. The cold had brought the smell with it, fresh and crisp.

"It's going to snow tonight," said Harry.

"How do you know?" Orville asked.

"I just know. It's time."

Harry's grandfather had taught him the tricks that nature knows well. It's what the land knows in its heart. Even squirrels know it. It's what all the old-timers knew, before weathermen with satellites and the Internet and round-the-clock predictions. Pioneers looked to the moon for their weather, good or bad. Was the moon tipped on its side, the horns pointing up? Does the smoke from that chimney rise straight or does it hang low? Are birds roosting close to the ground? If the bats are flying low, then rain is on the way. Old-timers asked the land, and the land answered them. Nowadays, Mattagash youngsters couldn't tell a raven from a crow. But they could download thousands of songs onto something called an iPod. They could cure viruses and scale Mount Everest with the click of a mouse.

"So, am I right?" Orville asked then. "This thing between you and me. It's because of Meg and that night at the dance."

It was in April of 1980. Emily was getting weaker by the day, the medicines not helping. She had packed a few items in a suitcase and Harry drove her to the hospital in Watertown. Mud season, April. The snow along the roadsides was half white, half brown. Cars hurled slush at each other when they met. Harry drove up to the hospital's front door and let Emily out there, so she wouldn't have far to walk. And that's when Orville Craft's car flew past, in a hurry to find a space in the crowded parking lot. Harry knew his car, a green Chevy in those days. He hadn't seen Orville much since high school. Harry had become a soldier in Vietnam and Orville had become a milkman in Mattagash. Roads so different they weren't on the same map. But Orville was at the hospital that day, the same day Emily would disappear inside forever. Harry remembered getting out of the car in a rush of anger. The front of Emily's coat, her legs, her shoes, were sprayed with wet and dirty water. She was already trying to make light of it. "For heaven's sake, Harry, it will wash out. It's not a big issue." For Harry, it was a major issue. Maybe it was because he felt so helpless that day. Maybe he knew that Emily wasn't coming home again. He knew, and yet he could do nothing about it. Once, near the village of Trang Chanh, he and Wally had pulled an old Vietnamese woman out of a burning hut before it came crashing down, had dragged her back into the trees where she would be safe from gunfire. She was weeping, so ancient she was toothless, her papery brown hands withered and bony. She kept muttering words to Harry in Vietnamese and pointing back at the inferno that had been her home. *She's telling us something about her husband,* said Wally, who had been learning all he could of the new language, with its many vowels and strange consonants. *Ah, shit. He's still inside the hut, Sarge.* He had taken Army food to children whose ribs showed through their skin. He had placed babies into the arms of medics, infants burned so badly their bodies were black. But he couldn't make those hospital doors open again so Emily would step back out, smiling and healed. "That son of a bitch," is what Harry said that day, watching as Orville's car found a parking space. For years, Harry carried in his mind a frozen picture of Emily's face, as if it were a photograph, the surprise when that wave of dirty water washed over her. Her heart weakening by the beat, Emily would stay in the hospital another two months before it was finally over.

"What are you thinking?" asked Orville.

It always amazed Harry how the mind has no borders, no need for gasoline to fuel it, to carry it 12,000 miles away or fifty years into the past. It can even carry humans to the future, as they think ahead to what they might do on Wednesday. Or in a year.

Twenty years. And it all happens in a second, with a snap of those neurons. A spaceship, the mind, a time machine.

"I was thinking of the last time Emily went to the hospital," Harry said.

"She was two doors down from my mother," said Orville. "Mother died in May."

"Emily in June," said Harry.

"I know," said Orville. "I see her stone every Memorial Day."

Harry knew that human beings often do battle over a parking space. Men go to war in tall office buildings over a window. Was it any less honorable than the wars fought over mountains? *Iwo Jima. Bloody Ridge. Pork Chop Hill. Hamburger Hill.* He would ask Blanche to drive with him to Connecticut, maybe for New Year's. He wanted her to meet Angie and the kids. But more importantly, he wanted to hold his only child in his arms again. He would stop being cantankerous. If Angie wouldn't come home for visits, he would go to her. He would listen to the city noises, the honking, the sirens wailing, the road rage. She was worth it.

"I got those two blankets," said Orville. "Wanna sit in my car?"

"Sure," said Harry. He couldn't remember when he had felt so cold. "Long as it's not too warm in there."

Harry sat in the passenger seat of Orville's car, beneath one of the blankets. He felt the cold creeping into the steel of the car, settling into the tires. Orville had been in there for a good part of the eleven hours. How large was the man's bladder? Harry had peed off the bridge three times but had yet to see any body activity from Orville. Maybe he had canisters in the mail car. Maybe mailmen were like astronauts and long-distance truck drivers. Maybe they peed as they drove and delivered letters.

"You got any big regrets, Orville?" Harry asked. It was the question Blanche had asked of *him*.

"I wish I hadn't retired," said Orville. "What about you?"

And that's when Harry Plunkett found himself talking to Orville Craft in the way he could never talk to Emily before she died, saying the things he might one day say to Blanche if the time was ever right.

"There was this kid in Vietnam," said Harry. "He was the best soldier in my platoon. Smart as hell. Always thinking on his feet. I was his sergeant, the man he respected most in that hellhole. So one night he tried to talk to me. He tried to tell me that he wasn't who I thought he was. He wanted to clear his conscience. He told me he was never going to marry that pretty girl he had waiting back in Philadelphia because she didn't exist. There was a soldier he met in basic, and this guy helped him understand who he was."

"You mean he was like Ray Ray," said Orville.

"He wanted to share his heart with me that night," Harry said. "He wanted to die with the truth if his time was up. But I didn't let him. We were ambushed just before dawn. I lost two men in my platoon. I'd have lost three more, including myself, if it hadn't been for Wally McGee."

Orville had been listening to the melodic sound of Harry's words. He said nothing for he had no language to give back, no words to express what he was feeling. This was a bigger war than the one he'd fought for three years over a mailbox. He had watched the real war on television, from a safe distance, with Walter Cronkite talking to America in that fatherly voice, deep and comforting.

"Tell me something," said Orville. "Where did you go that night of your welcome home party? I heard all kinds of rumors. Is it true you gave your Purple Heart to a hooker in Bangor?"

Harry looked over at Orville. And that's when he felt it again, that rush going through his body, as it had the second Wally died. He felt the rush of years, years wasted and years used wisely. He felt time moving through him, as if it were a ghost, a thing that can haunt a man's days and nights.

"I went to Craft Pond," said Harry. "Just me, a couple beers, and a sleeping bag." They were selling the medals of war on eBay now, collectors buying them from relatives and friends who no longer had use for them or needed money more. Harry had put his father's medal in his mother's hands before they closed her casket. At least that was one Purple Heart that wouldn't end up on the Internet for dollars. His own was another.

Orville was slowly getting it, running facts and rumors around in his thoughts until he knew.

"You threw your Purple Heart into my pond," he said. "*That's* why you go up there. It's got nothing to do with my trout."

Harry could never explain to anyone how safe he felt, those nights he camped on the banks of Craft Pond. When the stars twinkled overhead, when the owls hooted from the deep woods, when the crickets and night creatures came alive beneath the trees, skunks and raccoons, fox and porcupines, it was a world he *knew* and *understood*, a world he fit into. It was a world The Little People would never find. Some nights, it was as if he could hear that Purple Heart beating, up through the waters of the pond.

"I'm honored that you chose my pond," said Orville. "This will be our secret."

Harry nodded. He was grateful that Orville understood. Let the town think a hooker in Bangor had a Purple Heart tacked to the wall over her bed.

"You got an extra set of keys in here somewhere?" Harry asked. He was ready to get off the bridge. Some things weren't worth dying for. He was ready to find Blanche warm in her bed, hold her to his chest, feel the safety in her body.

"Of course I got an extra set," said Orville. "Don't you?"

"Yup," said Harry. He reached into his jacket pocket and pulled out a set of keys. When Orville heard them jangle, he reached into his glove compartment and found his own extra set.

"I'm gonna back up," said Harry. He opened his door and light flooded the car.

"No you're not," said Orville. "I am."

Unable to sleep, Edna Plunkett thumbed through the pages of her art book, looking at all the interesting paintings. There was that crazy Russian again, Marc Chagall, with things flying all over his canvases, even people and hens. Wasn't there such a thing as gravity in Russia? But there was one she saw that she liked. It was called *The Flying Lovers*, and the couple seemed to be sharing such a tender moment as they floated in the air. Unaware that it was snowing, Edna closed the book and snapped off her light. She snuggled close to Roderick for the first time in a week. And when she slept, she dreamed of a man flying like a bird in the dark sky. He wasn't in a glider, as Ward Hooper might have been. Edna couldn't see his face and then realized that he didn't *have* a face. There was a blank white oval where a face should be. *I need to learn how to paint faces* is what her dream mind was thinking. And that's when the man's face began to take form, as if an artist were putting strokes of paint on a canvas. Now she could see the nose and the mouth, the eyes. It was the face of her husband, Roderick Plunkett, flying high overhead. Edna knew he was peering down on all the pinpricks of light, the yellow sparks that mark the lives of those people who live in Mattagash. Would he know *her* light? Could he find their house in a snowstorm? If the flakes were so thick and white, would he fly away, certain that in the town of Mattagash all the lights were out and no one was home? "I'm right here, Roderick," Edna whispered, still asleep. "I'm here, sweetheart, so fly down and get me."

And that's when Edna realized that she was also flying, she and Roderick together, two lovers floating across the sky.

The dog, Bullet, raised his head and whined, as if sensing something nearby in the darkness. Billy opened his eyes. He had had another dream of strolling into Murray's Restaurant & Bar and there was Phoebe, in her pink uniform and showing everyone a new diamond ring. She was planning to marry someone and it wasn't William Thunder. Awake now, Billy smiled, thinking it a foolish dream. Phoebe Perkins would wait for him forever. He'd call her in the morning to tell her the money was on its way and ask if she liked dogs.

"It's okay, Bullet," said Billy. He had let Tommy Gifford name the dog. *I got a bullet with this dog's name on it*. Billy reached for the small light near his bed and snapped it on. He didn't notice the white flakes that were hitting the tiny windows of the camper. With all the excitement in town, he was behind in his reading. He flicked his *Playboy* open to Miss October. She was a brunette named Jordan Monroe, with great legs and a pretty little mouth, lips that pouted out to kiss every man who opened the magazine. *From Denison, Iowa, but attends the University of Nebraska, majoring in consumer sciences*. She had a great set of knockers. If *he* was freezing in the camper, what must she feel like, nothing on but a Hugh Hefner smile? Something about her eyes and her nose reminded him of Phoebe. But Phoebe would never take her pink uniform off and pose naked for anyone but

Billy. He was so sure of this that he returned to studying the consumer scientist in the centerfold.

Cuddled close to Meg, who was already snoring by the time he had arrived home cold and tired, as if he had been away at war, Orville Craft didn't see the snow filtering down beneath his yard light, turning his lawn white. Instead, he dreamed of his father. "I'm proud of you, son. You're a fine mailman." And Simon Craft would know a fine mailman when he saw one. He had died on the job, soldier to the end, sitting next to Amy Joy Lawler's mailbox, his heart ticking like a wound-down clock. Then, Simon gave his only son some advice. "Don't retire until they put you out to pasture, Orville. Don't hang up your spurs." Orville would think of that word for many years to come. *Spurs*. It made him dream then that he was a Pony Express rider on that dangerous trail from St. Joseph to Sacramento, his saddle bag full of important letters. He dreamed he was galloping across prairies, galloping through snow-covered canyons and icy mountain passes, galloping through heat and locusts, along muddy wagon ruts and through fields of swaying grass, through thunderstorms and hailstorms and snowstorms. Orville dreamed he was galloping.

Still cold from his hours on the bridge, Harry had kissed Blanche good night and then fallen asleep next to her. The dream this time was of flares being dropped from an AC-47 gunship, which was also firing thousands of rounds at the mountain below it. It was a mountain they could see from their camp. Magnesium flares, falling like sparklers attached to parachutes, igniting twenty seconds after the gunner pulled the safety pin and tossed them out the cargo door. It was the Air Force's way of letting American ground troops know the enemy's position in the jungle. "If Charlie so much as lights a cigarette, we'll find him," Harry was telling Wally McGee, as he had that night before Wally died. "There are heat sensors all over that mountain." Harry watched as bursts of light from the flares drifted down, soundless, painting the world below them a dazzling white. And that's when he realized they weren't flares at all but hundreds and hundreds of twinkling stars, maybe thousands. They were all the stars that the sky over Mattagash had held, ever since the first settlers came there to build the notion of a town. Millions of stars twinkling in unison. Then, so easily and gently it seemed to happen in an instant, the stars turned into white snowflakes. And that's when Sergeant Harold Plunkett knew that he had finally come home from the war.

17

MIDNIGHT

A fox slid from the shadows of the trees and onto the main road near Tommy Gifford's house. Upriver, the eastern sky had turned gray with snowflakes, hiding the stars that were flickering above it. The fox had already been to the dump and found nothing of food on that night. Seeing a light pop on in the darkness, the animal held its nose high, sniffing. The wind was bringing with it the smell of a human. Humans meant food or danger. The fox turned away, a reddish-black shadow moving toward the bridge.

At the first house above Tommy's, the porch light was on and Florence Walker was standing near the leafless lilac bush on her front lawn. It was still a couple minutes until midnight. She knew that in two hours the first logging trucks would come whooshing up from Watertown and St. Leonard, all men who worked in the Mattagash woods for the P. J. Irvine Company. They would use their Jake brakes just before the bridge and then fly across it, past Dump Road and then Florence's house. The trucks would appear as yellow headlights and disappear into red taillights, as if those headlights and taillights marked the years of a man's life. And for many men, they did.

Florence was wearing a coat over her nightgown, her boots with the fake fur around the tops, a knitted cap, and a scarf wrapped tightly about her throat. In her hands was the white poster board with the Word for the Week written in large black letters. Monday was always the toughest day, the day of the jokes. "Who will ever use a word like *heinous?*" But by Friday, lots of folks would be finding all sorts of things *hay-nous*, and Florence would once again be vindicated. Teaching is not an easy task. One must use whatever tools one has at hand. Harry Plunkett had offered to build for her the type of sign that had a plastic shield over it. That way, she could slide the poster inside and it would be protected from the rain and snow. But Florence didn't like the idea of plastic. Instead, when it rained, she came out with her blue umbrella and unpinned the poster from the sandwich board sign. She took it inside until the storm passed. But when it snowed, she let the fresh flakes enjoy the word too. She didn't mind making a new sign. Words, in her opinion, should be toiled for, respected. Human beings have fought wars over words. Florence's own father had been in the Argonne Forest in World War I, the war to "Make the World Safe for Democracy."

Florence Walker pinned the new word to her sign, and then stood back to admire it:

Denouement (day-knew-ma): the outcome of a complex sequence of events.

The fox had made its circling, cautious way toward the upper end of the bridge, its red coat now flecked with snow. It had found half a donut lying frozen in the grass and grabbed it quickly into its small mouth. That's when the fox noticed the dot of light, saw that it burned like a yellow fire on the flat by the river. It gazed down at Billy Thunder's camper, waiting to see if this was some kind of trouble. It didn't fear the humans as much as it feared the coyote. Sensing no danger, the fox searched the grass for the other smells. A piece of ham sandwich. A bite of cake. A potato chip. The Mattagash night, after all, belonged to the fox. With pupils that are vertically slit, with cells that reflect light *back out*, it saw what it needed and wanted of the night. Food gone, the thin body of the fox moved off, back toward the woods, safe at least for now. In its wake, and as if on cue, Billy Thunder said good night to *Miss October* and turned out his light. The dog waited in the darkness, its head tilted, its senses alert. Then, satisfied the fox was gone, it moved closer to Billy and slept.

On that night in October, a week after the harvest moon, no one could know what the new word would be on Florence Walker's sign. Or that satellite images had picked up the first big snowfall of the year, an early snow that came gusting in from the Canadian plains. They still did not know the *sequence of events* that lay ahead.

They didn't know that, in four months, Florence Walker would die of a stroke and all vocabulary lessons in town would cease. But first she would live from E, *epitome*, to P, *paradox*, giving the populace sixteen more precious words.

No one knew that once the bitter winter was over, Dorrie Mullins would form a group called Rename the Mattagash Bridge. Six women would gather in Dorrie's kitchen to discuss strategy and eat pizza. "The William Leonard Fitzgerald Bridge would be my choice," Lydia Fitzgerald Hatch would say. "After all, the first Lace Curtain Irish name to settle here was Great-Grandad Fitzgerald." And Dorrie, being the group's organizer, would reply, "But the name would be longer than the bridge." And that's when Lydia, grandmother to the only genius in town, would grab Owl's hand and take him home. "Wow, that wasn't the *day-knew-mah* I had hoped for," Dorrie would say, as she reached for a second piece of pizza.

Buck Fennelson didn't know that he would fail his paternity test with flying colors and be free of Mona. But that he would mourn her right up until the New Year's Eve party at Bert's Lounge in Watertown, when he would get a glimpse of Patty Ann, a simple and loving girl who would bear their children and cook them sensible New England meals like Chinese Pie and American Chop Suey.

No one in town knew yet that Mama Sal's daughter, Bertina, would marry an older man named Paul Bateman, her former boss from Tampa, and that she would move herself and her daughters back to Florida. Mama Sal didn't know yet that she would say, "Well, I guess the fourth time tells the story. Always a bride, never a bridesmaid. Let's hope she gets it right, now that there's money behind it and the groom is a regular Anglo-Saxon."

But Mama Sal also didn't know that the very next summer, while she was inspecting Edna's cucumber beds, a garter snake would slither across the top of her foot, prompting her to run for safety in front of Edna and the twins, leaving behind her aluminum walker and her alleged disability, if not the monthly disability check.

Tommy Gifford didn't know that he would never reconcile with his wife and daughters, that he would start driving a tractor-trailer out across the vast and exotic United States of America. Or that, one rainy night, he would fall asleep at the wheel, having done too many hours on the road for too little money. He would fall asleep and die in a fiery crash on the interstate north of Atlanta, Georgia.

No one knew that Edna Plunkett would paint her house a rose color the next spring. Or that the twins, Roddy and Ricky, would do very well in counseling, learning to control their identical anger before they became men and the anger turned to rage. "They need to find a balance between being exactly the same as another person and yet having their own identity as well," the counselor would tell their parents. And Edna would nod and say, "It can be *daunting*, can't it?"

Billy Thunder didn't know that the river would freeze over in December, sealing inside its belly the body of George Delgato until the ice ran free in the spring. That's when an excited Buck Fennelson would call Blanche's and ask to talk to Billy. "Are you sitting down?" Buck would ask, and Billy would say, "Well, yes, Buck, since I'm at Blanche's eating lunch. But I can lie down on the floor if it's necessary." And Buck would say, "They found the body of that man, Bill, the one you told me about. That George guy. And he's got a police record as long as my dick." And Billy would smile, thinking, *Ah, Bucko, I hope you're right on this one*. But all he would say to Buck would be, "Well, FuckYouBuckFuckYouVeryMuch." And Buck would collapse in laughter so Billy could hang up the phone.

That night in October, a week after the full harvest moon, the moon farmers used to gather their crops late into the night, Harry Plunkett did not know that he would buy the white Mustang from Tommy Gifford for two thousand dollars and give the car back to Billy Thunder. Or that he would offer Billy a job and a chance to pay off the loan. He didn't know that on Blanche Taylor's birthday, he would lean down to kiss her mouth and ask, "Will you marry me, sweetheart?"

Orville Craft didn't know that the very next week he would take back his job as mailman and would deliver letters for another five years before retiring for good. He also didn't know that he and Meg would soon begin a ritual, a social hour they would spend together, just the two of them at his cabin. They would each drink a martini and play rummy while they listened to classic songs on the oldies station, the one that never plays Faith Hill since she's still too young. Or that every blue moon, with no help at all from Pfizer and all the help in the world from nature, he and his wife would make love. Orville didn't know that twelve years after the incident on the bridge, and like his father Simon Craft, he would die of a heart attack as he chopped kindling. His hand would come up to his chest and his first thoughts would be, strangely, of the sun bouncing silver off his trout at Craft Pond. And there, through the clear water, he would see something shiny lying on the bottom, something with a purple ribbon. Then, his mind being a time machine, it would carry Orville Craft in his last seconds back to the island in the Mattagash River, the one you can see so well from the bridge, where the current takes trash thrown down by tourists, that island where there exists a laughter put in place one day when his father took him fishing and a crayfish bit his toe.

Even Billy Thunder, still cocky and self-assured on that night in October, didn't know that in two days, he and his dog would move from the freezing camper and into Buck's little house. He didn't know he would find a job with Harry Plunkett, who would teach him how to fix small engines and restore cars. Or that the first car they restored would be the white Mustang, the one with the perfect canvas top that went up and down on command once Harry fixed the hydraulic mechanism. He didn't know yet that Phoebe Perkins had fallen in love with Tony Cameron, who always came into Murray's Restaurant & Bar for just a glimpse of her.

Billy also didn't know that he would marry Little Lucy and they would have their own family. Or that he and Harry Plunkett would grow so close in friendship that he would feel at last he'd found the father he always wanted. He and Harry would add vintage motorcycles to their auto restorations, and Billy would build them a website so they could sell them to the nation. The world would have come to Mattagash by then, since Mattagash was too isolated and shy to go to the world.

No one knew that one day, in that spaceship of a future, Billy Thunder and his grandson would drive the same white Mustang in a town parade celebrating the completion of the new, two-way Mattagash bridge. Harry Plunkett would be there watching, one of the lucky American veterans who seemed immune to the effects of Agent Orange. At eighty-seven, Harry would have two more years to sleep next to Blanche, free of nightmares. He and his fishing buddy, Orville Craft, would never tell *anyone* who backed up first, that famous night on the one-way bridge.

But no one knew yet the *denouement.*

Florence Walker stood in the path of her porch light and watched the white flakes twirling down from the sky like tiny windmills, covering the mailboxes, the railings of the one-way bridge, rooftops, the bodies of pickups, and the hoods of cars, filling up the old mistakes with a new beginning. Then Florence went back inside her house and let the first storm of the year discover her word.

As midnight arrived, all the clocks in town, the modern ones with luminous faces and the old-fashioned ones with keys and knobs, clocks on nightstands, grandfather clocks, clocks on walls, clocks on shelves, and clocks hooked to watch straps—all the clocks felt it. Their numbers flicked, or their hands moved silently. As if taking one unanimous breath, they went forward into a new day, pulling everyone in town closer to the future, pulling all those threads in the tapestry tighter and tighter.

AUTHOR'S NOTE

This is my tenth novel. In all my other books, I may have a character mention a certain war now and then. Perhaps his or her father fought in Korea. Or died in World War II. But I have never tried to create a fictional character who has actually been in combat. It seemed too disrespectful to the real soldiers who fought real wars. And then, how to do it? Where to start? But writers don't always write about what we know, contrary to literary rumors. Sometimes, we write about what we should know.

This novel has several main characters. One is Sgt. Harold "Harry" Plunkett. I didn't want to write about a Vietnam veteran because I have never been to war. I've never been to Vietnam. I have never even visited a military base. As a writer, my wars take place around the kitchen table and in the bedroom. They are fought over lovers, leather purses, Christmas lights, and mailboxes. Sometimes, they last the weekend. Other times, they go on for years and my characters are in them for the duration. Those are *my* wars. Fictional. Easily erased. And as time passes, they are even quickly forgotten.

Harry Plunkett first appeared to me in 1991 while I was watching CNN late one night in Nashville, Tennessee, where I was living. A news clip was showing images of a one-way bridge being swept away like tinsel in an ice jam. *Allagash, Maine. The St. John River*. This was a bridge in my old hometown that crossed my childhood river. It was then that I realized I'd never used a one-way bridge in my fiction. As I thought about the metaphor of a *bridge* and all that it implies, Harry Plunkett and mailman Orville Craft began to take shape. I jotted down pages of notes and ideas for a possible future novel. That's when Harry announced that he was a Vietnam War veteran. "Okay, Harry," I told him. "But you keep quiet about Vietnam, or I'll cut you out of this book."

Here in this northern Maine town, the Vietnam War had a different impact on us than it did protestors in the big, faraway cities. We were proud of the men (no female soldiers from this town back then) who went to fight it, almost all of them having been drafted. We knew them personally, knew their hearts, knew the last thing they wanted to do was fight or die in a jungle halfway around the world. We saw them come home, some with medals, some wounded, some just glad to be alive. The Vietnam War played out differently in Allagash, Maine, than it did in San Francisco or Washington, D.C. There, the protests grew bitterly personal, and the anger was often directed at the soldiers themselves, instead of solely at our government. But it was still a war I only *heard about* from letters to and from soldiers I knew. And from Walter Cronkite's nightly reports. It was a distant war, and I was a safe girl in tiny and remote Allagash.

Over a decade passed as Harry and Orville rested on my shelf. By 2004, after I'd moved to the Eastern Townships of Quebec, I was ready to assemble my characters and notes and settle in to write the full novel. By the end of my first draft, Harry Plunkett began having flashbacks from his combat experiences in Vietnam. I was frantic. Writers know that characters take on lives of their own and suddenly start talking about *stuff*, and it seems as if we are only recording what they say. But, of course, it's all coming from that trunk of memories we keep in our subconscious minds, our own emotions, our fears, our joys, our loves, our hates. *We* run the show, not the characters we invent.

I could *not* delete Harry Plunkett, nor could I change what he was insisting on remembering, on reliving, on teaching me. He was too real to me by then. So I began reading about the Vietnam War and first-person accounts of the soldiers who had fought it. Some of them haunt me still. One incident involving an old Vietnamese man in a sampan was so horrific that I softened the facts for this novel. The truth was too over-the-top to be believable in fiction. That story would better serve a compelling and painful work of nonfiction. I was haunted for months by all I read, and yet I was safe in Quebec, doing research forty years after real soldiers suffered those heart-wrenching experiences.

I wrote a dozen drafts of this novel, eight years of drafts, which involved the necessary cutting of 360-plus pages. I wanted to tell *everything* I'd been learning, how artists were brought in during World War II (Norman Rockwell was one) to create colorful posters to be sent to post offices all over the country, propaganda that would engage the public in support of the war. I scolded the New York City public relations company who sent forth Nayirah, an ambassador's daughter, to lie about babies being ripped from incubators in Kuwait, thus helping push us into the Gulf War. "War is all in the words," Harry told me, so I let him say that in this novel. There were many pages where I angrily denounced George W. Bush for taking us into Iraq and a useless search for WMDs. I wore my research on my sleeve, that place it should never appear. Advice from a fellow writer was good enough to take: *You're a storyteller. You can't spend all that time on a soapbox about Bush and how heinous war is.* She was right. And by that time, 2010, George Bush and his war were already fading into our collective memory.

But one reader suggested I find a "less Hollywood" way for a soldier to die than by throwing himself on a grenade. (I had been so moved by the account of a young man who had done that heroic act that I chose it for a character in this novel.) It was years later, when checking his name listed under the Medal of Honor recipients—it's our country's highest decoration for bravery—that I found other names of soldiers who had also done this. And some lived to remember that day. Please go to the Internet and read the names of all the soldiers who received the Medal of Honor during the Vietnam War. Look at their pictures, study their faces. While no list can ever be complete in any war (over 200,000 American soldiers received the Purple Heart for bravery in Vietnam, as did my fictional Harry Plunkett), the Medal of Honor was given to a mere 248 soldiers. The most recent recipient was Leslie H. Sabo, 21, who died in Cambodia in 1970. His family learned just this year, 2012, of his amazing heroics on the day he died. Of those 248 men receiving the medal, seventy threw themselves on grenades or explosives to protect their comrades. Imagine that. And there may have been more, other Leslie Sabos.

A former Vietnam medic recently told me, "There is no one way to write about that war. Every soldier has a different story, a different way of dealing with it. Back then, we all had our own means of surviving." So I guess this is Sgt. Harold "Harry" Plunkett's version of the war and how *he* dealt with it. Are my facts and terms correct? I certainly tried to make sure that they were. Are Harry's emotional thoughts valid as I imagined them to be? I hope so. Did any soldiers in the Mekong Delta ever hear the *coop coop coop* of the Crow Pheasant, or was it only in the Central or Northern Highlands? I don't know. Writers take license at times for the sake of poetry. The harvest moon of 2006, for instance, did not occur when I suggested it did in this novel, but a week earlier. But that fact does not change the hearts of my characters.

If sometimes we write about what we *should* know, then I thank Harry for insisting I listen to him. And I thank the Vietnam vets, my friends, and those strangers I will never meet, for teaching me about their courage and their endurance. This book is for them.

ACKNOWLEDGMENTS

The people I *should* thank would outnumber the population of Allagash, Maine. This is my condensed list:

Tom Viorikic, my husband, and always the first to read.

My agent, the amazing **Jennifer DeChiara**, of the Jennifer DeChiara Agency.

Howard Frank Mosher, for encouragement and input so valuable it was indispensable. You are the godfather of the Delgato cousins. They belong to *you* now.

The gang at **Sourcebooks**, for all their hard work and faith in this novel: **Stephanie Bowen**, my editor; **Jenna Skwarek**, assistant editor; **Heather Hall**, production editor; **Heather Moore**, senior publicity manager; **Jennifer Sterkowitz**, digital content assistant; **Anna Klenke**, editorial assistant; **Valerie Pierce**, marketing manager; **Katie Anderson**, marketing coordinator; **Dawn Adams**, design manager; **Will Riley**, senior graphic designer; and **Chris Norton**, page production specialist.

Thank you **Peter Lynch** and, of course, **Steve Geck** at Sourcebooks Jabberwocky.

And **Michael Malone**, wonderful writer and wonderful friend. Thank you.

Friends who read early drafts: **Randy Ford, Rosemary Kingsland, Kathleen Wallace King, Nancy Henderson, Jay Selberg, Bill**

Andrews, **Larry Wells**, **Leroy Martin**, **Allen Jackson**, **Chad Pelletier**, and **Cherry Danker**, who is missed daily.

Bob Zimmerman, who told me many years ago about an electrical painting he once saw, on black velvet, of Venice, Italy. We miss you, Bob Z.

Jack "Doc" Mannick, former Vietnam medic, for your input and assurance.

Thank you to artist **Ward Hooper** of New York, for that wonderful watercolor that found a home in this story. And so did the use of your name.

And, as always, to those rescued animals who came, saw, and conquered, five fine and dignified dogs: **Lance**, **Wylie**, **Rosie**, **Bear**, and **Allie**. And a precious cat named **Mali**, or "Little One."

And I always thank Mama and Daddy.

ABOUT THE AUTHOR

Cathie Pelletier was born and raised on the banks of the St. John River, at the end of the road in northern Maine. She is the author of nine other novels, including *The Funeral Makers* (NYTBR Notable Book), *The Weight of Winter* (winner of the New England Book Award), and *Running the Bulls* (winner of the Paterson Prize for Fiction). As K. C. McKinnon, she has written two novels, both of which became television films. After years of living in Nashville, Tennessee; Toronto, Canada; and Eastman, Quebec, she has returned to Allagash, Maine, and the family homestead where she was born. She is at work on a new novel.

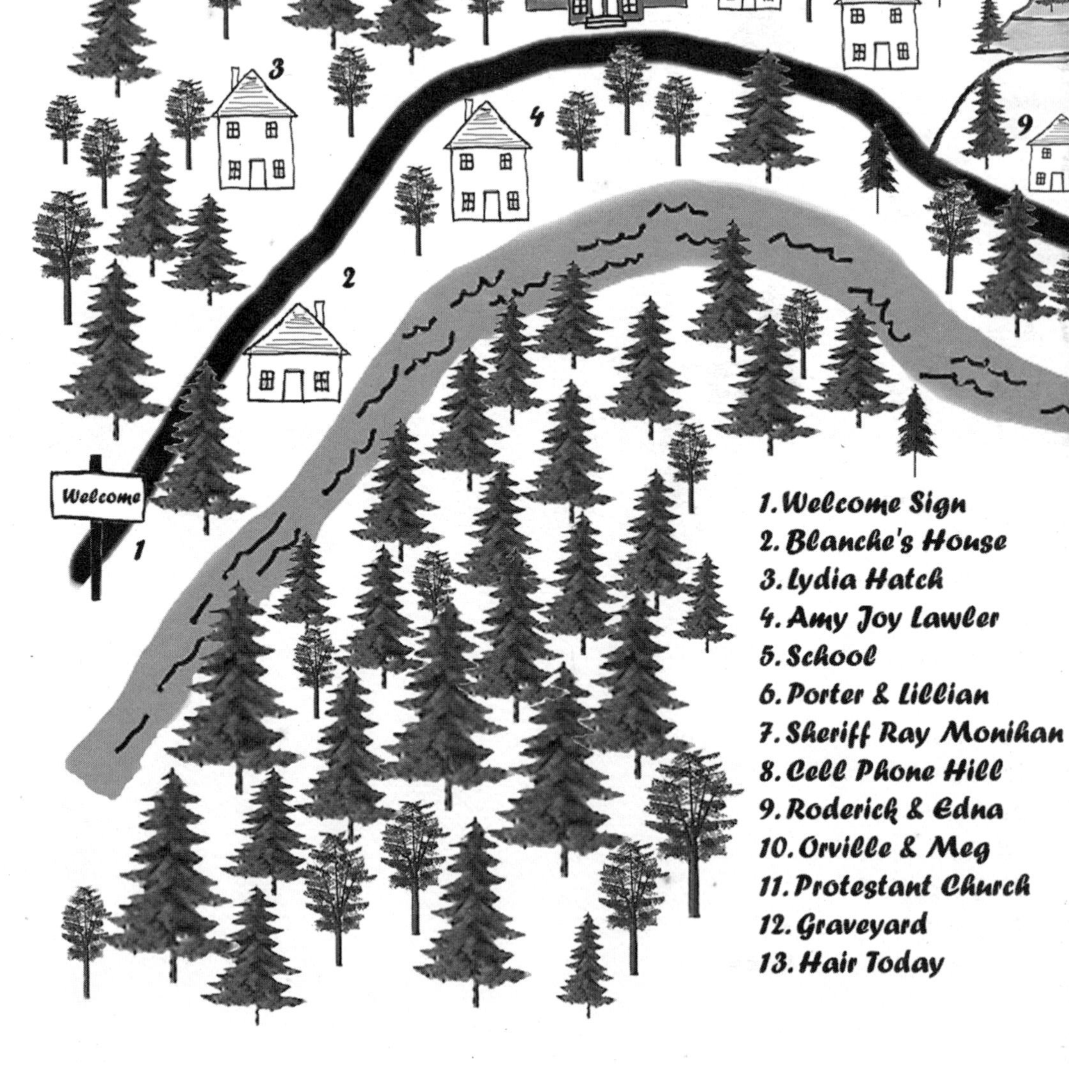

Welcome
1
2
3
4
5
6
7
9
1. Welcome Sign
2. Blanche's House
3. Lydia Hatch
4. Amy Joy Lawler
5. School
6. Porter & Lillian
7. Sheriff Ray Monihan
8. Cell Phone Hill
9. Roderick & Edna
10. Orville & Meg
11. Protestant Church
12. Graveyard
13. Hair Today